The Pro

If it hadn't been for Matty, Meggie might have been content to settle down in the workhouse. Unlike her brother she had never seriously expected her parents to come for them. She believed that they had been glad to be rid of her, that they blamed her for Nancy's death – as she blamed herself. It hadn't taken her long to realise that the harder she worked, the more she learned, the better equipped she would be to get a job and a room of her own. Then she would take Matty to live with her. It was what drove her on, making her shine in class, compelling her, even at her chores, to work twice as hard as the other girls, always hoping that she was learning skills which would help her to make a home for them both.

She planned constantly for the future, looking forward to the time when she and Matty could be a family again and was deeply hurt to see the way he looked at her, almost as if he hated her. If only she could talk to him, explain her plans, make him understand that she still loved him, maybe he would be able to smile at her. She would give anything to see her little brother happy again.

Anne Vivis was brought up in Fife, Scotland, where all her books are set. *The Provost's Woman* is her fourth novel; her first three, *Daughters of Strathannan*, *The Lennox Women* and *The Rowan Tree* are also available from Mandarin. She now lives in Warrington, Cheshire.

Also by Anne Vivis
and available in Mandarin

Daughters of Strathannan
The Lennox Women
The Rowan Tree

Anne Vivis

The Provost's Woman

Mandarin

A Mandarin Paperback
THE PROVOST'S WOMAN

First published in Great Britain 1995
by William Heinemann Ltd
and Mandarin Paperbacks
imprints of Reed Consumer Books Ltd
Michelin House, 81 Fulham Road, London SW3 6RB
and Auckland, Melbourne, Singapore and Toronto

Copyright © Anne Vivis 1995
The author has asserted her moral rights

A CIP catalogue record for this title
is available from the British Library

Typeset by Deltatype Ltd, Ellesmere Port, Cheshire
Printed and bound in Germany
by Elsnerdruck, Berlin

To Mum and Dad
for all your help
and support
I love you

and for Pete
ditto

and Deb and Ste
last but never least
ditto again

A Workhouse! ah, that sound awakes my woes,
And pillows on the thorn my racked repose!
In durance vile here must I wake and weep,
And all my frowzy couch in sorrow sleep.

Robert Burns
'Epistle from Esopus to Maria'

Part One

CHAPTER ONE

Inverannan, County Town of Strathannan
Autumn 1926

'**W**ell!' Mrs Elsie Laing managed to gasp her well bred outrage even as she felt her foot stumble over the edge of the kerbstone. While the word still hung on the damp September morning air her ankle twisted, dumping her inelegantly in the filthy gutter of Inverannan High Street. The small human bullet which had been the cause of her descent hurtled on without so much as slowing its speed.

Mrs Laing's first concern was not for her wrenched ankle, was not even for the possible ruin of her good coat. What bothered her most was that she, the Provost's wife, should have landed so soundly on her skinny backside in the town's busiest street, where every Tam, Jock and Harriet would be able to gloat at her misfortune. If they all got to glimpse her knickers into the bargain she would never be able to venture out in public again. Her face already puce with humiliation, she tugged at her hem, pulling it down over the exposed blue flannel. Modesty restored she looked up, expecting help to be at hand. To her chagrin no one was paying her the slightest attention.

'Stop him. Someone stop that wee bugger!'

Pursued by angry cries the youngster dodged through the crowd, slipping past outstretched hands with the evasive qualities of a desperate eel.

Ethel Muir followed the excitement until the young thief disappeared from view and only then realised that her

3

shopping companion was sitting on the wet setts. 'Och, Mrs Laing!' she screeched, her horrified tone alerting others who turned in time to witness Mrs Laing's predicament.

Elsie mustered her dignity and scrambled quickly to her feet.

'Are you all right, hen?' Billy Tonner asked, his face carefully schooled into an expression of deep concern, though he dearly wanted to laugh at the rare spectacle of the Provost's haughty wife being brought down a peg or two.

He was saved from what would have been an unforgivable social gaffe by a further disturbance in the crowd which parted to allow a tall, wheezing man through. In one hand he held a large cabbage. The other was firmly grasping a young lad's disintegrating collar.

'I got him,' he announced unnecessarily.

Billy Tonner crooked a finger at the boy who hung his head, all trace of bravado gone. Someone shoved him hard in the back and he stumbled forward.

'Right, lad. What did you think you were playing at, eh?' Billy observed the huge, shadowed eyes, the prominent bones, the boots with the toes cut out, the sores round the child's mouth and recognised the all too evident signs of poverty. He thought of his own well-fed, healthy children and felt the familiar surge of anger at a system which could allow bairns to sink to such a pathetic level.

Elsie saw the pity on Billy Tonner's face and pushed herself forward, eager to intervene before his soft nature got the better of him. 'Call a constable,' she ordered.

The boy looked up briefly, a flicker of fear in his hooded eyes.

'He's just a wean,' Billy muttered.

4

'It is your duty to put him in the hands of the law,' Elsie Laing insisted loudly. 'Inverannan is a decent town. There's no place in it for the likes of him. Someone go for a constable.' Her sharp, pale eyes raked the crowd. Everyone looked away, avoiding her gaze.

'Och, there's no need for that, Mrs Laing. If the laddie pays for the cabbage we'll forget about it. Just this once, mind.' Billy looked down at the silent child. 'Well, lad? It's a fair offer. You can't go round helping yourself to whatever you fancy. You have to pay for what you want, just like the rest of us.'

The boy's continued silence was starting to look like insolence, even to the generous-minded Billy.

'Mr Tonner, folk who steal should go to jail. Let him off with it this time and he'll think he can do it again,' Elsie lectured, grabbing the child's bony shoulder with cruelly sharp fingers. 'If nobody will call a constable then I'll take him to the police station myself.'

'No!' For the second time that day Elsie found herself the target of a young body. 'Leave him alone. Let him go. Get your hands off him.' Grubby fingers plucked at the fine wool of Elsie's best coat. Elsie gawped. No one had dared to speak to her like that in years, certainly not since her husband had become the Burgh's most prominent citizen. Shock loosened her grip and the wee boy stumbled free.

Mrs Laing found herself looking into a pair of furious brown eyes. Huge and luminous with anger they dominated a heart-shaped face, surrounded by a mass of dark, tangled hair, clumsily and unevenly shorn off at chin level. Painfully thin, the girl was tall, her eyes almost on a level with Mrs Laing's. She stood her ground defiantly and defended her brother.

'He's only ten and he's hungry,' she said, putting a protective arm round the boy's shoulders.

Billy sighed. 'Aye, lass, that's as maybe, but he can't go round stealing. Tell youse what,' he added kindly. 'You give me tuppence for the cabbage and we'll say no more about it.'

To his horror her pretty face flushed scarlet and she looked away in shame. 'We've no money,' she stammered.

The crowd murmured, half-sympathetic, half-condemnatory.

'Where do youse live?' Billy asked.

'Craigie,' was the muttered reply.

'Your Dad's a miner then? On strike is he?' The note of sympathy in Billy's soft tone was unmistakable. The crowd shuffled. Billy scratched his head in consternation, his conscience well and truly prodded. Craigie, as everyone watching the small drama knew, was a mining village. Existing on the outer edges of poverty even in better times, the miners and their families had been locked in a bitter strike since the beginning of May. After four months most were destitute. Some, the young, the weak and the aged, had already succumbed to malnutrition.

The prosperous citizens of Inverannan, a town made relatively and safely affluent by its thriving linen mills, were made uncomfortable by this graphic reminder of their less fortunate neighbours. Among the crowd were many, like Billy, who sympathised with the plight of the stricken pit villages and abhorred the greed of the pit owners whose exploitation had driven thousands of honest, hard-working men to this destructive impasse. But even more people persisted in the view that the miners should be grateful to have work and had brought this trouble on themselves. No one believed this more firmly than Mrs Elsie Laing, wife of the Provost, a man whose rise to eminence owed everything to the fact that his family owned the Strathannan Mining Company.

'Well, I should have known!' Mrs Laing's temper exploded. 'I know the type.' She turned back to the crowd. 'You all know the sort of people they are. Bone-idle shirkers, every one of them. Troublemakers, spending their relief money on drink and sending their children out to steal their food.'

There was a muted growl. 'A fair wage for a fair day's work. That's all we want,' a voice shouted to low approval.

'Rubbish!' Elsie insisted, incensed that anyone should have the temerity to argue with her. 'That's exactly what you had.' The growl grew louder, the crowd shifted.

'Not in your husband's mines we don't,' someone else yelled.

'What's going on here?'

Elsie whirled round and, with considerable relief, found herself facing an officer of the Strathannan Constabulary. In a few exaggerated words she described the events. 'If you do not take this child to the police station and charge him I will ask my husband to make a formal complaint,' she threatened.

'Right you are, Mrs Laing.' A huge hand descended on the boy's shoulders. 'Come along, lad. Your father'll have to be told about this.' And he led the boy away.

'You too.' Elsie turned towards the girl but the child wheeled round, dropping a small brown bottle as she did so. After a momentary hesitation while she stared in dismay at the shattered glass and sticky brown liquid, she shoved her way through the crowd. Nobody made any move to stop her.

* * *

7

Meggie McPherson raced along the slippery setts, then dodged down a side wynd, fleeing between the high, blank walls with no thought in her mind other than escape. It was a full five minutes before she felt safe enough to stop and lean, coughing and gasping, against a wall. Cautiously she crept to the nearest corner and peered up the hill towards the High Street, realising, with a hollowing of her already empty stomach, that her panicked flight had taken her almost a mile downhill in the wrong direction. The grey street was dotted with folk doing nothing more threatening than going about their own private business. Meggie drew a great shuddering breath of relief, though her heart still beat painfully under her ribs. But it was a different fear which was making her feel sick now.

She and her brother, Matty, had been trusted to walk the five long miles from Craigie to Inverannan that morning to buy a cough bottle for their baby sister, Nancy, who had thrashed and grizzled with fever all night. As the oldest of five children, thirteen-year-old Meggie knew exactly how hard it had been for their mother to find the shilling to pay for the medicine. And now, not only had she dropped the bottle but, on top of that, she would have to explain what had happened to Matty. Already she could feel the sting of her father's belt as he whacked it against the soft flesh of her backside. The thought was enough to drain the hectic colour from her face and it was a dejected, stooped figure who trailed back up the steep hill towards the road home.

It was late afternoon before Meggie cut off the main road and squirmed through a gap in a hedge, taking the usual short cut across a field to Craigie. She walked with her eyes firmly fixed on the dark soil, searching for tatties which might have been overlooked by the pickers who had cleared the field only two days ago. Not that there had been much of the crop left for the farmer to harvest. Driven to desperate measures the miners' families had already added most of it to their soup pots.

Meggie's keen eyes spotted a couple of half-buried tubers and she stooped quickly, barely altering her stride, and scooped them into her pocket, hoping that this small offering might serve to deflect the worst of her mother's wrath. Ten yards further on she found another, then another. Encouraged she walked more slowly, managing to scavenge enough to fill their bellies for one more night. Concentrating on the damp soil she quite forgot to keep one eye open for Farmer McCready. Only the frantic barking of a dog alerted her to danger. She turned in time to see McCready himself, roaring abuse and lumbering towards her, preceded by the huge, bad-tempered mongrel which had taken bites out of so many thin legs that he was developing a taste for human flesh. Ten minutes ago Meggie had thought she had barely enough energy to get her home. Now, faced with two stones of vicious dog and fifteen of furious farmer, she flew across the remaining ten yards of field, crashed through the sparse hedge and emerged at the back of Craigie's communal wash-house.

Though McCready's sympathies were generally with the miners – the evidence of their poverty was all too obvious on his own doorstep to be ignored – his good will was exhaustd. Despite the fact that he was always willing to sell his vegetables to the villagers, straight from the fields, at prices which were well below those charged by the shops, five acres had been all but stripped of potatoes, carrots and turnips over the past months, leaving him precious little to send to market and even less to put in the bank. He was tempted to force his way through the hedge and chase the young thief all the way to her home, but the mood of the villagers was desperate and ugly. Deciding that a few more stolen tatties weren't worth a bloodied nose McCreadie bellowed angrily at the dog to come back. It ran along the hedge, howling with disappointment then, tail drooping between its scabby legs, lolloped reluctantly back to its master.

Peering round the corner of the wash-house, Meggie watched until McCready's bulky figure had disappeared over the crest of the low hill before daring to walk on home.

The wash-house was the first building in the little village. Running away from it at right angles and following the undulations caused by the slow collapse of the ground over the mine workings beneath, were the rows of miners' cottages: four grim lines of single-storey dwellings, coated in the sooty smoke from two hundred chimneys. Smoke which lingered, caught in the natural dip which harboured Craigie, and blended with other, more offensive odours, unnoticed by the villagers themselves but causing visitors to choke and gag. There wasn't much in the way of smoke today. The only coal available was on the spoil heaps, or bings, at the back of the Dene colliery.

Like tatties, coal was gleaned by dark, furtive figures in the dead of night and then used sparingly. Most families were now reduced to one hot meal a week, existing on bread and lard for the rest of the time. The more enterprising households pooled resources and donated a lump or two of coal to light a single fire over which a huge soup pot greedily accepted anything which might simmer down into the glutinous mess which was then shared out among the children.

Even the wash-house had been still and silent for the length of the summer. Coal to fuel the boilers was brought in by the Strathannan Mining Company and the supply had ceased on the very first day of the strike, way back in May. The village women were reduced to washing their clothes in tubs of cold water, into which they added lumps of soda. The resulting greyness of their clothing added to the impression of grime.

Meggie's house was in the middle of the second row, facing across the stretch of rutted grass which was the main access route. It had the added disadvantage of having a privie – which was shared between four similar cottages – less than ten feet from its front door, a noisome fact which ensured that the single window on that side of the house stayed firmly shut. At the rear a small plot of garden backed on to that of a similar cottage. All along the rows men congregated on doorsteps, passing time which dragged slowly but Meggie barely raised her head in acknowledgement. Nor did she respond to the cheerful calls of her other two brothers, Perce and Bertie, newly released from school and intent on enjoying an hour or two of precious freedom before nightfall. Too soon she was outside her own home. Steeling herself for what lay ahead she opened the door and stepped inside.

After the daylight the inside of the house was gloomy. She could only just see her mother, seated in the creaking rocking chair, Nancy cuddled close in her arms. Meggie closed her eyes in a moment of sheer terror for what was to come.

'Well! You took your time.' Netta McPherson's words were harsher than her expression as she lowered the feverish child on to the box bed.

Meggie swallowed hard but before she had the chance to

lurch into her explanations, Nancy started to cry, a thin, unhappy wailing noise which brought her mother instantly back to her side. Netta, on her knees, stroked the child's hair back from her damp forehead and murmured gently to her. Nancy's eyes were bright with fever and her small chest gurgled as she breathed. Meggie felt tears sting her eyes as she watched her tiny, helpless sister.

'There, there,' Netta crooned, 'Lie still wee one. We'll soon have you feeling better.' Tenderly she wiped the hot head with a damp rag. Nancy's wails subsided and she looked at her mother with eyes that were filled with absolute trust. Meggie quailed, looked desperately towards the door and wondered whether she could simply run away. She might have done just that if the door hadn't opened at that very moment to admit her father.

Tam McPherson was leanly built. His shoulders were stooped from his years underground and an old injury had left him with a slight limp. His pale, short-sighted eyes were screwed up in an habitual squint, lending his appearance a misleading mildness, disguising both a stubborn pride and the complete inability to admit to fault or defeat. His devotion to the miners' cause, his gift for reasoned argument and persuasive speech had earned him respect and the place of spokesman for his colleagues. It was Tam who urged his workmates and neighbours to hold fast in the face of increasing hardship, determined that no man from Craigie should blackleg the strike.

He brought those same qualities to his family. Meggie could not recall him losing his temper, had seldom even heard him raise his voice. Such was the force of his personality that he never needed to. His family lived their lives in the shadow of his disapproval, knowing that misdeeds, big and small, were punished with emotionless efficiency, that pleas and apologies had little effect on him.

'Is the wean no better?' Tam asked his wife, glancng with a frown at the grizzling child.

Netta shook her head, loosening a strand of dull brown hair from the plait which fell down her back. 'She's worse,' she whispered. 'Where's the medicine, Meggie? Fetch a spoon and I'll give her a wee drop now.Maybe it'll ease her enough to let her get to sleep. She's exhausted as much as anything else. A sleep will do her the world of good.'

Meggie's mouth dried while her hands poured water. 'I've not got it,' she croaked.

'What?' Netta rounded on her daughter. 'What did you say?'

'I've not got it, Ma,' Meggie whispered, misery running the words together.

'Why not, lass?' Tam's voice was deceptively calm.

'I dropped it . . . I'm sorry, Ma.' Meggie looked at her mother in mute appeal but found no reassurance in the shadowed, grey eyes. 'Our Matty got caught stealing from the greengrocers. They got me too when I went to get him. The bottle fell from my pocket when I was running away from them. I had to run, else they'd have put me in the jail too.' She gabbled her story out to her silent parents. 'But I got some tatties from McCready's field on the way home.' She emptied her pathetic offering over the freshly scrubbed table, showering it with dried earth. 'I'm sorry . . .' she ended at last.

'You stupid wee bitch,' Netta spat, delivering a sharp slap across Meggie's left ear. 'Can you not be trusted with the simplest thing? And where's Matty now? You were supposed to look after him.' Her voice vibrating with

13

temper she raised her hand a second time but found it caught and held by Tam.

'Sit down, Margaret, and tell me exactly what happened,' he ordered.

Meggie shivered. He only used her full name when he was really angry.

Slowly she recounted the day's events. Her mother held the fretful Nancy, fighting to control her own seething anger. Her father simply sat still and listened to her without comment.

'This is your fault, lass,' he decided when she came to the end. 'It was your job to keep on eye on Matty.'

'I had to wait for the bottle to be made up,' she explained. 'Matty'd been messing about, touching things. Mr Beattie sent him outside. That's when he took the cabbage from Mr Tonner.'

Tam shook his head, his wordless disapproval cutting through her soul.

'I'm sorry, Pa,' she tried again, her voice cracking on tears she could no longer hold back.

'It's too late for sorry, Margaret.'

Anything else he might have said was pre-empted by a sharp knock on the door.

'Now then, Margaret, stop that snivelling. There's no need to let anyone else know our business.' Tam regarded his daughter coldly and waited until she had herself under control before moving to open the door.

'Mr McPherson?'

Meggie could just make out the form of a policeman silhouetted in the doorway, the figures of several interested villagers clustered round him. Her pounding heart missed a beat.

'Aye, that's me.'

14

'I've come about your son. Matthew.'

'Better come inside then.' Tam stood back and ushered the officer in. The look of contempt on the man's face as he glanced round the barely furnished room brought a flare of quickly controlled anger. Tam McPherson did not let it show on his face. 'Sit yourself down.' The policeman looked carefully at the chair before risking his clean uniform.

'I'm sorry to have to tell you that Matthew McPherson is at the police station in Inverannan, accused of stealing from William Tonner, the greengrocer in the High Street.'

'Aye. I know. My daughter has told me that much.' Pride kept Tam's voice firm.

'So, you're the wee lassie who ran away?' The policeman smiled grim encouragement at Meggie.

'I did nothing wrong.' Meggie defended herself stoutly, terrified that this huge uniformed man would bear her away to the jail, too.

'No, lass, no one's saying you did. But did you see what happened?'

She shook her head. 'I only saw that woman holding our Matty and shouting at him.'

'Aye, well, Mrs Laing'd every right to be angry. She says your wee brother attacked her. She's witnesses to prove it and a gey sore looking ankle, too.'

'Mrs Laing?' Tam interrupted. 'The Provost's wife?'

'Aye.'

For the first time, Tam McPherson's anger was visible on his face. 'If it wasn't for the likes of Mrs Laing and her husband my wee lad wouldn't have felt he had to steal his food.'

The policeman was well aware of the reasons for the miners' bitterness. Provost Laing and his family owned the

15

Dene colliery, a pit with one of the highest accident records in the county. And if this village was typical, Laing was one of the worst landlords, too. But it wasn't his place to comment.

'That doesn't make what your son did right, Mr McPherson. He's to face charges of stealing and assault in front of the magistrate the morn. You can fetch him home as long as you give me your word to have him back at the court room the morn's morning at eight o'clock.'

'Keep him there. A night in the cells to think on what he's done won't do him any harm.'

'Tam!' Netta couldn't stop that one word escaping her pale lips.

He silenced her with an icy glare. 'I'll be in court in the morning.'

'Right.' The officer nodded his approval. A sharp lesson was likely all the lad needed.

Tam opened the door, waited impatiently for the officer to leave, then closed it firmly, denying his inquisitive neighbours the chance to see what was going on.

'You,' he turned to Meggie, 'get off to your bed. And stay there until I fetch your brother back from the court the morn. Then youse'll both get the leathering of your lives.'

CHAPTER TWO

In all his short life, Matty McPherson had never been so frightened. After a lengthy interview with a vituperative sergeant he had been taken to the dank cellars which housed the Inverannan police cells. Sandwiched between two policemen, their footsteps echoing back at them from the flagged floor, Matty was led along a dimly lit passageway of heavy wooden doors, secured by the biggest bolts and padlocks he had ever seen.

Halfway down the corridor he was halted roughly and made to wait while one of the doors was unlocked and thrown open. That done he was shoved inside, so harshly that he sprawled painfully to his knees, grazing them on the concrete floor. Before he had time to get himself upright the door was slammed, the bolts were shot home and the padlock snapped shut.

He turned, his mouth open to yell but the sound died before it was born, silenced by the impenetrable wall of darkness which faced him. Matty stood, his eyes clenched shut, hoping that when he opened them again he would be able to see. That usually worked at home. Cautiously he lifted his lids. The darkness was complete. A solid, smothering blackness in which might hide all the bad things in the world. Fear paralysed him. A stifled whimper escaped his clenched lips.

Somewhere in front of him was the door. Shivering, his breath coming in tight, distressed gasps, he wrapped his arms round his thin body and took a tenative pace forward. Then another until his foot encountered wood. Slowly he unwound his arms and reached out, running his hands over the uneven surface of the door. Behind him he was aware only of the black void, the unknown, feeling it like a physical weight pressing in on him. Disabled by the numbing combination of fear and cold, he sank to the unyielding stone floor and curled himself into a tight ball. And there he stayed, shivering through the long night.

Long sleepless hours of unabated horror later, he felt the door moving against him. A sliver of light edged its way into the cell. Matty scrambled out of the way. His fingers and feet were numb and his head hurt. He was so stiff that he stumbled when he tried to get to his feet.

'What are you doing down there, lad?' The policeman's voice was bluff and cheerful.

Matty tried to speak but his teeth were chattering too much for words.

The policeman frowned and dumped the tray he ws carrying on the floor.

'Here lad, up you get.' He hauled Matty to his feet, wincing at the chill feel of his skin. 'By, and you're near frozen solid.' He glanced at the wooden shelf which acted as a bed, noted the still folded blanket, the undented pillow. 'Did you not sleep on the bed then?' he asked kindly.

Matty looked about him. Light from the open door bathed the cell in enough dull light for him to make out the sleeping arrangements. He shook his head, jerkily. 'N . . . n . . . no. I didn't know it was there. I couldn't see.'

The man guffawed then took a mug of strong, warm tea off the tray and placed it in the boy's hands. 'You daft wee tyke. Here, drink this. It'll warm you. And there's bread there too. Be sure and eat it all.'

Matty's teeth chinked against the thick china but he

drank the tea greedily, felt the warmth flood his empty insides.

Constable Sillars, recognisig blind terror when he saw it, waited until the bread had been eaten. 'Right then,' he said briskly. 'I've other jobs to be getting on with. Someone'll fetch you in about an hour and take you over to the court. Your father'll likely be there.' Unaware of the fresh horror he had injected into Matty's heart he turned to go.

'Please can you leave the door open, just a wee bit?' Matty pleaded.

'No, lad. I'm sorry but I have to lock the door. That's in the rules. Sit yourself on the bed there and wrap that blanket round yourself to keep warm.'

Matty watched the thin line of light contract and disappear. Then he huddled in the far corner of the narrow bed, drawing the blanket round his head and shoulders like a cowl, and waited.

Netta McPherson slid from her bed in the dead of night. Careful not to disturb baby Nancy, who had finally sunk into a hot, restless sleep, she hauled her skirt and jumper over her nightdress, shoved her feet into her battered boots, wrapped her heavy shawl round her shoulders and let herself out of the house. At the rear of the cottage she groped in the darkness until she located the pram, so recently vacated by her youngest child, but now black and filthy with coal dust. Pushing this in front of her she made her way cautiously through the village, stumbling on the rutted grass track. She walked with her head down, the shawl pulled up over her head, sensing that she was not the only one up and about illegal business at this hour of the night.

The air was cold, damp with incipient rain. Praying it

would hold off until she got back, Netta plodded towards the Dene colliery. She avoided the road which was the shortest route and led directly to the huge metal colliery gates, barred and guarded now, and made her way instead through the village and on to a narrow but well-trodden track, edged with nettles and brambles, the half-ripe fruit long ago stripped by the hungry villagers. A mile or so along this path she halted and set the pram securely in among the bushes of the hedgerow where it would be hidden from anyone else who might venture this way in the dead of night. Gathering her skirts between her legs she clambered over a rusty fence, broken and lowered here by the passage of many furtive bodies. Ahead of her loomed the dark mass of the pit bing.

She walked slowly, her eyes straining to see the ground ahead of her but there would be little on this side of the bing worth collecting. The small pieces of loose coal she was searching for had all been gleaned from here long ago. Instead she skirted the edge of the bing, making for the far side, the side which looked down over the pithead itself and where the risk of discovery was so much greater. And the danger was very real. The Strathannan Mining Company posted watchmen every night and several unlucky villagers had found themselves before the magistrates for stealing coal from this heap in the last few months. The fines imposed were impossible to pay and a prison sentence was the usual result.

Grateful now for the cover of cloud, Netta edged her way up the slope, forced every time she came here to climb higher in search of enough coal to fuel the stove and heat food for her family. Now she could make out the bent forms of half a dozen other people, all creeping carefully over the loose surface. Although she would know every one of them she, like all the rest, stayed well away from everyone else, kept silent and concentrated only on her task. They all knew how the slightest sound carried right down to the pit yard. A single careless move by any one of them could spell disaster for them all.

Tucked into her waistband, Netta carried a hessian sack. She took it out and, sinking to her knees, crawled over the hillside, searching out the precious lumps of coal. An hour later her sack was almost full but she knew that daylight would reveal at least half of it as worthless rock. Aching with tiredness she crept back to where she had hidden the pram and emptied her sack into it. For a moment, she was tempted to go on home. But if she did that she would only have to repeat the whole exercise in a night or two and tonight she had the added incentive of knowing that Nancy would need a warm room and hot food if she was to make a good recovery. Resolutely Netta set off again, returning an hour later with a second sackful. This time, the pram almost full, she set off for home.

It was raining in earnest now, soaking through her shawl and into her clothes, chilling her to the bone. Time and again the laden pram stuck in the muddy ruts of the lane, forcing her to manhandle it over them. By the time she got back to the rows her clothes were drenched, her skirts were clinging to her legs, her boots were lumpy with mud and she was staggering with exhaustion. And, overlaying all this discomfort, ignited by it but reducing it almost to insignificance, was deep, raging resentment.

Why, she grunted to herself as she summoned the last of her energy to haul the pram over her front doorstep, should she be the one to have to risk her health and freedom to go scrounging round the pit bing while her husband slumbered on in the warmth of their bed? Wasn't it enough that she toiled from dawn to nightfall, caught in the web of work and worry that keeping house and raising a family entailed?

It was the sweat of her labour, her ability to make every single ha'penny do the work of four, that kept them from the poor-house, while her husband, the man whose stubborn beliefs had reduced his family to living like tinkers, spent his time lording it over his colleagues, forcing them to ever more bitter deprivation in a useless battle that everyone knew they could never win. But Netta didn't have enough energy to feed her bitterness. Once her anger had run its brief course she was left with the knowledge that she was luckier than many of her neighbours.

Tam was a good husband, a man to be relied upon, a man she still loved. Any money that came his way was handed, untouched, to his wife and the best of the food on their table was given to the children, unlike some households where the men drank the relief money, returning late at night to vent their frustrations on women who wore the resulting bruises in the uncaring manner of absolute defeat. If Tam was strict with the children, demanding unquestioning obedience and insisting that their free time was mostly occupied by chores and schoolwork, it was because he wanted them to grow up knowing right from wrong, to stop them sinking to the level of some of their apathetic neighbours. As for allowing his wife to make these illegal trips to the spoil heap, well, all the women did it. If the worst happened and a woman was caught she was always careful to insist that her husband had no knowledge of what she was doing. If she was very lucky and the magistrate was sympathetic, she might get away with a week in jail. Any man being arrested, in addition to a fine or possible prison sentence, would find, when this strike was over, that he had no job to return to and no home to live in.

Sighing, Netta dragged the pram and the accumulation of mire clogging its wheels straight into the main room. To leave it and its illegal cargo sitting at the front door was to invite someone to steal it, or worse, to attract the attention of the company agent who was rumoured to walk the village at night looking for evidence of this very crime.

Using cold water from the bucket under the sink, Netta sluiced her hands and legs. The old clock on the shelf showed it was a little after half-past five. There was no point in slipping back into bed now. She would only disturb Tam and anyway, in just over an hour it would be time to get up and face another day.

Moving carefully she went to check on Nancy. The child was lying in her cot, her eyes closed, her skin frighteningly hot to the touch but at least she was still sleeping and her breathing, though harsh and noisy, wasn't any worse.

Quietly, Netta changed her wet clothes for her one remaining clean dress and settled herself in a chair to wait. Utter weariness overcame her. She felt her eyes close but forced them open again, afraid to sleep in case she failed to wake in time to light the fire and boil a kettle for Tam before he set out to Inverannan and the courthouse. But again her eyes drooped, her head sagged towards her chest and this time she slept.

She awoke with a jerk, her head spinning with weariness. Through the soot-dusted window she could see the first hint of dawn lightening the heavy sky and was relieved to realise that she had been asleep for less than an hour. In normal times the village would have been alive at this hour, busy with colliers setting out to start their shift at the Dene. But today, and for the past five months, the men were still abed, lingering there as late as possible, seeking any means of escape from the dull monotony of their workless days.

Outside nothing stirred. So what had wakened her? Her heart thumping with instinctive fear, Netta sat forward and listened, hearing nothing other than the regular ticking of the clock. But something had woken her, of that she was certain. Careful not to disturb Tam or Nancy, Netta crept to the back room, opened the door softly and looked in on the children huddled together in the bed there, wondering if one of them had cried out. There were three tousled heads instead of the usual four, but they were all sleeping peacefully.

Closing the door again Netta tiptoed past Nancy's still form and over to the stove, meaning to light it, ready for Tam getting up. She was on her knees, carefully filling it with wood, when she stilled suddenly. Fear gripped her so fiercely that she dropped the kindling she was holding and it fell to the floor with a dull thud. She knew now what had disturbed her and experienced a minute of sheer panic as horror enveloped her. Around her the house sank back into silence, the very silence which had wakened her. Silence when there should have been the laboured, rasping breathing of her sick child.

Slowly, she got to her feet and walked towards the baby's cot. Nancy was in exactly the same position she had been in the last time Netta checked on her, her little fists bunched outside the blankets, her mouth slightly agape. Trembling, Netta placed a gentle hand on her daughter's downy cheek. It was no longer hot, but cool. For a moment her heart leapt in relief as she thought it was all right, that the fever had left her, but even while the hope filled her mind the blood in her veins turned to ice. Stooping she gathered the still child into her arms and brought her face to the baby's lips, praying to feel the whispering touch of breath on her cheeks. There was nothing.

* * *

24

Later, much later, when the doctor had called and Ma Trale, who acted as midwife and layer-out, had attended to the baby, leaving her washed and dressed in the best of her handed-down clothes, when the two boys had been packed off, miserable and confused, to school, Tam, Netta and Meggie sat silently round the bare wooden table.

Netta, stiff-backed and white-faced, seemed contained. Her tears would be shed in the privacy of her bed. Tam, sat in terrible silence, his head in his hands, while Meggie, her eyes bloated with tears sobbed fitfully.

'We've not even got the money to give her a decent burial.' Netta's whispered words broke the silence which had lasted for more than an hour.

Nobody answered.

'Did you hear me, Tam McPherson?' she asked, her voice becoming shrill and angry. 'Our own wee bairn and she'll be buried in a pauper's grave, not even in our own churchyard but in Inverannan, away from everyone who loved her.'

'Be quiet, woman,' Tam hissed, his own control almost broken.

'Quiet! You tell me to be quiet when your own wean's dead! You're a cold, hard man, Tam McPherson. This would never have happened if you'd put your own family first, if you'd thought about what your own bairns were supposed to eat when you came out on strike. You're the one who talked them into it. You're the one who spends his time persuading the other men to hold out. What for?' she screamed. 'So that their weans can die too? Is that what you want?'

Tam pulled himself to his feet. 'Don't you go blaming me for this. This isn't my fault,' he told her, his voice clipped and unsteady with the effort of self-control.

'Whose fault is it then?' his wife demanded. 'Whose fault is it that she didn't have enough food to make her strong? Whose fault is it that this house is cold and damp? Whose fault is it that there was no money to have the doctor to her? You and your bloody strike . . .'

So fast that Netta barely saw the movement, Tam lashed out and struck his wife, catching her an open-palmed blow across the face. She staggered slightly, stared at him from shocked-filled eyes and raised a disbelieving hand to her hot cheek. Never before, not in fourteen hard years of marriage, had he struck her. And now, instead of the anger she had expected to read in his face, she saw only sorrow, etched in deep lines down the side of his mouth, across his brow and in his eyes.

'Och, Tammy,' sobbing now she collapsed back into her chair. 'Tammy . . .'

'Nay, lass, you can't blame the strike for what happened to our Nancy. She was never strong . . . Even when I'm working there's never enough money. You know that.' He reached across the table and took her hand.

She nodded. What he said was true enough. 'I know . . . I know.'

'It's Meggie who is at fault,' he said, careless of the terrible guilt he was inflicting on his appalled daughter. 'The wean would likely have pulled through if she'd been given that medicine.'

Meggie could only stare at him, her eyes flooding with fresh tears.

'She needed a doctor, not cheap medicine,' Netta murmured, but she too was oblivious to her daughter's pain.

'No miner can afford a doctor. A man can't keep a wife and five bairns on pit pay. Don't you understand? That's why we have to fight, to keep this strike solid.'

Even now, Netta thought, with his baby daughter dead, his son in jail, Tam cared more for the miners' cause than he did for his family. But he had always been like that and it was something she had admired in him.

'Tammy,' she cried again. 'What are we going to do? What are we going to do?'

Unable to offer any comfort to his wife, Tam turned away and shrugged himself into his jacket. 'I'll away to the town. See what's to happen to our Matty.' Anything was better than staying here, feeling his wife's accusing eyes on him.

Huddled in the damp-smelling blanket, Matty waited. Each time he heard footsteps echoing down the long corridor, the rattle and clank of keys, or the grating sound of a door being opened, he looked up hopefully. His stomach, empty and rumbling again, told him that much more than the promised hour had passed. At last there was the clank of the bolt being drawn and an ever-widening line of light round the door. He sat up, eager to face the magistrate, or even his father, anything rather than have to spend another minute here.

'Come on now, get a move on.' It was an officer Matty hadn't seen before, one who had no sympathy for young thieves, especially from the mining villages. 'Upstairs, and look sharp about it. This way.' The policeman gripped him by the arm and dragged him, blinking and confused, up to the relative brightness of the police station then out, on to the street and across the road, towards the imposing court building. He was hustled past the magnificent double entrance doors, led round the side of the building, down some steps and brought to a halt outside a single, iron door. The constable tugged on a bell set high on the wall and the

27

door opened. Encouraged by a determined shove between his shoulders, Matty stepped inside and found himself in a corridor very similar to the one in the police station.

'This way,' the constable ordered impatiently.

Matty trailed up some steep wooden stairs, waited at the top while another stout door was unlocked by someone on the other side and stepped through into the polished splendour of the courtroom.

He stopped, staring round in fear and confusion, awed by a sea of faces, all stern and unsmiling, and a great deal of dark wood. Rough hands led him forward to mount some wooden steps and he realised he was standing in a sort of box. On one side of the room, arranged in tiers on wooden benches, was a crowd of people, all strangers, all staring at him. On the other, behind a raised desk, his presence dominating the room, was a man, his expression as dark as his black robe. Matty looked round desperately searching for his father but failed to find him. He felt sick.

'Are you Matthew McPherson?' Magistrate Binns peered over his half-glasses at the trembling youngster and sighed. He saw too many lads like this, brought before him for childish pranks which would be better dealt with by their parents. A night in the cells and a stern talking to was often enough for a boy of this age but when the Provost's wife insisted on charges then there was no option but to bring the case to court, wasting time and money which would be better spent on dealing with real villains.

'Answer when you're spoken to,' the policeman standing behind Matty hissed in his ear.

Magistrate Binns, accustomed to a certain amount of confusion from his unwilling customers, repeated the question. 'Are you Matthew McPherson?'

'Aye.' Matty nodded vigorously, anxious to make a good impression.

'Aye, *sir*,' corrected the policeman.

'Aye. Sir,' Matty repeated, moving nervously from one foot to the other.

'Stand still, lad, and concentrate on what I am saying,' the magistrate ordered.

Matty froze, his face draining of all colour at the sternness of the magistrate's tone, understanding that this bad-tempered old man might very well send him to prison. He decided to grovel. It sometimes worked with his mother. 'I'm right sorry, sir. I know it was wrong and I won't do it again.'

Poor little bugger. Magistrate Binns smothered a smile and buried his head in a sheaf of papers. Still, no reason to let the lad think the court was soft. Give him enough of a fright to make him think twice the next time. He wished he could have been there to see Mrs Laing sitting in the gutter himself, though. That would have been a sight to feed off for weeks. He settled his glasses more firmly on his plump nose and glared at the boy.

'Right lad, I want you to answer these questions truthfully.'

Matty quaked. 'Yes, sir.'

'Now then. Did you or did you not steal a cabbage from Mr Tonner yesterday?'

'Aye, sir.' Matty looked miserably at his feet.

'Do you know you were wrong?'

'Aye, sir.'

'Well, that's something I suppose. But if you knew it was wrong, why did you do it?'

'I hadn't the money to buy one. I wanted to take it home for my Ma, for the soup. Sir.'

29

'Cabbage soup? Did she not give you the money for it?'

'No, sir. I wanted to take her a present.'

Magistrate Binns peered through his glasses instead of over them, bringing the boy into sharp focus. The marks of poverty were obvious. He sighed heavily. Still right was right and wrong was wrong. 'You're from Craigie?'

'Aye, sir.'

'Your father'll be on strike then?'

'Aye, sir.'

'So you thought to help out by taking your mother a wee present of a cabbage?'

'Aye, sir.'

'And what was a wee lad like you doing in Inverannan all on your own?'

'I wasn't on my own, sir. And I'm not wee. I'm ten.'

Binns frowned and looked even more closely at the lad who looked nearer seven than ten. All skin and bones, poor little sod. 'Ten? Well, that's big enough to know right from wrong, lad. And who were you with?'

'Our Meggie.'

'And who's your Meggie?' Binns asked kindly.

'My big sister.'

'She was supposed to be looking after you, was she?'

'Aye.'

'And do you know how old she is?'

'Thirteen,' Matty answered proudly.

'Aye, lad, thirteen is big right enough. Big enough to take better care of her wee brother, eh? Maybe she should be up there along with you?'

Matty considered this and nodded his head vigorously, wishing his big sister was indeed there beside him so that he could slip his hand inside hers like he so often did. And then it occurred to him to wonder why he was here on his own, why Meggie had run off and left him like that. For the first time anger displaced the fear which had been his constant companion since yesterday morning. He scowled.

'Still,' Binns went on, unaware of the train of thought he had provoked in the young lad. 'That doesn't make what you did any better.'

'I'm sorry.' Matty lifted huge round eyes and looked straight at the magistrate.

'Aye, lad, I expect you are. You'll not do it again, then? You know it's not right to steal?'

Matty shook his head then nodded it, desperately. Someone in the courtroom laughed. Binns smiled.

'Well, you'd better not let me see you here again or you'll be in real trouble. Understand?'

Matty couldn't believe his luck. 'Aye . . . Thank you. Sir.'

'Magistrate Binns!' Everyone in the small courtroom turned to look at the tall, beak-nosed woman who was awaiting Magistrate Binn's attention with an expression so sour that it would turn milk in the cow.

'Mrs Laing.' Binns groaned inwardly. 'Have you something to say to the court?'

'You know very well I have. This young ruffian attacked me. You can't let him go!'

'Attacked you?'

'He did. And plenty of folk saw him do it,' she insisted.

'Well, lad, what do you say to that? Did you attack Mrs Laing?'

'No, sir. I knocked into her by accident,' Matty told him. 'I didn't mean her to fall over.'

'Did anyone see this happen?'

'I did.' Billy Tonner stood up, ready to enjoy his moment of glory.

'Right then, Mr Tonner. Come to the front and say your

piece.' Anxious to be done with this and get away to his lunch Magistrate Binns abandoned all formality.

'The lad's right enough. He knocked Mrs Laing down but it was an accident.'

'Och! How can you say that, Mr Tonner, when the little devil stole from you?' Elsie Laing's outrage echoed round the room.

'Aye, he stole the cabbage right enough but he didn't attack you, Mrs Laing. It was an accident. I saw it.'

So Billy Tonner had seen her knocked into the gutter but hadn't lifted a finger to help. She would remember that. She stared at him icily but he grinned and looked right back.

'Is there anyone else here who saw what went on?' Magistrate Binns asked wearily.

Half a dozen eager citizens rose to their feet.

'Is there anyone who would swear on the Holy Bible that this wee lad deliberately attacked Mrs Laing?' Binns asked. No one moved. 'Is there anyone who would swear on the Holy Bible that it was an accident? Raise your hands if that is the case.'

Six hands stabbed the air.

'Well, that seems to be that. An accident,' he decided.

'How dare you? What sort of court is this? That boy should go to prison', Elsie screeched at him.

Binns clattered his pen down and glared at her. 'A fair court, Mrs Laing. One which doesn't waste the county's time and money. And one which doesn't send ten-year-old lads to jail for such a minor offence. Now, . . .' The look he gave her was enough to send her back to her seat. '. . . keep yourself quiet or you'll be the one up here answering a charge. There's no real harm been done, except to your dignity. The wee lad will apologise and that'll be an end to it.' He looked expectantly at Matty who, prompted by the policeman, mumbled, 'I'm sorry, sir.'

'Louder. And it's Mrs Laing you should be apologising to. Not me.'

Matty took a deep breath and decided to do the thing properly. 'I'm right sorry, Mrs. I didn't mean to knock you down.'

Mrs Laing kept her eyes firmly on her feet, knowing that the citizens of Inverannan would be laughing at her expense for weeks to come.

Binns grunted. 'Is this lad's mother or father here?'

There was a shuffling at the back of the room and Tam McPherson rose slowly to his feet. Relief flooded through Matty but faded again as soon as he saw the expression on his father's face.

'You are this boy's father?' Binns asked, pleased to see that the man appeared to be taking the proceedings seriously. By the look on his father's face the lad would be punished severely enough once he got home.

'I am.' Tam McPherson kept his tone of voice respectful but he would never resort to calling another man 'sir'.

'You understand that this is a serious offence?'

'I do.'

'Times may be hard for you miners, Mr McPherson, but I'll not have your children out on the streets, thieving from honest people.'

Tam swallowed an angry retort and stared stonily in front of him. 'No.'

'I shall hold you responsible for making sure that this lad of yours doesn't come before the court again. Take him home and leather his backside. Case dismissed.' Magistrate Binns rose, already contemplating his lunch.

The court emptied slowly. Matty waited until everyone

had gone before walking across to his father who was standing by the door.

As soon as his son joined him, Tam turned and led the way out of the building, up the High Street and through the town. He wore his anger round him like an impenetrable armour and they were well along the road to Craigie before Matty plucked up the courage to speak.

'I'm sorry, Pa,' he offered nervously.

Tam marched on in silence, leaving Matty to trail behind, knowing that he was walking towards the beating of his life.

His mother's greeting was even less encouraging. She was sitting at the table and, when he walked through the door, she burst into tears. Nothing she could have done would have made Matty more aware of how seriously they took his crime. Even Meggie gave him nothing more than a watery half-smile. Close to tears himself and still angry with his sister, he fled towards the bedroom.

'No!' Meggie's shout halted him.

'Sit down!' her father rounded on her. 'Hold your tongue, girl. Let him go in there and see what the pair of you have done.' He went to the bedroom door and flung it open.

Perplexed and miserable, Matty was glad to escape to the other room. He walked in and looked round, wondering what his father had been talking about. Nancy was asleep on the bed so he was careful not to make a lot of noise and wake her. He still couldn't see anything unusual so sank cautiously down beside his baby sister. At least if she woke up she would smile at him. He looked at her, willing her to open her eyes. He went on looking at her, knowing there was something about her that wasn't quite right but not understand what. It was a full minute before realisation hit him. Then he bolted from the room like an unbroken horse. His father caught him at the front door.

'Now do you understand what you've done?' he asked.

'It wasn't Matty's fault, Pa,' Meggie tried to intercede. 'It was me. I dropped the bottle.'

Tam gripped his son's upper arm and pulled the trembling child round to face him. 'If you hadn't stolen that cabbage Margaret wouldn't have dropped the medicine bottle and Nancy would be getting better by now.'

Matty merely stared, too shocked to speak. He barely registered the fact that Tam was loosening his thick leather belt, ready to inflict punishment on both children.

'Please, Pa, no . . .' Meggie begged.

'Be quiet. You are to blame for all of this. You were in charge of your brother. You are the eldest. It is your fault that Matty got into trouble in the first place. You should have been watching him. And you were the one who dropped the bottle.'

For Meggie the thrash of the belt on her bared buttocks was almost a relief. So guilty did she feel that she was glad of every spear of pain her father inflicted. She did not cry.

Matty was beyond pain. When it was over he crept away to the corner of the room and crouched there in utter silence. Like an animal.

Mrs Laing pushed her way through the smirking crowd outside the courthouse, string straight ahead, avoiding the malicious pleasure she imagined she would see on every face. The shame of it! For her, the Provost's wife, to be spoken to in such a manner by the likes of Magistrate Binns, who, everyone knew, was nothing more than a jumped-up mill-hand! Despite the glorious war record which had won him decorations for valour and field promotions to the officer class, his concern for those less fortunate than himself, and the position of eminence and respect he now held in Inverannan, Elsie would always remember Eddy Binns as the grubby, snotty-nosed lad who had started school on the same day as her. She, the only child of a well-to-do banker, had worn a clean woollen dress and good leather boots while he, fourth son of a carter, had turned up in hand-downs and bare feet. Elsie considered that to be a good enough reason to ignore all he had achieved since that time and look down her hooked nose at him for the rest of her life.

Anxious to get away from the scene of her humiliation she strode off up the bustling High Street, not even lingering to find herself a cab. In grim defiance of her forty-seven years she forced her proud, stiff-backed figure on at a fast pace and fifteen minutes later, she was half-way up the steep hill on which perched the town's most prestigious houses.

Officially named, 'Benalder Lodge', in memory of a honeymoon spent slaughtering the west highland wildlife, the Laing residence was more commonly known simply as, 'The Big Hoose'. Set at the very crest of the hill, slightly apart from and dominating the other houses, it was an impressively large but drab building constructed from the greying stone that gave the whole town its rather dour appearance. The effect of the large bay windows which were its best feature was nullified by plain white nets. The result was a blind, featureless appearance, an impression not helped by a dull expanse of severely trimmed lawn. Along one side of this ran a flower-lined driveway.

Kneeling painfully on the gravel, rooting among the precise rows of edging plants in endless pursuit of any weed, stone, or fallen leaf which might dare to mar the outward perfection of the Provost's home, was an elderly gardener.

Elsie ignored him, then came to a conspicuous, tongue-clicking halt in front of a wheelbarrow which lay in her path. The old man creaked to his feet and shifted the barrow a bare three feet to the left, so saving Elsie the inconvenience of walking round it. She walked on without even bothering to look at him. He muttered something deeply profane then hawked and aimed a satisfying amount of spittle at her favourite plant.

Elsie, exhausted by her fast-paced climb up the hill, was red-faced and breathless by the time she reached her own doorstep. She dashed a hand over the droplets of moisture beading her lip and proceeded to vent her temper on the pretty fifteen-year-old who had the misfortune to be her maid.

'Don't hold my coat like that! You'll crease it. Take it upstairs and hang it up. Now. Wait! Where do you think you're going? Take my gloves. And my hat.' She dumped both in the girl's outstretched arms, marched into her sitting room and immediately rang her handbell.

Beth, halfway up the stairs, hesitated then turned and ran back down, arranged her mistress's clothes on a hall chair, wiped the irritated frown off her face and hurried to see what Mrs Laing wanted now.

'Is my lunch ready?' Elsie asked.

'I thought you said you were eating in town?' Beth answered with a sinking heart.

'Don't you dare answer back!' Elsie rounded on her, her face and neck mottling in shades of red and purple. Indeed she had expected to take her lunch in town, to be able to crow to her acquaintances about the justice she had caused to be visited on the young thief, to reaffirm her position of superiority in the town.

'I can make you an omelette in ten minutes,' the girl suggested timidly.

'Omelette! Is there no cold roast beef left?'

'No, Mrs Laing.'

'And why not? What has happened to it?' Elsie raged in her most accusing tone.

'Och, Mrs Laing. It wasn't a very big piece of meat. Just enough for the three meals there was.' Mrs Laing, for all her husband's supposed money, was parsimonious in the extreme when it came to housekeeping. Beth couldn't imagine any other household feeding itself for three days on a joint of meat that had weighed little more than a pound to start with.

Elsie might have argued but her husband's tightfistedness and the resultant restrictions on her budget wasn't something to which she wanted to draw attention. Even she knew she was asking too much of a pound of topside. She capitulated with bad grace. 'Very well. An omelette will do.'

By the time she heard her husband's key in the lock that evening, Elsie Laing's temper had been fermenting dangerously for six hours.

'Good evening, my dear. I hope you have had a pleasant day.' The words were nothing more than habit. Wallace Laing, a tall, distinguished-looking man in his early fifties neither looked at his wife nor waited for an answer before sinking into his own chair and reaching for his evening paper.

Elsie knew better than to launch directly into a recital of her own complaints and simply replied, as she replied every evening, 'Good evening, Wallace,' before energetically ringing the chunky brass handbell to indicate that she would expect to see a perfectly cooked meal on the dining room table in exactly fifteen minutes.

In truth, she was somewhat in awe of her husband, more so now, after twenty years of marriage then she had been as a young bride. Success had changed Wallace, given him an air of authority which was difficult to challenge. He bore little resemblance to the eager young man who had been intent on learning the business of mining, industriously seeking ways to make the concern more profitable, ready for the day when his grandfather's shares in the Strathannan Mining Company should fall into his hands. In those days he had been as anxious as she to amass the material things by which his standing could be judged. There had been this house, a carriage, servants, modern furnishings and a regularly updated wardrobe of smart clothes in which to entertain guests at the lavish dinners he had enjoyed hosting. Over the succeeding years Elsie watched in dismay as Wallace lost the raw look of youth and matured gradually to become a handsome, grey-haired personification of success while her own slim figure aged into scrawniness.

Nor did she have his social ease. Wallace enjoyed the company of similarly-minded men and could converse impressively on the heavy subjects of politics and commerce, always relishing a lively, open discussion. Elsie sat through many boring evenings, the conversation beyond her comprehension. But when she made the effort to find out more, to play her part as an informed, intelligent spouse, she met with an icy wall of ridicule. He, he informed her coldly, irritated by her tendency to regurgitate poorly understood sentences from the morning papers, would worry about business, money and the state of the country. His wife should confine herself to womanly, domestic matters.

Disillusioned, she devoted herself to caring for their son, Oliver. When Oliver finally left school, taking his place beside his father, eager to join the male world of freedom and independence, her horizons closed in even more. Her life now revolved around her own reflected importance as Provost's wife.

Meanwhile, finding himself at an age when his peers were fast sinking into self-satisfied, paunch-ridden middle age, Wallace discovered that his wife had evolved into a bitter, ugly woman and looked for the rediscovery of his youth elsewhere. The process was an enjoyable if exhausting one, and, along with the shrinking company profits, accounted for the need to run this household with the minimum of expense. But this was not something he could explain to his wife.

Knowing that Wallace expected to eat his evening meal in peace, Elsie curbed her impatience, contenting herself by releasing her frustration on the unfortunate Beth, who was criticised both for the quality of the pastry on the excellent steak pie and the speed at which she responded to her mistress's summons. Then, leaving the resentful maid to clear the table, Elsie joined her husband in their over-furnished sitting room. The furniture was all good-quality, heavy stuff, every surface polished daily to a glaring sheen then covered by fussy, lace-edged runners upon which rested a glut of ornaments, photographs and pot plants. The claustrophobic atmosphere was exacerbated by dark wall-paper and several coats of treacle-coloured varnish on skirting boards, picture rails and doors.

'Really,' she exploded as she sat down opposite him,

unable to contain her ill temper any longer, 'That girl is quite useless.'

'Then get rid of her,' Wallace grunted, taking up the paper again.

'And where do you think I would find anyone else to work for the sort of wages you pay?' she demanded.

He lifted the paper and hid behind it, unwilling to be drawn into another confrontation about money. But Elsie was too disgruntled to be so easily deterred.

'Really, Wallace, I don't know how you expect me to run this house on the money you allow me.'

Wallace glared at her over the top of the paper. This had been a regularly resurrected topic for several months now and it was time for him to put a stop to his wife's constant carping.

'I give you more than sufficient to meet all the household expenses, Elsie. If you choose to spend it on new coats and hats and dresses and gloves . . .' He looked pointedly at the unflattering, dropped waist dress which was obviously a new acquisition.

Elsie, who had wrongly assumed that her husband never noticed the frequent additions to her wardrobe, flushed guiltily but defended herself vigorously. 'You are the Provost! As your wife I have a position to maintain. People judge by appearances, Wallace.'

He sighed in exasperation. 'Money is very tight at the moment, Elsie. You, like everyone else, will just have to economise.'

'But surely you can't be in difficulties, Wallace?' The prospect was so appalling that the words came out as a hoarse whisper.

'No, not in difficulties precisely.' He regarded her sternly over the top of the paper. 'Surely even you must realise that this damned strike is taking its toll. There has been no output of coal since May.'

'I understand that, Wallace. I am not stupid. But you haven't had to pay wages . . .'

'You understand nothing!' he thundered. 'The men aren't working but the pits still have to be maintained. The pumps have to be kept running, the workings must be made safe. There's been more damage in these five months of idleness than in ten years of regular work. The managers and officials have to be paid, then there's the watchmen . . . the expense is astronomical.'

'Oh . . .'

'Aye . . . oh.' He was scornful. 'Still, they can't hold out for much longer. They'll be forced to go back soon or starve to death.'

Elsie, who had only the sketchiest understanding of the inadequate pay and intolerable conditions which had driven the miners to the current confrontation, snorted. 'If they starve it's their own fault. It's disgusting, so it is, paying men to be idle when there's jobs waiting for them. If you ask me they don't know when they're well off.'

'Aye, well, the relief fund's all but exhausted. There'll be nothing at all for them in another week or so. They'll go back to work soon enough then, and for lower wages, too. It's that or the poorhouse.' There was no note of victory in Wallace's voice. Unlike many mine owners he was acutely aware of the dire conditions in which his employers existed and truly wished he was in a position to offer improvements. But, with increasingly inaccessible seams and inefficient equipment, a legacy of mismanagement handed down to him by his own grandfather, the Strathannan Mining Company had been poorly placed to take advantage of the brief upsurge in demand which had taken place two years ago.

Now the market had fallen away, made worse by the high price of British coal abroad. The Strathannan Mining Company, barely in profit, even before the strike, was facing a crisis. Unlike some other, more unscrupulous owners, Wallace Laing's claim that he could not afford to keep the miners' wages at their present level, now that the government subsidy had ended, was genuine. A rise in the wages bill would tip them into a collapse which would deprive the colliers of their jobs permanently, something Wallace was determined to avoid.

Elsie stubbornly refused to acknowledge any of this. 'About time too. There's been nothing but trouble with the miners. That boy I told you about . . . the one who knocked me over?'

Wallace was about to bury himself in his paper again. 'What about him?'

'His father's a miner.'

'Oh?' With the first sign of genuine interest, Wallace lowered his paper and Elsie gave herself up to an indignant recital of the morning's events.

'Binns let him away with it,' she ended. 'That man has no business being a magistrate. The boy should have been sent to the jail, made an example of. Now every miner's child will think it's perfectly acceptable to steal.'

Wallace frowned. For his wife to be publicly rebuked by a magistrate reflected badly on him. And in the matter of Magistrate Binns, a working-class man who made no secret of his support for the miners, he and his wife were in rare, perfect accord. 'The man's a damned disgrace. Everyone knows he's in sympathy with the strikers. Why can't men like him see what the miners here are doing to themselves?

They can't win. If this goes on for much longer there won't be any jobs for them to go back to. What'll happen to them and their families then?' The frustration was plain in his voice.

'Tch . . .' Elsie tutted her disapproval. 'The boy's father was in court this morning. Sly looking, rough, dirty . . .' She shuddered. 'One of yours I should think. He was from Craigie.'

'He was, was he? What was his name? Do you remember?'

'I'm not likely to forget it am I?' she retorted acidly. 'McPherson.'

'McPherson! I might have known he'd be causing trouble,' Wallace exploded.

It was a gratifying reaction and Elsie smiled. 'You know him then?'

'I know of him. Tam McPherson. Union man. Agitator. If it wasn't for the likes of him the men at the Dene would have been back weeks ago. Bloody Communist . . .'

'You'll not let this pass then, Wallace?'

'No,' he looked at her and shook his head slowly. 'I'll not forget Tam McPherson in a hurry.' Abruptly he folded his paper, set it on the table and stood up. 'I've business to attend to. Don't bother to wait up.'

Her husband's habitual abandonment of her usually irked Elsie. Tonight she went as far as to smile and say, 'Very well, Wallace,' before settling back in her chair with a look of satisfaction on her thin face.

CHAPTER THREE

Netta McPherson cut the last of the bread into two thick slices, smeared them with bacon fat and packed them in Tam's piece tin. She set this on the table beside a bottle of cold tea, knowing it wasn't enough to see him through a full shift. The last months had been difficult enough but the next two weeks, until he got his first pay, would be the hardest of all. She stood at the window, looking out across the rows. Most of the houses were still in complete darkness, the occupants no longer able to find the money to light the oil lamps on which these mean dwellings depended, but Netta knew that inside them, the women were up, seeing their men off to work for the first time in seven months.

She had yearned for today, for an end to the strife, but never had she imagined it would all finish up like this, that their struggle would be in vain. The long months of hardship, months which had seen weaker children die and made the strongest of them ill, had gained them nothing. The miners were returning to work but for lower wages and worse conditions, their spirit broken. And it was people like Tam, men who had worked passionately for the cause, who were being blamed for the resultant misery. It was all so unfair.

It was still half dark and mist lay eerily in low patches, caught in the hollows between the rows. As she watched, Tam emerged from the privie and walked slowly back to the cottage, his whole bearing one of defeat. Behind him, the dark figures of men started to drift through the gloom in the direction of the Dene.

She turned as Tam came in and watched as he jammed his piece tin and bottle into his jacket pockets. He nodded briefly before letting himself out again and merging with the tide of silent men.

A month ago Nancy would have been awake, hungry and wet, filling Netta's time until the other children had to be roused for school. Now the little house was still and quiet, almost as if it was completely empty. Grief swamped Netta, tightening across her chest until she could hardly breathe. Nancy, her youngest child, her last child, had been the most precious of them all. With the others all at school she had had time to enjoy her tiny daughter as she had never been able to enjoy the others.

Nancy had been a gift, an unexpected blessing when her failure to conceive again had made her believe that her child-bearing days were over. Even now she could recall how upset she had been when she had realised that she was wrong; could remember just how strongly she had resented this new drain on her energy; how clearly she had known they simply could not afford another bairn. But when Nancy was born, bigger than any of them, red-faced and lusty, Netta had loved her with every fibre of her being. And then had come the strike which had reduced them all to a diet of watery porridge and thin soup. One by one the children had succumbed to upset stomachs and bad chests. Nancy, who had always seemed so strong and resilient, had become thin, flushed and miserable. Finally, what had appeared to be nothing more than a feverish cold had refused to go away and had finally choked her lungs.

Netta roused herself from the lethargy which claimed her every unguarded moment and poked at the red embers in the stove, setting the half-empty kettle on them to heat. Then she wrapped her knitted shawl tightly round her shoulders and took the water bucket to the standpipe. Several other women were already there and she joined the back of the queue, offering a quiet greeting but getting only curt nods in return. Netta knew they blamed her, along with Tam, for the defeat. Ina Lennox, a young woman who was neater and cleaner-looking than many of the others, stood in front of her, a well-wrapped infant balanced on her hip. She alone turned and smiled kindly.

'Don't mind them,' she advised, not bothering to lower her voice, which carried clearly in the still air. 'Your Tam did his best. It's not his fault that they had to go back to work.'

'Look where it got us,' Doris Cree, a big-boned, loud-voiced woman rounded on them from the front of the line. 'We're worse off now than we've ever been. The men should never have listened to the likes of Tam McPherson.'

'If it wasn't for the likes of him us women and bairns would still be going down the pits alongside our men,' Ina retorted angrily.

'And what would you know about it?' Doris challenged. 'Been here for five minutes and you think you know better than us who've lived here all our days.' There was a low murmur of approval from a few of Doris's cronies.

'I know enough to see that the mine owners are getting fat while their workers starve,' Ina retorted furiously, taking a step towards her bitterest foe, while many of the women yelled their support.

Netta, who had witnessed many similar clashes in the dying days of the dispute put a restraining hand on Ina's arm. 'Leave it, Ina. We women held together all through the strike and we've all suffered too much to start fighting among ourselves now.' The others, disheartened and weary, nodded their agreement and went back to their chores.

'You more than most,' Ina said, turning back to her friend. 'Poor wee Nancy.'

'Aye,' Netta sighed and said, in an undertone, 'There's been many times when I've felt the way Doris Cree does. All those weeks of going without, just to end up with less than we started with.'

'Maybe, but you know Tam and the others were right. Don't let anyone tell you otherwise.' Ina picked up her bucket and stepped into the mire round the standpipe where she filled her bucket with icy water.

Netta took her turn next, watching her friend stride quickly back to her own home at the far end of the rows and wishing she had the same strength of character. She understood herself well enough to know that she was a follower rather than a leader and was content to let others make the decisions. The same was true of her marriage. Even though she was often irritated by Tam's obsession with the miners' cause and was frequently resentful of the way he seemed to take everything she did for granted, she was glad to have his strength to lean on. And, for all his faults, she still loved him. Without him she felt she would be nothing.

She hefted the heavy bucket home, topped up the steaming kettle and used a little of her fast-dwindling supply of oats to make a watery porridge for the children's breakfast.

That done she opened the door of the second room and shouted, 'Come on youse lot, up you get.' She stopped, frowning, then peered at the mattress on the floor where Meggie was supposed to sleep. Looking angrily back at the bed she counted four heads instead of the three which should have been there. Furiously she stripped back the blankets and coats which covered the children. Meggie was curled up, hugging Matty close against her while Bertie snuggled into her back with Perce, in turn, wrapped around him.

'Meggie McPherson! Get out of that bed this instant,' Netta roared.

Four pairs of almost identical dark eyes flew open and stared at her. Meggie, with difficulty, disentangled herself from her brothers' limbs and crawled out of bed to stand barefoot on the cold floor, facing her mother's wrath.

'How many times have I told you not to sleep with your brothers?' Netta demanded.

'We were cold and Matty was crying. He's feared of the dark,' Meggie explained.

Netta turned exasperated eyes on her middle son. 'Feared of the dark! At your age?'

'But we were cold, Mam.' Perce, the oldest of the boys, hauled the covers back over his shivering body.

'It doesn't matter. Meggie's got her own bed. She's no business getting in with youse.' She faced her unhappy daughter. 'If I catch you in with them again, I'll make you sleep under the kitchen table,' she threatened.

'But why can't I sleep with them any more?' Meggie asked. Until last month, she and her brothers had always snuggled in together and she didn't understand why it was suddenly wrong for her to do so now.

Netta eyed her daughter's budding breasts then looked away quickly. 'You're too big,' was her unhelpful reply. Not wanting to be trapped into embarrassing explanations she went hastily back to the kitchen, calling, 'Get yourselves dressed and ready for the school. And hurry up!'

Half an hour later Netta stood in her doorway, watching

her children walking down the rows towards the little school. Just four more grubby-looking weans in handed down clothes and bare legs, no different from any of the other ragged urchins who roamed the rows after school, getting up to mischief. Perce and Bertie ran, yelling their heads off, to join their own special friends but Meggie and Matty, as always, walked hand in hand. Netta felt the familiar surge of irritation with them. It wasn't right that they should be so close, they should each have friends of their own age. But Meggie and Matty were inseparable. More so since Nancy's death.

Netta, lost in her own grief, never realised the terrible guilt that Meggie and Matty felt while they, sensing a change in their mother's attitude towards them, believed they were no longer loved. In a way they were right. Netta knew it was wrong, knew Nancy would have died, even had she been dosed with the fated medicine, but somehow she couldn't help associating those two with what had happened.

Netta watched until all four had disappeared from view then went back inside and wearily started to gather the used cups and dishes, stacking them in the sink, knowing that there were a hundred chores which needed to be done in the never-ending battle to keep the tiny house even half decent. But instead of setting to work she sank down miserably in a chair at the table and rested her face in her hands, unable to rouse herself sufficiently to even make a start.

It was there that Tam discovered her when he came home fifteen minutes later.

Netta heard the door open and looked up with a start, her eyes red-rimmed and watery. 'Tam!' She shot to her feet as he tossed his piece box on to the table with a clatter. 'What are you doing home?' The expression on his face made her heart turn to lead.

'I've been put off,' he growled.

'Put off?' She repeated it dully, her head starting to spin.

'Aye. Sacked. Fired.' His voice was loaded with bitterness.

'Och, no!' she cried. 'But why, Tam? After all these years, why? You're one of the best. Mister Mickle said so himself.'

'There's not enough work. Not enough for me anyway. Too much to say for myself during the strike. That's what Mickle told me.'

'But they can't do that, Tam.'

'They can do what they bloody well like!' he retorted, collapsing on to a chair and lowering his face into his hands. Netta was appalled to realise his shoulders were heaving with suppressed sobs. Very gently she reached across to him and stroked his hair.

'It's not your fault, Tam McPherson,' she told him. 'You did your best. You always do your best.'

Her strong, dependable husband lifted tear-filled eyes and choked. 'I'm sorry, lass. I'm sorry.'

She took his hand, lifted it to her mouth and kissed his fingers. 'You did what you thought was right. You've nothing to be sorry for.'

'What are we going to do now, Netta? There's no work for me here. How will we manage?'

Never before had he turned to her for help. A flutter of fear clutched at Netta's heart even as it swelled with love for him. 'We will manage, Tam,' she told him fiercely. 'Somehow, together, we'll manage.'

The rows were in darkness. The children were in bed. Tam and Netta were sitting in silence in the shadowed room,

51

each immersed in their own dismal thoughts. A sharp rap on the door disturbed them. Netta rose and hurriedly cleared the dirty cups from the table before going to see who their unexpected visitor was.

'Mrs McPherson?'

'Aye.' Even in the darkness she recognised the company agent, Peter Bonar. 'Och, it's yourself, Mr Bonar.'

'I need to have a wee word with your man, Mrs McPherson. Is he at home the night?'

'Aye. Come away in, Mr Bonar.' Netta ushered him into the house then lit the lamp, burning oil they could not afford to replace.

Tam was standing with his back to the empty grate, his face hard, but he greeted the man politely enough. 'Mr Bonar. What can we do for you?'

Bonar shifted uneasily.

'It's not rent day yet, is it, Mr Bonar?' Netta asked, knowing that when it did fall due she was unlikely to have the money to pay him. But Bonar was a reasonable man. More than likely he would give them time, let a couple of weeks pass so that Tam could find himself another job. After all, they had always paid up on time before, even through the strike when many of their neighbours had fallen into arrears.

'No, Mrs McPherson. I'll be round on Friday for the rent, as always.'

'Then what are you here for, man?' Tam asked.

Bonar took a deep breath and relied on the authority of his position to get him through this. 'You'll be aware, Mr McPherson, that you are entitled to occupy this house only so long as you work for the Strathannan Mining Company?'

Beside him, Netta gasped. 'Och, you can't be going to put us out?'

'I'm sorry.'

'But Tam'll find another job. He's going to go round all the pits.'

'There'll be nothing for him with the company, Mrs McPherson.'

'Then he'll try the mills in the town. There's bound to be work for him there.'

'And no one wishes you success more than I do, Mr McPherson. But this house belongs to the company. You are no longer entitled to live in it.'

'I've a wife and four weans,' Tam roared, taking a threatening step towards the agent. 'You can't throw us out on the street. Where are we supposed to go?'

'I wish I could help you, Mr McPherson. As it is I have my orders. You're to be out of this house four weeks from today.'

'You bastard! Is it not enough for you that I've no job?' Tam brought his face close to Bonar's and snarled at him. 'Get out of my house before I knock your bloody teeth down your throat.'

'Tam . . ' Netta laid a restraining hand on her husband's arm.

Bonar stood his ground. This wasn't the first time he'd had to perform this unpleasant duty and he had known what to expect. 'Sit down, Mr McPherson. You'll not do yourself any good by threatening me.'

Tam glowered at him for seconds longer, then, realising the futility of fighting with this man, backed away slightly.

'Mr Bonar . . .' Netta pleaded. 'We've nowhere to go . . . no money . . . no work . . . nothing. What in the name of all that's right are we supposed to do?'

53

'I'm just doing my job, Mrs McPherson. You've got four weeks. I can't do more than that.' He proferred a sheet of paper. 'It's all written there for you. Legal and proper.'

Tam knocked it violently out of his hand and turned away to stare at the dead fire. 'Get out,' he growled. 'Get out of my bloody house.'

Bonar picked up the paper and slapped it pointedly on the table then made for the door. Netta followed him.

'I'm right sorry, Mrs McPherson,' he muttered. 'And you do understand that the rent will still have to be paid? You're a fortnight in advance so I'll be back on Friday for the last two weeks rent as usual.'

'You can try, Mr Bonar,' she retorted, slamming the door in his face.

Tam spent every day trudging round the pits, vainly seeking work. He borrowed a bicycle from Joe Lennox and went as far afield as Glencraig and Comrie in the neighbouring county, hoping to be put on by the Fife Coal Company. He always got the same discouraging replies. After that he spent days in Inverannan, visiting the linen mills, willing to take the most lowly position. But there was nothing for him there either.

It was Netta who, with under a week left to them in their tiny home, set him on the only path left open to him.

'You'll have to go to Bothlie and see Jim. He might know of something through there. And even if you don't get taken on in a pit there's a better chance of finding work, and somewhere to live, in a big city like Glasgow.'

Tam grunted. Jim McPherson was his only brother. He had enlisted in 1915 and, miraculously, survived unscathed for more than two years in the trenches. Then, with victory only months away, he had been wounded and found himself convalescing near Glasgow. When the war ended Jim had returned to Glasgow to marry a local girl. He had found work and housing in Bothlie colliery, a few miles outside the city. In all the intervening years he and Tam had met only twice. But there was no bad feeling between them and Tam knew that Jim would feel obliged to help as much as he could – as he would have done had the situation been reversed. Just the same, they and their four children would be an unwelcome burden on the other family and pride had made Tam reserve this desperate course of action as a last resort. Now there was no alternative.

The October day was fading before Tam dismounted from his borrowed bicycle and stood looking across the village where his brother lived. In some ways it was worse than Craigie. Low Bothlie was built on the very back of the mine. The pithead and bings loomed over the clustered houses, enveloping them in constant noise and dust. The surrounding countryside was bleak and exposed, scarred with mineworkings and offering none of Strathannan's redeeming soft beauty. The nearby towns were ugly, industrial places where factories, iron foundries and belching chimneys darkened the stone and choked the air. The houses themselves were almost identical to those in Craigie, low, dark and with the familiar stench of privies and coal mingling in the damp evening air. Here though, rather than straggling across the countryside in never-ending rows, the dwellings were clustered in several close groups around rectangular drying greens which took the place of the tiny back gardens in which the Craigie villagers were able to grow vegetables. Instead of the muddy tracks which linked the Strathannan houses, Low Bothlie had proper roads, each front door opening on to a narrow strip of pavement.

Tam, who had only been here once before, took a minute to work out where his brother's house was. Near to the shop, he recalled, and facing the pit itself. Wheeling the cycle tiredly through the streets he noticed the soft light coming from many windows and realised that this village had the advantage of gas. Perhaps when he told Netta that she would not mind coming here so much.

Propping the bike on the pavement aginst the front wall of the house, Tam knocked loudly. The door was opened by a tousle-headed lad of about seven or eight. His face was grimy, his legs were bare and his clothes were several sizes too large, but his grin was cheerful.

'Is your Dad at home, lad?' Tam asked him.

'Who wants to know?' the lad responded in a strong, Glasgow accent.

'Your Uncle Tam wants to know, that's who.'

'Tam!' The voice came from behind the half-open door. The wee lad was shoved aside and the door frame filled with a man of about Tam's own height and build. Plumper about the face than his brother, and with more hair, it was obvious that Jim McPherson was the younger of the two men, but the family resemblance was plain as soon as he smiled. 'Bloody hell, it is our Tam!' Jim grasped his brother's hand warmly then stood back and motioned to Tam to step inside. 'Is that your bicycle?' he asked.

'It's been loaned to me,' Tam explained.

'Best bring it inside. Leave it there and some wee tyke will make off with it before the door's right closed.' With that he grabbed the cycle and wheeled it indoors.

Tam followed and found himself in a small house, very similar to his own but brighter and warmer.

'Well, Tam McPherson, it's a gey long time since you came to pay us a visit.' Lil, Jim's wife, turned from the stove and subjected her brother-in-law to a searching frown. A woman more given to criticism than praise, Lil's face was prematurely lined, the skin dry and dull, the expression wary. Her instincts warned her that Tam's unexpected arrival could only mean he wanted something from them and there was little welcome in her manner as she rounded on her children. 'Right youse lot. Move yourselves and give your uncle Tam room to sit down.'

Tam watched while four children, not one of them older than eight, redistributed themselves around the room, finally making a place for him close to the fireside.

'I don't suppose youse mind of your uncle Tam?' Lil addressed her offspring. 'And I bet you don't even know which one's which,' she challenged her bemused brother-in-law.

Tam shook his head in a mute gesture of apology, sensing that somehow she had manged to put him in the wrong.

'The oldest one's James, after his Dad. Then there's Andrew and Sandy, in that order. And the wee one's Duncan.' Lil pointed to each of her grinning brood in turn, barely pausing for breath.

'Don't worry, Tam, you'll get them sorted out in time. I wouldn't know your weans either,' Jim laughed and nodded towards the bike. 'If you've come all the way on that thing you'll be fair starving.' He turned to his wife. 'Lil?'

'There's a scraping of stew left in the pot. I suppose you could have it if you want.' Lil offered her hospitality grudgingly then bawled at the children. 'Youse lot away outside for an hour. Go on. Out from under my feet!' She chased them outside and turned to clatter with her dishes.

Half an hour later Tam was mopping the last of the gravy from his plate with a hunk of fresh bread. 'By, and that was welcome, Lil. The best bit of stew I've tasted for a while.'

'Things have been bad across your way then?' Jim asked.

'Aye. We've not had meat on our table for months,' Tam admitted. 'Nor coal to light a decent fire either,' he added, nodding at the warm, orange glow in the grate. 'You've been back at work a week or two then?'

'Aye. Six weeks past. We couldn't hold out any longer, man. And you?'

'Four weeks in Craigie. Held out to the end we did.' He was aware of the bitter, critical note in his voice.

'Aye, and what good did it do?' Lil muttered.

'Would it have been right to do nothing?' Tam asked, but there was little conviction in his voice.

'Och, I know fine the way you feel, Tam, and I'll not argue with you about it, but the weans were starving. We had to go back. Everyone in Low Bothlie felt the same. No one broke faith. Everyone from our pit went back on the same day. A man can't stand by and watch his family suffer,' Jim said softly.

'I did.' Tam looked into the fire, unable to go on for a second or two. 'Our Nancy . . . she died, six weeks back.'

'Och, Tam.' The tragedy pierced even Lil's animosity and her eyes filled with tears. 'Och, poor wee mite.'

They sat in silence for a few moments, understanding Tam's need to collect himself. Then he said the words which cost him all his pride to utter. 'I'm in trouble, Jim. I've come to ask for your help.'

'Aye,' his brother nodded. 'I guessed as much.'

'I've done everything I could think of. I wouldn't come begging to you if there was any other way.'

Lil let her breath out in an audible hiss. Jim silenced her with a furious glare then turned to his brother. 'I know that fiine. And what are families for if we can't lend a hand where it's needed? We've not much in the way of savings, mind. A few pounds, that's all, but you're welcome to it.'

'I wish it was that easy,' his brother muttered. 'It's not money I'm after, Jim.'

'Well, lad, if we're to help you'd best come right out with it.' He and Lil pulled their chairs closer and sat in silence while Tam related the sad events of the past weeks.

'We've nothing,' he ended. 'I thought I'd have a better chance of work through this way. I'm willing to do anything, mind. It doesn't have to be in the pits. If you could just let us stay here for a wee while, until I can get something sorted out.'

'You know you're welcome here, Tam,' Jim said generously.

'But, there's six of us and six of you. We've only the two rooms . . .' Lil abandoned any attempt at goodwill. 'We'll never manage.'

'Lil,' Jim's voice was sharp. 'Surely we can work something out?' She stared at her iron-willed husband then dropped her gaze, knowing she was beaten.

'Aye,' she muttered. 'We'll work something out.'

Netta had been watching out for Tam for hours before she finally saw him wheeling the bike over the bumpy grass towards the house and knew at once that things hadn't gone as he had hoped. She chased the children off to bed, brewed the last of the tea, making it strong and black, and gave him a few minutes to rest. She was almost frightened to hear what he had to say. If there was to be no home for them with Jim and Lil they might all end up in the workhouse.

Tam took his time, not knowing how to tell her of the choices they had to make but finally he knew it was unfair to leave her wondering any longer.

'I saw Jim and Lil,' he began.

'Aye, I know that much, Tam McPherson,' she answered impatiently.

'Aye . . . Well, Jim offered us his savings. Eight pounds. It's little enough but it's all he's got and it's ours if we want it.'

'Och, I knew he'd help. He's a decent man, your Jim. And can we go to them for a wee while?'

'Aye.'

'Och, thank goodness! I've been that worried, Tam. I should have known things would work out all right in the end.' She was smiling now, something she had rarely done in the last hard weeks.

'It's not all right,' he stopped her abruptly, his voice echoing through the dark house.

'I thought you said . . .?'

'I did. Look, Netta, lass, we can do one of two things. Jim's offered us the money. We can take that, try to find ourselves somewhere else to live and hope I get another job before it runs out. Pay Jim back as soon as we can.'

'Eight pounds? That'll not keep us for very long, Tam and there'll be rent to pay and all.'

'Or, we can go and live with Jim and Lil. He'll need the money himself then, mind, to keep us.'

Netta thought for a moment. 'You know fine there's no work round here. We'll have a better chance through there.'

'Aye. There's no work at the pits just now, but Jim asked for me yesterday and they promised to keep me in mind when something does come up. Meantime there's plenty factories nearby. I could try them.'

Netta watched him closely, saw no sign of the relief she had expected. 'But?' she prompted him.

'Och, Netta. Lil and Jim, they've four weans of their own

60

in a house no bigger than this one. There's just not enough room for all of us, too. And Lil . . . well, she's not an easy woman to get along with.'

She turned away and thought about it for a minute. 'I should have realised,' she whispered. 'Och well, we'll just have to take the eight pounds . . .'

'No, Netta, you know that's not near enough to see us through. We'll end up losing it all and no hope of ever paying Jim back. That wouldn't be right.'

'So what are we going to do, Tam McPherson?' she demanded angrily. 'We've nothing! Your brother's offered us the only help we're going to get and you're sitting there telling me we can't take it?'

'We're going to go and live with him.'

'But you just said . . .'

'I know fine what I said. Just hear me through, will you?'

'I'm listening.'

'Right. Well, Jim's got four laddies. They'll manage to squeeze our three boys in with them, there's just enough space if we take that wee mattress Meggie sleeps on. And we'll have to sleep in the kitchen with Lil and Jim. They'll use the box bed and we'll have to make do with a mattress on the floor. It'll be a squash, not much privacy, but we'll manage.' He sighed heavily then went on. 'But there's nowhere for our Meggie. There's not the room and even if there was it wouldn't be right for her to sleep with the laddies, not at her age.'

'Och, Tam,' Netta breathed. 'We can't go and leave her behind.'

'It's for the best, Netta. What else can we do?' he asked wearily.

'But where will she go, Tam?'

'It'll only be for a few weeks. Maybe one of the neighbours will take her in, just until we're settled.'

'She'll not want to leave Matty.'

'Aye. I know. Maybe someone would take the two of them. It would be easier on the pair of them that way and better for Jim and Lil.'

'I don't know, Tam. It doesn't seem right.'

'Tomorrow, go and ask round the village. Ina Lennox might help. She's a decent lass. Ask her, Netta. It's either that or the workhouse for our Meggie.'

The next morning Netta shooed her brood off to school then hurried up the rows to see her friend, Ina Lennox.

'Och, Netta, I'd like to help but I don't see how I can. Now that I've got Joe's parents living with us, and only Joe's money coming in, I couldn't afford to take on your Meggie and Matty, too. And it wouldn't be good for them here, not with Joe's dad being so poorly.' Ina looked genuinely distressed. Her father-in-law's health had deteriorated rapidly during the strike and they all knew he would never work again. Ina had encouraged the older couple to give up their own home, hoping to ease the burden on her mother-in-law, but with four adults and a baby to keep and only Joe's wage to do it on, she was in no position to help her friend.

'It's all right, Ina. I understand. I shouldn't have asked.'

Nor did she meet with success elsewhere in the village. Although the miners were back at work, they were earning less now than before the strike and no family could afford to take on two more children, especially when Tam and Netta weren't able to offer anything towards their keep.

'We'll take Matty with us then,' Tam decided. 'But Meggie will have to go to the workhouse.'

'Tam . . .'

'Don't worry, hen. We'll fetch her back just as soon as I get myself a job,' he promised her.

'*No!*' Meggie screamed, holding her hands over her ears as if to block out the dreadful words. 'I won't go. You can't make me.'

'It's all organised, lass. I'm to take you to Inverannan the morn. On Saturday the rest of us will go through to your Uncle Jim's.' Tam couldn't meet his daughter's anguished eyes.

'You'll see, your father'll find himself a job and we'll all be together again before you know it.' Netta reached her arms out but Meggie pulled away and ran to stand with Matty, who slipped a hand into hers.

Netta and Tam had done their best to explain, to make this easier for Meggie, to try to make her understand that there had been no other way open to them, but the girl would not listen. Despairing, Netta slumped in a chair, not knowing what to say or do next.

'You'll never come to fetch me.' Meggie accused her parents bitterly. 'I know you won't. You just want to get rid of me.' She clutched desperately at Matty's warm hand.

'If Meggie can't go to Uncle Jim's, I'm not going either,' Matty spoke up now, setting his jaw defiantly at his father.

'You can't stay, lad. There's room for you with your cousins,' Tam told him gently.

'I'm not going! I'm staying with Meggie. You can't make me go.'

'You'll do what you're told,' Tam rounded on him coldly. 'Now, both of you get away to your beds.'

His son and daughter, their hands tightly linked, stared at him with identically rebellious expressions, but eventually

63

the girl turned away and pulled her brother towards the bedroom where Perce and Bertie were already sleeping.

Netta looked at her husband, desolation lining her face. Their eyes met and both knew what the other was thinking. It was Netta who put it into words. 'Maybe,' she whispered. 'Maybe they should stay together . . .?'

CHAPTER FOUR

Netta was up with the dawn. There was much to be done on this, their last day in Craigie for tomorrow morning the carter would be here to take them and their possessions to Low Bothlie. Not that there was much left to take. Before the parish would pay relief to the striking miners the bailiffs had removed all but the most basic household equipment. A place on a mattress for each family member, a table and a few chairs were all that remained in the way of furniture. The spare blankets, cutlery, cooking pots and even the solid wooden dresser which had belonged to Netta's mother had all been taken away to be sold. And now, before Netta could start dismantling what was left of her home, she had to say goodbye to two of her four remaining children, not knowing when she would see them again. Already there was a feeling of painful tightness in her chest.

Leaving Tam to make a skimpy breakfast out of stale bread and a scraping of lard she went to rouse the children. The sight of Meggie and Matty, curled defiantly together on Meggie's mattress almost destroyed her composure but, swallowing down the threatening tears, Netta woke them, sounding to her children's ears, as if this was just another ordinary day.

'You see,' Meggie whispered to her unhappy brother, 'she doesn't care that I'm going.'

'Come on,' Netta called. 'I've a cup of good hot tea for youse. Come and get it now.'

The children had become accustomed to plain water with

their meals and the unexpected treat did not go unnoticed, though neither Meggie nor Matty commented on it. Pale faced and utterly miserable they pulled their chairs closer together and sat slightly apart from the rest of their family. Perce and Bertie rushed through their breakfasts and said goodbye to their sister carelessly, eager to get their last day of school over and start out on this new adventure. Neither of them had been unduly disturbed by the news that Meggie couldn't come with them to Uncle Jim's. It didn't really matter. She would come home again as soon as they had their new house.

'Meggie, lass.' Netta knew she had to have one last try at making her daughter understand why they had to take this drastic step. 'It'll only be for a wee while. As soon as your father finds a job and we're settled in a place of our own, we'll come and fetch you. Och,' she went on, nervousness making her unusually talkative. 'You'll be better off where you're going. It'll not be much fun for us at your Uncle Jim's. There's six of them and four of us, there'll not be room to put a foot down.'

'Five of you', Meggie spoke for the first time that morning.

Netta flushed and shot an agonised appeal to Tam.

'Four of us. We've decided it'd be best for you and Matty to stay together. You'll not feel so alone that way.' Tam did his best to lighten the blow.

Matty grinned at his sister and kicked her leg jubilantly under the table.

Meggie scowled at him and drew away. 'Don't be so stupid,' she snarled. 'It's just a way of getting rid of you, too.'

'No, lass,' Netta protested. 'That's not true. It's just for a wee while. We'll soon be together again.'

Matty looked at his parents and then back at his sister with frightened eyes. But it was Meggie who he spoke to next. 'Are we going away for ever, Meggie?' he asked, uncertainty plain in his voice.

'No . . .' Netta cried.

Meggie ignored her mother. 'Aye. Forever. They're sending us away because of what happened to Nancy.'

'That's enough, Margaret,' Tam intervened. 'Don't go upsetting your brother with your stupid lies.'

'It's not lies!' The girl sprang to her feet and faced her father with apparent fearlessness. 'It's true! You know it is.'

Tam, worn down by the worry of the past month, was suddenly impatient to get this over with. He let his hand fall obviously to the buckle of his heavy belt. 'If you don't want to be taking the marks of my belt to Inverannan with you, Margaret, you had better watch that mouth of yours.'

Meggie fought tears and turned her face away. Matty nudged closer to her and groped for her clenched hand. 'It's all right, Meggie, I want to stay with you,' he told her. He depended on his big sister for everything, couldn't imagine how his life would be without her.

'Are you sure, lad?' Tam asked, salving his conscience by transferring the burden of decision to his ten-year-old son's thin shoulders.

'I'm staying with Meggie,' the boy insisted, jutting his chin out stubbornly.

'Maybe he should come with us, Tam,' Netta suggested in an undertone. 'It'll do him good to be separated from her.'

Tam looked from his defiant son to his hostile daughter as if unsure. 'Look at them,' he growled at his wife. 'If we split them up he'll be nothing but trouble. No, we were right. Matty can go with her. It'll be fairer to Jim and it's not as if it's for ever.'

'I'm staying with Meggie,' Matty repeated again, sealing the decision.

'Right. Then there's nothing more to be said. Fetch your things, say goodbye to your mother and we'll be off.'

Five minutes later the children and their pathetically small bundles of clothes were ready to leave.

'Two or three weeks, lass, that's all. We'll fetch you home before you know it.' Netta bent to kiss her daughter, felt no response as her lips brushed skin which seemed as cold and unyielding as the expression in the child's eyes. She drew back, fighting the urge to clasp the girl fiercely, to tell her that she didn't have to go, that they would look for another home and work here, in Strathannan. Tam, seeing the torment on his wife's face, hastily drew his daughter aside.

'Say goodbye to your mother, Matty,' he ordered.

Matty's huge eyes were already swimming with tears. He ran to his mother, threw his skinny arms around her and held on, pressing his face into her skirts.

'Och, Matty,' Netta breathed, stroking his hair.

As the first tear spilled over her cheek, Tam took the children's hands and led them away. Through a wavering mist Netta saw Matty look back. She lifted an arm and waved at his blurred image, then called out to her daughter, praying for a smile to remember her by in the weeks ahead. But Meggie walked on, her back rigidly straight, too hurt and angry to respond to her mother's plea. Completely bereft, Netta stood in her doorway and sobbed her grief to the cold morning air.

Inverannan workhouse was a tall, grey stone building, the austerity of its façade hinting at the severity of the regime within. Tam, grasping a child in each hand, felt a shiver of apprehension run down his spine. For a moment, in front of the strong double doors, he hesitated, feeling defeat overwhelm him. This was the place of which he and his kind lived in perpetual fear. To come here was to be shamed, to admit failure. For Tam McPherson it was the most bitter moment of his life, robbing him of the ability to speak tenderly to the children he was consigning to its care. Knowing there was no alternative, he jerked on the bell pull and waited, his face grim.

There was the distant sound of voices, the clack of sharp footsteps on a hard floor, the distinctive noise of a heavy key turning in a stout lock. Meggie's hand tightened involuntarily on her father's. And then the doors opened smoothly, revealing a plump, middle-aged woman, plainly dressed but with a smile illuminating her kindly face. 'You'll be Mr McPherson?'

'Aye.' It was gruff, choked. He pushed the children forward. They, sensing their shame, went with their heads bent.

'Two children, Mr McPherson?' There was a note of surprised disapproval in the woman's voice now.

'Aye. There's no room where we're going. And the weans . . . they're close . . . didn't want to be apart.' He did his best to explain.

'Well, better come with me.' She led them through two pairs of doors, carefully relocking them behind her. They found themselves in a hall, a vast, empty, echoing area, freezingly cold. The overwhelming air of bleakness was sharpened by the appearance of the walls, which were covered in yellowing, white tiles to the level of Meggie's head and, above that, were painted in a particularly unpleasant shade of green. A bare stone staircase rose from the centre of the hall, dividing on the back wall into two diverging branches, their upper reaches lost in shadow. The whole place reeked of disinfectant, reminding Matty unpleasantly of the police station in Inverannan. At the bottom of the stairs the woman stopped, turned and waited for them.

'Mr McPherson, wait here please. I'll be back to take the details as soon as I've settled these two. Now children, say goodbye to your father then come upstairs with me.' She turned and began to make her way up the stairs. Halfway up she turned and looked back to see Matty and Meggie standing holding hands and looking very frightened. 'Come along now,' she encouraged them briskly. 'Bring your things and we'll soon have you settled.'

'Goodbye, Pa,' Matty said, his thin voice wavering.

'Goodbye, son,' Tam rasped. 'You be a good lad now.'

With a jerky tug on her brother's sleeve, Meggie led him upstairs to the waiting woman. Once again she did not look back.

At the point where the stairs divided the woman waited. She smiled at them. 'I know you are frightened, but there is no need to be. If you are always obedient and industrious you will be well treated. My name is Mrs Cruickshank and I am the superintendent of the female house. Now Margaret, it is Margaret, isn't it?'

Meggie nodded then screwed up her courage and said, 'I'm called Meggie at home.'

Mrs Cruickshank smiled, admiring the girl's brave self-control. 'And what is your brother's name?'

'Matty,' Meggie answered.

'Matthew?'

'Aye.'

'Very good. Say goodbye to your sister, Matthew, then come with me.'

'But we're to stay together,' Meggie protested, clutching Matty's hand so hard his knuckles cracked.

Mrs Cruickshank frowned. 'You must learn to do as you are told, Margaret,' she chided gently. 'You will see Matthew later. Now, say goodbye.'

Meggie looked round desperately and saw, at the top of each branch of the stairs, a door. Written on one was the single word MEN, the other was labelled WOMEN. Strangely she felt reassured. It was just like school, she thought, where the boys went in one door and the girls went in another, only to join up again in class. 'It's all right, Matty,' she whispered bravely.

'Good girl,' Mrs Cruickshank beamed her approval. 'Wait here, Margaret.'

With that she climbed the left hand branch of the staircase, pushing Matty gently in front of her. He turned round just as the door closed behind him and Meggie got a brief glimpse of dark, frightened eyes. It was an image which returned to torment her often in the months which followed.

With surprising speed, Mrs Cruickshank reappeared. 'You go this way,' she smiled. Meggie picked up her things and followed her meekly through the door marked WOMEN.

To her surprise she found herself in a room with four huge bath tubs. Two women, almost totally encased in stiff, white aprons were waiting. Meggie, who had never bathed in anything other than a galvanised tub, in water heated in pans on the range, watched as hot water gushed from a roaring, cylindrical monster over the nearest bath. Frightened, she stepped back a little.

Mrs Cruickshank caught her and held her gently. 'This,'

she said to the two waiting women, 'is Margaret McPherson. When she is ready take her upstairs.'

'Yes, Mrs Cruickshank,' the women responded respectfully.

The door closed behind the superintendent and Meggie stood, clutching her things, feeling very much alone and frightened.

'Right, lass. Take your clothes off.' The smaller of the two waiting women smiled.

'Come on,' the other one ordered impatiently. 'Everything off and get in the bath.'

The woman had a determined look in her eyes and her sleeves, rolled above the elbow, showed beefy forearms. Meggie decided it would be best to do as she was told. Slowly, she took off her coat, slid her dress to the floor and then, blushing furiously, turned her back and stepped out of her knickers and vest.

Behind her one of the women chortled. 'Och, she's shy . . .' but it wasn't a kind sound.

Meggie shivered in the icy draught and covered her budding breasts with her hands before turning round.

'In you get.'

Struggling to maintain some degree of modesty, Meggie climbed into the tub. The water was scalding hot and she lowered herself slowly.

'Hurry up.' An unsympathetic hand descended on her shoulders and shoved her down into the water. The heat took her breath away. She was still gasping when she was pushed again, this time right under the water, then hauled upright, coughing and spluttering.

'Stop it!' Meggie cried, trying to clamber out. Instantly her arms were grabbed and she was pinioned inside the tub.

'Sit still.'

Meggie gasped again and protested sharply as carbolic soap was rubbed harshly into her hair, splashing into her eyes and making them smart. Again she was dunked under the water and the whole process was repeated. When they pushed on her shoulders to submerge her the third time she was ready for it and managed to take a breath before she went down.

Water streaming down her face she felt rough hands rubbing the coarse soap all over her body. 'Don't! I can wash myself,' she yelled, struggling to break free. But it was as if they didn't hear her.

'Stand up.' She was hoisted to her feet while they worked they way over her body, driving the soap between her legs and scrubbing away at the embarrassing hairs growing there. Meggie cringed with humiliation then screamed as her body was doused in cold water.

'Right. Out you get.'

She stumbled from the water and stood shivering and naked in the icy room.

Looking round frantically for her clothes she realised that they, and her small bundle of belongings, had vanished. 'Where are my clothes?' she screamed.

'They've been taken away to be cleaned. You won't need them in here,' the smaller of the two women replied, draping a coarse towel round Meggie's shoulders. 'Now, stand still.'

To Meggie's horror she felt a tug at her head, heard the snip of scissors and watched as clumps of wet hair fell to the floor around her feet. She jerked away violently. 'You can't cut my hair!'

Tall as she was, Meggie was no match for the two women, one of whom held her arms at her side while the other tried to finish the job.

'Och, stand still, will you,' she snapped as Meggie continued to twist her head away from the scissors.

'I don't want my hair cut.' She had been growing it since last Easter, hoping that it would soon be long enough for plaits, like Susan Menzies.

'It's the rules,' the smaller woman explained. 'Everyone coming in here has to have their hair cut. Now stand still. It'll look even worse if you don't let us do it properly.'

Meggie wrestled a hand free and raised it to her head. To her horror she found a great lump of hair missing from one side. Slowly she lowered her hand and stood perfectly still, jaws clenched, refusing to let them see her cry, while the women completed their task.

'Put these on.' Meggie was handed a coarse, cotton dress, in a dull beige colour, a pair of knickers, a greying vest and her own shoes. 'You get clean underwear on Wednesdays and Saturdays and a clean dress every Saturday,' the woman said, dragging a shapeless garment over Meggie's shorn head.

It engulfed her, hanging almost to the floor, the sleeves completely covering her hands. The taller woman laughed but the smaller one handed her a belt and said, almost kindly. 'This'll help. Turn back the cuffs too. There, that's better. Come on then, I'll show you where you're to sleep. You can make your bed up and then it'll be near enough time for supper.' She led the way out of a second door, along a narrow corridor and up some more stairs, talking all the time. Still shaking with outrage, Meggie tried to concentrate, sensing she would be in trouble if she made too many mistakes.

'You get up at six. Dress, wash, make your bed and go downstairs for morning prayers. Then you go to the kitchen to help with breakfast. All the new ones start off there. If

74

you work hard you'll get better jobs later on. Dinner is at twelve. You young 'uns have lessons in the afternoon then it's back to the kitchen to help with supper, which is at six. After that you tidy up the kitchen and then, if there's no complaints against you, you have an hour to read your Bible and do some mending. Then you have an hour for private recreation before bed at nine. Saturdays you'll be in the kitchen all day. Sundays are the same but you get time off to go to the kirk in the morning.'

They had arrived at yet another stout door. The woman opened it and led Meggie into a long, cold dormitory, wooden-framed beds lining either side.

'This is your bed. Keep it tidy. If you wet the sheets you miss supper. My name's Janet and I'm in charge of this dormitory so you must do what I tell you. Any questions?'

'Where's my brother?' Meggie asked, her voice quavering slightly.

'He's on the men's side,' Janet answered.

'I want to see him.' Meggie knew how frightened Matty would be.

Janet shook her head. 'Men and women are kept apart. He'll have lessons with you but lads and lassies are not allowed to speak to each other. You'll be thrashed if you're caught talking to him.'

'But he's my brother and he's only ten.'

Janet's face softened for a minute. 'Och, he'll be fine. There's lots of young lads to keep him company. I'll ask someone to tell him you're all right if you like.'

Already Meggie had heard enough to understand the futility of fighting the system. The only way to survive in such a harsh environment was to obey the rules and stay out of trouble. She forced herself to smile, grasping at this tenuous friendship. 'Thank you.'

'Just remember that Mrs Cruickshank's a fair enough woman but she's right strict. Work hard and you'll get easier jobs and, if you're lucky, when you get to fifteen, you'll be allowed out to work or maybe you'll be made an assistant, like me.'

'I'll not be here that long,' Meggie asserted fiercely. 'My Pa and Ma have gone to find a new house. They're coming to get me and Matty in two or three weeks.'

Janet looked at her pityingly. 'Aye, hen,' she smiled. 'They all say that.'

After supper, which was some kind of greasy stew, taken in silence at long tables, men in one half of the room, women in the other, Meggie, with thirty or so identically dressed women and girls, returned to the icy dormitory where various items of clothing and linen were distributed to be darned and patched while Janet read from the Bible. Netta had taught Meggie to sew but, a far from neat needle-woman, Meggie needed all her concentration to patch a torn sheet and was relieved when her work passed Janet's inspection and she was at last free to retire to bed.

The beds nearest hers were all occupied by older women. There were several girls, some even younger than her, but all at the other end of the room. One or two of them smiled at her but Meggie was too worried about Matty to respond. She fell into bed and wrapped herself in the thin blankets, shivering until, exhausted by the day's events, she fell asleep.

Through the dividing wall, less than five feet away on the men's side of the building, Matty hid his newly-shaved head under his blankets and wept until his neighbour, a foul-tempered old man who had been turned on to the streets by his married daughter, ordered him to be quiet. The words were accompanied by two hefty whacks across his ear. Matty subsided into terrified sobs which he stifled in the sour-smelling pillow.

After a fortnight Meggie realised that the workhouse was not as bad as she had feared. The other women were a varied lot but most were willing enough to help a newcomer settle in. The oldest was a wrinkled, eighty-year-old crone who talked only to herself, the youngest a six-week-old baby, the illegitimate daughter of a fourteen-year-old girl. It couldn't be called a happy place, the conditions were too harsh and the older women, in particular, were too miserable for that. These poor creatures, many too old or too poorly to support themselves in the outside world, knew they had no hope of ever escaping and spent their days in quiet resignation in the workroom, folding, pressing and packing the linen produced by one of the local mills. But among the younger ones there was a different atmosphere, a sense of expectation as they looked forward to the day when they would be old enough to leave. Few of them were consigned to the workroom. Before and after their afternoon lessons most were assigned duties around the workhouse itself. The work was arduous but it was Mrs Cruickshank's firm belief that this was a better preparation for the normal life to which she sincerely hoped most would return.

The female inhabitants of the Inverannan workhouse were unusually fortunate in their superintendent. Bertha Cruickshank was a kind-hearted woman who had genuine sympathy for many of the unfortunates who found themselves thrown on the parish spoil heap. Severely hampered by the petty mindedness of the governing board, who saw the inmates as little better than animals, she was not above bargaining personally with local traders and wringing every last farthing of value from the ridiculously small amount of money allotted to her.

But even she couldn't find the resources to heat the rooms or pay for the medicine which was so badly needed. She did her limited best to ease the humiliation of the elderly folk, who had been abandoned by their own families and actively encouraged the younger ones to have pride in themselves and to work to rise above their unfortunate start in life.

Above all she was strict, insisting on discipline, cleanliness, tidiness, good manners and consideration of others. The result was that many of the impressionable young girls who passed through her hands emerged as better human beings than they might otherwise have been. Once these girls reached an age where they could begin to make their own way in the world she was tireless in her efforts to overcome the snobbery and prejudice of Inverannan's citizens and was often successful in finding the better girls respectable jobs as shop assistants, or maids. Even the less bright ones could usually be found work in the linen mills and Mrs Cruickshank was proud that very few of her charges had to resort to walking the streets, as happened in so many other towns. She had been watching young Meggie McPherson closely and was glad to see that the lass was clean and polite, and a hard worker, too. With the right training, in another year or two, she would be able to find a job and lodgings of her own, and would very likely end up better placed than if she had stayed with her family.

Sadly, Mrs Cruickshank's enlightened attitude was not shared by her male counterpart. Andrew Carlyle had nothing but disdain for the men who ended up in his hands. His only aim was to ingratiate himself with the eminent members of the Relief Board and to run his half of the little community as parsimoniously as possible, making sure there was always enough of his meagre funds left to line his own pockets. The men and boys in his care saw no hope for their future and even the most optimistic of them soon retreated into sullen, exhausted silence. He ruled cruelly, delegating authority to assistants chosen for their ruthlessness, and cared not at all that the younger boys were bullied and mistreated.

Matty spent every day waiting for his father to come to fetch him home. Every time a door opened he looked up, hope blazing briefly in his tired face. Each disappointment deepened the shadows round his eyes and set his mouth more firmly in the ugly, downturned scowl which was rapidly becoming its most noticeable feature. At meal times and in the school room, his eyes constantly sought Meggie, sending her mute pleas for help. Aware of her brother's unhappiness but unable to offer any practical comfort, Meggie did her best to respond with bright, encouraging smiles. But, resentful of the apparent ease with which Meggie appeared to have settled down, Matty felt that, like his parents, his sister had abandoned him. When she smiled he twisted his face into a dark grimace of animosity and looked away, hoping to wound her.

If it hadn't been for Matty, Meggie might have been content to settle down in the workhouse. Unlike her brother she had never seriously expected her parents to come for them. She believed that they had been glad to be rid of her, that they blamed her for Nancy's death – as she blamed herself. It hadn't taken her long to realise that the harder she worked, the more she learned, the better equipped she would be to get a job and a room of her own. Then she would take

Matty to live with her. It was what drove her on, making her shine in class, compelling her, even at her chores, to work twice as hard as the other girls, always hoping that she was learning skills which would help her to make a home for them both.

She planned constantly for the future, looking forward to the time when she and Matty could be a family again and was deeply hurt to see the way he looked at her, almost as if he hated her. If only she could talk to him, explain her plans, make him understand that she still loved him, maybe he would be able to smile at her. She would give anything to see her little brother happy again.

CHAPTER FIVE

Lilian McPherson needed all her strength to lift the huge pan off the stove and drain it over the edge of the stone sink. Boiling water splashed over her wrist and she gave a bad-tempered yelp of pain. Thumping the pan back on the still warm hotplate to dry the tatties she then made a great fuss about ladling stew from an equally heavy pot on to the ten plates distributed over any spare surface in the cramped room.

'Will youse get out of my bloody way,' she snarled at the six children who had come from playing in the street in rapid response to her impatient summons. Only too eager to keep out of her way they flattened themselves against the walls.

'Let me put out the tatties for you, Lil,' Netta offered, the familiar feeling of helpless indebtedness doing nothing for her own temper.

'You know fine there's not room. You'll only be in the way,' was Lil's ungracious response.

Netta sighed and edged slowly round the room and out of the back door to call in the men. They, accustomed to the flarings of temper between the two women, had taken themselves out of range.

With ten people balancing plates on their knees, the small room was uncomfortably crowded. When Perce, rising to place his empty dish in the sink, inadvertently knocked against his eldest cousin, James, the older boy's plate slipped, landing upside down on the linoleum.

'Sorry . . .' Perce was quick to apologise, bending to

retrieve the plate and leaving a sticky mess on the newly polished flooring.

'Thickhead,' James snarled, jabbing his foot out and kicking Perce painfully on the shin.

Perce, never one to avoid a challenge, retaliated with a powerful shove of his own. 'Watch your mouth, snotbrain,' he yelled.

'That's enough!' Jim and Tam McPherson bellowed in unison.

'Outside the lot of youse,' Jim added, connecting the power of his boot with the nearest behind.

'Och, will you just look at the mess,' Lil wailed, falling to her hands and knees and rubbing at the spilled gravy with a damp cloth. 'And I spent all afternoon cleaning this floor!'

'Stop your fuss, woman. It's just a wee bit stew.' Jim sank back into his chair and polished off the remains of his own meal.

'Just a wee bit stew!' his wife exclaimed loudly. 'I'll have you know we can't afford to be throwing good food around, Jim McPherson.'

'I'm right sorry, Lil. I'm sure it was just an accident,' Netta muttered, her face scarlet with shame.

Jim clattered his plate into the sink, his face mirroring his own impatience. 'Bloody women. I'm off for a pint. You coming, Tam?'

Tam looked embarrassed. 'No . . . I don't think so, Jim. Not the night.'

'Suit yourself.' The door slammed as Jim escaped the tension of his own home.

'I'll just go for a wee walk,' Tam decided, setting his battered cap firmly on his head and escaping as eagerly as his brother.

'That's right,' Lil called after him, past bothering about

hurt feelings. 'Off you go. Leave me to clear up after youse. This isn't a bloody hotel, you know!'

'Och, let him be, Lil. You sit down and have a wee cup of tea. I'll wash the dishes.' Netta hurried to fill the sink with hot water.

'You will not! This is still my house, Netta McPherson, and my kitchen. And I like to have things done my way,' Lil insisted.

'Aye, and don't I know it,' Netta hit back.

'And what do you mean by that?' Lil challenged, rising to face the row which had been simmering for weeks now.

'You . . . you're making us feel terrible.'

'Och, I'm awful sorry!' The heavily accented voice was laced with sarcasm. 'Perhaps you'd like it better if Jim and I moved out and left the place to you and Tam?'

'Och, Lil,' Netta sighed. 'You know that's not what I meant.'

'Then what do you mean?' The other woman rounded on her, eyes blazing.

For a moment Netta was tempted to unleash her own carefully controlled temper, but it wasn't in her nature to give in to her emotions. For a long moment she met her sister-in-law's furious gaze then put a placating hand on her arm.

'Come and sit down. It's time we had a wee talk. Better to clear the air while there's no one else in the house.'

'There's work to be done, or hadn't you noticed?' Lil plunged her arms into the sink.

'Och, for goodness' sake! You are the most stubborn woman.'

'Aye, and that's gratitude for you!' Lil spat.

'Gratitude! Is that what you want? Well, here it is. I'm grateful to you for taking me and my family in, Lil

McPherson. I'm right glad to have lost my Nancy and to have put Meggie and Matty in the workhouse. I'm grateful for being put out of my own home and for having a man with no job. Aye, and I'm right bloody proud to let you and Jim feed me and my weans . . .'

To Netta's own astonishment her voice choked on a sob and tears spilled down her face. 'Och, aye, I've got such a lot to be grateful for,' she ended, turning away and rubbing frantically at her eyes.

Lil stared, her conscience momentarily torn by the raw pain on the other woman's face. Driven by the knowledge that her husband would be furious with her if the barely concealed animosity between the two women were allowed to flare into open warfare she did her best to make amends. Hurriedly wiping her hands on her apron she turned from the sink and put an arm round Netta's trembling shoulders. 'Och, Netta, I'm sorry. I didn't mean it.'

Netta sniffed and flinched away. 'Aye, but you did mean it, Lil. We both know you don't want us here.'

Stung by the rebuff, Lil's face flared into angry colour, her good intentions forgotten. 'You're right! I don't! We were on strike too, you know. You weren't the only ones to suffer. We'd to go without just like anyone else. But we managed! It's not our fault if Tam opened that big mouth of his once too often. It's all fine and good having big ideas of what's right and wrong, Netta, so long as you don't expect other people to pay the price with you. Why should Jim and me suffer because of your Tam's pig-headedness?'

Netta opened her mouth to defend her husband but Lil was too angry to stop now. The bitter words flowed relentlessly on.

'Jim's too soft. He'd give away his last penny if he thought Tam needed it. But I've my own bairns to think about and I'll not stand by and see them go without. And I'll not have another woman trying to take over my house.'

'I'm not trying to run your house, Lil. And I am grateful to you and Jim. Though I know I don't always show it.'

'Huh!'

'It's hard, Lil, not being able to pay your way.'

'It's not only the money. There's enough. Just. But . . . there's so many of us in this wee house, Netta. It's never tidy, there's no privacy. It's such hard work, the cooking and cleaning and washing and mending. There's never a minute for myself any more.' Now that the dispute was out in the open Lil's temper faded a little.

'But if you'd just let me help you, Lil. You've no need to do it all yourself. I know fine I don't do things the same way you do but I feel so . . . so . . . useless. I'm not used to being waited on and it's not right that you should run round after us. Let me at least do my share of the chores. I maybe can't make a pie as good as yours but I can peel tatties with the best of them and I'm damn sure I can wash a dish as clean as you can, any day.'

'I like to do it myself,' Lil insisted.

'Well, that's just plain stupid! Look at you. You're worn out. White as a sheet and always nagging at Jim and the bairns. Just so you can make me feel bad.'

'That's not true. It's just that I've got my own way of doing things.' Lil looked at her hands, which were red and chapped, refusing to meet Netta's eyes. 'And if I'm tired it's because I'm in the family way again. Though I don't suppose you've noticed.' She smoothed the front of her apron revealing a gentle bulge over her stomach.

Netta was immediately contrite. 'Och, Lil, why ever didn't you say? And you never off your feet from the minute you get out of your bed in the mornings! I'm right pleased for you, hen,' she added.

'That's more than I am,' Lil retorted. 'It's just another one to feed and worry about.'

'Aye . . . I suppose so.' Netta frowned. 'When are you due?'

'I'm four months gone already.'

'I'd never have guessed . . .' But under the shapeless pinafores Lil always wore it was hard to see any sort of figure. 'Tam had better find himself another job soon. There's no room for a mouse in this house never mind a new bairn.'

'Aye, well, I hope so, Netta,' Lil said pointedly. 'We can't go on like this.'

Netta sighed. 'There's no work at the pit. There's even talk of laying men off. But maybe he'll get something at the steelworks in Lairdstoun. He's heard they're setting men on there.'

'Aye, well make sure he goes over there the morn.' Lil smoothed her pinafore again. 'I feel right sad about what's happened to you Netta but it's your problem, not mine. The sooner Tam gets himself another job the better.'

'Do you think I don't know that?' Netta retorted. 'Still, it's better now we've had this wee talk. At least we understand one another. We'll never be friends, Lil McPherson, but Tam and Jim are brothers. Let's not come between them.'

'That's up to you and Tam. Get yourselves out of my house, Netta, and we'll all get along just fine.'

'Don't worry, we'll not stay a moment longer than we have to. In the meantime, you can at least let me pull my weight around here.' Netta strode purposefully to the sink

86

and, after a minute's thought, Lil sat back and put her feet up on the opposite chair.

'It's not much of a job,' Tam said glumly.

'It's better than nothing,' Netta insisted. 'Steel making's the same as any other trade, Tam. You have to learn a bit about it before you can expect to get on.'

'And how am I supposed to learn anything sweeping up the yard?' he demanded bitterly. 'It's a job for an old man. And it's only temporary until the regular lad's back. He dropped a crate on his foot. They reckon he'll be off for another three or four weeks. Then I'll likely be out of work again.'

'It's a start.' She glanced at him, seeing the way he slouched along, his hands buried deep in his pockets, as if he had no pride left. 'You'll get something else, Tam, you'll see. And you've been lucky to get this. You know fine there's no more work in these parts than there was in Strathannan.'

And how she missed the county of her birth. Maybe the pit bings were ugly things but there had been beautiful country all round about them, and the broad, silver river with beaches where the children could play in the summer had been no more than a pleasant walk away. There was none of that here. Lairdstoun was such an ugly place. Streets of blackened tenements, mean shops and grim churches all under the stench and shadow of the steel mills and foundries which were the backbone of the town. A town which ran on and merged with the next one, and the next, with hardly a green field between them and Glasgow itself. And this, she thought glumly, was where they would have to make their home. She watched as a gang of street urchins raced barefooted over the setted streets, screaming language which would shock even the miners of Craigie. At least there the children ran on grass and could escape to the freedom of the countryside to fish for tiddlers in clear running burns, skate on the ponds in winter or build hideaways in the woods. There would be nothing like that for Perce and Bertie in Lairdstoun, where the streets were the only place to play.

'Down here, I think.' Tam shattered her reverie and led her round a corner to yet another road of tall tenement buildings. 'Aye, this is it.'

She followed him into a dark close. Tam opened a door and they found themselves in an echoing hallway. It was dark, damp and malodorous. Paint peeled off the doors, the walls were stained and cracked and he stairs were of bare stone. At the back, half hidden by the gloom was a heap of household rubbish, broken chairs, a filthy old pram and a rusty, tin bath. Perched on the bottom stair, watching them with open curiosity, were two of the grubbiest children Netta had ever seen, their bare feet scuffing carelessly in the mucky litter which had blown in from the close.

Tam knocked on the nearest door. It was opened by an elderly man, his trousers gaping open at the top, his collarless shirt stained and unbuttoned, his face coarse with stubble.

'Aye?'

'Mr Cleary?'

'Who wants tae know?' Even from where she stood Netta could smell stale beer from his breath.

'My name's Tam McPherson and this is my wife. I'm starting at the steelworks on Monday. I was told there might be rooms to rent here.'

'So you'll be wanting number nine then? Wait here. I'll need to find the keys.' He shuffled off, leaving Tam and

Netta waiting in the cold hallway. It was a full five minutes before he returned.

'Off with youse, ye wee buggers!' Cleary cursed and aimed a kick at the urchins who scurried away down the close, shouting insults as they ran. Wheezing loudly and leaning heavily on the loose banister he hauled himself slowly up the stairway, obviously expecting Netta and Tam to follow. On the second landing he paused, fighting for breath.

'Bloody stairs,' he hawked loudly then straightened and shuffled towards a door, almost hidden under the rise of the stairs to the third floor.

'This is it,' he grunted, throwing the door open. 'Room and kitchen. Gas meter by the door. Wash-house and the usuals are out back, through the close. The women take their turn at cleaning the stairs and closet. Rent man comes on Friday nights.' He stood back and ushered them in.

Netta walked to the middle of a square room and looked round critically, depressed by the lack of light, the dingy paintwork and the all-too-evident traces of the last tenant, who obviously hadn't bothered to clean the place before leaving. There was a small fireplace on one wall, a grease-encrusted range and a deep, stained sink on another.

A box bed was built into a corner and beside it was an inner door. Netta pushed it gingerly and it swung inwards to reveal a large, damp-smelling cupboard, hardly big enough for a single mattress and without even the benefit of a window. This, she supposed, was what the landlord called 'the room'.

Knowing they could afford nothing better on the wages Tam would be drawing, she closed the door again and walked back to the single narrow window in the main room. The view, over an inner courtyard from which the sun was excluded by the height of the buildings on all four sides, was bleak. The towering tenements were uniformly black with soot, the windows like dark caverns in the stone walls. With an effort she unfastened the sash, raised the window and peered down, seeing at once the dark tunnels where the closes led in to this common central area, the wash-houses and privies clustered there, the rubbish spilling from open bins, the dogs scavenging for scraps, the dirty children and the fighting cats. An unpleasant smell drifted up, rotting vegetables, bad drains, boiling cabbage. Netta slammed the window down.

'It's filthy,' she said indignantly.

Cleary shrugged. 'Not up to me to clean the place. I just hold the keys. You want to complain you take it up with the landlord. S'nothing to do with me. You want the rooms or not?'

Netta looked desperately at Tam.

'Och, it'll not be so bad once you've given it a good clean out,' he said. 'And there's gas for light and cooking.'

'Look at this place, Tam,' she sighed. 'By the time we get our table and chairs in this room there'll not be space for anything else. It's right wee. And there's only just enough room for a single mattress in there.'

'It'll do for now, Netta,' Tam sounded resigned. 'Just like my job. It's better than nothing. Unless you want to stay with Jim and Lil for a bit longer? I suppose I could buy an old bike and ride up here to work every day.'

'No!' She startled him with the violence of her reaction. 'No. It's better if we leave as soon as we can, Tam, before we fall out worse than we have done already. You know it's hard for them with us all living there.'

'We'd have done the same for them.'

'Aye. But it's not easy. Not for any of us. It's their home.

And I want a place to call my own again. Even if it has to be here.'

'You're taking it then?' Cleary asked. 'Best make up your minds fast. I'm back off downstairs for my dinner.'

'We'll take it,' Tam decided. 'When can we move our things in?'

Cleary shrugged. 'It's all one to me.'

'Saturday then?'

'Right you are. I'll tell the rent collector when he calls.' With that he tossed the key at Tam and shuffled off, leaving Tam and Netta for a longer look at their new home.

Netta moved back to the grime-streaked window and stood looking out across the backs of the other buildings, becoming aware now of the constant background noise, the muffled thumps and bangs of everyday life, the muted voices of their neighbours through the thin walls, the barking of dogs, the distant wail of a baby, the squabbling of the children in the close far below. Behind every window in this terrifyingly alien tenement were strangers, people whose very way of speaking was different from her own. How she yearned for the comforting familiarity of folk she had known all her life.

She became aware of Tam behind her and leant back gratefully against the strength of his chest, feeling his arms close round her. He dropped a kiss on her head, a rare demonstration of the affection which still bound them. For his sake she smiled over her despair, knowing the adjustment would be even harder for him.

'We'll manage,' she whispered.

'Aye, lass, we will that.'

She turned and kissed his mouth, feeling a sudden surge of longing for him, a longing which had found no outlet in the cramped room they shared with Jim and Lil.

'We've no need to hurry away yet,' he whispered, kissing her purposefully, his hands already roving over her coat, working their way under the buttons. 'And there's a fine comfortable looking mattress on that bed.'

Netta glanced dubiously at the stained ticking but her doubts were pushed aside by pure physical need.

They made love there, on a grubby mattress, in a room bare of all comfort, returning, too briefly, to the passion which had made their marriage so strong. Later, lying beside her husband in the shell of their new home, Netta felt the first stirrings of hope. It was a new start, a second chance. Before long Tam would get a permanent job and a decent house so that the family could all be together again. Together they would make things come right.

Netta straightened stiffly, a hand massaging her aching back. She had been scrubbing, sweeping and polishing since first light, racing to get the rooms decent before Tam arrived with the hired cart and their few bits of furniture. There had been no room in Jim and Lil's house for the few things they had brought with them from Craigie. Everything, except clothes and bedding, had been stored in the lean-to against the back wall where three months of damp had taken the surface from the table, tarnished the cooking pots and warped the chairs. There had been no reasonable alternative to accepting Jim's renewed offer of the loan of eight pounds with which to pay the carter and buy essentials for their new home from the second-hand shop.

Chasing Perce and Bertie outside to investigate their new playmates, Netta attacked the range with hot water and caustic soda, laid faded rag rugs on the floors, hung mildewed curtains at the newly cleaned window, scoured her ruined pans fiercely and rubbed several coats of wax into the spoiled surface of her table. Only then did she stand back and examine the effect.

Even with only the table and its four hard chairs placed under the window, two mismatched easy chairs on either side of the fireplace, her pots, pans and dishes stored on the wooden shelves beside the sink, the place was full. Perce and Bertie would share the single mattress which was all the second room would hold.

'Where are Meggie and Matty going to sleep?' she asked Tam who had just come back after returning the cart.

He stared round the room, his face grim and it seemed a very long time before he answered her. 'Maybe they'd be better to stay where they are for a wee while longer,' he said finally. 'At least until I've found a proper job. I'll hardly be making enough money at the steelworks to pay the rent and buy food for the four of us. And we've that eight pounds to repay Jim and Lil.'

'Tam ...' Netta groaned, her chest tightening with anguish. But she knew he was right.

'Och, Netta, it'll not be for much longer. I'll find a steady job and as soon as we've repaid our debts we'll look for a bigger place to live. We'll fetch them home then.'

'It's been three months already, Tam. The weans'll think we don't want them with us.'

'I'll write. Let them know how we're going on,' Tam suggested.

'Aye! Do that. It'll give them something to look forward to. Och, I'd give anything to have them home again, Tam.'

Mrs Cruickshank took the envelopes from the postman and flicked casually through them, expecting nothing more than the usual bills. It was almost unknown for workhouse inmates to receive mail and the cheap envelope with its pencilled address caught her attention immediately. Despite the fact that it was clearly addressed to Matthew and Margaret McPherson, Mrs Cruickshank tore it open and read it through without compunction. Then, an angry expression on her face, she rose, took the single sheet of paper and poked it deep into the heart of the fire. It was better this way, she thought sadly. In her experience, once children were abandoned by their parents they were very seldom reclaimed and it wasn't as if Mr McPherson had even given an address where he could be contacted. This cruel letter was nothing more than a salve to his conscience, a string of thin excuses and empty promises which would merely unsettle the children. Kinder by far to leave them in ignorance of their parents' treachery.

CHAPTER SIX

Meggie, sandwiched between the other women while the Minister droned on and on, was grateful for the warmth of their bodies. The March chill seeped through the stone floor of the kirk, creeping through the worn soles of her boots and turning her feet to ice. Her breath emerged as a misty cloud, mingling with that of the other inmates who were herded together in the back pews, as far away from the rest of the congregation as possible – almost, she thought, as if their poverty was contagious. She turned her head, straining for a glimpse of Matty and found him, jammed in with the men on the opposite side of the aisle.

Several of the men were asleep, some even snoring gently as they gave in to the inevitable toll of exhaustion and poor nourishment. Matty too looked sleepy, his face was unnaturally flushed and once or twice he coughed. If anything he was even thinner than he had been when they arrived. His eyes were lost in deep, shadowed hollows and his face seemed devoid of all animation. When he finally looked at his sister he didn't smile but just stared back at her with the same blank expression which some of the older women wore.

Although members of the opposite sex were strictly segregated in the workhouse, it was possible, by dint of exemplary behaviour and a special request, for relatives to meet briefly on Sunday afternoons. Meggie had been granted this concession by a sympathetic Mrs Cruickshank each time she had asked, only to find that Matty's behaviour warranted no such reward from the male superintendent. To her distress she learned that Matty had earned a reputation for laziness and disobedience which effectively made authorised communication between them impossible. It was only after the weekly service, when everyone gathered outside for the half mile walk back to the workhouse, that there was sometimes the chance to exchange a quick word or two. But recently Meggie had felt that, even there, Matty was deliberately avoiding her. Worried because he was so obviously unwell, hurt by the coldness in his eyes, she was determined to speak to him today.

As usual the workhouse inmates filed out of the kirk first and waited in a silent group outside the building until Mrs Cruickshank and Mr Carlyle joined them from their places with the main body of worshippers. Keeping a wary eye on the male assistants who would have no hesitation in punishing Matty if he was caught talking to her, Meggie edged her way towards him.

'Matty!' she hissed. 'Matty.'

He turned towards her at last. 'What?' He seemed hardly interested.

'Are you not well?' she asked.

He shrugged. 'I've a cold.'

Meggie walked on, as if she was merely keeping on the move in order to stay warm, then turned casually and strolled back towards her brother. 'Why won't you ever smile at me?' she asked, genuinely dismayed by his obvious antipathy.

'What for?' he snarled. 'You don't care about me.'

'Matty! That's not true,' she whispered, but was then forced to walk away again, making a show of stamping her feet and blowing on her hands.

'It is,' he insisted, falling into step a few paces behind her. 'I see you with the other girls, laughing all the time. You like it here.'

'Och, Matty, no I don't! But we'll just have to make the most of it until I'm old enough to get a job and find somewhere for us to live. I'll take care of you, Matty,' she promised.

'Liar!' he nearly spat the word, the venom in his voice making her forget caution and turn to face him angrily.

'I am not a liar!'

'Aye, you are. You're just like Ma and Pa. They said they'd come for us. Where are they? And you said we'd be together, that's why I came with you. But you never even talk to me.'

'You know it's not allowed.'

'I hate you, Meggie McPherson, and I hate it here. I want to go home,' he cried, his eyes flooding with tears, misery written on every feature of his immature face.

'Och, Matty, please don't say that,' she pleaded, her heart wrenching with dread as his thin shoulders shook with a spasm of coughing. Matty had never been strong and there was no one to care for him in the workhouse, where three children had failed to survive the winter months. The sudden fear that he, like Nancy, might die, filled her with dread. In the seconds while she waited for him to get his breath back, Meggie knew she had to get Matty away from here, that he could not wait until she was old enough to find work. There was a sudden flurry of movement at the back of the crowd and she saw one of the male assistants pushing his way towards them.

'Matty,' she whispered, desperation making her rash. 'I'll take you away from here. I promise. Next Sunday. After church. Just be ready.'

'No talking.' Matty was grabbed and hauled away but he looked back over his shoulder and sobbed. 'I don't believe you, Meggie McPherson. I don't believe you.' The words were lost in another violent fit of coughing.

'I promise,' she called, not caring that she too would be in trouble now. 'I promise, Matty.'

She joined the line of women to walk back to the workhouse, heads lowered in shame. For once, Meggie was impervious to the hostile glances and sneering comments of the town's Christian citizens which normally made the weekly journey to and from the kirk such an ordeal. Her mind was fully occupied with the problem she had set herself, a problem to which she could see no solution. But, she told herself, a promise was a promise. Matty was ill and miserable, and all because of her. She must find some way of getting him away from the workhouse before it was too late.

The next Sunday morning Meggie felt as if her guilt was written on her forehead for everyone to see. She went about her routine chores conscious only of her hammering heart and the tell-tale bulge under her apron where she had stuffed bread and cold bacon scraps retrieved from the pantry when no one was looking. As soon as her jobs were done she rushed upstairs. As usual she was one of the last to get ready for kirk but today luck seemed against her and there was another woman in the long dormitory. Turning her back, Meggie changed her clothes, keeping the stolen food concealed inside her discarded dress.

Bessie Hardman, a slow-witted woman who spent her time scrubbing pans in the kitchen, walked down the room and waited by Meggie's bed. Deperate to get rid of her,

Meggie said, 'You go on, Bessie. Don't get yourself in trouble by waiting for me.'

To Meggie's horror, Bessie simply grinned inanely then, meaning to be helpful, leaned over and gathered her bundled dress, dropping it into the basket with all the other soiled clothes.

Meggie watched helplessly, knowing there was no way she could retrieve the precious food or put the rest of her plan into effect while Bessie was with her. Harmless though the woman was, she couldn't be trusted to keep a secret. She would just need to get her out of the room then make some excuse to come back, even though each passing second made discovery more likely.

'I'm ready now,' Meggie said, shoving Bessie out of the room in front of her.

They walked quickly along the narrow corridor and were at the top of the stairs before Meggie gasped and muttered, 'Och, look at my hands! Mrs Cruickshank'll kill me if she sees the state of them. You go on Bessie. I'll be as quick as I can.'

Before the older woman could protest, Meggie was flying back along the passageway, past the dormitory and on, to the walk-in closet where the inmates' personal clothing was stored. Yesterday evening, while the others were safely in the dining room finishing their meal, she had taken a huge risk by pretending an urgent need to visit the toilet and had spent a terrifying five minutes searching for her and Matty's clothes, knowing very well that the easily identifiable beige dresses and shirts would immediately betray them. Now she grabbed the bundle which she had stowed close to the door and raced back to the dormitory, stripping her clothes off as she ran.

She jerked her own old dress over her head, pulled

Matty's shirt on over it and covered both with the workhouse uniform. Diving into the linen basket she retrieved the bread and bacon from the folds of the dirty dress, delving down among the other garments for scattered bits. Frantically she stuffed the food down the bodice of the outer dress, squirming to distribute it more evenly round her slim frame. Finally she wrapped her thin, woollen shawl round her shoulders, hoping that it would disguise the tell-tale lumpiness of her figure.

Before she left the room she went back to her bed and, lifting the mattress, found the piece of paper she had hidden there last night and placed it on her pillow. The brief note merely said that she and Matty were going to Glasgow to join their parents. It would be enough, she hoped, to stop anyone looking for them.

Meggie was pink-faced and breathless when she finally joined the back of the queue forming up for the walk to kirk, but by great good fortune no one of importance seemed to have noticed her absence. Being at the back of the line, Meggie was last into church and managed to sit at the end of a pew, near the aisle. She looked round, desperately hunting for Matty and found him on the opposite side of the aisle, just one row in front of her. Making a pretence of dropping her prayer book she crouched to retrieve it.

'Be ready to come with me as soon as we get outside,' she hissed in his ear before sliding back to her seat.

Matty twisted round, his face confused but, aware that people were already looking at her, Meggie fiddled conspicuously with her prayer book and ignored him. Under cover of the general surge of movement when the Minister entered the Kirk, Matty looked round again. Meggie nodded her head vigorously and mouthed, 'Wait for me. Outside.'

For a moment he frowned as if he still didn't understand

and her pulse raced with frustration at the possibility that her carefully laid plan would fail simply because she couldn't make him realise what she intended to do. But then his eyes widened with dawning comprehension. Meggie smiled and nodded her head vigorously before repeating, 'Outside.'

To her intense relief Matty grinned, excitement making his face gleam. Everyone settled back in their pews and Meggie made desperate flapping signs with her hands, urging him to turn round again. He did, at last, and Meggie buried her burning face in her prayer book, hoping that their frantic exchange had gone unnoticed.

The service dragged. Meggie had to make a conscious effort to stop herself from fidgeting with impatience. In front of her Matty too wriggled on his seat and turned several times to look at her, almost as if seeking reassurance. As soon as the minister left, Meggie turned and walked quickly from the church, breaking into a run as soon as she was through the double doors, racing round the corner of the building and out of sight before anyone could see where she had gone. Flattening herself against the wall she watched for Matty. He appeared in the doorway, his eyes darting round, searching for her.

'Here. Over here,' she hissed desperately, knowing they hadn't much time if they hoped to avoid detection.

He saw her at once and ran over to her. Meggie grabbed his hand. Wasting no time on explanations she ran for the rear of the building. In a minute or two the superintendents would be out, marshalling their charges for the walk back to the workhouse. Meggie knew that she and Matty had to be well away from the kirk before their absence was discovered.

'Where are we going?' Matty wheezed.

'We've got to hide,' she gasped, never slackening her pace as she dashed through the back gate and across the road, narrowly missing a milk float, causing the old horse pulling it to whinny and the delivery man to shout a curse after them.

Darting down a side wynd they emerged in the High Street. To the left was the Town Hall; to the right, shops and offices. At the very bottom of the road, behind large ornate gates, was the town park. Meggie hesitated. The street was long, gently sloping and, at this time of a Sunday morning, relatively deserted. Anyone looking down it would have a clear view of everyone walking there. Her heart pounding with apprehension, she looked back in the direction of the kirk. It would be several minutes yet, she calculated, before anyone started to look for them. Just time for her and Matty to reach the shelter of the sprawling park.

'Come on,' she encouraged her brother. 'We'll be safer in the park.' Hand in hand they raced on, clattering past the police station and Billy Tonner's shop. Ahead of them an increasing number of Sunday strollers, released at last from their various places of worship, milled round the park gates, anxious to take advantage of the first bright weather of the year. But, halfway to their goal, Meggie slowed suddenly, pulling Matty to a jerky stop beside her.

'We can't go through the main gates,' she gasped in dismay.

'Why not?' Matty darted a frantic look behind him.

'Dressed like this?' She tugged at the drab, beige dress. 'Everyone'll know where we've come from. This way, come on.' She dragged him down a side road, towards Inverannan Castle, a ruin of collapsed walls, exposed cellars and the skeletal remains of an ancient tower which perched on a raised knoll, overlooking the eastern side of the park. A car rattled up the road towards them and Meggie shoved Matty into a doorway, holding him there until the road was empty again. Then, moving cautiously now, she climbed over the low gate to the ruins and led him inside, clambering over crumbling stonework until they were sheltered and hidden in the heart of the castle.

'Here.' Meggie wriggled out of her beige dress and handed Matty his own checked shirt, grateful that the lads wore nondescript grey trousers. 'Put this on.'

'My own shirt!' Matty beamed. 'How did you get it?'

'Never mind that.' She was impatient now, eager to get to the greater safety of the park. 'Give me that shirt.'

She bundled the workhouse clothing deep in a niche in one of the collapsing walls. Matty, looking like any normal lad now, scrambled up a pile of fallen masonry and perched there perkily.

'Get down,' Meggie cried, hauling at his legs.

'Why?' Instantly his face regained the closed, resentful look with which she had become so familiar.

'Because we shouldn't be here. The ruins are closed on Sundays. We don't want to draw attention to ourselves. Come on, we'll go to the park. Now that we've got our own clothes on no one will think anything of a couple of kids being there on a Sunday.'

Not wanting to risk the High Street again she picked her way carefully over the unstable walls to the far side of the ruined castle where a dangerously steep bank led down to a secluded corner of the park. Laughing, revelling in this new freedom, Matty levered himself over the dividing fence and slid down the brae on his backside, shrieking with glee. Meggie followed more cautiously, clutching at tufts of grass to slow her descent and finally arriving at Matty's side on a narrow footpath.

Matty turned to his older sister and felt for her hand. 'Where are we going now, Meggie?' he asked, all the old trust flooding back.

'We're going to find Ma and Pa,' she told him confidently, warmed by the feel of his hand in hers.

'In Glasgow?' Matty felt that he was setting out on a huge adventure.

'Aye.'

'Now? Can't we play in the park and go tomorrow?' he begged. 'Please, Meggie.'

Meggie glanced up at the clear blue sky and experienced the urge to have just one day of complete freedom. In any case, she told herself, it was already after twelve o'clock, and too late to start for Glasgow today.

'All right.'

Matty grinned and jumped up and down in excitement. 'I knew you'd look after me,' he told her gleefully.

Meggie smiled back at him, her heart full of love but there too was the first niggling doubt at her own ability to protect him.

He saw the flickering frown which dimmed the light in her eyes. 'You won't let them take me back to the workhouse, will you, Meggie?'

A cloud obscured the late winter sun, throwing them into chilly shadow. Meggie felt a shiver of cold terror on her skin. Then, as quickly as it had disappeared, the sun emerged again melting her momentary fear. When she turned to him her eyes mirrored only love and warmth.

'No,' she told him, squeezing his hand. 'I'll never let them take you back there, Matty. I promise.'

'So they've run off?' Carlyle faced his fellow superintendent over her desk. 'I hold you responsible, Mrs Cruickshank.

The girl was in your care and it was she who planned this, that much is obvious.'

'I am afraid you are right, Mr Carlyle.' Mrs Cruickshank's dislike of this harsh man was intensified by the knowledge that, in this, he was correct.

'And you think they have gone to Glasgow to join their parents?'

'So the girl's note said.'

Carlyle stared down at the dying embers of the fire, aware that the Parish board would take a very dim view of the youngsters' disappearance, that his own lucrative position might be threatened by any investigation.

'Then I think we should be very careful in what we tell the board, Mrs Cruickshank,' he said at last. 'As far as they are concerned, Margaret and Matthew McPherson have simply gone to join their parents. There is no reason for the full story to become known.'

Mrs Cruickshank was appalled. 'But Mr Carlyle! They are children. They have no money, no food. Nothing! I dread to think what might happen to them. We have to tell the authorities. Have a search made for them.'

'A search? And where do you suggest we start looking? They will be well on their way now and Glasgow is not so very far away. Children like these are used to fending for themselves. Two less for the parish to support, Mrs Cruickshank and no need at all to risk our own positions by reporting their disappearance.'

'Oh . . . I don't know, Mr Carlyle. They're so young.'

'Well, I have no intention of losing my post for a pair of ungrateful little thieves!'

'Thieves? Oh no, Mr Carlyle.'

'Aye, thieves! Did they not help themselves to clothes which were no longer theirs? And Matthew McPherson had already been up before the magistrates for stealing from Billy Tonner in the High Street. And nothing but trouble from the day he arrived here.'

'That may be so, Mr Carlyle, but Margaret McPherson is an honest child, and hard-working, too. I had high hopes for her.'

'High hopes?' he scoffed. 'For an ignorant little work-house skivvy? A thief just as much as her brother. I think you are forgetting the purpose of this establishment, Mrs Cruickshank. And you know, of course, that the board are already asking questions about why the women's section should cost so much more to run than the male house? You can't afford to bring more attention to the lax way you run the place.' He puffed his chest out, his own self-importance giving credence to the lie, then craftily changed tack, appealing to the softer side of his colleague's nature. 'You have already said that the parents wanted the children back so what is to be gained by admitting your mistake, Mrs Cruickshank? All that will happen is that your poor girls will lose their superintendent. Not every woman is as kind-hearted as you are. They will suffer if another, less caring, woman is put in charge. Is that what you want?'

Mrs Cruickshank was well aware of the fact that hers was a much more lenient régime than that in many similar institutions. The thought of her unfortunate charges being subjected to the same harsh treatment as the men unnerved her. 'No . . . of course not. I am very happy here. I feel I can do some very real good.'

'There . . . Then there's no more to be said. You may rely on my discretion, Mrs Cruickshank.' Carlyle smiled unctuously, sure he had managed to convince her of the safe course of action. 'I'll leave you to mark your records in an appropriate way.' He nodded politely and left the room before she had the chance to change her mind.

Mrs Cruickshank wrestled with her conscience for a minute or two before finally withdrawing the file marked MARGARET MCPHERSON from her drawer and noting that both children had been returned to their family.

'I'm still cold,' Matty complained, coughing and shivering in his thin shirt and jacket.

The bright March sunshine had faded. The delights of the day – the freedom to run on the grass of the park; playing with other children; watching with appalled fascination as two exquisitely dressed children were handed pennies by their mother which they promptly threw into the clear pool at the deep bottom of the glen; eating a picnic meal of bread and bacon scraps in the shelter of one of the park's many trees – had rapidly given way to creeping fear as night approached. Too late, Meggie realised that her plans had taken her no further than their actual escape from the workhouse and the nebulous aim of getting to her Uncle Jim and Aunt Lil's. Now night was falling rapidly and there was very little food left. They were both cold. Matty's jacket was thin and her own shawl would offer little protection in the long night. The enormous weight of responsibility frightened her but wouldn't get any less by sitting there and doing nothing.

'Come on,' she said, decisively, pulling him to his feet. 'We'll keep moving, that's the best way to stay warm.'

'I'm tired,' he jerked away from her hand. 'I don't want to walk any more.'

'Well, you'll have to get used to it,' she snapped, her patience eroded by his constant complaints. ' 'Cos walking's the only way we've got of getting to Ma and Pa.'

'Walk! All the way to Low Bothlie?' His pinched face wore an almost comical expression of horror.

Despite herself she chuckled. 'Aye, walk. And how else did you think we were going to get there?'

He shrugged. 'Bus?'

'We've no money, Matty,' she explained gently.

'I thought you'd made all the plans?' he accused her petulantly. 'We can't walk all the way to Uncle Jim's.'

Meggie's good humour evaporated again. 'And where do you think I am going to find money for bus fares?' she demanded.

'I'm not walking,' he insisted stubbornly.

'Fine,' she retorted.'Then go back to the workhouse. I'm going to find Ma and Pa.' Turning her back on him she started to march away.

Matty stared after her for a long minute, expecting her to relent. When she didn't he aimed a destructive kick at some early daffodils, then broke into a run and caught up with her, tugging at her sleeve. 'Wait for me, Meggie.'

She walked on, ignoring him.

'Meggie. Wait. Please.' Still she ignored him. 'I want to come with you, Meggie. Please wait.'

At last she stopped. 'Are you sure?'

'Aye,' he nodded, his urchin's face creasing in an anxious monkey-like grin.

'Och, Matty . . . Look, sit here a wee minute and let me talk to you.' She steered him towards a bench. 'You're a big lad now,' she told him. 'And if you want to find Ma and Pa you've got to help me. It's no good sulking and complaining every time things get hard. I meant what I said, Matty. If we don't find Ma and Pa we'll both of us end up back at the workhouse.'

'I'm not going back there.'

'So you'll have to help.'

'All right,' he agreed sullenly, staring at his feet.

Suddenly the evening air was pierced by three shrill blasts on a whistle. Meggie jumped up and looked around her anxiously, suddenly realising that the light was fading, that the sounds of children playing had gradually died away, that there was nothing but the occasional cry of a bird and the rustle of the breeze in the tree tops to disturb the peace of the park. In the distance she saw a keeper, rounding up the last of the park's visitors and herding them towards the gate, sounding another warning on his whistle as he did so. 'Everyone's going home! The park's closing.'

'I don't want to stay here for the night,' Matty whined, eyeing the dark, threatening forms of the trees and shivering again.

'We're not going to! We'll go back to the castle.'

'No!' The thought of a night among the eerie ruins terrified him.

'Have you got a better idea?' she demanded.

He shook his head miserably. 'It's cold,' he muttered, wrapping stick-like arms round his body.

'I know.' He looked so pathetic that she felt ashamed of her impatience. 'But it'll be more sheltered in the ruins. Anyway, our other clothes are there. 'We'll need them to keep us warm.'

'I suppose so,' he agreed doubtfully.

They avoided the patrolling park-keepers and clambered unchallenged up the bank and over the fence into the ruins, scrambling over the low remnants of ancient walls until they reached the spot where they had changed that morning. Meggie delved into the deep recess and withdrew their crumpled workhouse clothing.

'Put it on under your own shirt,' she told him.

Matty rapidly stripped off his own clothes and donned the beige-coloured shirt, flinching as the damp fabric touched his skin. 'I don't like it here, Meggie,' he muttered, looking at the shadowed walls which surrounded them, his eyes luminous with apprehension.

'Och, Matty, what did I just say to you? You've to be brave for a night or two,' she said, determined not to let him see her own fear but then jumping as a bird rose screeching just over their heads, loudly objecting to its night time roost being disturbed. 'And look, there's a braw sheltered place over there. We can snuggle in under that wall.' She pointed to what had once been a huge fireplace, still intact and sheltered enough to offer some protection from the night.

They picked their way carefully along the remains of a wall then jumped down into what must once have been a cellar, now exposed to the sky, and cautiously examined the old fireplace.

'There's plenty of room here,' she said, determinedly cheerful. 'If we go right to the back and snuggle up together we'll be fine and warm.' She led the way, inching forward on hands and knees and found there was room to sit quite comfortably against the back wall. 'Come on, it's braw.'

Matty crawled in beside her and they lay down together, cuddled up like kittens. The town clock struck nine and the gentle noises of Inverannan gradually faded away as they drifted towards fitful sleep.

Meggie woke cramped, chilled and alone. A horse clopped slowly along the cobbled road behind her and she could hear the milkman's tuneless whistling, the metal segs on his boots ringing sharply in the clear morning air as he hurried about his deliveries. Moving stiffly, Meggie crawled out of the shelter and stood yawning on the damp grass which now covered the floor of what had once been a kitchen where sumptuous meals for King James V had been prepared when he visited the town, centuries before. For Meggie and Matty breakfast would consist of dry bread and hard bacon scraps.

There was no sign of Matty and she was on the point of going to look for him when he came clambering over a wall on the far side of the ruins and ran towards her, grinning and clutching something in his hands.

'See what I've got,' he held out his offering proudly.

'Milk!' Meggie looked aghast at the bottle of creamy liquid.

'Aye. I waited until the milkman was away up a close then helped myself. It was easy.' He tipped the bottle to his mouth, drank deeply, wiped the froth of milk from his upper lip and passed the bottle to his sister.

'You shouldn't steal, Matty. It's wrong and you'll end up in the jail again if anyone catches you.'

'It's early yet,' he said. 'There's no one around. And I was careful.'

'It's still wrong,' she insisted, longing for a sip of the cool liquid.

'Aye, so's running away, but we did that, didn't we?' Still he held the bottle out to her. 'Go on, have some.'

Meggie gave in and helped herself to a long, refreshing drink. 'Don't do it again,' she told her brother. 'Water'll be fine until we find Ma and Pa.'

Matty just grinned. 'Close your eyes. I've got something else.'

'Matty!'

'Don't fret yourself. It's not stolen,' he insisted, still grinning widely. 'Go on, close your eyes and hold out your hands.'

Reluctantly she did as she was asked and listened to the unmistakable noise of rattling coins.

'You can open them now,' he said, holding his own clasped hands over her cupped ones.

Meggie looked on in horror as he opened his fingers and allowed a fistful of coppers to fall into her hands. Before she managed to gasp out her astonishment his hands delved back into his trouser pockets and came out with yet more money. Pennies, half-pennies, farthings and even a couple of three-penny bits slid from her nerveless fingers and showered over the damp grass.

Meggie found her voice at last. 'Matty! Where . . . where did you get this?' She knew that this amount of money could not have been come by honestly. 'Who did you take it from, Matty?'

'No one,' he laughed.

'Don't lie to me!' she screamed. 'Where did you get it? Was it from the milkman? Did you steal it from him?' She grabbed him by the shoulders and shook him.

He squirmed away from her, still laughing. 'Och, keep your hair on. I told you, I didn't steal it. Honest.'

Meggie sank to her knees, still hardly believing what she was seeing. When she looked up at him again her eyes were cold. 'I want to know where you got this, Matty.'

Matty dropped down beside her and raked the money together. 'I got it in the glen.'

'Och aye! Of course you did,' she sneered.

'Aye! From the pool. You remember. You saw them chucking money in there yesterday.' He chuckled aloud, hugely proud of himself. 'I climbed down the bank and into the water. All this was just laying on the bottom.' He picked up a penny still smeared with mud and examined it thoughtfully. 'Why do folk throw money into the water, Meggie?' He sounded genuinely perplexed.

Meggie suddenly realised that Matty was barefooted, saw streaks of mud on his legs and the pink wrinkling effect of the water on his toes. She took picked up a coin and turned it over in her hands. 'They throw money in and make a wish. It's supposed to be lucky.'

'It's stupid,' Matty declared.

'Aye.' Now Meggie was laughing, too. 'It is, isn't it?'

'See I told you I didn't steal it. If it was thrown into the pool it doesn't belong to anyone, does it, Meggie?'

His sister considered this for a moment. 'No, I don't suppose it does,' she agreed at last.

'We can go to Glasgow on the bus now, can't we?' he asked.

Meggie hastily counted the money. 'I don't know how much it costs, but they don't charge much for children. I think there'll be enough.'

'We won't have to walk?'

'No, Matty. We won't have to walk. Not now.' Excitement bubbled up inside her and she crawled across the dewy, early morning grass and hugged him tight. 'Everything's going to be all right, Matty. I know it is.'

Before the middle-class homes were properly astir, Meggie and Matty were walking towards the bus stance. Even at such an early hour the streets were busy. Trams and the occasional bus transported folk to work. Milk carts and coal carts, their horses straining under their loads, carried supplies to the outlying areas. Fish merchants rushed the morning's catch inland from the fishing villages further up the Strathannan coast. There were workmen, walking and on bicycles, setting out for another shift in the linen mills and women too who would spend up to twelve hours a day in the mills for half the pay a man would get and then struggle home, bone weary, to tend to husbands and children.

No one gave the two youngsters a second glance.

CHAPTER SEVEN

Neither Matty nor Maggie had ever been on a service bus before. At first Matty sat with his nose pressed to the window, watching the passing countryside but, but quickly becoming bored, eventually fell asleep. For Meggie too, the novelty rapidly wore off, leaving her with a strange, apprehensive feeling in her stomach. Although she had courageously attempted to obliterate the pain of her family's rejection by immersing herself in the strict routine of the workhouse, she had been unable to overcome the suspicion that she and Matty had been sent there as a punishment; that, because of what had happened when Nancy died, her Ma and Pa no longer loved them. Her father's failure to keep his promise to return for them had hardened that suspicion until it was absolute conviction and she was far from certain that they would find a warm welcome at the end of this journey.

'I wonder which is Uncle Jim's house,' Meggie whispered, when they were finally deposited in Low Bothlie.

'I don't know,' Matty reached for his sister's hand.

'Well, it's not a very big place. We'll ask. Someone's bound to know.'

'Aye, lass. That's it, right over there. Third one from the end.' A miner, returning home from his shift, pointed the house out to them.

Outside the front door Meggie ran her fingers through Matty's hair and spat on a corner of her cuff before rubbing it over his face to remove traces of dirt from round his mouth, anxious to make the best possible impression. That done she rapped sharply on the door.

'Aye?' It opened to reveal a bad-tempered stranger.

'Are you Aunty Lil?' Matty asked, stepping forward.

The woman stared at them, her mouth gaping open. 'In the name . . . !' she gasped. 'You're never Meggie and Matty, are youse?'

Relief made Meggie's tired head spin. Everything would be all right now. Someone else would take responsibility for her brother and she could go back to being just a schoolgirl again. She looked up at her aunt and smiled shyly.

'We came to find Ma and Pa,' she said.

'But they're not here! They've been gone since before the New Year.'

Meggie's smile became a set grimace of pain. 'Gone?' she repeated softly.

'Och, youse had better come in for a wee minute.' Lil stood aside and ushered them indoors, her mind working furiously. She was tired, the last weeks of pregnancy making her back ache and draining her of all energy. Tasks which had taken minutes a month ago now took half an hour and the last thing she wanted was to be saddled with two extra children. She would give them a bite to eat and set them on the road to Lairdstoun before Jim came home.

She set the cooling teapot on the hob, gave it a couple of minutes to heat, then dispensed tepid, amber liquid into cups, not bothering to add milk or sugar, then smeared margarine on two slices of bread. The children looked at it as if too shocked to eat or drink.

'Och,' she said, striving to instil some cheer in them and, hopefully, get them on their way all the quicker. 'They're not that far away. I'll put you on the right road as soon as you've eaten.'

116

'Drink your tea, Meggie,' Matty said, nudging her, frightened by the bleak look on his sister's face.

She jumped slightly then drained the cup and made herself eat the stale bread. 'Where are they, Aunty Lil?'

'Lairdstoun. It's just three or four miles down the road. You'll get there in time for tea. Are youse ready then?' She struggled to haul her bulk from the chair and opened the front door. 'Come here and I'll show you the way.'

Meggie and Matty stood despondently on the pavement and followed the direction of her pointing finger.

'Go to the main road and turn right. Just keep on walking until you come to Lairdstoun. You'll not miss it.'

'Do they live near there?' Meggie asked.

'Aye. I think so. Your Pa had a job with the steelworks so they'll be able to give you his address.'

'Don't you know it?'

'No, I've not seen them since they left.' Lil looked away, unable to meet the girl's searching gaze, discomfited by such wise old eyes in so young a face. And there was certainly no need to tell them about the bad feeling between the two families. 'Your Pa's busy working. There's been no chance to visit.'

Meggie took her brother's hand and started back through the village. She hadn't liked her Aunt Lil and didn't bother looking back. The front door slammed behind them.

By the time they found the Lairdstoun steelworks the streets were thronged with folk returning home from their day's work. The two youngsters, who had walked the four weary miles in near silence, wove through the tide of men and found themselves at the main gate.

'We'll have to ask here,' Meggie told Matty.

He nodded and leant tiredly against a wall to wait.

117

Meggie walked to the big wooden gates and stepped boldly into the yard.

'Hey! What do you think you're doing?'

She turned and found herself facing a huge, brawny man, his face hidden under a bushy beard. He was so tall that it hurt her neck to look up at him.

'I'm looking for someone,' she said bravely.

'Aye, but you shouldn't be in here, lass. Employees only.'

She watched as the last few men straggled through the gate, making for their homes. 'Has everyone gone home now?' she asked.

'Only the day shift.'

'I'm needing to find a Mr McPherson,' she said as he took her arm and propelled her back towards the gate. 'Do you know if he's still here?'

'There's hundreds of folk work here, hen and McPherson's a common enough name.' He pushed her firmly outside the gate. 'Best to come back tomorrow when the lassies from the office are here. They'll be able to tell you if he works here.'

'I need to find him tonight,' Meggie insisted, refusing to move another inch. 'We're going to his house to stay but I don't know his address. We'll have nowhere to sleep if you don't help us.'

The man scratched his beard, disturbed by the intensity in the girl's eyes. 'There's not much I can do the night, lass. I just watch the gate. I know the faces but not the names. What does this Mr McPerson look like?'

'His name's Tam,' Meggie told him. 'He's not awful big and he walks a bit funny 'cos he once broke his leg in the pit. He's not been here very long.'

'Wait a wee minute! Did he used to be a miner . . .

118

somewhere in the east? Let me think . . . where was it now . . .'

'Craigie. In Strathannan,' she prompted him urgently.

'Aye! Strathannan. That's it. Got paid off after the strike. Well, you're in luck. Tam worked here right enough, in the yard. We sometimes walked home together.'

Meggie beamed, the smile transforming her face. 'Can you tell me where his house is, please?'

'Aye, though, come to think of it, I've not seen him for a week or so. Still, he lives in Mungo's Close, off the Rutherglen Road. You'll find it easy enough. Just down past the church there and turn right.'

Meggie was already hurrying away. 'Thanks mister,' she called back. 'Come on Matty. We're almost there,' she laughed, her flagging spirits miraculously revived.

Ten minutes later they were standing in Mungo's Close, peering into the dismal interior of a tenement building. The grimy paintwork, the dark stairs and fusty smell made no impression on the two excited children.

'I wonder which door it is?' Matty asked.

'We'll just have to ask,' Meggie decided, walking determinedly to the nearest one and knocking loudly.

It seemed a very long time before the door opened a fraction and a scruffy grey head peered round.

'Wha' do youse want?' Cleary asked.

'Please, we're looking for Mr McPherson. He lives here,' Meggie said, stepping back out of range of his foul breath.

The door opened wider and the old man stepped out, hauling at his sagging trousers with one hand and scratching at his backside with the other. 'Och aye, number nine. Mr McPherson and his high-and-mighty wife. Always complaining she was. And what do youse two want with them?'

'We've a message for him,' Meggie said, unwilling to admit they were searching for their parents for fear of being sent back to the workhouse.

'Well, you'll not find him here. They've gone. And good bloody riddance.'

Meggie thought she was going to be sick. 'When? Where to?' She managed to choke out the words.

He shrugged, not caring. 'How the bloody hell should I know where they've gone? Dunshill way I think. Aye. Try up by Dunshill. Now bugger off and leave me in peace.'

He slammed the door in her face. Meggie collapsed on to the bottom stair and gave herself up to overwhelming despair. After a minute of waiting in vain for her to look up and tell him what they were going to do now, Matty sat beside her and slid his body close to hers, huddling together in the draught from the close.

Unaware that her son and daughter were less than five miles away from her, Netta McPherson took the kettle out to the tap on the landing and filled it, ready for Tam's tea.

It had been a mistake to come through here, she thought bitterly, as she peeled tatties and threw them into the pan of water already boiling on the gas stove. Work was scarce and the best Tam had been able to find after getting paid off from the steelworks was another temporary job with Dunshill town council, sweeping the streets, something a proud man like Tam found demeaning. But it was too late to go back to Strathannan now. They had nothing beyond what Tam earned and that was barely sufficient to pay the rent and feed them, wasn't even enough to repay the debt they still owed Jim and Lil, never mind pay to have their things carted back to Strathannan.

Rinsing off the scrubbed peelings she put them to one

side, ready for tomorrow's stewpot then went to stand at the window, watching for Tam, the view deepening her depression.

They had moved to Dunshill, a cheerless little town of tenements and factories, three weeks ago and had been lucky to find this two-roomed, tenement flat close to the council depot. Netta was starting to wonder if this was to be the pattern of their lives, moving from one grim tenement block to another every time Tam changed his job. Not that there had been any alternative to moving, she accepted that. Tam's hours were long and the wages so low that paying tram fares was out of the question.

At least this was an improvement over the place at Lairdstoun. The two rooms were bigger, cleaner and there was the advantage of a water pipe on every landing. Here they were at the front of the building, looking down over the street instead of the clutter and smell of the inner courtyard. But it was a busy road, teeming with carts, cars, buses and people, and the constant noise disturbed her. There were times when she wondered if she would ever get used to living in the bustle of the town and longed for the relative quiet of the countryside. None of that would matter, she thought, if Matty and Meggie could come home.

They, more than anything, disturbed her peace of mind, keeping her awake long into the night, worn out by constant arguing with Tam. But he was right, she admitted to herself, they still couldn't afford to feed and clothe two extra bairns. And this was no life for children.

Perce and Bertie, forced to change schools yet again, had both been bullied by the local youngsters who all belonged to one or another of the gangs which roamed the streets, amusing themselves with acts of petty crime and general mischief. It was exactly the same here as it had been in Lairdstoun, where the very fact that they were new to the area and spoke with different accents had marked them out as targets – until both had demonstrated that they knew how to use their fists and were not frightened to stand and fight when necessary. Now they would have to prove themselves all over again. She hated to think what might become of timid, babyish little Matty in such a place. Yes, Tam was right. Better to leave Matty and Meggie where they were until Tam had a regular job and the family could find a better place to live.

She saw Tam walking slowly along the street, his shoulders bent, his limp more pronounced now than it had ever been. Even from this first-floor window she could see the bleak expression on his face. She turned away, unable to look and busied herself setting the meal on the table.

Meggie and Matty, hungry and penniless in a strange town, spent the night huddled together in a cubbyhole under the tenement stairs. They were woken before first light by the tramp of heavy boots as the menfolk left for work. Like two frightened animals they peered round the corner of their den, instinctively fearing discovery. All around them the thin walls allowed sounds of everyday life to escape as families rose to face another day. In the grey light of dawn Meggie and Matty felt more alone and frightened than they had done since leaving the workhouse.

'We can't stay here,' Meggie whispered to her brother, who was doing his best to stifle his incessant coughing.

'Are you going to find Ma and Pa today?' he asked.

Meggie felt a surge of anger. He expected so much from her, seemed unwilling to think for himself. In the past she had protected him fiercely but now, cold, hungry and frightened herself, she was resenting his dependence on her.

She rounded on him angrily. 'Why does it always have to be me?' she demanded. 'You're the one who wanted to run away.'

Matty's huge, dark eyes immediately filled with tears. He turned away and hunched miserably in the corner, his shoulders shaking with muffled sobs, interspersed with coughing. She sighed, feeling a surge of guilt. Matty wasn't well, he wasn't strong or clever, like her. He had always relied on her and until they found their Ma and Pa, she was all he had. Gently she put her arm round his thin shoulders and pulled him against her.

'I'm sorry, Matty,' she whispered. 'Don't cry. Please don't cry.'

Slowly the sobbing stopped and he looked up with accusing eyes. 'You promised,' he reminded her. 'You said we'd find Ma and Pa.'

'I know,' she said, her heart heavy.

'You won't make me go back to the workhouse, will you?' he asked.

Meggie shivered.

'No,' she assured him. 'We'll find them, Matty. It'll just take a wee while longer, that's all. Come on. We'd better get out of here before anyone sees us.'

They emerged on to the grey street and mingled easily with people setting off for work. Meggie hesitated for a moment, then waylaid a woman who frowned at being delayed.

'Can you tell me the way to Dunshill, please?' Meggie asked.

'Dunshill? Aye. Down there to the steelworks then left

and on up the main road as far as Sunter's bar, then left again on to Craighill Road. It's on down there.'

'Is it far?'

'Five or six miles. There's a tram every half hour.' The woman brushed past them and hurried on.

'I don't want . . .' Matty started, then, seeing the scowl on his sister's face, rapidly changed his tone. 'Hurry up, our Meggie. I'm starving and the sooner we find Ma and Pa the sooner we'll have something to eat.' He set off along the pavement and this time it was Meggie who hurried to catch up with him.

They found Craighill Road easily enough and stood for a moment gazing into the distance where it crested the top of a rise and disappeared. For as far as the eye could see there was the same vista of tall, grim tenements, punctuated by the occasional shop or kirk. As they walked Maggie felt as if she was passing the same buidings again and again. It was only when they reached the top of the hill and looked back to see the Lairdstoun steelworks dominating the skyline behind them that she believed they had made any progress at all. In front of them the road dropped away gently until it came to a junction with another main road. With aching legs they went on.

At the junction they hesitated, uncertain about the direction in which to go. To the left the road seemed as unending as the one they had just walked down, but to the right, they could see shops and open barrows on the pavement. The area was teeming with people.

'We'll go that way,' Meggie decided.

The pavement bustled with housewives doing their daily messages, the air hummed with the banter of the barrow boys and the gossip of the women. No one took any notice of the brother and sister as they walked past bakers, fleshers and grocers, their empty stomachs contracting painfully at the sight and smell of so much food. Matty's eyes widened as he peered at the tempting display in a baker's window, his stomach growled and his steps slowed bringing a sharp reproof from his sister.

'I'm hungry,' he complained. 'And we don't even know where we are.'

'I'll ask someone.' Meggie looked for a friendly face, then approached a woman serving behind a fruit and vegetable barrow.

'Aye, lass?' The woman smiled encouragingly. 'What's it to be? The carrots are braw the day and the tatties are good and firm. You'll not find cheaper round here.'

'I'm not wanting to buy anything,' Meggie apologised, trying not to look at the tempting array of fruit on the front of the barrow. 'I'm looking for Dunshill.'

'On up the road, lass. A mile or so. You'll know you've got there when you see a pub called the Pot Man on the left-hand side.' She pointed back the way Meggie and Matty had just come.

Meggie sighed, thanked the woman and looked round for Matty. He had disappeared. Frantically she wound her way through the shoppers, searching for him. She was on the point of turning round and going back to look in the opposite direction when she heard him calling to her.

'Psst! Meggie.'

She looked round and saw him grinning at her from a side close.

'Matty! What do you think you're doing?' she scolded.

'Did you find the right way?' he asked.

'Aye. It's back up here,' she sighed. 'We turned the wrong way.'

'Never mind,' was his unexpectedly cheerful comment.

'Look, see what I've got.' Chuckling he produced two shiny, red apples and three or four carrots from his pockets and held them out to her.

'Matty!' Meggie was truly appalled. 'Did you steal those?'

'Aye.' His face closed in a sullen expression and he snarled the words at her. 'I thought you'd be pleased. You told me to help you and we've had nothing to eat since before we got on the bus.'

'But I told you before, you mustn't steal, Matty. It's wicked.'

'Bollocks!' he repeated a word he had often heard in the workhouse, knowing it would shock her.

In one fast, fluid movement, Meggie bent down and delivered a stinging slap across the backs of his bare legs, very much as her mother would have done. 'Don't you dare speak to me like that, Matty McPherson. You ever say anything like that again and I'll tell Pa. You know fine what he'd do if he heard you.'

Matty's predictable reaction was to dissolve into tears. 'I was only trying to help,' he sobbed.

'Aye, I know. But you'll not use words like that again.'

'All right, but you're hungry, too, I know you are. We've spent all the money so how else are we going to get anything to eat?' Tentatively he offered her the biggest apple.

She took it reluctantly, knowing he was right. Surely it wasn't such a wicked thing to take food when you were so hungry? Their father had always insisted on total honesty, even in little things, and every fibre of her being told her that what Matty had done, what he might need to do again, was wrong. But what other way was there? They were very hungry, her own head was spinning with lack of food and

Matty wasn't even as strong as she was. Deliberately she bit into the apple.

'We'll only take what we need,' she told him, her conscience still uneasy. 'And you be careful. If you get caught we'll both end up in the jail and then we'll never find Ma and Pa.'

His stinging legs forgotten, Matty grinned and attacked his own apple, following it quickly with a raw carrot as they walked on along the road.

A few minutes later, they passed a run-down pub with THE POT MAN written in peeling letters above the dirty windows. 'This is it,' Meggie cried. 'This must be Dunshill.'

They looked round expectantly but all they could see was the now familiar street of blackened tenements and equally drab housewives. Meggie approached the nearest woman and asked, 'Is this Dunshill?'

'Aye, lass, that it is.'

'We're looking for a Mr and Mrs McPherson. Do you know where they stay?'

'McPherson? Nay, lass. The only McPherson I know of is old Mrs McPherson on Ladywell Road. And she's a widow woman.'

Disappointed, Meggie led Matty further up the street, stopping every so often to ask after their parents but with no success. After that they resorted to trailing up and down the various streets, knocking on doors. Brought up in a close, village community where everyone knew everything about everyone else, Meggie hadn't imagined it would be so hard to find her family in the teeming tenements of the town. Four or five times they found someone who did know of a family of McPhersons and their hopes would rise, only to be dashed again when the family in question turned out to have six children, or to have lived in Dunshill for years or to be a newly married couple. None of them could possibly have been their parents.

Meggie and Matty spent another night huddled under the stair of a tenement house and a second day combing the maze of streets and alleys that made up Dunshill, without success. If their parents had come here to live, no one seemed to know them.

'Maybe that man was wrong and they didn't come to Dunshill after all,' Meggie suggested as they trailed through the late afternoon drizzle, her head spinning from lack of food. Beside her Matty coughed constantly.

'What we are going to do now?' he asked.

'I don't know,' she admitted. 'I suppose we'll have to find somewhere to sleep and then go back to Aunty Lil's tomorrow.' But she knew that they both had to have something to eat before then. There were still a few barrows lining the road and they were surprisingly busy with housewives in search of a late bargain, women who eked out their wages by buying at the end of the day, knowing very well that the pies, bread and meat would not keep until tomorrow. Meggie eyed one barrow which had half a dozen meat pies piled temptingly near the edge, then turned reluctantly to Matty.

'If I talk to the barrowman, could you take a pie?' she asked, knowing that what she was suggesting was wrong, but seeing no other way of feeding them.

Matty looked startled, then grinned. 'Aye, course I could,' he assured her, anxious to make her see how useful he could be.

Meggie pulled her damp shawl up over her head to that it half hid her face. She waited until there was no one else to be served, then stood at the far side of the barrow, well away from the pies, and called to the man who was starting to pack up. She had asked the same questions so many times now that the words came out quite automatically.

'McPherson? No lass. I've not heard of anyone of that name moving in round here.'

Meggie was so nervous that she hardly heard his answer. She saw her brother's grubby little hand snake out and take one pie, then another, but something in her manner alerted the stallholder and he too looked round, just in time to see a choice mince and potato pie disappear under a street urchin's dirty jacket.

'Hey!' he bellowed.

Matty was already off, tearing along the street, dodging round the back of the barrows and then down a side road and into a tenement close. Maggie too acted instinctively, backing away then racing after her brother, struggling to see where he went. She rounded the corner of the street just in time to see him disappear up a close. Checking to make sure they hadn't been followed, she ducked in beside him. Coughing and spluttering, Matty proudly offered her a pie. Laughing with relief they sat on the bottom stair and ate ravenously.

'Thieving little tinks!' the barrowman roared, knowing there was no point in giving chase. They would be well away by this time.

'Wee tykes,' one woman commented to another as they waited their turn to buy the last of the day's bread at a knock-down price. 'Need a good thumping, kids these days.'

'Aye,' Netta McPherson, swathed in coat and shawl against the persistent rain, agreed distractedly. She had caught only a brief glimpse of the girl as she sped away but, dirty and unkempt though she was, just for a second she had reminded her of Meggie, reviving the lump of pain under her heart. When she turned to ask for a plain half loaf her eyes were so misted with tears of longing that she miscounted her money and gave the barrowboy a penny more than he asked for.

'We can't stay round here,' Maggie said, as they stepped back on to the pavement. 'That barrowman'll recognise us and anyway, I don't think Ma and Pa can be here.'

'I don't like it here.' Matty looked at the grim tenements and thought longingly of the cottage in Craigie.

'But where else can we go, Matty? Even as they talked they retraced their route, turning out of Dunshill and back up the hill until there, before them in the distance, was the spread of Lairdstoun steelworks. Like her brother, Meggie longed for familiar faces, warm food and somewhere safe to spend the night, all things they had known in Strathannan. Without consciously making the decision, they began to make their way back there.

It took them a full week to get to Inverannan. Luckily the weather held because they had to walk the whole way. They slept wherever there was somewhere sheltered and dry, twice in tenement buildings, twice in barns, once in someone's shed and once under a hedge. They survived by scrabbling through the hay in one of the barns for eggs hidden by the hens who also lived there, then eating them raw, but mostly by reverting to the now familiar tricks of stealing from unsuspecting milkmen and shopkeepers. On their second morning Matty discovered that this particular milkman also delivered bread and helped himself to two pan halves, as well as a full pint of milk.

At last, exhausted, filthy and disheartened they were back in the shelter of Inverannan Castle's decaying walls and

Meggie forced herself to face the prospect of returning to the workhouse.

'No!' Matty stamped his feet, his face scarlet with rage and fear. 'You promised! You promised! You're just like Ma and Pa. You don't care what happens to me.'

'That's not fair, Matty. You know I tried to find them. But we can't go on like this. We've nowhere to live and we can't keep stealing food either. We'll get caught and then we'll both end up in jail.'

'No, we won't. Summer's coming, we'll be all right.' He refused to listen to reason.

'But how are we going to pay for our food?' she pleaded.

'You could get a job. You're tall. Everyone will think you're old enough.'

'I couldn't. I don't look fifteen.' Despite her height Meggie knew that her ragged haircut, her too thin body and dirty clothes gave her an exaggeratedly childish appearance.

'Yes, you do. Please, Meggie. Try,' he begged her, his dark eyes filled with apprehension.

She sank back in the corner of the old fireplace and groaned. What sort of job could she possibly do? She knew nothing, hadn't even finished her schooling. But she did know something! She sat forward slightly, her mind assessing the possibilities. She had worked in the workhouse kitchen and knew that girls had left to take up jobs as skivvies in big houses or hotels in the town. It wasn't much but it would be better than what they were doing now. But how did you go about finding work like that? By knocking on doors until you were successful, she answered her own question. Maybe if she had a good wash and tidied herself up a bit she could pass for fifteen.

Matty had watched the change in his sister's expression in silence. Now he said, 'Will you try, Meggie? Please?'

'Aye, I'll try,' she promised. But then the burden of responsibility seemed to drain all her energy, making her see the impossibility of her plan. She rolled herself in her shawl and turned away from him so that he couldn't see the rare tears of despair running down her cheeks.

CHAPTER EIGHT

After nearly a fortnight of living rough, Meggie's hands were ingrained with dirt, her fingernails were rimmed with black and her hair was nothing more than rats' tails. Although her shawl was dark enough to hide the dirt, her dress was badly marked and her boots were encrusted with dried mud. But, with no money to visit the public baths or even to buy a single piece of soap, how could she hope to clean herself up?

The only way she could get herself even half presentable was to wash in the burn which ran through the park's sheltered glen. It would be better than nothing, though, and Matty too was in desperate need of a thorough scrubbing. So, early in the morning, when the only other people about were either exercising their dogs on the wide stretches of open grassland or taking a short cut to work, she dragged her protesting brother into the park.

Avoiding the ornate hothouses where gardeners were already at work they skirted the children's paddling pool – still empty of water so early in the season – and hurried past the pavilion tea rooms. Meggie had always been drawn to this sophisticated place and couldn't help staring through the open doors. She had a tantalising glimpse of snowy white tablecloths and the flash of silver cutlery as a waitress, neatly garbed in a black dress and crisp white apron and cap, prepared the tables in readiness for the town's matrons who had made the pavilion their favourite place for morning coffee and lunch. And there, just inside the main entrance were two doors. On one was written LADIES. On the other, GENTLEMEN.

'Matty.' Meggie tugged urgently on her brother's arm.

'What?' He asked impatiently, thoroughly disgruntled by the prospect of a cold wash.

'There. LADIES and GENTLEMEN.'

He stared, not comprehending, his limited scholastic accomplishments making it difficult for him to read even his own name.

'Toilets,' she explained impatiently.

'Don't need,' he shrugged and started to walk on.

'I know! But that's a posh place. Maybe they've got sinks and warm water in there.'

The waitress worked briskly, moving steadily across the room, further and further away from the watching children. Meggie awaited her moment, then swiftly pushed Matty through the main door and into the ladies' washroom.

Half an hour later they re-emerged, looking vastly improved. Meggie's hair hung wetly round her face and her dress had dark, damp patches where she had scrubbed at the worst of the marks, but both would soon dry in the fresh air. Their faces glowed from the energetic rubbing she had given them and even her fingernails were almost clean. Meggie looked at her brother and grinned, feeling her mood lighten, as if it had been sluiced away with the layers of dirt.

'Come on then, if I'm going to find a job today, I'd better hurry up.'

Meggie's mood of buoyant optimism lasted until she knocked at the back door of the City Hotel, the largest of the burgh's two 'good' hotels. Her halting request for a job was met with scornful disbelief by a girl, not much older than herself, who refused even to let her enter the building.

At the second, a smaller establishment near the railway station, a rosy-faced, middle-aged woman looked her up and down with a critical eye then said kindly enough, 'Well, as it happens we've a place for a skivvy in the kitchen. Washing up and such like. Do you have references, lass?'

'References?' Meggie repeated blankly.

'Aye.' There was a trace of impatience in the woman's voice now. 'Something written down by someone who knows you to tell me you're honest and hard-working.'

'I've nothing like that,' Meggie admitted.

The door was already closing on her. She dragged herself back to where Matty was sitting on the edge of the pavement, waiting for her. Seeing the grim set of her mouth he said nothing but slipped his hand into hers and they walked away together.

They spent an equally unproductive afternoon and evening touring the larger houses. It was after ten at night by the time Meggie and Matty made their way back through streets which glistened wetly, the streetlamps casting a muted yellow glow over the rain water pooling between the setts. Their feet were wet, their clothes were saturated, clinging to their chilled bodies and adding to the misery of gnawing hunger. Darkness had brought gusting winds, clouds and heavy showers and although the early springtime days were mild, the nights were still bitterly cold. Neither child relished the prospect of another night in the open.

Ahead, clearly silhouetted against the scudding clouds, loomed the castle ruins, eerie and unwelcoming. Directly in front of them, on a street corner, stood the Houlets' Nest. The windows of its public bar were ablaze with warm, golden light and the sound of laughter pulsated over the quiet street each time its doors swung open to disgorge another satisfied client.

Above the door the sign creaked on its rusty chains, the houlets' eyes catching the glow from within and shining eerily in the darkness.

Notorious for the fights which regularly broke out on its premises the Houlets' Nest was popular for more than its excellent beer. The landlady, an astute woman of somewhat blousy, if faded, charms, made a substantial profit from the half-dozen or so girls who populated the hotel bedrooms. The enigma of such a business being tolerated in a town whose citizens flocked piously to the kirk at least once every Sunday was explained by the fact that she and her girls provided a discreet service to several of the burgh's more eminent citizens, including the Chief Inspector of Police.

Meggie and Matty, of course, knew nothing of this. Drawn by the sounds of revelry on such a cheerless night, they sought shelter from the latest shower, huddling in the doorway and basking in the warmth escaping from within.

They had been there for only a few minutes, watching as the rain gradually eased, when the door opened and a man emerged. Meggie had seen enough miners rolling home on a Saturday night to recognise a drunk when she saw one and stepped back, out of his way.

The man staggered slightly as the cool night air hit him, then seemed to make a determined effort to collect his wits, straightening his tie, smoothing the collar of his coat and setting his hat firmly on his head. Only then did he realise that he was being watched.

'Well, well,' he laughed pleasantly. 'Have youse two no home to go to?'

'We were just sheltering from the rain,' Meggie said quickly.

'By, and youse look near frozen,' he said, the good whisky and even better company he had enjoyed making him mellow. 'Youse could do with something to warm yourselves through.' He delved into his trouser pockets and withdrew a handful of coins. 'Wait a wee minute,' he ordered, shoving open the door and bellowing, 'Two of your hot meat and tattie pies out here, Moira.' He tossed the money into the depths of the smoke-filled room, then, with a wink and another laugh he was off, leaving the children staring after him, their mouths gaping.

They were still watching him when the door opened again and a young woman peered out. She looked away up the street to where their anonymous benefactor was following an erratic path up the hill. 'Are these pies for youse?' She looked doubtfully at the youngsters in the doorway.

'Aye!' Matty, the rich, fatty smell making his head spin, reached out greedily and grabbed the pies, biting into one and holding the other out to his sister. 'Go on. Eat it,' he ordered.

The girl shrugged. 'Might as well,' she smiled at Meggie. 'They're paid for.'

Meggie could wait no longer. She took the second pie from Matty's hand and sank her teeth into it, swallowing the unchewed mouthful before she had a chance to taste what she was eating. In seconds the pies were gone and Matty was licking the greasy remnants from his fingers.

'My, and you were hungry weren't youse?' The girl was watching them now, her eyes sharp and alert. 'Wait here and I'll fetch youse something to drink.'

She came back a minute later with two glasses of lemonade. 'Here, wash it down with this.'

Meggie, her stomach warm and comfortable for the first time in days, smiled back and thanked her.

'Now then, what are youse two doing on my doorstep at this time of the night?' Unnoticed by either child, an older woman had followed the girl and was now watching them from the doorway. 'All right, Moira. You go back inside. Leave this to me now.'

'Yes, Mrs McDonnell.' The girl winked at Meggie then hurried back to the bar.

'Well? Have youse lost your tongues?'

'N . . . n . . . no,' Meggie stammered, wondering if they had done something wrong.

'Well then, I asked you a question. What are youse two doing here at this time of the night? Shouldn't you be home in bed?' She propped the door open with her ample hips, allowing light to bathe the youngsters, and missed not a single detail in her rapid appraisal of them. 'Come along. I'm not going to eat youse,' she smiled warmly, encouraging them to trust her. 'It looks to me as if youse two are in some sort of bother. Maybe if you tell me about it I could help.'

Cold, lonely and desperate it was tempting for them to accept this woman's offer of friendship. But Meggie was cautious, wary of coming out with the whole story. Instead she looked up, met the woman's small eyes firmly and said, 'I was looking for a job.'

'At this time of the night?'

'Just washing dishes, or cleaning up. Anything.' Meggie raced on. 'I'll work hard and I'm honest and reliable.' Assets which seemed to be high on the list of necessary requirements for even the most menial job.

Mrs McDonnell looked hard at her again. The girl was too thin, that much was obvious even in this light. But then again, she mused, she had the almost waif-like quality that appealed to some types.

'Well,' she said. 'I might have something to suit . . . I'll

138

tell you what. Why don't you and the wee boy come round the back? You can have a warm at my fire and when I've closed up here we'll have a wee talk about it.'

Meggie gaped, unable to believe her good fortune.

Mrs McDonnell gave her a gentle shove. 'Round the back. I'll meet you there.'

Half an hour later, divested of their damp clothing, washed, wrapped in warm blankets and settled one at either end of a huge sofa with a cup of cocoa in their hands, Meggie and Matty were sleepily pondering the sudden change in their luck.

Mrs McDonnell, having cleared her bar and seen that the other side of her business could do without her for a while, smiled at her guests, relieved them of their empty mugs and settled them more comfortably on the couch.

'Not to worry, lass,' she said to Meggie who, thinking of her job prospects, was struggling to wake up. 'You get a good night's sleep. Our wee chat'll keep till the morn.'

If the previous night's trade had been good, none of the women in the Houlets' Nest stirred much before mid-day. The clearing up and lunchtime opening was attended to by Mr McDonnell, a diffident, grateful little man who was only too happy to live his life on a different timetable to that of his wife. By the time Mrs McDonnell appeared in the sitting room, swathed in a voluminous, floating creation which billowed behind her, threatening to sweep ornaments from shelves, Meggie and Matty were just emerging from the deep sleep of almost total exhaustion. Meggie, blinking her eyes open, stared at the majestic figure in front of her and wondered if she was still dreaming. The strident voice with its thick Strathannan accent soon brought her to full alertness.

'Well, youse two. Up you get. Breakfast first and then we've got some talking to do.' Mrs McDonnell tossed a pile of clothes at them, their own things, somehow washed and dried since last night.

Breakfast was as substantial as any main meal they had eaten. Matty stared at the heaped plate of bacon, black pudding, dumpling and eggs, too intimidated even to pick up his knife and fork.

'Get on with it, lad. You look as though you could use a bite of good food.' Mrs McDonnell, not particularly fond of small boys, had taken a liking to this wide-eyed urchin. If it wasn't for her aversion to 'unnatural' practices, she might have been tempted to use him to widen the scope of her business. But even she could see he was far too young. Nevertheless, she filed the thought away for future reference.

'Right.' She settled her impressive bulk on a chair and faced them sternly. 'Now I've given youse good food and a bed for the night. I may or may not have a job for you. That will depend on whether I get the truth. First time round, mind. No second chances. The truth now or forget the job and back out on the streets with youse.'

Inwardly Meggie groaned. Once Mrs McDonnell knew all about them there would be no job. She looked up, found herself staring into the woman's shrewd eyes and knew there was no chance of getting away with an untruth. In any case she was no good at lying. She always went pink and stammered too much to be convincing. 'Yes, Mrs McDonnell.'

'First off, what are your names?'

'Meggie and Matty,' Meggie answered.

'Meggie and Matty what?'

'McPherson.'

'And how old are you?'

'Fourteen. And Matty's just eleven.'

'Eleven! He doesn't look eleven. More like eight or nine.' Mrs McDonnell shook her head.

'He is eleven. Honest!' Meggie was desperate to be believed. 'I know he's not very big, but he was eleven last month.'

'So, you're quite a big lad then? Big enough to do some work yourself?'

Matty puffed his chest out with pride and nodded furiously. 'Aye.'

'Now you can tell me the rest of the story.' Mrs McDonnell, satisfied that what she had heard so far was the truth, sat back and waited. What she heard sent the girl up several notches in her estimation. Tall and slender with a waiflike appearance, huge eyes and that thick mane of clumsily cut, dark hair, Meggie McPherson was on the way to becoming an unusually beautiful young woman. She was also resourceful, tough enough to adapt and yet young enough to be moulded. Yes, Mrs McDonnell had the feeling that things would work out very nicely indeed.

'Well, there's no one from the workhouse looking for youse,' Mrs McDonnell told them later that afternoon and smiled to see the obvious relief that flooded the girl's face. A brief conversation with Mr Carlyle, who had been persuaded to part with the information on the promise of a free night's entertainment, had cleared up her one area of concern over Meggie and Matty McPherson. 'So, you're safe enough staying here, if that's what you'd like.'

'You mean I can have a job?' After the relief and euphoria of last night, Meggie was getting suspicious. In her limited experience no one went out of their way to help unless they were getting something in return.

'Aye. If you want it.'

'But why? No one else would take me.'

Mrs McDonnell smiled. 'Let's just say I've taken a liking to youse.' She saw the girl's doubting expression, the glint of intelligence in her dark eyes and added, 'And don't go thinking I'm soft enough to be taking you on as charity cases. You'll both have to work and work bloody hard, too. You'll get bed and board and pocket money, to start with anyway. I get a bargain and you get a roof over your heads. That should suit us all.'

'Matty should be going to the school,' Meggie suggested boldly, concern for her brother uppermost in her mind.

'School!' Mrs McDonnell's over-pencilled eyebrows disappeared in the ruts and ridges of her forehead. 'And what use would a schoolboy be to me? If it's an education you want, get off back to the workhouse.'

'Meggie,' Matty's voice was pleading. 'You promised.'

'But you need to learn things, Matty,' she insisted. 'How will you ever get a proper job if you don't go to the school?' She turned back to Mrs McDonnell. 'If he went to school he could still work for you in the evenings and at weekends.'

'Och, use your head, lass. If he goes to the school they'll be asking all sorts of questions. They wouldn't think it right, youse two staying here. You know fine that you're neither of youse old enough to be working. They'd have you back in the workhouse before you could snap your fingers.'

'I'm not going back there, Meggie.' Matty was adamant. 'I want to stay here. I like it here.'

Meggie shrugged helplessly, seeing little alternative. 'I suppose . . .'

'That's settled then.'

'What'll we be doing?' Meggie asked.

Mrs McDonnell laughed, a brief, humpfing sound.

'Doing? Anything I or Mr McDonnell tell you to do. In the kitchen, cleaning the bar, cleaning the rooms, washing, anything at all, lass. But just you keep out of the bar in opening hours. I catch you in there and you'll be for it. Not that a bright young face like yours wouldn't cheer them up, mind, but it's against the law and I've no mind to lose my licence.'

'Yes, Mrs McDonnell.'

'Good lass. Now then, come with me and I'll show you where you'll be sleeping.'

Meggie stirred restlessly, easing her aching limbs to a more comfortable position on the sagging mattress. On the other bed, Matty laid, splayed on his back, snoring gently.

Somewhere on the floor below them, a door banged and there was the sound of muffled laughter, then rapid footsteps. It was the same every night. Mrs McDonnell insisted that Meggie and Matty were safely in their beds before the serious business of the night began. After rising at six and working until after six at night, Meggie was glad enough to creep away to her room as soon as she had eaten her dinner. But there was always this constant noise and commotion from the other girls' rooms. Matty too worked hard enough to fall into bed without complaint but, unlike her, he slept soundly, reassured by his sister's presence and by the comforting human sounds which seldom faded away until the early hours.

The other girls, six of them in all, were something of a mystery to Meggie. Apart from on Sundays, when nobody worked, she saw little of them and the floor which housed the girls' rooms was strictly off limits. She assumed they worked in the bar, serving drinks, but if that was the case how come so many of them seemed to be in their rooms in the evenings when the hotel was at its busiest?

But, all in all, Meggie thought, turning over yet again, they were happy enough at the Houlets' Nest. They worked hard, that was true, but in return they were well fed, had clean beds and warm rooms to sleep in and even had every Sunday off. That was the best day. The whole place had a relaxed, good-tempered feel about it on Sundays. The bar was closed to the public, but more often than not the girls gathered there, laughing and chatting among the debris of the night before. On wet Sundays Meggie and Matty sometimes sat with them, playing cards or dominoes. The girls were pleasant enough, but Meggie sensed that, for some reason, they weren't at ease when she was there. Not that it really mattered. Now that summer had arrived, Meggie preferred to spend her free time in the open. More often than not she took Matty to the park where he soon made friends with some other lads while she sat under a tree engrossed in one of the books she borrowed from the Kirkgate library.

It was Matty who had benefited most from their new situation. Working on an endless round of odd jobs under the eye of Mrs McDonnell's self-effacing husband, Arthur, Matty was flourishing. Though still small for his age he could no longer be mistaken for an eight-year-old. The good food and exercise had already put some flesh on him and he coughed less, had more energy and seemed brighter, more alert than he had ever done. Determined that he wouldn't grow up to be ignorant, Meggie did her best, using the daily paper and library books to teach him to read, and was delighted when he finally seemed to grasp their meaning.

They were sitting in the kitchen one Sunday morning,

Matty reading the headlines aloud, while Mr McDonnell attended to his account books, adding the long columns of figures with much sighing and scratching of his head. Arthur McDonnell was an unremarkable man with such a talent for blending with his background that few people even noticed his existence. He wore bottle lenses, was slightly deaf, half his wife's girth and an inch or two shorter, all of which meant that he had to peer up at her when she spoke, giving him the appearance of a frightened squirrel. Having only her father's example to draw on, Meggie was astonished to discover that Mr McDonnell was in awe of his strong-willed wife and lived in fear of upsetting her. But he was not an unkind man and was endlessly patient with Matty who took shameless advantage of his good nature.

'You're doing well with the reading, lad,' he said, dropping his pencil in exasperation and pushing his spectacles up on to his forehead. 'It's a pity you can't tally figures for I could do with a hand with these.'

It was jokingly said but Meggie, who had grown to like this gentle-natured man said, 'I know how to do arithmetic, Mr McDonnell.'

He looked at her, then shook his head. 'Aye, lass, I daresay you do but this is difficult stuff.'

'I was top in my class,' she insisted, anxious to both help and learn.

'Go on then, Miss Smarty Pants,' he teased her. 'Sort that lot out for me and I'll give you a tanner each.' He shoved the book and a pile of papers across the table at her, sure she wouldn't be able to make sense of them.

Meggie peered at the lines of figures with a sinking heart. The roughly pencilled numbers were almost illegible and the totals at the bottom of each column so changed and crossed through that she couldn't read them.

'What does this say?' she asked, pointing to the nearest total.

Mr McDonnell laughed. 'Aye, Mrs McDonnell's aye complaining about my writing, too. That's why I do it in pencil first. When I've got it to balance I ink it in. See.' He flipped back a page and showed her the completed entry for the previous week. It was horribly untidy and still practically indecipherable. She grimaced and he laughed. 'I bet you could write it in neater than that.'

She laughed back. 'I think I could,' she agreed, frowning again at the figures. 'Och, I see. This side is what you've taken in and this is what you've paid out. These are bills and receipts.'

'Aye.' He was impressed with her now. 'That's it. And that figure, at the top there, is what we started the week with and this one is what we've got now.'

'So you add what we started with to what we've taken and then take away everything we've paid out and that should be what's left?'

'That's the idea. But somehow it's not right this week. Mrs McDonnell will fair go her dinger if we're short.'

Meggie bent her head to the book and counted furiously, noting her answers on the back of one of the bills. At the end she shook her head in frustration. 'It's still not right.'

'Here, give it back to me lass. I'll have another go,' Mr McDonnell offered.

'No, let me try again,' she pleaded, more anxious to prove she could do it than to claim the sixpence he had promised for success. Now she checked off every invoice, again using the back of one of the bills. 'I see it!' she exclaimed, her face alight with pleasure.

'Where?'

'There. You'd put this bill in twice. That makes it exactly right.'

'Och . . .' He sighed his relief and rattled round in his pocket for two sixpenny pieces.

'I reckon you've earned that, lass.'

'I'll write the figures in for you, if you like.'

'You're a glutton for punishment. You want to be careful or you'll find yourself landed with this job every week.' He pushed the pen and bottle of ink over to her. 'Try not to make any blots. Mrs McDonnell hates to see blots.'

'I won't.' Meggie leaned over the paper, concentrating fiercely and didn't see Mrs McDonnell coming into the room.

'Well, that's a fine job you've made of that, lass.' She pulled the book towards her for a closer look. 'Neat, too. Do you like numbers, Meggie?'

'I enjoyed doing that.'

'Good,' Mrs McDonnell was brisk. 'You can do them every week.'

'Och, that's hardly fair on the lass,' her husband objected.

'Fair? She's paid to do what she's told and I daresay it'll make a change from washing dishes and scrubbing floors. Anyway, you're no bloody use at it!'

With that she sailed from the room.

'I'm sorry, lass. I think I've landed you with more work,' Mr McDonnell apologised.

Meggie was far from upset. 'But I like doing it,' she insisted. And it was something else, more experience being stored up for the time when she could go and look for a proper job.

* * *

'I'm right pleased with you, Meggie.'

Astonished, Meggie looked up from the sink where she was working her way through a huge pile of dinner dishes. Mrs McDonnell wasn't an easy woman to work for and relished finding fault.

'You're making a braw job of keeping the books.'

Meggie turned, a smile brightening her pretty face. 'I really like doing it, Mrs McDonnell.'

'Keep it up then and maybe, just maybe, if you work hard at it, we could start you on something else. Something more interesting.'

As she spoke Mrs McDonnell's keen eyes assessed the girl again. In the few months she had been here, Meggie had begun to grow into her youthful promise. Her hair, now long and trimmed neatly to fall softly round her shoulders, framed a face of rare and memorable beauty. Exotically high cheekbones with a pleasing touch of peachy colour, balanced, wide, thick-lashed eyes. Her full-lipped mouth was very nearly sensual, curling readily in a smile that displayed even, white teeth and made dimples in her cheeks. And her figure was developing nicely, too. Her breasts were youthfully firm and well defined by the thin cotton of her working blouse while her legs were long and shapely, leading the eyes up to gently flaring hips and an enviably slender waist. But despite her ripening assets, Meggie had an air of untouched innocence. And it was that freshness which Mrs McDonnell knew would appeal to certain of her customers. One thing was certain; the girl was wasted here, skivvying in the kitchen, and there were plenty of youngsters who would be glad enough to do the menial work. Mrs McDonnell had an altogether different future planned for Meggie McPherson but she would need to ease her into it very carefully indeed.

* * *

Meggie twirled in front of the mirror in Mrs McDonnell's bedroom. Her cheeks were flushed with excitement and her dark eyes sparkled.

'It's braw,' she sang, turning yet again, smiling as the soft, white fabric billowed round her legs.

Mrs McDonnell laughed. Meggie's innocent delight was infectious and for a moment she quite forgot exactly why she had chosen this virginial white.

'You're a picture, lass, a bonny picture. And this other one is just as braw.' She fingered the blood red velvet, enjoying the rich feel of the fabric. The contrast could not have been more marked. The red, low cut dress complimented Meggie's dramatic colouring, making her look wild and wanton, while the white was demure, innocent. Oh yes, they had been inspired choices. The investment in a few yards of material, some decent underclothing and pretty shoes would be as nothing compared to the business the lass would generate.

'I don't know which one I like best,' Meggie admitted. Nor did she know what had prompted this sudden act of generosity. Instinct told her there had to be a purpose behind it. 'Can I wear one of them on Sunday?'

'To run round the park in? I should think not!' Mrs McDonnell helped her out of the dress and hung it carefully inside her wardrobe. 'These are for working in. You'll have to be careful and keep them decent.'

'Working in!' she exclaimed in dismay. 'I can't wear these in the kitchen. I'll never keep them clean.'

'Never you worry your pretty head about the kitchen. I've a new lassie starting in there the morn. As soon as you've shown her the ropes you'll be coming to work with me. On the hotel side.'

'The hotel side?' Meggie repeated, awed. The hotel was

still an area of mystery. She had seen the door marked PRIVATE, which was reached by walking through the bar and into the small back hall. She knew that behind that door was another, smaller bar area, richly decorated and furnished with deep, plush sofas. She had also discovered that this was where the other girls worked.

'Aye. Would you like that, lass? The pay will be better, of course.'

Meggie nodded, keen to better herself and be rid of the harsh routine of cleaning which had been her lot until now. And more pay would mean she could buy Matty some new clothes. Perhaps she might even be able to put aside a few shillings for his future.

'Yes, please,' she answered eagerly.

Mrs McDonnell smiled. 'It'll mean a later start. No more getting up at six in the morning. But you should be able to get away to your bed by eleven o'clock most nights, to start with at least,' she added wondering how long it would be before the girl had her own room along with the others, on the first floor. 'We usually close the private bar when we close the pub doors. Unless there's a special client, of course.'

'Special client?'

'Aye. But don't bother yourself with all that now. Away back downstairs and finish your chores. I'll explain it all to you later.'

CHAPTER NINE

'It's very simple really,' Mrs McDonnell explained on Meggie's first evening in her new job. 'All you have to do is sit here and look pretty. But remember, if anyone asks, don't tell them your age. Mind that now. We'll all be in trouble else.' Not that she had any serious doubts about Meggie now. In her new clothes and with a touch of powder, rouge and lipstick she looked satisfyingly older than she really was.

'Is that really all I have to do?' Meggie sensed there was more to it than that.

'Well, not quite. There's the money to look after and the list to keep, but that's not going to be difficult for a bright lass like you.' Mrs McDonnell patted the girl's hands and drew a stiff covered book towards her. 'When a guest arrives you smile, make him feel welcome – that's important. Take his coat and hat, settle him on one of the sofas and take his drink order to the barman. The regular clients will expect you to know their favourite tipple without asking but you'll soon get used to that. Then you ask which young lady he'd like to see.' She glanced at Meggie and, pleased to see that the girl was attending, went on. 'Check in the book. If she's free, fetch her down. If not, explain that she's engaged and ask if there's anyone else he'd like to spend the evening with. If he wants to wait for a particular girl, that's fine, the longer they're in the bar the more money they spend on drink so look after them while they're down here. Ah, and this is the most important thing of all: before the girl takes a gentleman upstairs, he must pay. Take the money, note it in the ledger and make certain you fill in the man's name, and the time, against the girl's room number. That way you can see instantly whether a girl is free or not. Understand all that?'

'Yes, Mrs McDonnell.' Meggie gazed round the room, impressed again by the splendid furnishings, so much in contrast with the public bar.

It would be a relief, Mrs McDonnell thought, to be rid of this job. It was deeply depressing to realise how infrequently her own services were required these days and, to be honest, she had lost all taste for the work since middle age had started to wreak havoc with her body, forcing her to admit that her once plump flesh was now simply flabby; that the laughter lines around her eyes had deepened and spread a web across her whole face; that her jowls sagged as much as her breasts and that her nightly desires ran to nothing more exciting than a warm bath and eight hours' sleep.

'Do all the men go upstairs?' Meggie asked.

'Most of them. Och, there's always the odd one who won't stay if he can't have the girl he wants. Then there's those who will have another drink when they come back down. Some even go upstairs a second time. It's your job to keep an eye on them. But you mind this, if anyone wants to buy you a drink you ask for a gin and tonic and that's what they'll pay for. What you'll get is soda water. We can't have you falling around drunk now, can we?' She cackled.

'I suppose not. But isn't that . . . well, it's not right, is it? Charging them for something they're not getting?'

'Every time someone does that, you get half the price of the drink, lass, so don't go turning your nose up at it,' Mrs McDonnell replied sharply.

'What do they do upstairs?' Aware that she had said the

wrong thing, Meggie changed the subject by asking the question which had been bothering her since she came to the hotel.

Mrs McDonnell hesitated momentarily, certain Meggie knew little about what went on between a man and a woman. It was her hope that by close contact with the clients and other girls who worked here Meggie would gradually come to understand and accept the real nature of the business. Young, fresh and innocent as she was, Meggie could turn out to be a very valuable asset indeed and it was vital not to frighten her.

Choosing her words with circumspection Mrs McDonnell said, 'Well . . . men like nothing better than to spend the evening in the company of a pretty lady. Some of them, och, they're poor, lonely souls, married to miserable, sour-faced women. They come here to relax, to have an hour or so with a bonny young lass. It's natural and there's no harm in it. It makes them feel good and they go home to their wives in a happy mood so everyone benefits.'

'Ten pounds just to spend the evening with a girl?' Meggie was astounded and the feeling that there was something else, something Mrs McDonnell wasn't telling her, persisted. But there wasn't anything difficult about the job and it seemed only right to do as she was asked, to repay the kindness Mrs McDonnell had shown her and Matty. And, at last, she would even have the opportunity to earn some money. Resolutely putting aside her embryonic doubts she smiled.

'I'm sure I'll manage fine, Mrs McDonnell.'

'Good. Now, don't worry about anything. I'll stay right here with you for the first couple of nights, just until you know what you're doing.'

Reassured Meggie nodded and settled herself on her seat, waiting for the first customer of the evening.

It was three weeks later, and a Friday, always one of their busiest nights. This evening, being so close to Christmas and New Year, business was especially brisk. The small private bar was crowded. Running between customers, serving drinks and attending to newcomers, Meggie glimpsed a man leaving and assumed it was the client who had gone upstairs with Hilda an hour before.

'Here's your drink, sir.' She handed a large gin to a portly newcomer and, with her best smile, asked, 'Who would you like to see?' With the faint flush on her cheeks matching the vivid colour of her dress and emphasising the lustre of her dark eyes, Meggie sparkled, drawing the eye of every man in the room.

'Well, if I can't have you, I suppose I'll have to settle for Hilda,' he said, teasing her.

'Of course. Enjoy your drink and I'll see if she's free.'

The girls often came into the bar between clients but there was no sign of Hilda so Meggie hurried upstairs and along the corridor. Sometimes, if it had been a particularly busy night, the girls would refuse to entertain anyone else and she had to check before sending the next customer up.

Hilda's door was closed. Meggie knocked but got no reply so opened the door quietly in case the girl had fallen asleep. What she saw froze her to the spot in shock.

There was no way of misinterpreting what the two naked bodies were doing. In the minute that she stood in the doorway, her eyes fixed on the scene in front of her, Meggie understood everything. Knew what her parents had done to make the box bed creak and rattle at night; knew why her mother had made such a fuss about her sharing a bed with her brothers; understood what the women in the work-house had laughed so coarsely about. And knew exactly what Mrs McDonnell had planned for her.

Hilda, looking up and finding her performance observed, froze and gaped over her partner's shoulder.

'What the bloody hell . . . ?' He client, alerted by her sudden stillness, looked round to see an open-mouthed child, apparently on the point of fainting, framed in the dooway. Finding himself unable to continue in the face of such obvious horror, he clapped a hand over his deflating manhood and made a dash for his trousers, muttering furiously about a refund.

'Out!' Hilda gathered her spread limbs and rushed at Meggie, shoving her none too gently into the corridor and slamming the door on her back.

Meggie sagged momentarily against the wall then, seem-ing to collect herself, ran frantically to her own room.

Alerted by an unamused Hilda, Mrs McDonnell, a poor substitute for Meggie, in an over-tight, off the shoulder dress which relentlessly exposed the crêpe-like flesh of her heaving bosoms, did her best to calm the ruffled feelings of the clients still waiting in the reception area before stomp-ing upstairs and confronting Meggie.

'Why didn't you tell me?' Meggie, her shock ripening into anger, challenged as soon as the older woman opened the door.

'I thought you'd have worked it out for yourself by this time!'

'You should have told me,' Meggie blazed. 'It's . . . it's horrible.'

'Och, take that look off your face,' Mrs McDonnell exploded, exasperated by the whole incident. 'My girls are all here because they want to be. No one forces them to do

155

it. And they make good money. Half of what every client pays goes to the girl. They've a bloody sight better life here than they would have working in some mill somewhere, or married to some pig of a man who takes it for free whenever he feels like it. And it's a damn sight better than being in the workhouse. You just think on. This is a decent place. I look after my girls. I'm fussy about who I let through that door. There's no rough trade, they're all clean and no one hurts my girls. We're providing a service, that's all and there's nothing wrong with that!' The tirade brought flecks of spittle to the corners of her mouth and she dabbed at them with her fingers, smearing crimson lipstick down towards her quivering jowls.

Meggie, who had had no guidance from her mother in these matters, had no standard by which to judge the other woman's views. Only instinct warned her that what she had witnessed was wrong. Confused, Meggie looked away and asked, in a small voice, 'Am I to be one of your girls?'

Mrs McDonnell sighed but knew the time had come to be perfectly honest. 'That's what I hoped, lass. That's why I put you in reception, so you could get used to the idea. From the minute I set eyes on you I knew you'd be one of the best. You're young and pretty, and you've a nice wee figure. There's plenty men would ask to go with you.'

'Some already have,' Meggie admitted. 'I didn't know what they meant.'

'Well, now you do!' Mrs McDonnell's voice held no hint of sympathy. 'Still, it's up to you. I'll not force you. I'd meant to let you settle in, find out gradually, maybe talk to some of the girls, see for yourself that it's not a bad life for lassies like you. I was trying to do you a favour, to give you the chance to make some money so you can look after that brother of yours properly. But it's your decision.'

'Couldn't I just be the hostess?'

'No, that wouldn't work. The clients are already asking for you. They wouldn't like it if you weren't available to them.'

'And if I don't want to?'

'Then I'll be sorry to lose you, Meggie. I've taken quite a liking to you and that brother of yours. Still, I can't afford to have you here if you're not going to earn your keep.'

'You'd put us out?' Meggie gasped.

'I'd have no choice. I'm a businesswoman. I need girls who can pay their way. And I'll not keep the lad without you.'

Meggie sank her face into her hands and groaned.

'Och, for goodness sake, don't take on so. It's not as bad as you think. I'm sorry you had to find out that way but it was time you knew the truth. Anyway, you think about it. I was going to give you another month to settle in before I said anything to you so why not wait and see how you feel in a couple of weeks? Wait until after the New Year before you make up your mind.'

'I don't know.'

'Talk to the other lassies,' Mrs McDonnell advised before leaving Meggie to think things through. 'But you'll soon see that you and your brother are safer here with me. And it is him you have to think about, isn't it Meggie?'

Meggie spent a sleepless night. The noises filtering through from the floor below had a new, more sinister meaning, now. Beside her Matty breathed heavily, a constant reminder of her promises, her obligations, her responsibility. Mrs McDonnell had been right. It was him she had to think about.

What real choice did she have, she wondered? She

already knew that because of her background she had small chance of getting a decent job and, without a job, there was absolutely no possibility of finding anywhere to live. The best she could hope for was some place where she would be paid a pittance for slaving in a kitchen. But what chance was there of finding a situation where Matty would be welcome too? She was wise enough now to know that no one of her age could expect to earn enough to support two people, pay rent on a room, and buy clothes, food and all the other things a growing boy needed to keep him safe and healthy.

Getting out of the crumpled bed she wandered over to look out of the window. Above the slated roofs the ruins of the castle loomed ghostlike in the darkness, reminding her of those cold nights when they had had no food, no clothes, no future. She shivered. She couldn't take Matty back to that, not now that he was so much better, so much happier. Nor could they return to the workhouse. He would never forgive her if she did that to him, and he was all she had now that their parents had abandoned them. The thought of her parents brought a sudden rush of anger. If they hadn't left her and Matty, this would never have happened. It seemed so long since she had last seen them. Perhaps she should have one more try at finding them. It would be her very last chance of seeing them because if she stayed here and did what Mrs McDonnell was suggesting she would be too ashamed to face her mother ever again. But it would be even harder to find them now than it had been before.

She turned away from the window and looked thoughtfully at her sleeping brother. If it was just herself she had to worry about she would have managed somehow. If it was only herself she would never have left the workhouse in the first place, she thought, fighting feelings of resentment. She was trapped. Because of Matty she was trapped. But not forever, she told herself, slipping back between the sheets. They would have to stay here and she would have to do what Mrs McDonnell wanted her to do. But only until she had some money behind them. As soon as she found a job which paid enough for her to support them both she would take Matty and leave.

The next night she was back, playing her role as hostess with a new, brittle lift to her smile, a harder edge to her voice.

'And which young lady would you like to see tonight, Mr Smith?' she asked, smiling at a gentleman who was a regular visitor.

He grinned, displaying tobacco-stained teeth. 'Well,' he boomed, twirling the end of his moustache between the thumb and forefinger of one hand and grabbing her knee with the other. 'To tell the truth, I'd like to have some time alone with you. You're a tasty little piece. I bet I could teach you a thing or two, eh?' His laughter barked across the room.

Meggie blushed so furiously that her face almost matched the red of her dress. He wasn't the first client to ask her to accompany him upstairs but so far she had managed to deflect their attentions by the sheer naïvety of her replies. Until yesterday. One brief minute in the doorway of another woman's bedroom had brought the end of her innocence, changed her life forever and was now making her see this man's comments for what they really were.

The knowledge that in a few short weeks she could be the one taking Mr Smith upstairs brought a fresh flush of shame to her cheeks.

Firmly she removed his hand from her knee. 'I'm sorry,

sir,' she said, her lips quivering with the strain of maintaining her sunny smile. 'I'm not available tonight. Is there anyone else?'

'Another night then?' He still grinned at her.

'Perhaps,' she whispered, feeling sick.

'Then I'll take whoever's free tonight,' he said, licking his lips. 'It doesn't matter who.'

'Yes, sir.' She walked away, hoping her disgust wasn't obvious. Anyone would do. The girl herself wasn't important, just her body. Was that the way all men saw women, she wondered bitterly as she looked in the book to check which of the girls were free.

With her new-found understanding, Meggie discovered she was looking at the other girls through different eyes. She saw how Moira, the oldest of the girls, relied on Meggie sending up the clients, as if she didn't care who or what they were. The men who went to her room re-emerged more quickly than they did from any other. Hilda, a slim, dark-haired girl with a quiet voice and a gentle smile, seemed almost shy, but she had a regular core of customers, many of whom were prepared to wait as much as two hours in order to see her. In contrast, Sadie was blonde, brash and loud, favouring tight, low-cut dresses. She preferred to choose her own clients and as soon as she had dispatched one she would appear in the reception area, flirting shamelessly, drinking glass after glass of gin between customers and, more often than not, ending the night in a drunken haze.

Eva was Sadie's closest friend, also blonde but not naturally so. She was abrasive and argumentative with the other women, and prowled the bar, anxious to take as many clients as possible. A huge proportion of her 'gentle-men' paid the maximum fee and Meggie soon realised that Eva offered something 'extra', though she still didn't understand exactly what that was. Lise, a tall, sultry brunette drifted among the men with a cigarette constantly burning in a long, tortoiseshell holder. Meggie was astounded to discover that Lise was only a year older than she was herself. Like Eva, Lise wanted as much work as possible, sometimes seeing as many as eight men in one night, but made no secret of the fact that she despised them all. She was the most cynical, the most outspoken and most shocking of the girls and seemed to go out of her way to embarrass Meggie, sneering at the younger girl's naïvety.

'Take no notice of her,' Ellie, the sixth girl, advised Meggie. 'She's just worried in case you take too many of her clients. She didn't think you'd stay. None of us did.'

Ellie was fast becoming Meggie's friend. Disarmingly honest about what she did, she was never coarse and it was her attitude which finally made Meggie decide to stay. Young, like the embittered Lise, Ellie was the one girl who seemed unaffected by the life she led. Although she was another one who spent much of her free time in the bar, she seldom drank, preferring to perch on a stool, talking either to Meggie or to the barman and never openly advertised her body. In fact she did nothing at all to enhance her looks, refusing to wear make-up and keeping her wavy, sandy-coloured hair simply styled. Compared to the others she looked natural and unspoiled and this, added to her pale colouring and slender build, gave a misleading impression of meekness. But when she was angry, Ellie's grey eyes had a steel-like quality, her voice could be chilling, her words cutting. She, more so than any of the others, was not intimidated by Mrs McDonnell's frequent displays of temper. Of them all she was the most selective and though it regularly attracted Mrs McDonnell's wrath, she was adamant in her refusal to go with any man who did not meet her own criteria for acceptance. Despite the way she earned her living, there was something remote and dignified about Ellie which, although it alienated the other girls, Meggie admired.

'How did you end up here?' Meggie asked her one Sunday morning, having already confided her own story. To Meggie's still inexperienced eyes, Ellie who was slim, sandy-haired, neat and well-mannered, could easily have found a more conducive job.

Ellie shrugged and smiled softly. 'I know. I'm not really the type, am I? Any more than you are.'

'I soon will be,' Meggie retorted.

'You don't have to be like them,' Ellie insisted, nodding towards Sadie, Evie and Lise who, in various stages of undress, were loudly discussing last night's business. 'They've given up. They'll always be exactly what they are now. We're not like them.'

'I will be this time next week,' Meggie persisted.

'Pretend. Think of it as playing a part – like an actress. Be two people. The girl who has sex for money hasn't got anything to do with the real you. Keep your mind out of it, don't let them see who you really are.'

'Is that what you do?' Meggie asked.

'It's the only way I can do it,' Ellie replied, frowning. 'But not for much longer.'

'You're not leaving?' Meggie was dismayed at the thought of losing her new friend so soon.

'As soon as I've saved up enough money, I'll be gone. And so will you if you've got any sense. This is just a way of getting what I want. I can still respect myself all the time I'm

162

working towards something. If I stayed here, like them,' she nodded towards the others again, 'just because it was a way of life, I would never be able to live with myself. I hate it, Meggie, but it's not me, it's not what I really am. All the time I've got something to aim for, all the time I know it's not forever, I can still have some pride. Do you understand?'

Meggie nodded. 'I think so. But if you hate it so much, why are you here? You could get a real job somewhere.'

'What sort of job would pay me what I'm earning now? It's just the same for me as it is for you. You need money to look after Matty, money you can't earn anywhere else at your age. I need money to go to my brother.'

'Your brother?'

'He's in Australia. Went there five years ago when mum got married again. He was lucky,' she added with a rare trace of bitterness. 'He got away. I was too young to go anywhere then.' She looked up and caught her friend's shrewd eyes. 'It was my step-father,' she explained. 'He's like the men who come here only he didn't have to pay for it. He forced me before I was even properly grown up. When I told my mother she said I was just trying to make trouble. That's what really hurt.' She shrugged again and looked away, the memory causing pain even now. 'So now you see. I ran away and ended up here, just like you.'

'I'm sorry,' Meggie muttered.

'Don't be,' Ellie rounded on her. 'It was my choice. Just like it's yours. Mrs McDonnell doesn't force any of us to do this. Just remember, Meggie, it's only a way of getting somewhere else. Use it to get what you want, because there's no other way for the likes of you and me. Then get out as soon as you can, go somewhere else, a place where no one knows you. Start again, in a real job, and forget you were ever in Inverannan.'

Meggie stared at Ellie as if she was suddenly seeing things clearly. The other girl was right, she could see that now. And she would remember what she had said. In a year's time she would pack her bags, take Matty, and go. She would find a proper job and forget that the last twelve months had ever happened. There was no other way open to her. For the first time since realising what Mrs McDonnell had planned for her, Meggie felt easier in her mind. But, she told herself, staring out of the window at the rain which was keeping everyone indoors, before that she had to get through the next week – her first week as one of the girls.

Mrs McDonnelll glanced at the door then stood up to welcome one of her most valued clients, relieved that he had arrived at last. Meggie was nervous and the sooner the deed was done, the better for everyone.

'Good evening, sir. I'm so glad you could come. Let me get you a drink before I take you upstairs.'

Charlie Sutherland allowed himself to be seated and accepted a large Scotch without feeling obliged to offer payment. No doubt Mrs McDonnell could afford the price of a dram or two from the enormous charge she was making for this evening. He settled back in the deep sofa, seeming quite at ease in his surroundings, crossed one leg carelessly over the other and surveyed the two other men already there with a faintly supercilious stare. Sniffing at the tumbler of malt he then swirled it round the glass before sipping and letting the liquid roll round his palate. Satisfied he threw the rest back, nodded and held his glass out to his hostess for a refill. Her fixed smile never wavering, Mrs McDonnell took it back to the bar, wondering if he had been quite the right choice for Meggie's initiation.

A large man, not yet fat but far past the streamlined proportions of his youth, Charlie Sutherland, at the age of forty-nine, was a man of some importance in the town. Through his father he had inherited an exaggerated opinion of his own status and the controlling interest in the Nethertown Mill, the largest, most advanced and certainly the most profitable of the burgh's linen mills. On the face of it, he had everything a man of his age could want; a beautiful but boring wife, chosen for her breeding and decorative qualities; two sons who had been packed off to boarding school at the earliest opportunity; a daughter for whom he intended an advantageous marriage; an impressive, fully-staffed house; a series of motorcars, changed every year; an equally disposable string of mistresses and, above all, power. But the ability to have almost anything he wanted had led to increasing staleness. The ceaseless search for something new with which to spike his jaded palate led him to an occasional patronage of the Houlets' Nest, the best of the town's two brothels.

Mrs McDonnell, as much a business person as he, understood that Meggie's untouched qualities would bring premium prices and, casting her net for someone who could afford the sum she had in mind, had come up with Charlie Sutherland's name. Now though, she wondered if he might not be too experienced, too demanding for Meggie. But, knowing it was too late to renege on the deal she closed her mind to the suspicion that he might be too rough in his handling of Meggie. The girl had to be broken in by someone who knew what he was doing, someone practised, someone who would appreciate what he was getting. And that man was Charlie Sutherland.

'I hope I am not going to be disappointed, Mrs McDonnell,' he drawled, taking the second drink. 'This girl is a virgin?'

'Of course. And she is a very special girl, Mr Charles.' In common with the vast majority of her clients he preferred the spurious protection of a sobriquet. 'Completely inexperienced. You may need to be, ah . . . gentle with her.'

He frowned. 'She does know what to expect? I don't want any difficulty. No fits of hysterics.'

Mrs McDonnell's fixed smile stiffened a little. 'Of course not. I have spoken to her myself. Explicitly. In the hands of a man such as yourself, Mr Charles, I am sure she will be a very satisfactory partner,' she assured him, taking his glass and refilling it for the third time.

'And young? You know I like them young,' he said, his face flushing red with premature excitement, a sheen of sweat breaking out on his forehead.

'She is little more than a child.'

The sweat beaded and broke, running down the side of his forehead. Downing his whisky he got up eagerly. Bending to retrieve his glass Mrs McDonnell let her eyes skim over his body and saw the all-too-obvious evidence of his anticipated enjoyment. Perhaps it would be better for him to wait a minute or two, to take the edge off his urgency, for Meggie's sake.

'Have just one more drink and I will go and make sure that she is quite ready.' She hurried to the bar, settled him back in his seat and, with a promise that she would not keep him more than five minutes longer, rushed upstairs.

'Drink this,' she ordered Meggie, bursting into the room, thankful that some premonition had sent her here before Charlie Sutherland. The girl was perched stiffly on the edge of her bed, her face ghostly pale, her breathing shallow. A

166

pearl of perspiration had formed in the hollow of her throat.

Meggie took a swallow of the clear liquid, wrinkled her nose in disgust and coughed slightly as it caught at the back of her throat. She shook her head and handed the glass back.

'Is he here yet?' she asked.

'Yes. Mr Charles is just enjoying a drink downstairs,' Mrs McDonnell assured her. 'Now you drink that all up. It'll help.'

Meggie made a face but tipped the tumbler back obediently and gulped down a triple measure of gin in two mouthfuls. She gasped, gagged, then belched faintly but already there was a curious, not unpleasant, sensation of warmth spreading from her stomach to her head.

'You've done what I told you to keep yourself safe?' Mrs McDonnell asked.

Meggie flushed at this reminder of the rubber cap, supplied after a humiliating examination by the rough-handed, sweating-faced doctor who, for a not-inconsiderable sum, looked after the girls' health. She forced her head to nod and was surprised that it felt so heavy and loose on her neck. She knew it was the gin and wished there was more of it.

'Good, lass. Now just relax and enjoy it. There's nothing to it.'

Dressed only in a flimsy negligée, Meggie sat on the bed, her legs curled underneath her. In the distance she heard the dull thud of heavy footsteps approaching along the landing. She closed her eyes in a moment of sheer terror but opened them again when everything started to spin. Then, as the room steadied itself, she realised the door was opening. She watched in silence as a tall, powerfully built man strode into the room. Behind him, Mrs McDonnell winked encouragement, a gesture so absurd that Meggie had to stifle the desire to laugh. It had the effect of bringing a wide smile to her face. Mrs McDonnell breathed a sigh of relief, shut the door behind her and hurried back downstairs.

Charlie Sutherland was not a man to waste time, especially when there was this insistent throbbing in his groin to drive him on. Stepping fully into the room, his eyes raking the pleasing young body in front of him, he slipped out of his jacket, pausing only to drape it tidily over the back of a chair. His tie was ripped from his neck, his shirt dragged over his head, his shoes kicked off and his trousers dropped in the time it took Meggie to wriggle between the sheets, unconsciously putting another layer of defence between herself and this sweating man.

Licking his lips, Sutherland dropped his underpants and turned round with deliberate slowness, proudly displaying the thing which stood so purposefully in front of him. He watched the girl's face, gratified to see the blink of shock, the widening of huge, dark eyes which he interpreted as signs of admiration. He saw too the involuntary move backwards, the modest hugging of the sheet and his arousal became unbearable. He almost ran at her, a distance of ten feet, launching himself onto the bed and diving under the sheets. Immediately his hot hands sought Meggie's private places and his mouth searched for hers. As he pressed himself into her he looked down at her face and was reassured to see a welcoming smile.

Meggie, startled by the suddenness of the attack was doing her best not to giggle. Relaxed by the unaccustomed alcohol, the ridiculous sight of a middle-aged man, naked but for his socks, running at her with the roll of fat round his middle wobbling, had seemed ridiculous. Now, seeing nothing to fear in this undignified creature she did not find his mouth unpleasant, and laughed again as his tongue tickled behind her teeth and hardly felt anything at all when he entered her.

The subsequent violent motion of the bed focused all her attention on her swimming head and caused her to cry out when she thought she might be sick. When he finally groaned, bucked and then collapsed over her she gave a huge sigh of relief and took a series of deep, gulping breaths, in an effort to still her queasy stomach.

Sutherland heard the moans of what he believed could only be pleasure, heard the replete sigh, saw the way she still gasped with the aftermath of excitement and congratulated himself. For a virgin she had been a highly satisfying experience. 'There,' he chuckled. 'That was better than you expected wasn't it?'

Meggie, her head and stomach settling slowly, nodded. 'Yes,' she agreed, quite truthfully, for in fact, she had been aware of very little but the effects of the gin.

Gently, Sutherland pushed her over the bed, making room for himself at her side. He had no intention of leaving yet. For the money he had handed over he would expect to perform to the limit of his endurance, which, with four huge whiskies inside him, was a great deal less than he expected it to be.

Meggie rolled on to her side. While he waited, Sutherland encouraged his potency to reassert itself by stroking her youthful body, sending warm, relaxing waves through her and easing her into a deep sleep. When he was ready he entered her again, from behind, lost in his own alcoholic haze, rutting away until he was purple with exertion and drenched in sweat. Afterwards, when he had his breath back, he peered over her shoulder and smiled to see the satisfied curve on her lips.

He waited, hoping for a third chance but his body remained stubbornly uncooperative. Glad that the girl had fallen asleep and would be unable to report his relative failure he dressed, taking care to appear as immaculate as he had on arrival. Swinging his umbrella, whistling between his teeth, he strolled downstairs, nodded farewell to Mrs McDonnell and went home to his wife.

Without the deadening effect of the alcohol, Meggie found the succeeding nights a disgusting and debasing experience. Between clients she cowered in her bed feeling miserable and dirty, clinging to the forlorn hope that if she didn't appear downstairs they might forget about her. Even Ellie who made time every night to look in on her friend, could do nothing to rouse her. Meggie's clients found her submissive, obedient, and totally cold. Too many of them looked into her eyes and were repelled by the blankness they found there. Few asked to see her again. Meggie wouldn't have recognised their faces even if they had come back. She always looked away, kept her eyes closed so that she didn't have to think of the thing that heaved and grunted over her as a human being. She had impressions of weight, of rolls of fat or the sharp feel of bones; of the texture of skin on the hands which fondled her; of bodily smells, the nauseating stench of stale breath; of animal-like noises. Terrified of losing the only home she and Matty had, she did her insufficient best to make her mind a blank and get on with her job.

Mrs McDonnell, anxious to realise a quick profit from what she considered to be her most valuable asset, vetted her clients carefully and invited only those who would be prepared to pay highly for the privilege of visiting Meggie's room. Invariably these were drawn from the better class of businessmen, older men who appreciated fine things and who expected value for money. So, her patience was severely tried when the second customer in a row complained about the unresponsiveness of the newest girl.

'You pull yourself together, lass,' she warned, hauling Meggie out of bed. In truth she was shocked by the girl's appearance. Meggie's heart-shaped face was blotched and bloated from constant tears, her lips were dry and her beautiful eyes were lost in folds of puffy flesh. Her long dark hair was lank and tangled, the bed was a rumpled heap and the room had a sour, stale smell about it. 'Get yourself into the bath, brush your teeth and wash that hair. I want you clean and sparkling for tonight. I won't have one of my girls giving me a bad name,' she ordered furiously.

Meggie wrapped a dressing gown round her shoulders and wandered off along the corridor to the bathroom where she steeped herself in water so hot that it scorched her skin. When she got out, half an hour later, she still felt dirty.

Back in Meggie's room, Mrs McDonnelll had straightened the bed and flung the windows open, letting damp air flood in. 'Feeling better?' she asked.

'No!' Meggie retorted savagely, sickened by the realisation of what every night would bring, bitterly regretting her decision to stay but seeing no possible way of escape which would not risk Matty's health and happiness. Not that she saw much of her brother these days, she thought bitterly. The fact that he hardly seemed to miss her, didn't seem to care that they no longer shared a room and took more notice of Mr McDonnell than he did of her, hurt her deeply.

'Never mind the cheek!' Mrs McDonnell yelled. 'It's time you learnt when you're well off. I'm doing you a big favour,

171

keeping you here and at your age. I'm taking a proper risk with you, Meggie McPherson. If the law ever found out about you I'd get the jail. It's about time you showed some gratitude.'

'I didn't know it would be like this,' Meggie said, anger bringing vivid colour to her cheeks.

'Like what?' Mrs McDonnell was scornful. 'You're not doing anything that doesn't happen between men and women the world over.'

'But not like this! Not with anyone who can pay for it. Not for money.'

'If you don't like it pack your bags and get out. Take that brother of yours with you. He eats more than he's worth. I'd be better off without the pair of youse. Nothing but bloody trouble. Aye, since you're so unhappy after I've done my best for youse, get off out of it. Right now. Go on.' She flounced dramatically to the door and flung it open.

Meggie blanched. 'Please . . . give me a week. Just until I find somewhere to live,' she pleaded.

'Somewhere to live! And just who do you think would take in two kids like youse? But that's nothing to do with me. Leave the dresses. They belong to me. Take what you came in and get out.'

'No . . . please,' Meggie begged, looking out at the rain which had seemed to pour down all winter long. 'Matty can't live on the streets in this weather.' She sank to the bed and buried her face in her hands in a gesture of despair.

Mrs McDonnell watched her in silence for a full minute before saying, 'So, changed your mind, have you? Want to stay now, do you?'

Meggie nodded.

'Well, get up off that bloody bed and tidy yourself up. But you listen to me, Meggie and you listen good. You buck your ideas up, lass, or I will put you out. You're here to do a job, just like all the other girls. Pull your weight or go. There's plenty lassies round here who would be willing enough to work for me and think themselves lucky to get the chance. One more complaint and you're out, both of youse.' She retrieved the hairbrush from the floor and tossed it back at the girl. 'Do something with that hair and be downstairs, smiling and willing, at seven o'clock.'

The door had hardly closed on her when it opened again to admit Ellie. If she was shocked by her friend's appearance she managed to conceal it. Perching on the edge of the bed she took up the brush and started to run it through Meggie's still-damp hair.

'Just remember,' she whispered. 'You're not alone. I'm here and I know just how you feel. And it won't be for ever. Remember what I told you before? You're here because you've got no other choice. You're doing it for Matty.'

'I hardly ever see him any more.'

Ellie stopped brushing and squatted at Meggie's side. 'Let's make ourselves a promise.' She took her friend's hand and squeezed it. 'I promise that I won't stay here for one single day longer than I have to.'

Meggie gave a watery smile and croaked, 'And I promise that I won't stay here for one single minute longer than I have to.'

Meggie leaned forward and the two girls held each other tightly, fighting an emotional battle against tears. When they parted, they both felt strengthened. Ellie picked up the brush again and went back to smoothing Meggie's hair, saying nothing now, lost in her own thoughts. Meggie, exhausted by sleepless nights and tear-filled days, allowed the regular rhythm to soothe her, grateful for the other girl's sympathetic silence.

'Now, slip into bed and get some sleep,' Ellie advised when she saw Meggie's eyelids droop. 'I'll wake you later.'

'Ellie.' Meggie dragged herself back from the brink of sleep. 'I'm glad we're friends.'

'Me too,' Ellie whispered.

CHAPTER TEN

'**I**'ll see the new girl. The dark-haired one.' Provost Wallace Laing's request set Mrs McDonnell something of a problem. The man wasn't a regular visitor – he was rumoured to keep a mistress somewhere in the town – but when he did patronise the Houlets' Nest he was prepared to pay well for the girl of his choice. Furthermore, he was an influential man and she couldn't afford to upset him.

'Are you sure, Mr Wallace? Meggie is very young and inexperienced. Perhaps one of the older girls, one who knows how to please a man of the world like yourself?'

It was the wrong thing to say. Provost Laing was a man who expected to get what he asked for, without challenge. 'I'll take the new girl or no one, Mrs McDonnell,' he insisted.

'Very well,' she sighed. 'Follow me.'

'Thank you.'

'Meggie,' she announced, opening the girl's door without knocking. 'This is Mr Wallace.'

Meggie didn't bother to turn round from the dressing table nor did she raise her eyes to seek her client's reflection in the mirror.

Wallace Laing, accustomed to a more effusive welcome, hesitated, his eyes drinking in the slender build of her young body, the tantalising glimpse of smooth skin, the shimmering curtain of dark hair as she pulled the brush through it. Slowly he crossed the room and stood behind her, entwining a hand in the silky tresses. 'You have wonderful hair,' he murmured, as Mrs McDonnell quietly slipped away.

Meggie tensed, expecting the usual assault on her body, steeling herself to get through it. But when his hand travelled to her shoulder, Laing felt the stiffness there and sensed the girl's reluctance. Gently he turned her towards him.

Her eyes still lowered, Meggie sat unmoving. Laing put a hand under her chin and tipped her face up, enchanted by what he saw, recognising in Meggie something far removed from the usual run of girl in places such as these. She was young, incredibly young, hurt-looking and quite astoundingly beautiful. A heart-shaped face, clearly defined cheekbones and long, thick eyelashes which rested on ivory clear skin. He saw too the blue shadows underlining her eyes and the tense line of her full lips and sensed her fear, her unwillingness. And, in that moment he knew he wanted her more than he had ever wanted any woman before. Something inside him tightened, bridling desire with the urge merely to hold and comfort for now, knowing that she would be worth a little patience, determined to make her respond to him.

Stroking her face he said, 'Och, lass, there's no need to be frightened of me. I'll not hurt you,' and was as surprised to hear himself saying the words as Meggie was.

Slowly she opened her eyes and gazed at him, wondering what sort of a man he was. She saw a tall, smartly dressed, middle-aged businessman with warm, brown eyes and greying hair which grew back from a marked widow's peak. He looked distinguished, she thought, and not unkind.

Laing stared into the huge dark pools which were regarding him so intently, saw his own face reflected there and smiled.

176

'Come on, lass.' He drew her to her feet and led her to the bed, laying beside her, still fully dressed, content for now simply to hold her, to be patient with such a young and desirable girl.

Meggie found her head cradled on a reassuringly steady chest, his breathing slow and easy, nothing like the panting urgency which overcame most of her clients. For long minutes his hands stroked her, almost as if she was a cat, skimming softly over her cheek and down her throat. But when he brought his mouth to hers she tensed again and drew away. When his hand grasped a breast she squeezed her eyes tight shut and lay rigidly, just praying for it to be over.

'No, lass, that isn't good enough,' he said, moving away from her and looking down on her strained face.

Thinking he was going to leave her without taking what he had come for and knowing that one more complaint would see her and Matty out on the street, Meggie panicked. 'I'm sorry. Please don't go.' But despite her words her body remained stiff and unwelcoming and her hands were clenched into tight fists.

Laing felt his own desire quicken, stirred again by the girl's obvious youth and loveliness. But he had never taken a woman against her wishes, expected willing compliance and mutual enjoyment, even when he was paying for the pleasure.

'There's no enjoyment in it if you're not willing, Meggie,' he told her.

'But I am,' she assured him frantically, sitting up and doing her best to smile.

With any other girl Laing would have stormed from the room, complaining bitterly, but there was something about Meggie which held him there. Again he watched her, drinking in the beauty of her face, the perfection of her long limbs, arrested by the inescapable sadness in those huge, dark eyes, and felt the incredible need to comfort her, to win her trust, to have her for his own. Accepting the challenge, he sank on to the bed and took one of her cold hands.

'No, Meggie, you are not willing,' he insisted. 'My lass, just look at yourself. You're shaking like a leaf and frightened half to death.'

'I'm sorry,' she muttered, looking away.

'Why, lass? You've done this before, surely? Is it me that's so awful? Is an old man like me such a horrible sight to a young lass like you? Eh?'

Meggie looked up again, astonished by such gentleness from one of her customers. There was warmth in his eyes and understanding. 'You're not awful,' she murmured, feeling embarrassed now.

'Well, I'm glad to hear that,' he joked. 'You're just new to this, is that it?'

She nodded, feeling shame flood her face.

'Well then, you just trust me, lass. I'll not be rough with you.' His hands moved back to her skin, stroking her again, gently, patiently.

Meggie closed her eyes, but, responding to his kindness, managed to play her part fairly convincingly, grateful for a consideration none of her other clients had shown her, even when lust finally overcame his patience and it ended as it always did.

Wallace lay back, satisfied that his performance had been almost equal to what it had been twenty years ago, knowing that it had been this girl's tender years and inexperience which had roused him so satisfactorily.

Watching her from under partly closed lids as she feigned sleep, Wallace imagined what it would be like to have this girl as a willing, enthusiastic partner for his own, exclusive use. Better by far than attempting to find any sort of enjoyment in his wife's cold bed, better too than visiting places like this, taking pot luck with the women, always living with the fear of being seen, of contracting some sort of infection. And it wasn't as if he hadn't made similar arrangements in the past. He missed the company of his last mistress, Alice, a woman of great skill who had served his needs for the past two years. But, like his wife, she had become too demanding, loudly dissatisfied by the limited material comforts he was prepared to offer her. Eventually she had found herself a younger, more generous provider and he hadn't been sorry to see her go. The relationship had gone stale and her body had become as familiar and unexciting as his wife's.

Perhaps this fresh, young creature might give him a new lease on life, help to prolong the illusion of youth and virility he craved so desperately. But that, he told himself, was impossible. A mistress, some discreet and respectable woman like Alice, set up in a nice little house at the bottom of the town where he could come and go without attracting attention, was one thing, but installing a professional whore, a girl young enough to be his granddaughter, was quite another. He grunted, half amused by this bizarre line of thought, and shifted his weight slightly, running questing hands over Meggie's still form, relishing again his gratifying reaction to her firm, young flesh.

Meggie blinked her eyes open and looked up to find him smiling down on her. Recognising that he hadn't finished with her, she turned towards him invitingly. He was kind, gentle and, strangely, made her feel safe. Better, she thought, curling an arm round his neck, to keep him here as long as possible. That way at least she wouldn't have to deal with yet another stranger and Mrs McDonnell would be pleased with her at last.

It was just after seven the next night when a light tap on Meggie's door announced her first customer of the evening. She frowned. No one usually bothered her until well after nine o'clock and she had been hoping for another two hours of privacy.

'You have a special visitor, Meggie,' Mrs McDonnell announced from the doorway, sounding pleased with herself.

'Good evening, Meggie.' Wallace Laing shoved the door shut, almost sending it into Mrs McDonnell's nose, and strode quickly across the room.

'Oh . . . !' Meggie was so surprised that she smiled and stepped towards him, conscious of an enormous flood of relief.

'So you are as pleased to see me as I am to see you,' Wallace teased her, kissing her cheek and sliding her robe from her shoulders. He had been anticipating this moment all day, had known, even as he left her last night, that he would not rest until he saw her again. A strangely unsettling feeling for a man of his age, he thought wryly.

Meggie looked away, knowing he had misinterpreted her welcome.

Wallace laughed, a great gusting guffaw. 'No need to be shy tonight, lass. We know one another now, don't we? And you know I'm not going to hurt you.'

She nodded.

'So, let's get to know one another even better.' In a matter of seconds he had her on the bed, delighted to discover that the intoxicating effect of her nubile young body had not been the passing thing he had feared it might have been.

From a generation which expected compliance but not active participation or even enjoyment from their women, Wallace was content to have Meggie as a willing partner and was delighted with his own rejuvenated performance. Realising that very little was asked of her beyond willing submission, Meggie was grateful for the undemanding way in which he satisfied himself and, for the first time, did her limited best to please.

'You're doing me the power of good,' he told her later as they lay side by side on the bed.

'I like you being here, too,' she admitted. And it was true. The whole thing was bearably quick with Mr Wallace and she appreciated the way he lingered afterwards, talking to her as if she was a real person, not just a body to be used then discarded.

'Good,' he ran a hand over her breasts, marvelling again at how firm and small they were. What wouldn't he give to have her for himself, available to him and him alone. Sighing he glanced at his pocket watch, placed on the bedside table, and reluctantly hauled himself off the bed.

'You can stay if you like,' she offered, panicking at the thought of another man visiting her tonight.

'I'd like that, Meggie, but I've an appointment.' With his wife at the dinner table. He was already late and no doubt Elsie's face would be sourer than ever because of it.

'Good night, Meggie,' he said, bending to kiss her cheek, a nicety which had seemed ridiculous with the other girls he had had occasion to use here.

'Good night,' she whispered.

Back downstairs, Wallace decided to treat himself to a small whisky before going home to face his wife's inevitable bad temper. He settled on the comfortable sofa and took a sip from his glass, his mind still filled with images of

Meggie's splendidly nubile young body. He was just starting to consider making a move for home when Mrs McDonnell returned and addressed the bar's only other occupant, a youngish man with noticeably greasy skin.

'Meggie is ready for you now, Mr Michael,' she said.

The man jumped to his feet, releasing a lingering odour of stale sweat, barely able to contain his impatience.

The warm smoothness of Mrs McDonnell's best malt turned to sulphur in Wallace's mouth. He gagged, almost choking and had to fight the impulse to launch himself at the young man's back, to render him incapable of visiting the young girl who, just minutes ago, had been his own partner.

Conscious of the barman's curious stare he thumped his glass back on the table and headed towards the back door, not even bothering to put his coat on before he left, his pleasure destroyed.

Outside, in the bite of a stiffening breeze he stopped, and took time to gather his wits. What the hell was he thinking of, he asked himself when his blood had ceased to pound behind his ears. A man of his age and a fifteen-year-old girl he had met but twice? Beautiful and beguiling though she was, she was nothing but a common prostitute. Angry with himself, astonished by the muddle of emotions flooding through him, he strode away up the hill, suddenly anxious to get home, where an hour of his wife's constant complaints would surely restore him to some semblance of normality.

When the not unexpected knock came on her door, Meggie tensed, steeling her whole body against the inevitably unpleasant encounter, wondering how much longer she could go on with this. With each new night the way she earned her living became more and more abhorrent. She had only managed to force herself to remain here by reminding herself, before, during and after each client, that Matty's well-being was at stake.

Each morning, exhausted by the night's work, she forced herself out of bed while the other girls were still asleep and trailed round the small town, approaching hotels, public houses, shops and offices, desperately searching for work. The response was always the same. Every potential employer wanted references or the name of some responsible adult who could vouch for her character. Clearly Mrs McDonnell, the only person Meggie could possibly ask for such a recommendation, was not suitable. Even to give her address would be to give herself away. Without a reference, unable to account for the last year of her life, Meggie was turned away time and time again. The few places which were willing to consider her offered the most menial of jobs at wages which wouldn't allow her to support herself, never mind Matty as well. Knowing that she couldn't face working at the Houlets' Nest for much longer, accutely aware of her brother's dependence, Meggie was getting more desperate with each passing day. Now, the knock which signalled another client actually made her feel sick. Forcing herself to stand up and face the door in a false display of welcome, she shivered.

'Come in,' she called, aware of the dead sound of her own voice.

'What sort of a welcome is that, Meggie?' Wallace Laing threw back the door and stood smiling at her, his bulk filling the frame.

She gaped, then, almost faint with relief, ran to greet him. 'Mr Wallace.'

It was more than a week since he had visited her last and she had thought she would never see him again.

Wallace gathered her to him, gratified to feel her arms tightening round him in a genuine display of delight. 'That's better,' he teased.

Meggie flushed slightly, well aware that this was not the way to feel about a paying customer, a man who, kind though he was, could only see her as a willing body, to be used as he thought fit. But of all her clients he was the only one who had treated her as a thinking, feeling human being and he had made an indelible imprint on her mind.

Looking at her, enchanted afresh by her youth, the misleading air of innocence, her sheer beauty, Wallace felt a vigorous surge of desire flame through his groin. But, confusingly he did not want the usual, quick coupling, an act which was nothing more than a necessary release for physical tension. To his own consternation he realised that he yearned for something more. Suddenly it was important that he had time to talk to her, to get to know a little about her, simply to hold her; to ensure that she too, enjoyed his visit. But that was absurd, he told himself. And anyway, the girl had her living to earn and wouldn't appreciate him taking up too much of her evening. The kindest thing would be for him to get it over with as quickly as possible and leave. To expect anything else was stupidity. Most likely she would ridicule an old man's obsession for a young girl.

Turning away he stripped himself of his clothes, grateful that she stirred him to such a response that his performance would at least be equal to that of many a younger man.

Meggie slipped off her own scanty covering and climbed into bed, confident that she had nothing to be afraid of in this strikingly handsome man. Watching him in her mirror she wondered what his age was. At least fifty, she guessed from the character etched into his face and the iron grey of his hair. His body, broad shouldered, slim hipped and firm, could have been that of a much younger man, but despite his gentleness he carried the distinct air of authority that could only belong to someone of power and experience. He turned round and caught her watching him. Humiliated she flushed violently and looked away.

Wallace smiled and crossed quickly to the bed. 'Don't be embarrassed Meggie. I'm flattered that you want to look at me.' He stroked her face with a gentle finger. 'So long as you allow me to look at you, too?'

He waited until Meggie looked up at him, a shy smile lifting her mouth. 'I don't mind you looking at me,' she said, her eyes straying to the unavoidable evidence of his own arousal and feeling a disturbing but as yet unrecognised pulse of desire between her legs.

'Good.' Wallace drew back the cover then lowered himself on to the bed beside her and began to kiss her naked body, starting at her toes and working up, burying his hand in the dark hair between her legs, finding the core of her sex and teasing it lightly with his fingers while his mouth moved on, covering her breasts, her throat and finally her lips. When he lifted himself over her he felt her clinging to him, raising herself to meet him and knew that, this time, she was a truly willing partner.

Afterwards, Meggie lay stunned by the treachery of her own body. To think that she could have allowed a client, a man who paid to be in her bed, to reduce her to such a state of trembling wantonness. The fact that she liked and was attracted to Mr Wallace only made it worse.

Wallace stirred and consulted his watch. With sudden rising fear, Meggie realised he was going to leave her. Within fifteen minutes there would probably be another man in her bed. She turned away, knowing she couldn't let him see the rare tears that flooded her eyes.

Wallace looked at her in time to see the way her mouth fell at the corners, the visible tremor of her lower lip, the suspicion of tears in her eyes.

'Not to worry. A pretty young thing like you will soon have another visitor,' he bluffed, feeling the words stick in his throat, almost choking him. The thought of anyone else pawing this beautiful girl sickened him.

To his dismay her only answer was a stifled sob. Thoughtfully he finished dressing then sat beside her on the rumpled bed. 'Are you going to tell me what's wrong?' he asked.

'I don't want you to go,' she sobbed.

He laughed, flattered but wary of encouraging the sort of clinging affection which could so easily become an embarrassment. 'I'm too old for you, lass. You need some nice young man of your own age.'

Meggie's sobbing stopped abruptly as she realised what he assumed she had meant. The thought that she might seriously fancy herself in love with him was so absurd that she smiled and admitted, 'I didn't mean that.'

'Oh! Well, what did you mean?' he asked, relieved and disappointed at the same time.

The smile faded abruptly as the reality of her situation hit her yet again. 'Just, if you go now they'll send someone else up.'

He shifted, making himself more comfortable, thrusting the unpleasant picture of his wife simmering away at home to the back of his thoughts as tempting possibilities invaded his mind. 'But that's what you do, isn't it? That's how you make a living. With men?'

'No! I mean, aye ... but I don't like it.' She knew she sounded pathetic but couldn't help herself.

'Then why stay? Surely you could find something else? In the mills, a shop ...'

'No,' she shook her head and strands of fine, dark hair clung to her damp face.

'Do you want to tell me why?' He cradled her protectively, almost as a father would and listened as she poured out her story, flattered by her trust.

'You won't tell Mrs McDonnell I told you, will you?' she begged when she came to the end, regretting the weakness which had made her confide in him.

'No, Meggie. I won't say anything,' he assured her, standing up and putting his coat on. In truth he was glad to move away so that she couldn't see the anger on his face. He was appalled by what he had heard, horrified to know how Mrs McDonnell had exploited her innocence. There was even an uncomfortable pricking of guilt in his own conscience, one he salved by saying, 'Now, you get some sleep and don't worry. I'll make sure no one else comes to you tonight. And maybe I've got an idea, a way of getting you out of here. Monday morning, you put on your best clothes and meet me by the big statue in the park.'

She stared at him, not sure she had heard him correctly. 'You want to meet me on Monday?'

'Aye. Eleven o'clock sharp.' Even as she still gaped he left her and she heard his footsteps echoing down the corridor.

Downstairs he paid Mrs McDonnell again, a sum twice as large as he had parted with on arrival. 'No one else, Mrs McDonnell,' he told her, reinforcing what he had just said.

'No one else, Mr Wallace,' she agreed, taking the money greedily. Aye, she thought, helping herself to a large gin to toast her success, perhaps the day Meggie McPherson had arrived on her doorstep had been the luckiest day of her life after all.

Meggie's heart sank as she hurried towards the statue of Queen Victoria, which dominated the centre of the park. It was a dull day of squally showers and only rare glimpses of sun. Water glistened on the grass and dripped from the trees, puddling on the deserted footpaths. She was five minutes late but there was no sign of Mr Wallace. Her spirits sinking to match the weather, Meggie sought shelter from yet another shower in the lee of the grim-faced statue. How could she have been stupid enough to believe him and his promise of help? Why would a man as obviously wealthy and respectable as him bother with a girl like her?

With rain seeping through to her skin, shivering and alone in the vastness of the empty park, Meggie abandoned herself to misery. Deserted by her parents, taken for granted by her brother and forced to earn her living in a way which was slowly destroying her, it seemed that there was nothing in her life which gave her even the smallest degree of pleasure. As the rain continued to pour down, making the trees appear dank and sinister, she gazed despondently over the long slope of saturated grass which dipped gently towards the banks of the Annan.

The river, high after the heavy rainfall, was a ribbon of churning, thundering water which seemed to draw her towards it. Walking slowly, unheedful of the rain soaking through her clothes, Meggie crossed the grass and stood looking down at the racing current. She closed her eyes, letting her imagination take her in, gasping at the cold of the water against her skin, smiling as it closed over her head, welcoming the sensation of lasting peace which would come with it. She moved a pace forward, balancing on the very bank of the river, peering into its depths, and willed herself on.

But, with her foot trembling on the crumbling bank, her courage failed her. The same thing which had driven her to agree to all Mrs McDonnell demanded of her prevented her from taking that final step. Matty. And, dreadful though her life was, Meggie's fear of the unknown was even more powerful. In that last critical second she realised that she wanted to live her life through, to have the chance to change things. With vision-like clarity she saw that only she held the key to her future; that she herself, not Matty, nor Mrs McDonnell, would control her fate, and, swaying there, on the verge of disaster, that was suddenly something Meggie longed to do.

Opening her eyes she was shocked to see the water just inches from her feet. Understanding just how close she had come to throwing her life away she lurched backwards. Still the water seemed to want to lure her. Frightened now, she scrambled desperately up the bank, her shoes sliding on the wet grass, her heart beating with terror at what she had so nearly done. And there, when she reached the top, in the distance, near the statue, was the unmistakable figure of Mr Wallace.

She fought the impulse to call out, to run to him like the frightened child she still was and forced herself to walk forward at a steady pace. When she was less than ten yards away he turned and saw her, his face breaking into a broad smile, softening his habitually serious expression.

'I thought you'd changed your mind,' he said, pulling her under the shelter of his large, black umbrella.

'You weren't here so I went to look at the river,' was all she said, giving him no hint of the turmoil which had so nearly claimed her.

Wallace made no apology for his lateness. He resented having to account for his time, to anyone, and this lass would need to make that one of her first lessons if his plan was to succeed. 'We'd best hurry,' he said, guiding her towards the lower end of the park. 'I can't be away from the office for too long.'

Meggie almost had to run to match his long, fast stride but, though it was still raining, her face bore the hint of a smile. And in place of the despair which had been her close companion for too many months, almost as if the traumatic events by the river had purged her mind, was the first glimmer of hope. Whatever Mr Wallace had planned for her, she told herself, a job as a millhand or as a skivvy somewhere, it could only be better than the way she was living now.

'Well, Meggie, what do you think?' Wallace settled himself in a worn but comfortable armchair.

Meggie stood in the middle of the room staring round with wide eyes, an expression of amazement on her face. 'It's wonderful,' she said at last. She had never imagined living in a place as well furnished and comfortable as this, could still hardly believe that Mr Wallace was seriously suggesting that she should move in here.

It was a flat, the first floor of a converted house in a quiet back street at the bottom of the town. From this room, at the rear of the house, there was a view over the lower end of the park. On the other side of the corridor which dissected the house was a small kitchen and, facing out over the street at the front were two bedrooms, one large, one small.

Next to the front door was a lavatory, tacked on to the back of the house as an afterthought. A flight of external stairs led to a tiny back garden, the province, Meggie already knew, of the downstairs tenant. Meggie had surveyed all this luxury in awestruck silence, oblivious to the threadbare patches in the carpet, the sun-bleached stripes on the curtains, the slightly battered appearance of the tables and chairs or the sagging mattress on the bed. Nor did she think to wonder why this flat was tucked away in such a seedy backwater of the town.

Wallace watched her, enjoying her unashamed wonder. Already it was as if Alice had never been here, as though young Meggie was imposing her own personality on the place. And despite her dubious origins, she would make an agreeable little companion, he thought, a touch complacently. She was young and still impressionable, had suffered sufficiently to be truly grateful to him and was still malleable enough to let him lead her, to teach her what pleased him, something which neither his wife nor Alice had permitted. And, by all she had told him, she would be grateful for his company and wouldn't sneer if he was unable to acquit himself as vigorously as a younger man. Nor would she nag him about the quality and condition of the furniture as Alice had, and complain about the less-than-salubrious nature of the neighbourhood.

From Wallace's point of view the flat was ideally placed. In a forgotten road which had been left behind by the town's northward development, it was conveniently close to the southern end of the park so that anyone seeing him on his way to or from his mistress's arms would assume he was simply out for a healthy stroll. It was also far enough away from the smarter residential areas to make the chance of anyone he knew seeing him here extremely unlikely. In any case, as most of the dozen or so houses were paid for by men like himself, local discretion was almost assured. All in all, this should be a very comfortable arrangement, one which would suit them both very nicely.

He quietened his lingering scruples by telling himself that it wasn't as if she was a real whore, she hadn't been doing it long enough for that. It was clear that she hated what she did, that at heart she was a decent lass who had merely fallen on bad times. The way she cared for her brother proved that and showed an admirable sense of responsibility. He frowned faintly at the reminder. The boy was the only flaw in this arrangement, but, provided she kept him out of the way when he called to see her, there should be no trouble there.

Meggie tore herself from contemplating the view and looked at Wallace in time to catch the self-satisfied smile which was curling his lip. She felt a glimmer of apprehension as she contemplated this latest change in her circumstances. The one thing Mrs McDonnell had taught her was that no one did anything for nothing.

'Why me?' she asked, coming to stand in front of him, facing him with a determination he hadn't realised she possessed.

After a moment of indecision he opted for the truth. Better they both knew exactly where they stood and then there could be no recriminations later.

'Because you are a bonny young lass and I want you for myself,' he admitted. 'You make me feel like a young man again, Meggie, and that's worth the money you'll cost me. I am doing this as much for myself as for you,' he told her candidly. 'But you'll be better off here than you were in that place. I like you, lass, but I'll be damned if I'll share you with anyone with a spare couple of pounds in his pocket. I'll keep you here and give you a wee bit to spend on yourself each week for just as long as we're both happy with the arrangement and as long as you understand that you'll get no more from me than I'm offering now. I can get complaints and bad temper from my wife any time at all. What I want from you, lass, is a warm welcome, whatever time of the day I choose to call on you. Do you think you can do that for me?'

Meggie met his eyes boldly, pleased that he had been honest with her. 'I'll be happy to do that,' she said, her face quite serious. And she would be. Mr Wallace was a kind man, she knew that already, and anything was better than the Houlets' Nest. Especially for Matty, who had too clear an understanding of what went on there and was growing wilder and cheekier by the day. Here, with just the two of them, away from the careless, indulgent influence of Mr McDonnell, with a room of his own and the park to play in, she would be able to get close to him again, to make sure he grew up to be a young man their parents would be proud of. But would they be equally proud of her? She suppressed a shiver and accepting Wallace's hand, allowed him to lead her through to the bedroom.

An hour later Wallace pulled himself back from the edge of sleep. 'Come on, lass, wake up,' he said, running a finger down her warm, still-flushed face. Her eyelids fluttered and for a moment he saw confusion in her eyes as she stared round the strange room. He was touched by her vulnerability and reminded again of how very young she was.

Seeing him looking down at her, his mouth curved in an affectionate smile, Meggie relaxed. 'I'd forgotten where I was,' she admitted.

'It's time I went back to the office,' he said.

'I'd like to stay here for a wee while longer. If that's all right?' Just to make sure this wasn't a wonderful dream.

'This is your home now, Meggie. You can stay for as long

as you want.' He straightened his tie then came to sit on the edge of the bed, beside her. 'Here.' He put his hand in his pocket and put something cold and metallic into her hand. 'The keys are yours. And I've something else for you, too.'

Now he placed a small, square, suede-covered box in her hands and waited, enjoying the expression of uninhibited delight that lit her face.

'Can I open it?' she asked, her eyes sparkling with excitement.

He laughed. 'Well, how else will I know whether you like it or not?'

Using her thumbs, Meggie pushed back the hinged lid. There, nestling on a bed of silk was an exquisite gold bracelet, studded alternately with jet and diamond chips.

'Oh . . .' Meggie gasped and stared at it. 'I can't . . .'

He silenced her with a kiss. 'I'll be hurt if you won't accept it.' He lifted her unresisting wrist and fastened the bracelet round it. 'There, doesn't that look fine?' Against the whiteness of her skin the bracelet shone and sparkled.

'It's beautiful,' she mumbled, feeling quite choked. 'Thank you . . .'

'No, lass. Thank you.'

'You what!' Mrs McDonnell shrieked, her mouth agape. The other girls, all gathered in the bar before going off to prepare for the evening's work, eavesdropped without shame.

'I'm leaving,' Meggie repeated.

'Oh no you don't, not after all I've done for you.' Mrs McDonnell could hear the rustle of money as it blew out of her grasp. She comforted herself with a second measure of gin.

Meggie ignored the outburst. 'So if you could just pay me what you owe me.'

'Owe you? What do you think I am, a bloody charity? You've had all you're getting from me.' She shook her head, causing the elaborately pinned hair to collapse, and reached again for the gin bottle.

'That's not fair, Mrs McDonnell. You're supposed to pay us half of what you take from the men. You should pay Meggie what she's earned,' Ellie intervened on behalf of her friend. Mrs McDonnell turned on her with a venomous glare.

'Half of what each client pays, that's what we agreed. We've checked in the book and written it down here.' Encouraged by her friend's support Meggie handed the neatly printed page to Mrs McDonnell. 'And you still owe me my wages for the time I was hostess.'

Mrs McDonnell almost choked over a mouthful of gin. 'And what about your keep, all the food you and your brother have eaten, the rent on your rooms, your clothes? Eh? What about all that?' She rounded on Meggie, her face a mottled mass of wrath, but was stilled by what she saw in the girl's eyes. It seemed that Meggie McPherson had grown up overnight. Instead of the whingeing, apathetic creature who had cowered in her bed all day, or even the ragamuffin child, so anxious to please, who had first arrived on her doorstep, there was now a determined and coldly angry young woman.

'I've earned more than enough to cover that and so has Matty. You took advantage of me, Mrs McDonnell, and now I want what's owing to me.' Meggie knew she couldn't back down now. Mr Wallace might be prepared to keep her, but she needed the extra security of some money of her own.

'Or what?' Mrs McDonnell challenged her.

'Or I'll make sure the police know exactly what goes on here. And that some of the girls are under age,' Meggie bluffed, understanding that to do that would only land her and Matty in serious trouble.

'Half our clients are policemen!' Mrs McDonnell scoffed. But she was worried now, knowing that the slightest hint of scandal would be enough to drive her customers away.

'You can't do that.' Evie, spurred on by the other girls, surged to her feet, hands on hips, almost spitting fury at Meggie. 'Selfish wee bitch. What about us? How are we supposed to earn a living if the polis close us down?'

'The same way you do now,' Meggie flung back at her. 'But you could keep all of what you earn instead of giving most of it to her.'

'Check the books for yourselves. She's cheating us all.' Ellie nodded calmly towards Mrs McDonnell who rose majestically from her stool by the bar and tottered across the room on outrageously high heels.

'You watch your mouth or you'll be out of here and all,' she threatened.

'Let me see that book.' Sadie rushed to the little desk, grabbed the appointments book then peered uncomprehendingly at the columns of figures.

'Here,' Ellie produced another sheet of paper. 'Meggie and I have worked out what all of us should have been paid for last month.'

The girls gathered round, their voices rising in squeals of outrage as they realised just how much they had been cheated.

Meggie allowed herself to smile.

Mrs McDonnell felt sweat break out under her arms. 'All right. I'll check the books. I suppose there might be a pound or two owing,' she conceded. 'Och, youse all know I'm not very good with figures.'

Howls of derision greeted this and over Mrs McDonnell's perspiring head, Ellie winked at Meggie.

'Here,' Mrs McDonnell yanked open the till drawer, withdrew a modest handful of notes and thrust them at Meggie. 'That's all you're getting. Now get your things and get out.'

Meggie made a great show of counting the money. 'That's about right,' she smiled sweetly. 'Thank you, Mrs McDonnell.'

'What about us?' The other girls clamoured angrily.

'You too,' Mrs McDonnell snarled at Ellie. 'Pack your things and get out. Bloody troublemaker. Get out and good riddance.'

'Not until you pay me,' Ellie, her face completely untroubled, insisted.

'And us,' the others chorused.

'Tomorrow!' Mrs McDonnell roared, tears filming her eyes as she thought of the damage this would do to her bank account. 'Tomorrow. I'll pay the lot of youse tomorrow.' Grabbing the gin bottle she filled her glass to the brim and tossed most of it back in one mouthful, refilled it and drank that down, too. That done, she felt for the seat of the stool, hauled herself inelegantly on to it, and sat, tightly gripping the bar which seemed to be rising and falling like the sea in a storm. She belched and muttered, 'Ungrateful. Ungrateful wee whores . . .'

The girls, reduced to silence by this display, watched the disintegration of their autocratic employer with round eyes and open mouths.

Meggie giggled, a strange shrill sound of relief which rang round the quiet room. Then Hilda laughed too, and

197

Sadie. Before long they were all wiping tears of mirth from their eyes while Mrs McDonnell did her inebriated best to fix them with a baleful stare over the top of her empty glass, still muttering, 'Ungrateful bitches . . . ungrateful . . . after all I done . . .'

'But what about you?' Meggie, her expression sombre again, turned to Ellie. 'What will you do now?'

'Celebrate!' was the firm answer. 'By the time she pays me what's owing I'll have enough money to go out to my brother.'

'But I'll miss you,' Meggie choked.

Unexpected tears blurred Ellie's vision. 'I'll miss you too,' she admitted as they hugged one another. 'But now we'll all have a wee drink. On Mrs McDonnell.' Drawing determinedly away and dashing a hand quickly over her eyes she ran to the bar where, to the cheers of the others, she dispensed huge drinks to all the girls.

Mrs McDonnell groaned and laid her thumping head on the bar.

'Going?' Matty was astounded. 'Where? Not back to Ma and Pa?' Meggie saw the veiled, faintly hostile look on his face and was saddened to realise that a reunion with their parents was no longer something Matty wished for. In the time they had spent at the Houlets' Nest, Matty had enjoyed greater freedom than he had ever known. Kept to his chores until three o'clock in the afternoon, he was then free to run wild. With Meggie working all evening and Mr and Mrs McDonnell busy with their various customers, there was no one to insist that he went to bed at a sensible hour, no one to wonder where he had been. Meggie knew that he had become cheeky and disobedient and, on more than one occasion, had found him with sweeties or cheap toys which

198

he had not the money to buy for himself. When challenged he always insisted that someone had given them to him, but Meggie, not liking the way he avoided her eyes, had found herself doubting him. She pushed these unwelcome thoughts out of her mind by telling herself that once they were living in Mr Wallace's cosy little flat she would soon be able to pull him back into line.

'No, not back to Ma and Pa,' she said now.

'Where then?'

'I've got us a nice wee flat. Near the park.'

He looked at her with the eyes of an old man. 'Och aye?' he sneered. 'And how are you going to pay for it?'

'A friend of mine . . . a Mr Wallace.' Under Matty's appraising stare her stomach tightened, her face flushed. It was as if he knew. But he was still a child, how could he know.

'A man! Aye, it would be a man.' He turned away in disgust. 'I'm not coming. I'm staying here.'

'You are not!' She grabbed his shoulder, surprised by the bulk of it, realising just how much he had filled out since coming here. 'Don't you cheek me, Matty McPherson. You are coming with me and that's an end to it.'

'I like it here,' he insisted petulantly.

'Well, I don't.'

He glared at her, defiance darkening his eyes, but she met his gaze evenly and it was he who looked away first.

'You're always spoiling things,' he snarled. 'It was your fault Nancy died.' Meggie gasped, cut by the cruel reminder. He went on. 'I'd still be with Ma and Pa if it wasn't for you. And now you're making me leave here, too.'

'But Matty, it's for the best. So we can be together.'

He tossed his head and spat past her, into the fire, in

faithful imitation of Mr McDonnell. 'I hate you! A slag, that's what you are. I hate you.'

The anger built inside Meggie until she could control it no longer. Raising her hand she delivered a sharp slap across his face and watched in grim satisfaction as he staggered then looked up at her in hurt confusion, suddenly a child again.

'I hope that hurt,' she hissed. 'And yes, that's what I am. But before you call me that again Matty McPherson, just remember that I did it for you.'

Coldly she turned away and went upstairs to say goodbye to Ellie.

CHAPTER ELEVEN

Straining to see herself in the oblong mirror over the fireplace, Netta McPherson brushed her long, light brown hair back, then wound it deftly into a tight bun. When she was sure it was securely pinned she topped it with a rather drab felt hat and wrapped her best shawl over her black coat, arranging it so that the threadbare shoulder seams were hidden. Her stout, lace-up shoes were old but freshly polished and her brown lisle stockings were hardly worn, undarned and not yet sagging at the ankles. Satisfied that there was nothing more she could do to improve her appearance she turned to her husband, checking that he too was respectably turned out. The collar of Tam's old tweed jacket curled stubbornly and his trousers were baggy at the knees, but his shirt had a crisp new collar on it and his shoes, from Mr Stein's pawn shop, were nearly new.

'Ready?' he asked.

'Aye.'

'Right then, we'd best be on our way if we're not to miss the bus. You take the weans to Mrs Craig and I'll meet you outside.'

'Youse two behave yourselves,' Netta told Perce and Bertie when she left them with her neighbour. 'We'll hear all about it mind, if you don't.'

'Och, away with you, hen and don't be worrying about the laddies. They'll be good and if they're not, well, Mr Craig has a fine strong belt on the back of the door.' Mrs

Craig winked at the boys as she said it and they grinned back.

'It's gey kind of you, Mrs Craig, keeping the lads for me,' Netta said.

'Och, think nothing of it, hen. It'll be a pleasure to have young 'uns about the house again.'

'Are you going to fetch Matty and Meggie home with you, Ma?' Perce asked, not at all sure that he relished the idea. His brother and sister were nothing more than fading memories and from what he did remember Meggie was bossy and Matty was a cry baby.

'Aye. Then we'll be a proper family again,' Netta said.

Bertie, sharing his brother's sentiments, made a wry face behind his mother's back.

'Off you go then, Netta. You'll miss that bus if you don't hurry,' Mrs Craig said.

Netta stooped and kissed her sons' cheeks. 'Be good boys now and I'll see youse in a couple of days.'

'Aye. Aye,' they said, anxious for her to go so that they could get back outside to join their pals.

The bus journey seemed interminable but, as they crossed the border into Strathannan, it seemed to Netta that the countryside changed, becoming softer, greener, instantly familiar. Ahead of them the skyline was dotted with pit bings, spoil heaps from the four pits which constituted the Strathannan Mining Company, and very soon the bus would pass by the villages of Valleydrum, Oakdene and Blairwood.

Then, slumped under the ever present haze of smoke, half-hidden in a dip in the ground, there was Craigie. Netta sat forward on her seat and strained to catch a glimpse of the familiar rows of cottages, smiled to see steam seeping from the wash-house and fought to contain tears of nostalgia as she looked at the village she still thought of as home.

How she missed it, the comforting feeling of living among folk she had known all her life, the knowledge that they were all the same, bound by the poverty of life in a mining village. Hardships forgotten, she recalled summer days when, work done, the women left their front doors wide open and gathered on the grass between the rows, drinking in the sun while they exchanged gossip. How different it was to where they lived now, strangers in a street of teeming tenements, outsiders, objects of curiosity. No sun managed to penetrate to the back courts and the women congregated instead on the hard concrete of the front steps, or yelled back and forth through open windows. Not that the women were unfriendly once you got to know them, and she had good-hearted neighbours, but the truth was she wasn't one of them, hadn't been brought up there and, outside of her close, she knew very few people. Making all this even harder to bear was the uncertainty, the constant fear of Tam being without work, the worrying possibility of having to flit to yet another house, of having to seek acceptance in another new neighbourhood.

It would have been easier if they had had Jim and Lil to visit from time to time but the two families had parted on bad terms and, in any case, there had not been the time or money to spare on trips to Low Bothlie. Shamefully conscious of their debt, Tam and Netta had scrimped and saved every spare farthing to repay the money they owed Tam's brother. The letter of thanks and reconciliation which Tam had finally sent with full payment of the loan had elicited nothing more than a terse, written acknowledgement which had made it plain that the rift would not heal easily. But everything would change for the better now, Netta thought, deliberately tearing her mind away from such depressing thoughts. Tam had at last found a permanent job at the Lairdstoun steelworks. They could stay where they were, start to make real friends and most important of all, they could afford to fetch Meggie and Matty home.

As the bus trundled through the outskirts of Inverannan, then across the arched stone bridge which spanned the river Annan, Netta felt her mouth dry with sudden apprehension. It was almost two years since she had seen them last. Two years in which never a night had passed when she hadn't prayed to have them back; two years in which she had seen her husband reduced to a slouching, dispirited man, his pride destroyed because no one would offer him regular work. A man who could read and write better than some of the bosses, a man who had toiled underground with barely a day's sickness since he was fourteen years old, was suddenly deemed capable of only the most menial work, sweeping streets, collecting rubbish, cleaning up after others. He had seemed to shrink before her, his fierce pride withering away under the disrespect of the people he worked for. Would Meggie and Matty understand? Would they know just how difficult it had been to find work, to rent a suitable place, to have enough money to fetch them home? It had been such a long time, such a very long time.

'We should have something to eat first,' Tam said, handing Netta off the bus and leading her through the chaos of lumbering horse-drawn carts, motorised trucks and impatient cars to the other side of the busy road.

'No. Let's wait. We could all have something together. If we're careful we've got enough money for that,' Netta told him, so nervous now that she couldn't bear the thought of any delay.

'It's a fair wee walk to the workhouse. Right to the bottom of the town. By the time we get back up here again it'll likely be too late to get anything to eat.'

'Och, Tam. Come on. It'll get no easier by putting it off. And they'll be waiting for us.' She squeezed his arm, understanding more than he realised. Walking ahead of him she started off in the direction of the High Street.

'Not here?' Tam stared at Mr Carlyle.

'Sit down, Mr McPherson. Mrs McPherson.' Carlyle settled himself behind his desk and looked at the couple uneasily.

'But I wrote. Surely you got my letter? You knew I was coming for them today.'

'It only arrived yesterday, Mr McPherson.'

Netta sank into the chair and felt the room spin round her. 'How can they be gone?' she whispered.

Slowly, Mr Carlyle explained what had happened. 'After all, Mr McPherson,' he ended, 'according to the note your daughter left they went to join you. There was no reason for us to think that they hadn't, in fact, gone home. Of course, if you had kept us informed of your whereabouts . . . ' He dumped the blame squarely on them.

'But where are they?' Netta asked, her voice shrill.

Carlyle shrugged and spread his hands. 'I couldn't say.'

'You couldn't say? But they were in your charge. I left them here . . . to be cared for . . . ' Tam rose to his feet, anger overcoming shock. 'They're just weans. You had no right to let them go.'

'I had every right, Mr McPherson. You signed forms relinquishing the care of your children on the day you left them here. Still,' he added rapidly, 'I am sure they are all right. If anything . . . anything had happened to them, we would have been told.'

'We've got to find them. Please, Mr Carlyle, help us,' Netta pleaded, her face bleached of colour. 'Perhaps the police?'

Carlyle stiffened faintly. He would have to do something but any close enquiry into the children's disappearance could result in him losing his job, especially if anyone ever found out that he knew they were at the Houlets' Nest. He would have to have a word with Mrs McDonnell, warn her, give her the chance to get them off the premises. 'Yes. The police,' he agreed. 'Leave it with me. I'll call at the police station right away.'

'We'll come with you,' Tam offered.

'No, Mr McPherson. Your wife is in no condition to undergo questioning from the police. And I'm sure it wouldn't be a pleasant experience for you. In fact, it would only complicate matters. For instance, they are certain to want to know why you have left it so long before making enquiries about your children. They might even decide not to return them to you, when they are found. No, better if I deal with it. They know me. Leave it to me.'

Tam started to argue but Netta whispered, 'Do as he says, Tam. He's right. What if they won't let them come back to us?'

'There's nothing you can do here for the moment. Come back later this afternoon and I'll tell you what the police say.' Carlyle rose purposefully from his desk. 'My advice is to go and have a cup of tea somewhere. You'll feel better then. Now then, if I'm to go to the police station you will have to excuse me.' He held the door open and, totally defeated, they went out.

* * *

'The police will do everything they can to trace your son and daughter, Mr McPherson,' Carlyle assured them smoothly, four hours later, much relieved to have discovered that the McPherson children had moved on from the Houlets' Nest without telling anyone where they were going. 'But I should warn you, it will take some time.' He stared at some point above Tam's head, unable to meet the man's tortured eyes.

'Tam . . .' Netta shot an anguished look at her husband.

'But they did agree with me that it is unlikely that they have come to any serious harm. If they've been in trouble of any kind it will be on record somewhere. The police are checking that, but anything worse . . . if they had been . . .' He left the terrible word unsaid. 'We would already know. But, for now, there is very little any of us can do.'

'There must be something,' Tam insisted, still unwilling simply to accept what had happened.

'The police are doing everything they possibly can, Mr McPherson. There is nothing you can do. Take your wife home. I have your new address and as soon as we find them I will contact you. You have my word on that.'

Outside, stranded on the pavement with the big wooden doors locked behind them, Netta seemed lost.

'Oh Tam . . .' she looked at him, relying on him as she had always done in the past to find some solution. 'Is there nothing we can do?'

For a moment it was as if he hadn't heard her but then he looked at her sharply and said, 'Aye. Of course there is. They're our wains. We know them better than anyone. Our Meggie's a bright lass. Where would she have gone, Netta? How did she plan to find us?'

* * *

'Well, well. Look who's here,' was Lil's inadequate welcome. Her hair scraped back under a scarf, a howling infant wriggling in her arms, she was ill-prepared for unexpected visitors. 'And what brings youse all the way out here? Not out of work again, are you, Tam?'

They told her.

'Aye, well,' she prevaricated, unwilling to admit just how eager she had been to get rid of her niece and nephew. 'They were gey anxious to find youse. I told them you'd gone to Lairdstoun. I knew Tam was at the steelworks there. I showed them the way.'

Tam stared at her, fury plain in his taut face. 'You sent them to find us? On their own?' he exploded. 'Could you not have kept them with you?'

'They wouldn't stay. Right determined they were,' she lied, already dreading what Jim would say when he found out about this. 'Anyway,' she added bitterly, 'it's your own fault. You should have written and let me know your address.'

Netta blanched, knowing there was at least some justification for the cutting remark. 'It must have been about the time we moved to Dunshill. No wonder they never found us. And we've been in three different places since then. It's only since we came back to Lairdstoun and Tam got a job at the steelworks that we've had a proper place to stay.'

'You did a wrong thing, Lil. A very wrong thing. To turn your own nephew and niece out on the street!'

Tam's voice was deep, full of pain and, looking at him, Lil felt that he had seen into her mind, read the guilt there. She looked away and busied herself with the child, unable to meet his eyes again.

'Come on, Netta. We'll not stay here,' he said, gently taking his wife's arm. He turned back to his sister-in-law.

208

'I'll not forgive your cold heart, Lillian McPherson. I hope you rot in hell for what you've done.'

'We'll go to all the places we stayed in,' Tam told Netta, leading her away from his brother's house. 'Ask if anyone's seen the bairns, leave messages in case they're still looking for us.'

'But it's been so long, Tam,' Netta whispered.

'They'll turn up, lass. Never fear, we'll find them,' he told her with an assurance he was a very long way from feeling.

At about the time Tam and Netta were leaving Lil McPherson's, Meggie stood in the window of her sitting room, gazing out over the park, hoping for a glimpse of Matty. The wooden clock which ticked so loudly on her mantelpiece struck four-thirty and he should have been home ages ago. As the minutes passed she got more and more angry. Matty knew that Mr Wallace, or Wallace as he preferred her to call him, always came to see her on a Friday night, arriving just after five o'clock and staying for an hour or two before rushing home to have dinner with his wife. The antipathy between Matty and Wallace had been obvious from the start and, usually, Meggie took care to give her brother his dinner and send him to his room with reading and copying out to occupy him while Wallace was with her. Resenting this deeply, Matty had become more and more uncooperative as the months passed.

Matty's increasing intransigence disturbed Meggie. Sullen, surly and secretive, he spent too many hours out of the house, often leaving before she got up in the mornings and seldom coming home before dinner time, frequently with items he could only have obtained dishonestly and not even caring that she saw them. He treated her with barely concealed scorn, was openly derisive about her relationship with Wallace and dismissive of her attempts to educate him by setting him simple reading and writing exercises. Sometimes she barely recognised in this aggressive youngster the affectionate younger brother for whom she had made such huge sacrifices. The shy, slightly backward child was no more, replaced by an old man in an adolescent body. The way he looked at her after Wallace had been to see her, his hooded eyes showing only contempt and a sneering understanding of what went on between them, filled her with shame.

She wished she could make Matty understand how much better it was for them both to be here, under Wallace's indulgent protection, than to have remained at the Houlets' Nest. Meggie's initial gratitude to Wallace who was wise, gentle and good-humoured, had grown to become a real fondness. Her pleasure at seeing him was always absolutely genuine, her willingness to please him, unfeigned. Her innate realism warned her that this situation could not be permanent and she did make some amorphous plans for the distant future, thinking vaguely of a time when she and Matty would both find jobs and be able to afford to rent their own little home somewhere. But, for now, she was content to enjoy the relative peace and security of the present.

That peace and security depended largely on Wallace and one of the few things that upset him was finding her to be out when he called. On the two or three occasions when she had been walking innocently in the park, disappointment had made him angry. Not wanting to let him down again, she now tried to plan her time, to warn him in advance, even when she was doing something as mundane as going to the shops but, inevitably, she spent most of her time indoors. Much as she looked forward to the diversion of his visits, being confined between walls on days when the leafy freedom of the park beckoned, sometimes irked her. To a girl of not yet sixteen, the little house could seem claustrophobic. Meggie spent many long hours gazing out of her bedroom window, up the hill towards the grey slate roofs of Inverannan, longing for company. If it weren't for Sally, her lively neighbour, Meggie would have been almost completely isolated from people of her own age.

The only other cause of discontent was the problem of keeping house. Making do on the modest sum of money which Wallace gave her every week was a constant battle. As if trying to make up for earlier deprivation, Matty had developed a prodigious appetite and Meggie needed every penny of Wallace's allowance to keep him adequately fed. His recent sudden spurt of growth had necessitated second-hand trousers, shirts and jumpers. Far from saving a little against the day when she and Matty would need to fend for themselves again, Meggie was eating steadily into the few pounds she had brought with her. She had been tempted to tell Wallace of her problems but pride, and the knowledge that he had already been more than generous in agreeing to support both her and her brother, stopped her. Bearing in mind what Wallace had said to her on the day he had first brought her here she was determined to ask for nothing more than he already gave her.

Meggie pulled herself out of her reverie to look at the clock and saw it was already a quarter to five and still no sign of Matty. Taking her temper out on the mince which was simmering on the stove, she slapped it messily on his plate and shoved it in the oven to keep warm, no longer caring that it would probably dry out long before he ate it. That done she went into the small bathroom and washed, then changed her clothes, making sure she was neat and attractive for Wallace. She had just finished brushing her hair, long now and falling well past her shoulders in a burnished curtain, when she heard the front door open.

'Matty, where have you been? You know you should have been home hours ago,' she shouted, hurrying to meet him.

'Good evening, Meggie,' Wallace greeted her with amused pleasure. The very sight of her was enough to invigorate him. The youthful freshness which should have emphasised his own advancing age and failing powers never failed to excite him. The naïvety and inexperience which had first captivated him was still evident enough to rouse him to the kind of performance he had seldom achieved with his wife, even in the early days of their marriage. And, under his delighted tutelage she was gradually learning the art of seduction, understanding that he gained as much pleasure from her arousal as he did from his own. That he felt a full decade younger than his fifty-eight years was entirely due to Meggie McPherson.

Hanging his coat on the hook behind the door Wallace glanced at the bedroom door with a keen sense of anticipation.

Meggie greeted him with a kiss, allowing him to grasp her buttocks and pull her against him. 'Wallace! I thought it was Matty.'

The mention of the boy's name brought a fleeting scowl to Wallace's face. Although Meggie was worth every penny he spent on her, keeping a mistress was a noticeable strain on his finances. To know he was also supporting her gutter-snipe of a brother, a boy who made no secret of his animosity and would not even make the effort to be ordinarily polite was galling, to say the least. But Meggie's devotion to her younger brother was unshakeable and

Wallace knew that unless he went on supporting them both, he would lose her – something he wasn't prepared to contemplate.

At that moment the door opened again and Matty himself sauntered in. He ignored Wallace and brushed rudely past him into the kitchen. 'Where's my dinner?' he demanded.

Leaving Wallace, whose temper was souring by the minute, standing in the narrow hallway, Meggie ran into the kitchen and drew the hot plate out of the oven. 'Hurry up and eat it,' she ordered furiously.

Without bothering to wash his hands, Matty sat at the table and prodded the dried-up mess. 'I'm not eating this,' he snarled, shoving the plate away. 'It's all dried up. What else is there?'

'What else?' Meggie's voice was shrill with indignation. 'If you'd come home when you're supposed to it would have been fine. Eat it or go without.' She could feel Wallace's irritation even through the dividing wall.

'Och, that's bloody wonderful,' Matty sneered. 'Never mind me, Meggie, I'm just your brother. Away you go to your fancy man. Leave me with nothing to eat.'

'Don't you talk about Mr Wallace like that!' she hissed furiously. 'It's his money that buys your food so eat it and be grateful you're not back in the workhouse.'

Slowly, insolently, Matty got to his feet. 'Eat it your bloody self,' he said, deliberately knocking the plate to the floor then barging into her on his way out of the room.

She followed him into the hallway just as he reached the front door. 'Matty!' she yelled. 'Don't you dare go out of that door.'

'Try stopping me,' he challenged.

'Matty,' she called again.

'Och, away fuck yourself,' he muttered.

Meggie gasped, appalled to hear the word on her brother's lips. Even as she took the first step towards him, Wallace emerged from the sitting-room doorway where he had been listening to the exchange. In two swift steps he had the boy by the collar, swung him round and hit him hard across the mouth.

'Insolent little bugger,' he swore, his face puce with anger. 'Don't you dare speak to your sister like that.'

Matty staggered slightly, then stood rubbing his face as if he didn't quite believe what had happened to him. 'Bastard,' he spat, searching his mind for the filthiest insults in his limited repertoire.

Wallace hit him again. Calmly now, as if the physical effort had taken the fire out of his fury, he turned the key in the lock and put it in his pocket. 'Get to your room,' he ordered, his face set like granite.

For a moment Matty's eyes burned into Meggies's. She stared back, grappling with her own conflicting emotions. One part of her resented Wallace's interference, the other knew that Matty badly needed disciplining. She looked away.

Beaten, Matty pushed past them both and stormed down the hallway to his own small bedroom. Turning in the doorway he yelled the words which time had taught him hurt Meggie the most. 'I hate you Meggie McPherson. I hate you.'

As the bedroom door slammed Wallace rounded on Meggie. 'When I come here to see you,' he bellowed, 'I don't expect to have to deal with nasty little scenes like that.'

'I'm sorry, Wallace,' she muttered, ashamed for him to have been forced to see how little respect her brother had for her.

But Wallace was incapable of remaining angry with Meggie. Sighing, he put his arms round her and drew her head on to his chest. 'Och, lass, I'm not blaming you,' he said gently. 'You do your best. The lad needs a father's hand but maybe I'm the wrong person to be trying to discipline him. I'll not have made things any easier for you.' He raised her face and kissed her lips. 'Now then, forget about him. Come and make an old man happy.'

When Meggie woke the next morning, bright winter sun was streaming through the window. Instead of the quiet satisfaction she usually experienced after an evening with Wallace her head thumped unbearably, her eyes were heavy and her stomach felt queasy. She groaned and turned over, yearning to go back to sleep but the movement caused a rush of nausea that sent her running for the lavatory. Five minutes later, her eyes red and swollen from the effort of violent retching, she made her way shakily back towards her bedroom. An insistent banging on her front door forced her to retrace her steps.

'Sally,' she greeted her neighbour without her usual enthusiasm. Sally lived in the corresponding flat next door. Big boned, generously fleshed and overflowing with cheerful energy, Sally was the product of a huge family from the poorest, roughest area of Inverannan – an area the burgh's more prosperous residents pretended did not exist. Her vocabulary was worse than anything Meggie had seen or heard in Craigie but she was so kind and generous that this shortcoming was simply not important. Although five years older than Meggie her present circumstances were similar and the girls had become firm friends. A visit at this early hour of the morning, however, was not usual.

'Are you all right?' Sally asked, taking note of Meggie's blotchy face and puffy eyes.

'Aye,' Meggie answered, heading for the kitchen. 'Why?'

Sally followed her. 'I heard a lot of shouting yesterday evening,' she went on. 'Did he hit you then?'

'Hit me? Wallace? No.' The idea was absurd. Meggie had never felt under any threat of physical violence from Wallace and in spite of what he had done to Matty last night, she knew he would never hit her.

'Then who did? Your face is all swollen,' Sally persisted.

Meggie's head pounded sickeningly, she felt nauseous again and didn't have the energy to argue. 'No one hit me.'

'What was all the noise about then? Had a row with your Wallace?'

'No!' Meggie snapped. Then, realising that Sally was probably the only friend she had, admitted, 'It was Matty's fault,' then went on to tell her exactly what had happened.

'Aye, well, he's a right cheeky wee sod, that brother of yours. You're too soft on him. It's about time someone sorted him out.' Sally was blunt.

'Matty's just upset. He knows Wallace doesn't like him.' Still she had to defend him. 'And I was in a rotten temper when he came in last night. He's a good boy, really, and he's just young yet.'

'Good boy, my backside!' Sally exploded. 'He's a right wee tyke and old enough to know exactly what he's doing. I've seen him and that gang of lads he hangs about with. A right load of trouble they are. Thieving things from the shops, giving cheek. They had the delivery boy from Hough the grocer off his bike the other day. Made off with half his stuff, they did. And the lad too feared to let on he knew who did it. He lost his job for that. And if you don't believe me, ask his sister. She's the ginger one three doors down.'

Meggie's head felt like it might explode. 'Matty wouldn't do anything like that,' she insisted stubbornly.

Sally shrugged. 'Suit yourself. But take it from me, I know what I'm talking about. My dad's been in and out of the jail all his days and I've watched my brothers going the same way. Just like your Matty they are. No bloody good.' She looked at the younger girl's blotchy face and relented a little. 'Och, away and sit down. I'll make some tea and toast. You'll feel better after that.'

Meggie trailed into her sitting room and hunched miserably on the old sofa. Five minutes later Sally bustled in with steaming tea and buttered toast. 'Eat this,' she ordered.

'Thanks,' Meggie said, smiling wistfully and reaching for the toast.

As soon as she put it to her mouth she knew she was going to be sick again. Dashing from the room with her hand clamped over her face she left a startled Sally staring after her. When she came back she was white and trembling slightly.

'Bloody hell!' Sally leapt to her feet and helped her into the room.

Meggie tried to fall on to the sofa but Sally held her, looking at her closely. 'You're never . . .?'

'Never what?' Meggie asked wearily.

'Stand still.'

To Meggie's astonishment Sally's hands were feeling around her abdomen. Affronted she pulled away. 'Stop it!'

'Bloody hell,' Sally looked at Meggie with pity now. 'Have you been sick a lot?' she asked.

'No, of course not.'

'Feeling funny then?'

'Well . . . sometimes. Just a bit. It's because I lie awake at night, worrying about Matty.'

'And when did you get the curse last?'

Sally's bluntness embarrassed Meggie, who had been taught never to discuss her bodily functions in anything but a hushed undertone and then only in an absolute emergency. Her time at the Houlets' Nest had done little to overcome the conditioning of childhood. 'I . . . I don't know.'

'Well think! It's important, Meggie.'

'I don't know! I've never really kept track.'

'You've got a proper little round belly there,' Sally commented.

Meggie, the first hint of trouble dawning on her, felt her own hands exploring the faint, tight curve in an area which had always been concave before. 'So . . .?'

'And you're bigger here?'

'Well, I expect I'm still growing.' But her mouth was dry with unexplained fear now and it was true, her good blouses hardly did up any more.

'You're in the family way, Meggie,' Sally said softly. 'You stupid wee bitch.'

CHAPTER TWELVE

Meggie and Sally walked along a road of grim, smoke-blackened, terraced houses. It was an unusually warm, late autumn day and the air rang with the sound of children playing and of women gossiping on their doorsteps.

But, even in the sunlight, this narrow street, one of five or six clustered around the back of the Netherton Mill, was dark and cheerless. Barefooted children, peeling paintwork, and boarded-up windows all gave evidence of underlying hardship, or neglect. Weeds straggled up through the uneven setts and mangy dogs lolled in the gutters, scratching half-heartedly at flea-infested coats. Clearly audible under the sounds of everyday life, was the steady throb and hum of the ageing steam engines which still powered the mill. The deep, sonorous rhythm was like a heartbeat, pulsing on, even after the sharper clack and rattle of the weaving sheds had fallen silent. On the rare occasions when the engines hissed into stillness, it was as though life itself was suspended. Overshadowing the streets of Netherton, just as surely as it dominated the lives of its inhabitants, was the blackened sandstone bulk of the mill itself.

To be in Netherton was almost like stepping back thirty years, certainly few improvements had been made in that time. Originally built for the mill workers, the houses had been sold to private landlords when Charlie Sutherland took over the mill and now accommodated the very poorest of Inverannan's citizens; families whose menfolk had been killed in the war, or whose main breadwinner couldn't, or wouldn't, seek work. People on the very edge of survival. Not that they were in any way an embarrassment to the more comfortably-off residents of the town. Tucked out of sight with the blank wall of the mill on one side and a slimy, rubbish-cluttered burn on the other, Netherton had a shunting yard behind it and was approached only through a murky tunnel which ran under the main railway line. The small community was effectively isolated from the rest of the town and was completely invisible to those who did not want to see it. Meggie, who had never known of its existence in a town which had seemed uniformly affluent, stayed close to Sally, feeling faintly threatened.

'This is it.' Sally, chirpy as ever, was oblivious to her unappealing surroundings. She stopped and pushed on the four bare planks which constituted the front door of her family's house. When it failed to yield to her pressure she lifted her daintily shod foot and delivered an almighty whack to the lower edge. The door creaked inwards and Sally ushered her friend inside.

After the warm sunlight the interior of the house was dim, the details hard to see. All Meggie was aware of was the smell, a horrible mélange of age, staleness, and unwashed humanity. As her eyes adjusted she looked round shocked by the bareness of the room, and recognised poverty so dire that even in the extremity of the strike, no house in Craigie had ever been as mean as this one.

'Wait here. I'll find Mum.' Sally disappeared through a curtained doorway and Meggie heard a shout of delight and the obviously warm greeting between Sally and her mother. Then the voices became muted and Meggie knew Sally was explaining the purpose of their visit. Her stomach turned and she wondered if she could run away. Desperation kept her where she was. She looked up when the curtain shifted and Sally, followed by an older woman, came back into the room.

'Well, lass, so you've got yourself in a wee bit of bother, have you?' Meggie found herself looking at a faded, worn version of Sally. Mrs Keir's face was lined, drained, aged before her time, but there was compassion there and understanding. Meggie instinctively liked and trusted her.

'I'm not sure,' she muttered. 'I think so.'

'Och, lass . . .' Mrs Keir sighed. 'Sit yourself down and you and me will have a wee chat. Sal, you take yourself outside for ten minutes.'

Sally winked and went off willingly enough. Meggie heard her shouting for her younger brothers and sisters, then laughter as they ran to greet her. As if reading her mind, Mrs Keir chuckled, 'Aye, we've not much, lass, but we do have love.' It cut Meggie as nothing else could have done, making her ashamed of the contempt which she had felt on walking into the house.

'Now then, Meggie, I've been delivering weans round here for the best part of twenty years, so I know what I'm about. Let me have a wee look at you. There's no need to be embarrassed.'

Gently she opened Meggie's blouse, looked quickly at her swelling breasts and darkened nipples, then ran a soft hand over the almost imperceptible mound of her belly. Then, after asking much the same questions as Sally had asked, she sat down on the room's only decent chair, a varnished wooden rocker.

'Sit down, lass.'

Meggie sank carefully on to an upright chair which tilted wildly on its uneven legs and waited, her eyes dark with apprehension.

'Our Sally's right enough. I'd say you're about four months' gone.'

'Oh . . .' Meggie felt faint, but passing out wasn't going to help her so she closed her eyes and concentrated on not making a complete spectacle of herself.

'What are you going to do, lass?'

'I don't know . . .'

'Well, you'll need to be quick and make up your mind. If you want, I can help you but it'll have to be done now. You're too far along to wait.'

'Help me?' Meggie looked up, her dark eyes puzzled as she wondered how a woman who obviously had so very little could help. 'How?'

'You really don't know much, do you?' There was a note of exasperation in the woman's voice now. 'I could get rid of it. It's easy enough. Painful, mind, but maybe the best thing.'

Meggie, whose understandings of the process by which babies arrived was still rudimentary, had no way of knowing what she meant. Mrs Keir saw the blankness in her eyes and explained.

'It happens all the time, lass. It's easier when you catch it early but I've done it for women as far along as five months. You're young and strong, you'll be fine.'

'But how? What do you do?' Thinking back, Meggie had heard vague stories in the Houlets' Nest, tales of hot baths and strong gin.

'A knitting pin. That's the best way.' Avoiding too much detail, Mrs Keir gave the briefest of descriptions. 'I'll not say it won't hurt, mind, but you'll soon forget,' she ended, doing her best to sound reassuring.

Meggie blanched with shock, her mouth filled with saliva and she fought to contain the nausea which was struggling for release. 'I can't,' she mumbled. 'I couldn't.' Until now she hadn't known such a thing was possible but the whole idea appalled her. There was already so much in her young life of which she was ashamed, but she knew that if she did as Mrs Keir was suggesting she would never forgive herself.

Mrs Keir rose from her chair and came to crouch beside her young visitor. 'It's your choice, hen,' she said, putting a comforting arm round the young shoulders. 'And I'm not saying that's what you should do, just letting you know that there is a way out, if you want it.'

'I can't,' Meggie repeated, more strongly now.

Mrs Keir nodded, admiring the determination she saw in the girl's face. 'All right, but what will you do, lass? Will your mother take you back?'

'I don't even know where she is,' Meggie admitted.

'Och, hen . . .' Mrs Keir's voice was soft and full of sympathy. 'Poor lass . . . Look, if you've nowhere else to go, you can come here till after it's born. We've a bit of spare room now the lads have left home. So long as you don't mind sharing with the lassies, we'll manage.' She laughed. 'I get by on nothing as it is, another mouth to feed won't make that much difference.'

Meggie's fragile composure almost shattered. The kindness was so genuine, so freely offered that she didn't know what to say. Her eyes flooded with tears and she mumbled, 'Thank you . . .'

'It's nothing,' Mrs Keir said briskly. 'And you could give me a hand round the house. I'm run off my feet most of the time.' She reached over and squeezed the young girl's hand. 'I hate to think of a lassie like you trying to manage all on her own. You think it over and let me know.'

At that point there was a thump on the front door, which

burst open letting Sally and three younger children into the room.

'Well?' she chased the youngsters into the scullery and looked at her friend.

Meggie smiled faintly but looked away again.

'I think Meggie needs time to think about it,' Mrs Keir suggested. 'Talk to her, Sal,' she said in an undertone as the girls took their leave. 'She's gey young to be having a wean and she'll find it hard if she goes through with it.'

Sally kissed her mother's dry cheek. 'Thanks, Mum.'

'Thank you, Mrs Keir,' Meggie said, already knowing that to impose herself on this family would be too much of a burden.

'My door's always open, lass, even if you just want someone to talk to.'

She stood in her doorway, watching as the girls walked back up the hill. Shaking her head sadly she went back inside.

The two friends took the long way home, walking arm in arm through the park, surrounded by a vivid display of gorgeous autumn colours as the trees prepared for the coming winter. All around them well dressed young mothers strolled serenely, soaking up the last of the season's sun, their offspring running and tumbling on the lush grass, the sounds of their carefree laughter filling the air. The contrast between these smartly dressed, pampered children and the barefooted urchins who had swarmed round Mrs Keir's house, seemed almost obscene to Meggie.

Sally tugged gently on Meggie's arm and pulled her towards an empty seat. 'Come on, let's enjoy the weather while it lasts.'

Meggie raised her face to the sun, smiled wistfully, then shook her head.

'I can't. I'll have to get back.'

'In case Wallace turns up?' Sally mocked her.

'Aye.'

'Och, Meggie, it's two o'clock in the afternoon. You're entitled to be out and about.'

'I know . . .'

'Well, another half an hour won't make any difference and it's a damn sight better than sitting all alone in that flat of yours,' Sally insisted. She strode away, settling herself determinedly on a bench, where she sprawled, shoving her sleeves up and hoisting her skirt to just above her knees, ignoring the shocked expressions on the faces of two elderly ladies on the neighbouring seat. When they got up, muttering, and stalked away, she giggled.

'Sally!' But, despite all her problems, Meggie had to smile. Resignedly she flopped down beside her friend.

'So, are you going to let my mum help you or not?' Sally asked brightly, as if, thought Meggie, she was asking whether there was soup or stew for tea.

Meggie shook her head. 'I can't.'

'Mum knows what she's doing. There's no need to be scared.'

'I'm not scared, not of that, anyway. It's just . . . not, not right.'

'Aye, and it's not right that you're an old man's mistress either,' Sally said with brutal frankness. 'But that doesn't stop you doing it.'

'It's not the same,' Meggie rounded on her friend angrily. 'I'm not hurting anyone.'

Sally snorted. 'His wife might not see it that way.'

'You can talk!' Meggie edged away, putting a space between them. 'I'm not doing it. I can't. I won't.'

'Then what the hell are you going to do?' Sally demanded.

'Tell Wallace.'

'Tell Wallace!' Sally almost screamed the words. 'And what bloody use do you think he'll be?'

'It's his child.'

'You tell him and he'll have you out of there so fast you won't have time to pack a bag,' Sally warned her. 'Bloody hell, Meggie. Don't you know anything yet?'

'No, he won't,' Meggie argued. 'Wallace is a kind man. He'll look after me.'

'Aye. Sure.' Sally was scornful. 'He's just like all the rest, Meggie. He wants a bit of fun, without any complications. You tell him about the baby and that'll be the end. You'll be out on your ear and you'll never hear from him again.'

Meggie turned her face away, her expression stubborn and angry.

Sally sighed. 'Och, there's no point in talking to you. But make sure you've got somewhere to go before you break the news to that man of yours. And leave it for as long as you can. You're hardly showing yet. If you've got any sense you'll get every penny you can out of him. Come on, let's go home.'

The next day, frightened that she might have missed Wallace the previous afternoon, Meggie would not leave the house and contented herself by sitting by her bedroom window, letting the autumn sunshine flood in as she turned her problem over and over in her mind.

She was no nearer a solution when a sharp rap on the door startled her. Expecting Wallace, she was disappointed and then surprised to find a uniformed policeman on her doorstep.

'Do you have a brother, lass?'

She nodded. ' . . . Aye.'

'Is he here?'

'Yes.' Matty had come home about an hour earlier and had gone straight to his room.

'I'd like to speak to him then,' he said, pushing his way into the house. 'He's in his bedroom,' she said, moving to block his way down the hall. 'Why do you want him? Is he in trouble?' Her heart was thumping against her ribcage.

'Maybe.' He walked around the sitting room, seeming to fill it. 'Is your mother not here?'

'No.'

'Your father?'

She shook her head, the palms of her hands growing sweaty.

'Where are they?'

'Meggie swallowed hard. 'Out.'

'At work?'

'Aye! At work.'

'When will they be back?' He watched as she struggled for an answer, well aware of the status of most of the residents of this little street. But surely a girl of this age, not a day over sixteen, could not be one of them?

Colouring under his watchful eye Meggie said, 'I'll fetch my brother,' and fled to his bedroom.

'What do you want?' Matty shoved something hurriedly under his bed and scowled at her.

'There's a polisman here to see you,' she hissed. 'What is it about, Matty? What have you done?'

'Nothing!' he insisted, but his face lost some of its

227

cockiness and for a moment he looked like a frightened little boy again.

'Is your brother there, miss?' the policeman called.

'Yes . . .' Meggie stood back and let Matty walk in front of her to the sitting room.

'And what's your name, son?' the policeman asked.

'Matty McPherson,' Matty said sullenly.

'Right, Matty, and where were you this afternoon?'

'Here,' Matty said with a convincing display of indignation and surprise. 'Why?'

'Here were you? And why weren't you at the school?' the policeman asked.

There was a moment of stunned silence before Meggie gathered her wits and lied, 'He was sick last night. Mam said he was to stay home.'

The constable raised an eyebrow. 'Looks well enough to me.'

'I am now,' Matty insisted. 'It was just last night. Terrible belly ache.'

'You weren't in the High Street with your friends then?'

'No!'

'Well, I hope not, lad, because if you're hanging around with that gang of lads who're lifting things from the shops you're going to be in right trouble.'

'I've been here, all day. Honest.' There was a note of panic in Matty's voice now.

'Aye, so you say, but I don't believe you lad. I'll know where to come next time there's trouble,' the policeman threatened. 'And I'll be back for a word with your father later tonight.' With that he settled his cap on his head and let himself out, hoping the warning would be enough to keep the lad out of trouble in future.

228

'Matty!' Meggie rounded on him as soon as the door closed. 'How could you?'

'Och, aye, Meggie, that's right. Believe him, never mind what I say,' he retorted with a show of affronted righteousness.

Ignoring him, Meggie ran to his room, fell to her hands and knees and groped under his bed. In the dust which had gathered there she located several lumpy items. She dragged them out and gasped at what she found. Two pullovers, a brand-new shirt, a shiny penknife, several bars of chocolate, some cigarettes, a box of matches, three tins of meat, four oranges, a half-bottle of whisky and, in a paper bag, six pound notes.

'Where did you get all this?' she asked, her voice cold.

He shrugged.

'Tell me where you got them,' she demanded.

He simply stared at her, a faint grin hovering round his lips.

'If you don't tell me, Matty, I'll take them to the police station,' she threatened.

'You wouldn't dare,' he sneered, grinning openly now.

Losing her temper she grabbed his shoulders and shook him so hard that his head wobbled. 'You little thief,' she screamed.

Matty tore himself away from her grip. 'I was going to give you the money,' he lied. 'I was trying to help. Honest, Meggie.'

'By stealing?'

'I did it before, when we went to find Ma and Pa. You didn't mind then.'

'That was different.'

Matty knew he had to convince her. 'I did it for you,

Meggie,' he pleaded slyly. 'I know you've spent all your money on clothes for me. I was just trying to help. Honest.'

Meggie couldn't make herself believe him, knew, in her heart, that he was lying. Even so, he was her brother, all she had in the world, and he was right, she had been glad of what he could steal when they had gone to look for their parents. Maybe this was her fault as much as his. Now it was up to her to make sure he never did it again.

'It's wrong to take things without paying, Matty. You know that. I've told you before.'

'I'm sorry, Meggie. I won't do it again,' he promised, wrapping his arms round her.

Meggie sighed and rested her head on his shoulder. 'All right. I believe you. But promise me you won't ever steal anything again.'

'I promise,' he assured her blithely, smiling to himself.

But nothing Meggie said could keep Matty at home. He continued to run wild, staying out until long after dark and refusing to say where he had been. When she pressed him he accused her of not trusting him. Every day she checked under his bed and in his drawers but never found anything else to justify her nagging suspicions. And by now her own problems were becoming too urgent to ignore.

Dressing in the chill of a December morning she struggled to fasten the catch on her skirt and, turning to look at herself in the dressing table mirror, realised that her condition was becoming noticeable. She couldn't put it off any longer. She would have to tell Wallace about the baby.

It was Friday, an evening when he regularly visited her. She washed, brushed out her hair until it shone, dressed carefully and fastened the jet and diamond bracelet round her wrist, anxious to appear at her best. In fact she looked better now than she ever had. Her skin was clear and glowed with gentle colour, her eyes sparkled and her slightly fuller figure suited her.

Wallace, assuming these subtle changes were the happy result of her improved circumstances, found himself freshly enchanted by her. He needed no encouragement to follow her to the bedroom that evening. A good day at work going over the books and finding the Strathannan Mining Company to be making a small but steady profit had invigorated him. He felt almost young again and fell on her with an energy more common in a thirty-year-old.

Afterwards, flushed and warm with exertion, Meggie laid her head on his chest while he still fondled a breast and she knew there would never be a better moment to break her news.

Shifting slightly she moved her weight away and taking his hand, laid it on her stomach. 'Can you feel anything, Wallace?' she asked.

He slid his hand down through the curling mat of hair between her legs and laughed, delighted by her wanton invitation and feeling himself harden again. Grunting slightly he heaved himself up and straddled her, admiring the milky quality of her skin, running a hand over her breasts, across her curving stomach and between her legs.

'Not there,' she said, taking his hand again and placing it back on her belly. 'Here. Look.'

Wallace's feverish eyes lighted greedily on the accentuated mound of her stomach, obvious now against the slenderness of the rest of her body. His erection died along with the desire which had raised it.

'Are you telling me you are pregnant?' he asked, his eyes widening in horror, his face sagging and adding a good ten years to his age.

Meggie, looking trustingly into his eyes, feared that Sally had been right. 'Yes,' she said, struggling to keep her voice steady. 'About five months.'

He clambered off the bed and pulled himself hastily into his clothes, not looking at her, trying not to let her see how much her news had disturbed him. His mind raced. A child was a complication he had not foreseen, assuming she knew enough to prevent such a thing happening. One thing he was sure of: he could never acknoweldge the child as his own, not in his position. The resulting scandal would be the end of his civic career and bring shame on his whole family. And without the support of a husband what hope was there for Meggie? She, and the child, would be marked for life.

'What are you going to do?' he asked when he could finally trust his voice not to tremble with shock.

'I don't know,' she answered miserably.

'Och, Meggie . . .' He fumbled for words. 'Do you know anyone . . . anyone to take care of it . . . help you get rid of it . . . a doctor?' There must be someone in the town who could help. He'd ask around, maybe visit Mrs McDonnell at the Houlets' Nest, surely she would know of someone.

'I won't have it taken away.' There was an unusually stubborn note to her voice.

'But, Meggie, you can't have it,' he insisted. 'Think, lass. I'm a married man. I can't give you the support you need. The child would never have a father. It's a terrible stigma.' He spoke as gently as he could, seeing the pain in her lovely eyes, sensing how hard she was fighting to remain calm. 'I'm not a wealthy man. I can hardly afford to look after you and that brother of yours . . .'

She interrupted him. 'It's too late to have it taken away. I'll have to have it now.'

'Bloody hell!' he swore, suddenly angry. 'Why didn't you tell me before? When I could have done something to help?'

'I didn't know.' She slid off the bed and wound her arms round his neck. 'It'll be all right, Wallace. No one will know. So long as you look after us we'll be all right.'

He broke her grip roughly and moved away, desperate to get out of the house, to think. 'I've got to go. My wife . . .'

'You will take care of us, won't you, Wallace?' she pressed him, scared that if he went now he might never come back.

He sighed, knowing he was behaving badly, and bent to kiss her face. 'You know I will. Just give me time,' he said. 'I need to think about this, to sort something out.'

Meggie watched helplessly as he stumbled hurriedly from the house. Only pride stopped her from calling out and begging him to stay.

A week passed and there was no sign of Wallace. The money he had left had almost run out and she would soon be reduced to using the pound notes she had confiscated from Matty. Within a week that would be gone too. To add to Meggie's worries, Matty hadn't bothered to come home at all the previous night. Standing at the sitting-room window, watching for him, Meggie felt as if she was living some kind of horrific nightmare. Panic rose in her chest when she thought about what might happen if Wallace never came back. Too late she realised how very little she knew about him. She didn't even know his real name, had no idea where he lived or worked and had absolutely no way of contacting him.

She felt the cold sweat of fear break out on her face, closed her eyes to steady the spiralling terror and opened them to see a capped head bobbing up the stairs. It was swiftly followed by the uniformed figure of the policeman who had visited them before. Meggie's instinctive reaction was to dodge down, out of sight, but even as she moved he looked up and she knew she had been seen. Nervously she went to the door.

'Good morning, miss.' He removed his cap and stepped inside.

'What do you want this time?' she asked wearily.

'I've come to see your father, miss,' he said grimly.

'He's not in.'

'I see, and when will he be home?'

Meggie avoided an answer. 'Why?'

'It's your brother, miss. There's been a spot of bother.'

'What bother?' she demanded.

'I'd best discuss that with your father.'

'I told you, he's not here,' Meggie said, crossing the room and sitting down before her jellified legs collapsed under her. As she did so her skirt tightened round her body and the constable saw her condition. It confirmed what the woman downstairs had just told him.

'Now then, lass,' he said sternly. 'I think you had best be honest with me. Your brother's at the police station. He's in a lot of trouble and you will be too if you don't tell me the truth.'

Privately Meggie thought things could hardly get worse for her. 'What do you want to know?' she asked dully.

'It's just you and the lad living here, isn't it, lass?'

'No! My Mam and Dad are at work,' she insisted desperately.

'In that case, I'll just wait until one of them comes home.' He tossed his cap on to the table and made a show of settling himself comfortably in a chair.

Meggie screwed her hands together. 'It'll be ages yet.'

'No matter. I'll wait anyway.' He sat there solidly immovable.

'You can't. I have to go out,' Meggie tried.

'I don't think so, lass. Just sit yourself down and wait.'

Half an hour passed, the clock on the mantel ticked loudly, marking every passing second. Constable Buller sat on with the air of a man who was determined to wait, until Doomsday if necessary. Meggie found it impossible to sit still. She paced the room, stared out of the window, sat down, then got up and resumed her restless prowling. Buller waited a full hour before he broke his silence.

'Now, lass,' he said, not unkindly. 'I think this has gone on long enough. And before you say anything, I've already had a wee talk with the woman who lives downstairs, so think carefully before you tell me any more untruths. Are you and the boy alone here?'

Meggie sighed, knowing it was useless to pretend. 'Aye.'

'And how old are you?'

'Almost sixteen.'

'Fifteen?'

'Aye.'

'That's gey young to be on your own. How do you manage?' He watched her, wondering how an obviously bright and pretty girl came to be living in circumstances like these.

Meggie shrugged. 'We just do.'

'Your brother goes out and steals for you, is that how you get by?'

'No!' she protested, appalled.

'Do you have a job?'

'No.'

'So lass, how do you manage?' he repeated the question. Shame flushed over Meggie's cheeks, making her look

235

away, unable actually to put into words what she did to keep a roof over their heads. The constable, who had seen similar situations in his twenty years on the force, said it for her.

'You've a gentleman friend, is that how it is?' Though gentleman was hardly the word he would have used to describe a man who took his pleasure with a fifteen-year-old.

Meggie nodded miserably.

'I see. You do know, don't you, lass, that it's against the law, at your age? And lass, you're far too young to be expected to look after your brother all on your own.'

Meggie nodded again.

'And when will he be coming to see you next, this gentleman of yours?'

'I don't know . . .' Meggie only realised she was crying when the words emerged as a choked sob. 'I don't think he's coming back. I haven't seen him since I told him about the baby.'

The constable sucked a sharp, angry breath through closed teeth. 'So you're all on your own then?'

'There's Matty,' she sobbed, then remembering her responsibilities asked, 'Why is he at the police station? What's he done?'

'He was caught trying to steal cigarettes from a shop on the High Street last night. He'll have to go before the magistrate.'

'Oh, Matty,' Meggie wailed, tears flowing down her face.

'Now then, lass, don't go upsetting yourself. He's safe enough at the police station and that's where I'm taking you too – just until we see what's to be done with you.'

Wallace had had a miserable week, his mind consumed by

the problem posed by Meggie's condition. Understanding more clearly than she how hard her life would be with an illegitimate child to raise, even if he did his best to support them, he was convinced that the wisest thing to do was to end the pregnancy. Finding the means of doing that safely had been a risky and time-consuming business, taking him eventually to Edinburgh. Now he was anxious to see her again, to reassure her and try to persuade her to his way of thinking. As he made his way up the outside stairs of the little house that evening, he had, in his pocket, seventy pounds and the address of an eminent Edinburgh doctor who as reputed to be both skilful and discreet. That very afternoon he had made the necessary appointment and had even gone so far as to book a room in a quiet hotel where Meggie and Mattie could spend a week while she recuperated. He would fabricate some excuse to Elsie and visit Meggie to make certain she was recovering properly. But Meggie had seemed set on having the baby. If she wouldn't be persuaded, then he would have to make some alternative arrangement, perhaps find her a small house in another town, devise some way of settling her future. Though his mind baulked at the thought of the danger of discovery, the complications inherent in any such arrangement, he knew he owed her that much at least.

He knocked loudly on the door, then, to his dismay, realised that the house was in darkness, apparently empty. Frowning he delved into his pockets, found his own key and let himself in. From the shadowed hallway, the small flat was absolutely still. His heart thumping with apprehension, Wallace opened the door of Meggie's bedroom. He saw at once that the surface of the dressing table was bare, her brushes and combs gone. Desperately he flung open the wardrobe. The cavern-like interior yawned emptily back at him. And there, on the centre of her pillow, was the suede box. He picked it up, withdrew the delicate bracelet and ran it through his fingers, picturing it on her slender wrist. Sadly he collapsed onto the bed and sank his head into his hands, knowing he was too late.

It was the very next morning when Wallace's secretary announced that Chief Inspector Knight of the Strathannan Constabulary was waiting in the outer office. With no premonition of trouble, Wallace stood up as she ushered the uniformed officer in, then grasped him warmly by the hand.

'Well, Bill, what can I do for you? Not come to arrest me, have you?' His laughter boomed across the room. There was no response. Realising that his old friend's face was set in disturbingly serious lines, Wallace motioned him towards a seat. 'Come on then, man, out with it.'

Knight cleared his throat and looked pointedly at Laing's secretary, a thin-faced spinster who was hovering at the back of the room, hoping to pick up any interesting gossip with which to regale her church group.

'In private I think, Wallace.'

'Aye . . . of course. Thank you, Mildred.'

The woman sniffed and left, closing the door with exaggerated care then pressing her ear against it. Hearing only muted mutterings she frowned and gave up, sitting herself back behind her desk and thumping the keys of her typewriter in frustration. Astute or attractive she was not, but she compensated for those failings by the possession of a nose which was finely tuned for the first hint of trouble. And trouble, she thought, a touch smugly, was what she had seen on Bill Knight's face.

Inside Wallace Laing's mahogany and leather office,

238

Inspector Knight was not relishing the task ahead of him. 'I have to ask you some rather awkward questions, Wallace.'

Wallace sat back in his chair, inserted his thumbs in his waistcoat pockets and waited, his face inscrutable. Behind the calm, brown eyes, his brain churned, searching for the petty sin which was all that could have brought the Chief Inspector here. Some slight infringement at one of the mines likely, or maybe a minor traffic offence. Aye, that was probably it. Whatever it was, it was something he could do without, especially with this worry about Meggie. Fixing a half smile on his face he encouraged Knight to go on.

'Do you own the house at 12 Beath Street?' Knight saw the slight twitching of a muscle at the side of Wallace's mouth and knew he had struck a raw nerve. 'A house which is divided into two flats.'

'Why do you ask?' Laing fiddled with a silver paper knife, trying to sound casual.

'Do you?' Knight persisted with a smile, as if it was a matter of only passing interest.

Laing quickly realised that there was no point in denying something which could be so easily proved. 'Aye. I've had it for the past six years.'

'And you know a young woman called Margaret McPherson who is living in the top flat?'

Laing shrugged, opened his arms wide and smiled in a precisely calculated gesture of frank openness, understanding that his whole reputation now rested with this man. 'Och, just trying to help. Pretty little thing, down on her luck. Only a temporary arrangement and . . . well, I'm sure you understand, Bill, not something I'd want to become known. People wouldn't understand.'

'No,' Knight agreed then waited, deliberately letting the silence lengthen, hoping the other man would be forced to say more. But Wallace Laing was wilier than most and sat on the other side of the desk, outwardly calm and smiling, still fiddling with the paper knife.

Suddenly Knight leaned forward, bringing his face close to the other man's. 'She is only fifteen years old,' he hissed.

Laing allowed the knife to clatter noisily on to the desk. 'Fifteen?'

'Are you trying to tell me you didn't know how old she is?' Knight asked.

'Fifteen! No of course I didn't. She told me eighteen and she certainly doesn't act like a fifteen-year-old.' He allowed his head to sink into his hands for a moment. 'Bill, look, can this be off the record?'

Knight nodded. 'For now.'

'I won't deny that I was keeping her, in return for . . . certain favours. But I swear to you, I had no idea, no idea. I brought her out of the Houlets' Nest, how was I to know she was so young? Just a child . . . If I'd known I would never have . . .' It was a bravura performance denied only by his heightening colour, the drops of sweat trickling down the side of his face. 'Surely, brother,' he added slyly, self-preservation uppermost in his mind, 'you might have met her at the Houlets' Nest yourself?'

Knight flinched, his own conscience not entirely clear, uncomfortable at this untimely reminder of their shared Masonic brotherhood and his own aspirations to the Master's chair which could be greatly facilitated by this man's influence.

'It's a nasty situation, Wallace,' he said. 'We stumbled on her by accident after her brother was picked up for theft. We went to Beath Street to speak to his father and found just the girl.'

'Aye, the lad. Ungrateful little swine. But the girl was

doing her best for him. Abandoned by their parents, some years ago I believe. You see,' he said, warming to his theme, 'that's why I felt I had to help them.'

'Quite.'

'And where is the girl now?'

Knight didn't miss the note of concern in Laing's voice. 'We thought it best, in the circumstances, a lass of her age, to keep her and her brother at the station overnight. The parents are on their way.'

Wallace let out a huge sigh of relief. 'Maybe that's for the best.'

'Maybe,' Knight was non-committal.

'Look, Bill, you and me, well, we've been friends for a long time. You know enough about me to see I'd never have taken the girl on if she'd been honest with me about her age.' Even as he spoke Wallace was aware of rising shame, knew he was letting Meggie down. But what else could he do? Now that Meggie was in the hands of the authorities, he could do nothing to help her. To admit he knew her age could land him in court, ruin his career, might even destroy the company and would certainly bring shame on the entire family.

'Um . . .' Knight knew no such thing.

'And, for a man in my position, if this gets out . . . I'd be ruined, Bill. Ruined. And all because I was trying to help. I'm sure there's nothing to be gained from taking this any further.'

'The law's the law, Wallace, even for the Provost.'

'But Bill, surely you can see that if this ever came to court, well I'm an honest man and the whole story would come out. The Houlets' Nest, the men who go there . . . very awkward it could be, Bill. Very awkward indeed, especially for a professional man like yourself.'

241

Knight's success in remaining unruffled by such a blatant threat was admirable. 'Difficult thing to hush up, Wallace. Constable Buller's a man who likes to see a thing through. He's very concerned about the girl. Got lassies of his own, see.'

'Then there's the Lodge, Bill. Wouldn't look good for your chances there if it got out that you like an hour or two at the Houlets' Nest.'

Bill Knight stood up and settled his hat firmly on his greying head. 'As you say, Wallace, very unpleasant.'

'Aye. Look, call round tonight, I've a couple of cases of best malt in the cellar. I'm sure they'd be to your liking.'

'Best malt, eh?' Knight tried not to smile.

'Aye. Best malt. Och, we're men of the world, Bill. We understand one another. No need to make something out of nothing?'

'Indeed not, Wallace, Indeed not. About eight o'clock then?'

'Aye.' Wallace led him to the door and pumped his hand. 'Eight o'clock.'

Bill Knight was grinning as he nodded farewell to Mildred. Disappointed that her instincts had, for once, let her down, she hammered furiously at her keys, mistyped three words in a row and then tore the paper from the carriage and hurled it at the wastebin.

Wallace leaned against the door, his heart thumping painfully, and caught the sharp smell of his own sweat. Feeling faintly unsteady on his legs he went to the cupboard, withdrew a bottle and not bothering with the refinement of a glass, swallowed a good two inches of neat whisky.

CHAPTER THIRTEEN

When Tam and Netta McPherson walked into the Inverannan police station, Netta's face was radiant with joy. While her husband spoke to the desk sergeant she looked round expectantly, impatient for her first glimpse of the children she had been frightened she would never see again.

'Ah . . .' The sergeant smiled grimly. It was his task to introduce this unsuspecting couple to the unpalatable facts about their son and daughter. 'Maybe youse should come with me. There's a wee room through here that's more private.' He flipped up the counter shelf and led the way to a small, cold room. 'Sit yourselves down and I'll fetch the lad.'

Netta looked at Tam and smiled, happiness sloughing years from her face, giving her back, if only temporarily, the colour and sparkle of her youth. He reached over and squeezed her hand, his own expression unreadable. Unlike Netta, Tam had sensed something was wrong from the minute the message had been delivered by a dour Glasgow policeman who, despite Tam's questions, had communicated nothing other than the fact that Meggie and Matty were in the Inverannan police station.

'Right, lad. In you go.' It was the tone of the sergeant's voice that alerted Tam, warning him that, as he had feared, all was far from well. His first glimpse of his son confirmed his worst suspicions. Instinctively he turned to Netta, grasping her hand more tightly, wishing he could shield her from whatever was coming next.

Netta stared, the smile of welcome frozen on her face. The stocky, sullen-faced youth who had shuffled into the room and was looking at her with no vestige of warmth in his expression couldn't be Matty. Matty had been small, childish still, loving and affectionate. Matty would have run to her, flung his arms round her neck and grinned.

'Well, son, aren't you going to say hello to your mother?' Tam prompted gently.

Matty, who had expected to meet the full force of his parents' wrath was momentarily surprised, then, quickly realising that they didn't yet know about the trouble he was in, grinned and ran towards them. 'Ma. Pa.'

Netta's sense of relief was enormous. As soon as her son smiled she recognised the familiar, impish sparkle in his eyes. He was still her Matty. Bigger and with all trace of babyishness gone, she remembered that at his age two years could make a great deal of difference. She opened her arms and hugged him tightly, taking pleasure in the solid, bulky feel of him, relieved that he was healthy and strong, that no harm had befallen him. Her heart swelled with emotion, her throat tightened so that she couldn't speak. But she refused to cry. Not here. Uncomfortable with such exposed feelings she kissed the top of his head then pulled herself away.

Tam, never a demonstrative man, contented himself by thumping his hand on Matty's shoulder then settled himself purposefully in his seat, making much of straightening his crumpled jacket.

'Sit down then, lad. We'll need to have a wee talk, your folks and me.' The sergeant who had waited in the doorway now took charge, sitting himself next to Matty on one side of the table, facing Tam and Netta.

'When can we take him and Meggie home?' Netta asked,

anxious to be gone from this place, to return them to the warmth and comfort of their family.

'I don't know about the lassie but the lad here won't be going home with you. Not yet a while.'

Netta darted a look at Tam who looked resolutely in front of him. She then gazed at her son who fidgeted and stared at the table top.

The sergant, a man with small sympathy for young criminals or their parents, said, 'Your son is in a great deal of trouble, Mr McPherson. Stealing; selling stolen goods; resisting arrest; attacking a police officer . . .'

'Matty!' Netta's voice was weak with horror. 'Surely not? Och, Sergeant, you must be mistaken. Matty's a good lad. He would never steal.'

'With all due respect, Mrs McPherson, the lad has been in front of the magistrate before so I think we can say there's no mistake. Then again, you'd hardly be in a position to know, would youse, seeing as you've not seen the boy for two years.' The condemnation was clear. Netta flushed and looked down at her hands, twisting them desperately in her lap.

'Maybe you should tell us what happened?' Tam suggested warily, then listened in growing shame as Matty's crimes, proven and suspected were reeled off.

'A bad record for a lad of his age,' the sergeant ended.

'What in the name were you thinking of?' Tam exploded. 'You were raised to know right from wrong.'

'It wasn't my fault,' Matty protested.

'What will happen now?' Tam turned to the sergeant. 'Is he to go to court?'

The sergeant laughed, a hard, unsympathetic sound, and grinned at them, obviously enjoying his role. 'He was up before the magistrate yesterday afternoon. And a very poor impression he made, never saying sorry, bragging about all the things he'd stolen. Cocky little bugger. Got what he deserved in my book. It's the likes of him that'll give this town a bad name unless they're taught a sharp lesson.' This is what made his job worthwhile. If he had his way no villain would be allowed in Inverannan. They'd be driven out, along with the left-footers, the prostitutes and the English, leaving the town clean for God-fearing folk to enjoy. He waited a minute, relishing the interplay of frowning glances, dawning comprehension, fear and disappointment between the boy and his parents. 'Tomorrow he's to go to the Stathannan County Institution for Boys. A place of correction. A reformatory,' he added, in case there should be any misunderstanding.

'He's being sent away?' Netta gasped, comprehending only that her son was being snatched away from her again.

'Aye. For twelve months.' The sergeant nodded in satisfaction. 'Well, I daresay he's a fair bit of explaining to do. I'll give youse a wee while to yourselves.'

'Thank you,' Tam muttered, unable to meet the sergeant's eyes, ashamed to know that this could happen to a son of his.

'Meggie!' Netta shouted as the sergeant reached the door. 'What about Meggie?'

'Och aye, the lassie. Sort the lad out first. I'll bring the girl down later.' With that he went back to his duties a happy man, detailing a constable to stand guard outside the door.

'You stupid little bugger.' Tam's fury unleashed itself the second the door closed.

'It wasn't my fault, Pa,' Matty muttered.

'Not your fault? How do you make that out?' Tam was on his feet now, his face white with the effort of control.

'Tam, Tam,' Netta pleaded. 'Listen to him. Give him a chance.'

Tam looked at his wife then back at his son who was sitting with his shoulders hunched, his head lowered, a picture of misery. 'All right.' He sank back on to the chair and waited impatiently for his son to justify his disgrace.

Netta leaned over and squeezed Matty's shoulder. 'Go on, son. We're listening,' she encouraged him gently.

'What's the point?' he asked bitterly. 'You won't believe me. No one believes me.'

'I will believe you, Matty,' she promised him. 'Tell us what happened. When we know the truth, maybe we can help you.'

'It wasn't my fault,' Matty repeated. 'It was Meggie. She made me do it. We had no money so she made me steal things.'

'Meggie?' Netta couldn't keep the sharp disbelief out of her voice.

Meggie was mischievous, prone to getting herself into scrapes but surely, as fiercely protective of Matty as she was, she would never have sent him out to steal?

'See! I knew you wouldn't believe me,' Matty accused, allowing tears to trickle down his dirty face. 'I knew you'd be on her side.'

Netta felt ashamed, knew she hadn't even given him a chance. 'I do believe you, Matty,' she assured him, touched by his desperation, his unhappiness. 'Tell me exactly what you did.'

'It was Meggie. She hated it in the workhouse. She said we should run away and find you. Och Ma, I missed you, I wanted to come home.'

Netta smiled at him. 'So you ran away?'

'Aye. Meggie said she'd look after me. We went to Aunty

Lil but she told us you weren't there any more. I wanted to go back to the workhouse then but Meggie wouldn't go. We didn't have any money so she sent me to the barrows to nick something to eat.'

'But you know it's wrong to steal, Matty,' Tam interrupted him.

'Aye. I know, but we had no money, Pa, and nothing to eat. Meggie said it didn't matter if I nicked a few things so long as I didn't get collared.'

Tam watched as his son spoke, feeling flickers of disquiet at the easy use of gutter slang, the way the boy's eyes rarely met his. 'And what happened then? Did you stay there or did you come back here?'

'We stayed a wee while but then we came back here. We lived in the castle ruins for a while and Meggie sent me out to steal food. It was easy, Pa. I took milk from the milk cart and bread . . .' He stopped himself just in time, knowing he sounded too proud of what he had done. 'Then we got jobs at the Houlets' Nest.' He waited to see if his father recognised what sort of place this was. Tam's tight frown, the sudden jerk of shock told him he did.

'Jobs? At your age?' Netta asked, appalled. 'In a public house?'

'Aye. I helped in the kitchen. And Meggie helped the other girls, you know, with the men. Then she met Mr Wallace.' He delivered the damning words with a cunning show of innocence.

'Men . . .?' Netta's face drained of colour, she felt sick and clutched wildly for Tam's hand. He didn't respond, frozen by shock.

Matty went on. 'I didn't like him, Ma. I didn't want to go, Pa, but she made me. We had a wee house, all to ourselves. Mr Wallace paid for it and gave Meggie money for food, but she made me go out every night when he came to see her. It was cold outside, Ma,' he whined now. 'And sometimes I had to stay out all night.'

Netta shook her head, unable to speak.

'I told Meggie we should go back to the workhouse, Pa, but she wouldn't. Mr Wallace, he never gave her enough money so I had to go and nick things, things to sell so we could buy food. I didn't want to but she made me. Honest, Pa, I didn't want to.'

'And that's when you got caught?' Tam asked, his voice hard.

Matty nodded, forcing tears to flow again. 'I was glad. I knew if I got caught that the police would find you. I'm sorry Ma, I didn't mean to do wrong. I was only trying to help.' He broke down into noisy sobs. 'I wanted to come home, Ma,' he choked.

'Och, Matty . . .' Netta ran round the table and gathered him into her arms. They clung together, her tears dripping into his hair while Tam looked on, his mind reeling.

'I'm sorry, Ma,' Matty sobbed. 'I know I've been bad but I didn't mean it.'

'I know, son. I know,' she soothed.

'It was Meggie, Ma. She wouldn't listen. She's changed, Ma.'

For want of somewhere else to put her, Meggie had spent the night in a police cell. Now, heavy-eyed from lack of sleep, she slumped despondently in the corner of the narrow bed and wondered what was going to happen to her. She viewed the future with a peculiar detachment, knowing that, for now at least, it was out of her hands. She was almost glad, relieved to be rid of the constant worry, the responsibility, the sense of failure which always over-whelmed her when she thought about Matty. Exhausted, she felt her eyes close and jumped when the door opened.

'Right,' the sergeant was shouting at her even before he appeared in the cell. 'Tidy yourself up. Your mother and father are upstairs.'

Momentarily confused, Meggie blinked herself awake. 'Ma and Pa? They're here?' Her tired eyes cleared, then brightened with excitement. She leapt off the bed and hurriedly sluiced her face and hands with water from the metal bowl which stood on the floor in the corner. Carefully she eased open the top button of her skirt so that it didn't strain so noticeably across her stomach, then pulled her loose cardigan over her blouse, confident that it would be enough to keep her condition hidden, at least until she had had time to make her parents understand why she had been forced to behave as she had.

'Upstairs,' the sergeant barked impatiently, his whole manner contemptuous. When they arrived outside the room where Matty and her parents were still talking, he opened the door and shoved her inside.

Her Ma and Pa looked exactly as she remembered them. Meggie simply feasted her eyes on her parents, too choked to speak, her face alive with joy, tears making her eyes unnaturally bright. She stood there for what seemed to be a very long time, smiling at the way her mother was embracing Matty, waiting for them to turn to her. Perhaps they hadn't noticed her. 'Ma,' she whispered. 'Pa?'

Slowly Netta raised her face from Matty's head and stared at her daughter. The coldness in that look chilled Meggie to the bone and she could only stand, frozen in the doorway.

While Netta still glared at her daughter the sergeant

250

pushed into the room and caught Matty roughly by the arm. 'Time to go, lad. Say goodbye to your parents.'

'Ma!' Panic-stricken, Matty appealed desperately to his mother. 'Don't let them take me, Ma.'

Netta held on to her son's arm. 'No, he's not a bad boy. Let him come home with us.'

'Aye.' At last Tam seemed to find his senses. 'We'll take him home. He'll not be any more bother.' Still he hadn't looked at his daughter.

'Sorry, sir. It's by order of the court. There's nothing I can do. The lad's to go to the reformatory this afternoon. I daresay you'll be able to visit if you want to.' He tugged hard on the boy and Netta allowed her hand to drop limply away.

'Matty . . .' Meggie held out a hand to her brother.

He stopped and stared at her, cold hatred in his eyes. 'This is all your fault, Meggie,' he hissed. 'I hate you. I hate you . . .' He was still screaming it when the sergeant dragged him from the room and slammed the door, leaving Meggie alone with her parents.

Now Tam rose and walked slowly across the room to face his daughter. Meggie saw the cold anger on his face and for the first time in her life, was truly afraid of him. She backed against the door. 'Pa, listen to me. Please,' she begged.

'Whore,' he roared, slapping her face, making her ears ring. 'Bloody little whore. A prostitute at the Houlets' Nest, kept by a man and taking Matty, *my son,* with you. Letting him see your evil ways, showing him things no child of his age has any right to know. Sending him out to steal for you.'

'Ma, please try to understand,' Meggie begged, turning to her mother. 'I was just trying to take care of Matty.'

'By making him a thief, by locking him out while you fornicated with a man?' her father asked.

'No!'

'Don't bother with your lies,' he spat. 'You've ruined your brother. He'll carry the mark with him for the rest of his life.'

'I didn't,' she cried, but knew he wasn't listening. 'Ma,' she appealed frantically to her mother who was watching her in silence. 'Please. I want to come home.'

Netta ignored her, wouldn't even meet her eyes. She spoke instead to her husband. 'Take me away from here, Tam.'

Tam McPherson put his arm round his wife's shoulders and led her to the door.

'Pa, please don't leave me here,' Meggie pleaded as they walked down the passageway.

It was Netta who answered, turning to face Meggie at last, her eyes filled with sadness. 'I can't take you home, Meggie, not with what you are, what you've done. I've the other weans to think about. I couldn't have you living in the same house as the weans, not now.' Her voice was soft, broken, as if her own sorrow was too great to bear. Mercifully unaware of the even greater disgrace hidden under Meggie's shapeless cardigan, Netta tucked her hand firmly in her husband's arm, held her head high and together they walked out of their daughter's life.

Two hours later Meggie, her face still ravaged by misery, found herself being subjected to the humiliating routine of admission to the workhouse. Naked, aware of the shameful bulge of her abdomen, she shivered as rough hands scrubbed at her skin and then doused her with freezing water.

'Get out. Dry yourself and get dressed.' Agnes Meikle-john, a bitter-tongued girl Meggie remembered from before, watched as she hurriedly dragged the shapeless, beige dress over her damp hair.

'Aye, you thought you were better than the rest of us, didn't you, Meggie McPherson?' she sneered. 'And look where it got you. Now everyone can see what a slut you really are.'

Meggie bit her lip, refusing to be goaded.

'Aye, that's right, say nothing. Better that way. No decent lassie will want to speak to you now, not after what you've done. And you'll not be able to hide it for long, not in that dress.'

'You'll make sure everyone knows anyway,' Meggie retorted, her fighting spirit not yet dead.

'Watch your mouth! I'm the senior assistant now and you show some respect. Now, pick up your things and come with me. Mrs Cruickshank wants to see you.'

Meggie knocked on the superintendent's door in some trepidation. She had liked and respected the older woman and was conscious both of having let her down and of her own disgrace.

'Come in.' The voice, loud, deep and firm was the same as she remembered it. Nervously, Meggie turned the handle and went in, keeping her eyes lowered, fully expecting to face a tirade of accusations.

'Margaret McPherson.'

'Yes, Mrs Cruickshank.' Meggie spoke up bravely, only the slight tremor in her voice betraying her nervousness.

'Come in, lass. Sit down.' Mrs Cruickshank's voice was kind.

Meggie sat stiffly on an upright chair, across the desk from Mrs Cruickshank, who looked at her closely. Dear

Lord, she thought sadly, noting the pallor of Meggie's cheeks, the deep shadows under her eyes, the downward quiver of the pretty mouth, what had happened to Meggie McPherson to change her from the bright, responsible girl she remembered into this defeated creature? Thoughtfully she got up and walked round the desk, pulling another chair up so that she could sit close to Meggie.

'Now, lass, don't be frightened. I'm here to help you.'

Meggie, expecting condemnation, finding only kindness, finally looked up. 'I'm going to have a baby,' she said, needing to know now whether the sympathy she thought she had heard would endure once the full extent of her disgrace was known.

'I know.' Mrs Cruickshank patted her softly on the shoulder. 'Perhaps you should tell me all about it, Meggie. Tell me what happened to you, from the day you left here. Then we'll work out what's to be done about it.'

'I can't,' Meggie shook her head, the dark hair, still damp, falling to cover her face.

'Aye, you can, lass. You need someone to talk to. You'll make yourself ill if you carry your troubles all inside yourself. And you've got the wee one to think about now. However bad you might think it is, I'll have heard worse. There's nothing you can say that will shock me, Meggie.'

As if in response to the words the child moved, kicking unmistakably, rippling the skin of Meggie's belly. Instinctively she put a protective hand over it. Stunned, she realised for the first time that this was a living creature. Wide-eyed, she looked at Mrs Cruickshank. 'What am I going to do?' she asked.

Gradually, over the next hour, Mrs Cruickshank drew her story from her. Then, an arm round the exhausted girl's shoulders she led her upstairs and, under the curious eyes of the other women, helped her into bed.

'Rest now,' she told Meggie. 'You're safe here for now. I'll talk to you again the morn.'

Meggie's eyes fluttered and closed even as she spoke.

Downstairs, in her own bedroom, it was a long time before Mrs Cruickshank managed to fall asleep.

'You could stay here,' she told Meggie the next day, relieved to see some colour creeping back into the girl's cheeks. 'Or, if you'd prefer, there's a home for unmarried mothers near Kirkcaldy. Maybe you'd rather go there, where no one will know you?'

Meggie knew that the workhouse was just that, that even the elderly inmates were expected to work for their keep, knew too that although married women were sometimes allowed to have their children here, the unmarried girls were usually sent to suffer their disgrce elsewhere. After all she had been through she was desperate to cling on to the sympathy and understanding she felt emanating from this misleadingly stern-faced woman. 'Can I really stay here?' she asked.

A woman who was inspired in her work by a genuine desire to help those who were unable to help themelves, Mrs Cruickshank felt desperately sorry for this young girl. And more than that, she liked Meggie. There was something about her – the lack of bitterness, the determined way in which she had adapted to the workhouse routines before, striving to learn the skills which would eventually give her independence – which demanded admiration. Even the ill-fated bid to find her parents had been motivated by loyalty, the deep feeling of responsibility Meggie had for her young brother. And underneath all this, Mrs Cruickshank was aware of her own sense of guilt, the nagging knowledge that by failing to report the youngsters' escape she had contributed to the tragic circumstances which had brought Meggie back to the workhouse. The girl had been let down and betrayed too many times. Mrs Cruickshank resolved, to do her very best to help her now.

'According to the rules you can stay for as long as you can work for your keep. You're a bright lass, Meggie. I don't see any reason why you shouldn't help me with the paperwork right up until the baby's born. From what you say you've done that sort of thing before.'

Meggie flushed slightly at the reminder of her days at the Houlets' Nest. 'I'd like that,' she murmured.

'Good, that's settled then. But what will you do then, lass? Have you thought about what you'll do after the child is born?'

Meggie shook her head. 'I don't know.'

'Does your mother know?'

'I don't think so.'

'You know, lass. I think your mother and father are good folk. They brought you here because they honestly thought it was for the best. From what you've told me about yesterday they were deeply shocked by what had happened to you and Matty. But maybe, after they've had a wee while to calm down, it would be a good idea to go and see them?'

'No!' Meggie was horrified, knew already what her father's reaction would be.

'Think about it, Meggie. On your own and with no man to support you you'll never manage. Folk in this town look down on lassies like you. It's wrong, but the wean will be made to suffer, too. If you can't persuade your mother and father to take you in the best thing would be to have it adopted. Let it go to some loving home and leave yourself free to get a job and start a life of your own.'

'My mother and father will never accept a baby.'

Mrs Cruickshank knew Meggie was probably right and it wasn't an unusual reaction. Almost all the pregnant young girls who came through here had been thrown out by their own parents. 'Well then, it'll have to go for adoption,' she said firmly, adding, when she saw the lingering doubt in the girl's face, 'It's for the best. All our babies go to good homes. It'll get things you could never give it. It'll be hard for you, Meggie, but it is the right thing to do. For both of you.'

'I suppose so. But couldn't I stay here with the baby?'

'No, lass. It's not allowed. This workhouse is supported by the church. The board won't allow it.' But she knew it wasn't so much the moral issue which was behind this ruling, as the economic one. The board members believed that allowing the mothers to keep their children prevented them from going out and finding work to support themselves, giving the parish the burden of two extra mouths to feed.

'Would I know where it went?'

'No. It's better to make a clean break.'

'I don't think I've got much choice,' Meggie said, with such sadness that Mrs Cruickshank felt her own stomach twist in sympathy. But when she spoke her voice was deliberately brisk.

'Nor do I. Now then, fetch those files over here and we'll see whether you can do the book-keeping for me.'

Meggie settled down to the routine of the workhouse easily enough. If the other women, jealous of her favoured position were hostile, she refused to notice it and simply busied herself with her job.

The books, meticulously kept by Mrs Cruickshank

herself, posed no great problems for Meggie, who was grateful for something which kept her mind off the future. Her day was spent behind a desk in the inner hall and her duties included admitting visitors. Because of this, her standard beige dresses were newer and smarter than those worn by the other women and gave them further grounds for resentment. She was glad that the dresses were loose enough to hide her condition though she knew that before long it would be only too obvious to everyone.

'The board are coming for their annual inspection at two o'clock tomorrow afternoon, Meggie,' Mrs Cruickshank told her during her second week. 'Make sure you are neat and tidy and, when they arrive, greet them politely, ask them to wait in the hall and tell me right away.'

'Yes, Mrs Cruickshank.'

Certain that Meggie could be trusted to greet the visitors politely, the superintendent hurried away to set a vigorous cleaning plan in action.

Meggie was neat in a freshly-laundered dress, her hair tied tightly back, her shoes polished and her desk newly dusted and tidy. She worked diligently at the books, keeping one eye on the door, anxious to be seen to be fully occupied when the board arrived.

When the bell jangled at precisely two o'clock she rose from her seat, smoothed down her dress, pulled in her stomach and hurried to open the door.

'I believe we are expected.' Mrs Elsie Laing, chairman of the board, spoke over Meggie's polite welcome and strode into the main hall. She was followed by half a dozen other august personages, including her husband.

He, not having bothered even to glance at the menial who had admitted them, avoided his wife and made unimportant

258

conversation with the minister, wishing only to be done with this irksome obligation and get back to his office. Being Provost was a position which guaranteed him respect and prestige but it did have its share of unpleasant duties.

'I'll tell Mrs Cruickshank that you are here.' Meggie, uncomfortably aware of her shameful bulk, kept her eyes downcast, so failing to notice Wallace, and hurried to knock on Mrs Cruickshank's door.

'Ah . . .' Mrs Cruickshank eyed the waiting inspection team without pleasure then, turning to Mr Carlyle who was in bad-mannered occupation of her chair, asked, 'Are you ready?'

Carlyle rose, took his time about extinguishing his foul-smelling cigarette, straightened his tie, then, with an unexpected burst of speed, pushed past her, almost flattening her against the doorpost, and strode out into the foyer.

'Mrs Laing! How very nice to see you and how very well you are looking, my dear,' he lied unctuously, extending a hand which she ignored.

'If we could just get on with it,' Elsie Laing snapped.

Snubbed, Carlyle scowled. Mrs Cruickshank smiled and stepped forward. 'If you would like to follow me,' she invited with the blend of deference and self-assuredness which had won her respect on several similar occasions. 'The usual short tour of the building first, I think.'

Judging the amount of respect shown by the other woman to be correct, Mrs Laing allowed herself to nod and smile graciously. 'Thank you, Mrs Cruickshank.' She turned, rounding up her fellow board members with one imperious sweep of her eyes. They fell obediently into line behind her as Mrs Cruickshank led the way up the stairs. Carlyle, inwardly fuming, brought up the rear, skulking at their heels like a bad-tempered dog.

259

Back at her desk, Meggie trying to make herself as inconspicuous as possible, bent her head assiduously over her work. Behind her, Wallace climbed the stairs, his gaze resting disinterestedly on the drab female who had admitted them. The shock of recognition was so great that he missed a step and stumbled, grabbing the banister for support. The unexpected sight of Meggie, her hair scraped back, the muddy hue of the shapeless dress drawing the colour from her face, shook him deeply. Until now his conscience had been partially appeased by the genuine belief that she had returned to her parents, without a doubt the best place for a girl in her situation. But now, here she was, in the workhouse.

The depth of his betrayal of a girl who was little more than a child, a girl whose family had obviously rejected her, just as she must think he had, suddenly seemed unforgivable. But, much as he longed to see her again, he knew it would be impossible to resume the relationship, or even to offer help, without exposing himself. Preoccupied, still light-headed with shock, he trailed round the workhouse, seeing the dormitories with their lines of metal-framed beds, their thin blankets, their lack of privacy, with new eyes, knowing what such a place would do to a proud, independent girl like Meggie. There must be something he could do to help her without risking his own reputation. But what?

Back in his office Wallace Laing ignored the letters, invoices and demands awaiting his attention and stood staring out of his window over the dark roofs of the town. In the distance, the workhouse was easily distinguishable, its forbidding, grey exterior only hinting at the bleakness inside. His gaze settled on it and stayed there.

An hour later he donned his hat and coat and walked through the town to the office of his solicitor.

'Sell the little house,' he instructed the elderly man. 'And when it is done I want the money in cash.'

The solicitor who had drawn his own conclusions about the precise use to which the house had been put, was wise enough to make no comment, even when the terms of the legal letter which was to accompany the money were explained to him.

Satisfied that he had done all he reasonably could, Wallace abandoned all thought of work and, much to the amazement of his wife, returned home early.

Two months later, looking surprisingly unsure of himself, Wallace welcomed Mrs Cruickshank into his office.

'Come in. Sit down,' he said, shutting the door firmly and lowering his voice to a confidential whisper to avoid all chance of his secretary overhearing.

'I must say I was surprised when you asked me to come here, Mr Laing,' Mrs Cruickshank admitted. 'If it is some matter concerning the workhouse, then all my records are there.'

'It is a personal matter, Mrs Cruickshank, though not unconnected with the workhouse. But first, I must ask you to respect my privacy and keep everything I will tell you in strict confidence. Do you follow?'

Intrigued, she responded briskly, 'I am not a gossip, Mr Laing. Nothing you say will be repeated by me.'

'Aye . . . well, I am sure we understand one another then.'

There were two or three minutes of uncomfortable silence as Wallace wondered how best to say what had to be said. Mrs Cruickshank peeled off her gloves, easing out each finger at a time, then laid them with neat precision along the edge of his desk. Smiling, betraying no sign of the impatience and curiosity she was feeling, she sat back and waited.

'The girl Meggie McPherson,' he started.

So that was it! Those four words, together with the incomplete facts that Meggie had given her, told her everything. 'Yes?'

'I have something for her.' He fiddled with a sealed envelope. 'I . . . I knew Meggie before she came to the workhouse. Aye,' he blustered now. 'She's a sweet wee thing and deserves better. I'd like to help.'

'I am sure you would, Mr Laing.'

Wallace frowned at the rather acid quality of that comment but, committed now, had to go on. 'I wish to give her a sum of money – to help her, you understand. But there are certain conditions, set out in this letter.' He handed it to her and went on. 'The money will only be handed over if the child she is carrying is adopted. Until then you will keep it for her. My name must not come into it.'

'Meggie McPherson is far from stupid, Mr Laing. She will know where it came from.'

'I daresay she will. But there will be no written proof. Even my solicitor does not know the name of the recipient.'

'I see.' Her lip curled in disdain but then she softened. At least he was doing something for the girl. Too many men simply walked away and closed their minds to the heart-break they caused.

'Now, I know as well as you do that under the rules of the workhouse, inmates are not allowed to receive personal gifts, that, strictly speaking, this should be paid into the parish funds. That, Mrs Cruickshank is why I have to throw myself on your mercy.'

'You are asking me to break the law, Mr Laing?'

'Aye. I am,' he admitted, looking her straight in the eye. 'And you know why, Mrs Cruickshank. Meggie McPherson is a good girl, though she'll have a hard time convincing anyone of that after what she's been through. I believe you are fond of her yourself else you'd have shuffled her off to one of those homes for fallen women.' He watched her closely and knew he was right. Encouraged he went on. 'This is the only way I can help her. What I want to know, Mrs Cruickshank, is will you help me?'

Mrs Cruickshank rose slowly and went to stare out of his window. 'If this should become known, Mr Laing, I could lose my position.'

'There is no reason why anyone should know. And I am even more vulnerable than you.'

'Yes.' It was non-committal, discouraging.

'Surely you can see that I have a moral obligation, Mrs Cruickshank?'

'I certainly do see that, Mr Laing,' she agreed tartly.

'Mrs Cruickshank, I do not much care what you must think of me, but I will tell you that I have a very real fondness for Meggie. I can't let her life be ruined because of an old man's folly,' he ended with surprising candour.

When Mrs Cruickshank turned round she was smiling. She walked towards him and offered her hand. 'Very well, Mr Laing. I will help you. For Meggie's sake.'

'Thank you.' He grasped her hand and shook it firmly. 'And you will advise her, help her to use the money wisely?'

'I will do my best,' she assured him. 'My very best.'

CHAPTER FOURTEEN

$\mathbf{M}$eggie queued with the other women for the portion of lumpy porridge with which the workhouse inmates started their days. As usual, she stood alone, ignored by the other women who, resentful of the apparent favouritism shown to her by Mrs Cruickshank, had seized on Meggie's pregnancy as a reason to make her the target of much spitefulness. Meggie defended herself by retreating into silence and conducting herself with as much dignity as her situation allowed.

Balancing the bowl on the ledge created by her swollen abdomen Meggie reached for a mug of tea. As she did so she was jostled violently from the side. The porridge clattered to the ground, splattering over her dress and across a wide area of the flagged floor. Beside her someone sniggered. Angrily she whirled round and found herself facing Agnes Meiklejohn, the senior assistant.

'What did you do that for?' Meggie demanded.

'Do what?' Agnes asked, feigning innocence.

'You pushed me,' Meggie blazed.

Around the two girls the other women fell silent, relishing the climax to an argument which had been brewing for weeks.

'I pushed you?' Agnes spoke loudly, making sure of her audience. 'I wouldn't lower myself to touch the likes of you, McPherson!'

Meggie tried to walk away but found herself surrounded by half a dozen of Agnes's friends.

'Look at you,' Agnes sneered. 'Mrs Cruickshank's wee

pet. Trying to make out you're better than the rest of us when all the time you're just a dirty little scrubber, a wee tramp from the Houlets' Nest. A prostitute.'

Meggie felt sick but stood perfectly still, determined to deny them the pleasure of seeing how badly shaken she was.

Agnes grinned then spoke to the assembled women. 'Aye, she's been with hundreds of men and any one of them could have fathered that wean.'

'*No!*' Meggie screamed in outraged defence of her unborn child.

'Aye.' Agnes grinned, then leaned over and, quite deliberately, tipped a mug of tea over the floor where it mingled unpleasantly with the congealing porridge. 'Now get that mess cleared up.' Agnes waited for the explosion of temper which she hoped would result in an unfavourable report to Mrs Cruickshank and the withdrawal of all privileges, including the loss of Meggie's job – one she coveted for herself.

Shaking with fury, Meggie opened her mouth to yell at Agnes, to give full rein to the emotions which were burning in her mind. But when she saw the avid way the other woman was watching her she swallowed the angry words, understanding that Agnes was deliberately goading her. And then she realised that the worst had already happened, that there was nothing they could say or do which would hurt more than she was already hurting. That knowledge gave her added courage. When she faced Agnes again it was with chilling determination to stand up for herself. 'Do it yourself,' she said, her voice carrying clearly to the watching inmates.

'What's going on here?' Carlyle, the source of Agnes's information, came from the back of the room.

'McPherson won't do as she's told,' Agnes simpered.

'Clean this mess up. Now!' Carlyle ordered.

'No.' Meggie's voice was flat and her face was expressionless. But there was something about her that warned Carlyle that she would not submit. To have her openly disobey him in front of the other inmates would only make him look foolish. He stared at her, allowing his baleful gaze to rest obviously on her distended belly.

'As you have no shame of your own, I will ask the minister to point it out to you, as a lesson to the other women and in the hope that you will mend your ways. And until you can come and apologise to me for your lack of respect and convince me that you are truly repentant for your evil ways, you will take your meals alone, after everyone else has eaten.'

'Yes, Mr Carlyle,' Meggie answered clearly, her dark eyes meeting his pale ones without flickering.

Carlyle recoiled from the contempt he read there. It was he who looked away first and he hurried from the room, calling back as he went, 'Get that mess cleaned up, Agnes.'

It was a white-faced and exhausted Meggie who filed into the kirk that Sunday morning. There was a dragging sensation in her lower back and the child, as if exhausted too, was still, like a lead weight dragging at her every movement. All she really wanted to do was sleep. As the service got under way she allowed her mind to drift, not even noticing when the minister ascended the pulpit steps and began his sermon.

It was a full twenty minutes later before she gradually became aware of a restlessness around her and stirred, refocusing her attention on her immediate surroundings. To her consternation people were turning round and staring at her with open disapprobation. Too late she remembered

Carlyle's threat and looked up to find the minister glaring straight at her as he delivered the final words of a humiliating public denouncement.

'Fallen women can have no place in decent society,' he thundered. 'But, as Christians, we shall pray for this child to see the error of her sinful ways.' With a final searing glance in her direction he bowed his head and launched into a lengthy prayer.

Heart thumping, face bleached of all colour, Meggie wished she had never been born.

The walk back to the workhouse seemed harder than ever before. Meggie's legs felt unnaturally heavy and the child pressed down on her, draining her of all energy.

While the other inmates ate their dinner she sat miserably in the scullery, glad to have been separated from them, knowing she couldn't face their scorn today. Mrs Cruickshank, appalled by the minister's callous words, came to check on her and was shocked by her pallor.

'Here,' she said. 'I've saved you some dinner.'

Meggie shook her head. 'I'm not hungry.'

'I know you're upset, Meggie, but you must try to eat. For the child's sake.'

Meggie looked at the single thin slice of greyish, fatty meat, the lump of congealing potatoes and the watery cabbage and felt her stomach heave. Again she shook her head.

'Then drink some milk.' Mrs Cruickshank filled a mug straight from the churn which was delivered every day and put it in the girl's hands. As she did so she felt them clench, saw Meggie's jaw tighten and heard the sharply indrawn breath of pain.

'So,' she said with deliberate lightness. 'It's time, is it?'

'I think so.' Meggie's eyes were shadowed with fear.

'Don't be frightened, Meggie. Be glad. A few hours and it'll all be over. As soon as you're strong again you'll be able to get out of here. Isn't that what you want?'

'Aye.' Above all else. 'But where to, Mrs Cruickshank? Who would give me a job now?' The last hours seemed to have drained her of hope as well as energy.

'We'll find you something, lass. In a few weeks you can put all this behind you. If it gets hard for you, you just think of that.'

There was such certainty in the older woman's voice that despite herself Meggie felt cheered and managed a weak smile.

'That's better. Now come away upstairs. There's a bed all ready for you in the infirmary and I'll ask the nurse to come and see to you.'

Alone with a hard-faced, impatient nurse, Meggie laboured to give birth to her child. By evening the pain was constant, assaulting her body in hot, cramping waves of agony.

The nurse settled herself comfortably in a chair at the bottom of the bed and concentrated on her knitting, unmoved by her patient's pain and stirring only occasionally to make a rough examination between Meggie's legs. She offered no encouragement, no sympathy and when Meggie asked how much longer this would go on, shrugged dismissively.

'It hurts,' Meggie gasped as her body tightened in another fierce contraction.

'Should have thought of that before you got yourself in this state.'

Meggie clenched her teeth, bit down on the pain and held on to the metal rail at the top of the bed, determined not to give anyone the satisfaction of hearing her cry out. Just before midnight the pain changed, becoming sharper, more urgent, bringing a greater sensation of pressure with it and the imperative urge to push. Meggie resisted for as long as she could, then gave way and strained downwards, grunting and red-faced.

The nurse placidly finished her row, folded her knitting and placed it in her bag before rolling up her sleeves and shoving the sheets off Meggie's perspiring body. 'At last,' she said.

The next hour passed in a haze of pain. Not once did Meggie cry out, not even when the pain became so extreme that she feared she might not survive the birth. She knew it was possible, had heard the other women in their loud talk of death and blood and pain. And then, when she thought she could bear no more, there was a feeling of movement. The mass which had been pressing down on her and causing such agony moved. Moments later, with a huge last effort the child slipped between her legs, bringing instant relief. Meggie raised her head and caught a glimpse of a red, wrinkled body, of tiny, clenched fists and a shock of dark hair. Before she could see more the midwife turned away to the bowl which was standing ready and Meggie heard the gentle splashing of water, followed by the miraculous sound of an infant's cries.

'Let me see,' she pleaded, holding out her arms.

The nurse turnd round, the child in her arms now wrapped loosely in a white towel, and for a moment her heart went out to the girl on the bed. Like most women of her generation she had nothing but contempt for girls like Meggie, had seen at first hand the unhappiness which resulted from illegitimacy. But, despite her hardened manner, she could not help admiring this girl who had endured her labour with such silent stoicism.

'Please,' Meggie begged again.

'Just for a minute then.' Gently the nurse lowered the child into Meggie's arms.

Meggie touched the baby's face, marvelling to see a fringe of dark eyelashes, the fine line of eyebrows, the perfectly formed nose, the delicate pink mouth, and smiled. So completely feminine was she that Meggie knew, without looking any further, that she had a daughter. Instinctively she cradled the child close and smiled when the tiny mouth turned in towards her breasts.

'Give her back to me now, lass.' The nurse's voice was soft and kind now, her resistence undone by the pure emotion of the moment.

Meggie looked up, her eyes wide with horror. 'No!'

'It's for the best, lass. You know you can't keep her.' Firmly the nurse extracted the child from Meggie's arms. As if sensing the finality of the separation, the baby mewled, her little fists waving outside the warm confines of the towel.

'No! Please. Let me have her. Just for a minute.' So many times Meggie had agonised over the child's fate, reluctantly accepting that to keep the baby would be to deny it the chance of a happy, secure future. It had all seemed so sensible, so logical. But now, with the first touch of that warm, delicate skin, all rational thought had been abandoned. She yearned to cradle her child, to protect it and lavish on it the love which was swelling in her heart. But then, in a flash of desolating clarity, Meggie saw that to do so would be an act of unforgivable selfishness which would condemn them both to a life of poverty and, worse, ostracism. 'Please. Let me say goodbye.'

The nurse shook her head and turned away so that she wouldn't have to look at the pain on the girl's face; then, rocking the child gently to try and silence its cries took her from the room.

It was then that Meggie screamed, the heart-rending sound echoing round the high-ceilinged room and along the empty corridors.

A week later, looking strained and pale, Meggie emerged to take her place in the workhouse routine. Her eyes seemed dull, as if some vital spark had been extinguished, and she moved among the others like a wraith, seldom speaking, never smiling.

Mrs Cruickshank got her back to her job, piling unnecessary work on her in an effort to over-ride her misery. But it was six weeks before she got the first flicker of response and a further week before Meggie said unexpectedly, when they were checking the accounts together, 'Thank you.'

Mrs Cruickshank closed the ledger and sighed. 'You've been through a difficult time, lass, but you must put it behind you now.'

'I know,' Meggie sighed 'You were right. It's better this way. But it's so hard. . .'

'I know, lass. I know.' Mrs Cruickshank squeezed Meggie's hand and swallowed hard to contain her own emotion. 'You can't stay here, Meggie. You do know that, don't you?'

'Aye.' But suddenly the thought of leaving, of going out to face the world alone, frightened her. 'Couldn't I work here? I wouldn't want any wages. I can earn my keep.'

'Och, Meggie, this is no place for you. Anyway,' she added briskly, 'the board wouldn't allow it. This is for folk who can't support themselves. Folk who are too old, too young or too ill to fend for themselves.'

'Then what will I do?'

'I've been meaning to talk to you about that. I've something to give you.' Bertha Cruickshank unlocked the drawer of her desk, pulled out a plump envelope and slid it across the desk. 'Open it. It's yours.'

Meggie pulled out four thick bundles of notes and then sat staring at them, too stunned to speak.

'There's a great deal of money there, Meggie. Enough to set you up.'

'But it can't be . . . can't be for me.'

'It is for you.'

'But . . . how? Where did it come from?'

'I can't tell you that. But it is legally yours.'

'Wallace . . .' Meggie breathed, knowing that he was the only possible source of such a vast amount of money. She looked up at Mrs Cruickshank and the woman's silence was enough to confirm her suspicions. 'It was him, wasn't it?'

'I can't say. Please don't press me, Meggie. Just take it and put it to good use.'

'But why didn't you give it to me before?' Now there was anger in her voice. 'I could have kept my baby . . .' She ended with a strangled sob. 'Why didn't you give it to me before?'

Mrs Cruickshank knew she had to lie, that to do otherwise would plunge Meggie back into the deep depression which had held her in its grip for too long now. 'This has only just been given to me.'

Meggie groaned, then said softly, 'I want my baby back, Mrs Cruickshank. I can look after her now.'

'It's too late, Meggie. The child has already been adopted.'

'But she's mine.'

'No. Not any more. You signed the papers and the child was taken for adoption. There is no going back on it.' She sighed heavily. 'Och, lass, even with this money, you, a lass on her own, can't give the child the home she deserves. She's with good, caring folk and you should be grateful that she'll be happy and well cared for.'

'Then I don't want it.' Meggie shoved the money away from her.

'Pull yourself together, Margaret McPherson!' Mrs Cruickshank spoke angrily, startling Meggie. 'You've had a terrible time of it and now that you've got the chance to better yourself, to get out of here, you've got the arrogance to tell me you don't want it.'

'I don't,' Meggie insisted.

'You listen to me! I'd have given anything for a piece of luck like this. The other poor souls in here would be grateful for five pounds each, never mind what you've got there. Take it. Use it so that you never have to go back to a place like the Houlets' Nest, so that you never have to rely on being kept by a man again.'

Meggie flinched. 'I'll never do that again.'

'You might have to.' Mrs Cruickshank was deliberately cruel. 'There aren't many places for girls like you to work, Meggie. Not many folk will take a chance on a girl from the workhouse, especially if they ever find out about the baby. And they might. This is a small town, word soon gets round.'

Meggie thought about all the people in the kirk who had witnessed her public disgrace at the hands of the minister. The stubborn look softened and was replaced by doubt. Mrs Cruickshank saw it and pounced, thrusting the money back at her.

'It's your freedom, Meggie, for goodness' sake take it.'

'But what would I do with it?'

273

Relief made Mrs Cruickshank laugh. 'I've an idea, though maybe you won't like it.'

'What?'

'After lunch I'll take you to see someone, a friend of mine.'

'Where?'

'Wait and see.' And she refused to be drawn further. 'Off you go and finish those books. I want them in perfect order before you leave here.'

And with that, Meggie had to be content.

The little grey town was luxuriating in summer warmth. As the two women stepped out that afternoon the sun was shining, the trees were dressed in lush greenery and folk went about their business with smiles on their faces. Meggie felt her own heart lifting, felt the weight of misery easing, as if melted by the sun.

They walked slowly, strolling along the prosperous High Street, past the ornate gates which guarded the town hall and on, until they were in a steep street of terraced houses. All built of greying stone and topped by darker slates, their windows sparkling, their doorsteps freshly scrubbed and with paintwork in conservative shades of green and brown, they were a fine representation of the solid respectability on which the town prided itself. In the distance, crowning the very top of the hill, were the burgh's largest, most impressive residences, the homes of the rich and successful. Between them and these modest, working-class terraces were the semi-detached villas, bungalows and detached houses of the office workers, managers and tradespeople, a ladder of bricks and mortar by which relative status and affluence could be easily assessed from position on the hillside.

Halfway up the hill, at the point where another road crossed the one they were walking up, Mrs Cruickshank stopped, her face flushed and her breathing slightly laboured from the long climb. 'Here we are,' she announced.

Before Meggie could ask any questions Mrs Cruickshank stepped into a little general store of the type found on many a street corner. Intrigued, Meggie hesitated for a moment, then followed her inside and blinked as her eyes adjusted to the gloom. Mrs Cruickshank greeted the elderly woman who was behind the counter, then turned and beckoned to Meggie.

'Meggie, come and meet my friend, Mrs Binnie. Mildred, this is Margaret McPherson, the lassie I was telling you about.'

'Hello, lass.' Meggie's hand was gripped by a tiny, snowy-haired woman, who peered up at her through palest blue, slightly milky, red-rimmed eyes. Her skin was a crazed multitude of fine lines and the hand which held Meggie's was bony and so slight that Meggie was frightened to return the pressure. But Mildred Binnie's frail appearance was belied by her lively smile, the surprising firmness of her handshake and the unexpectedly youthful lilt of her voice.

Meggie warmed to her immediately. 'Hello, Mrs Binnie.'

The bell above the door pinged and three children came in, taking ages to decide which sweeties to buy with their precious pennies. Mrs Binnie let them choose, laughing with them when they changed their minds and finally slipping extra goodies into the cone-shaped paper bags in which they took away their purchases. Meggie noticed how they all vied for Mrs Binnie's attention, their liking for the elderly lady quite obvious, and saw too that Mrs Binnie enjoyed serving them and knew them all by name. No sooner had they left than others took their place, coming into the shop in twos and threes on their way home from school.

'Aye, I'll miss the bairns,' Mrs Binnie said wistfully, when the shop finally emptied. 'It fair makes my day to have them coming in for a wee chat after school. Now then, come on round the counter, lass. Have a look at it from this side.'

Smiling, Meggie did as she was asked.

'You'll see why it's all getting a bit too much for me,' Mrs Binnie said cheerfully. 'My old joints aren't up to all this standing and bending and there's not much time to sit down. There's aye someone coming in.'

As if to demonstrate the point a man came in, asking for tobacco and cigarette papers, closely followed by a woman who bought a paper.

Meggie, who was now beginning to suspect what was afoot, turned to Mrs Cruickshank, who shook her head and raised a silencing finger to her lips.

When the shop emptied again the two older women chatted for a while leaving Meggie free to wander round the shop. Behind the wooden-topped counter, huge jars of sweets filled a whole shelf, under that, on the floor were bottles of pop. One half of the counter itself was hidden under newspapers, the other half held cardboard boxes of loose sweets. Other shelves held basic items such as eggs, bread and milk and there were also sacks of flour and sugar, and a set of shiny brass scales with strong blue paper bags stacked beside them.

'Well, lass, what do you think?' Mrs Cruickshank asked when Meggie had had a chance to look round.

'I don't know anything about working in a shop,' Meggie admitted. 'But I think I'd like it.'

'If you can add up you can work in a shop,' Mrs Binnie told her.

'But we were thinking that as well as working here you might like to own it,' Mrs Cruickshank said.

'Own it!' Meggie was flabbergasted. 'But I couldn't . . . I don't know enough.'

'There's nothing to it. You'll soon learn,' Mrs Binnie assured her. 'Look, youse two away upstairs, have a wee look round the place while I see to these customers.' She pulled aside a heavy curtain behind the counter and ushered them through. 'Mrs Cruickshank knows her way around, lass. She'll tell you all you need to know.'

In a daze Meggie followed the superintendent through what was obviously a storeroom, then out to a paved backyard where a toilet was housed in a rather dilapidated stone outhouse. Back inside, a narrow flight of stairs led to four more rooms. In the first one a stove, a huge sink and some cupboards were hidden behind a curtain while the main body of the room held a fireplace and an assortment of furniture. It was dark, old-fashioned stuff, well-used and worn but comfortable with a homely air about it. The window looked out over the main street which was bustling with life. Two of the other rooms were bedrooms. What had obviously been a tiny third bedroom now housed a second toilet, a bath with a huge geyser over it, and a basin.

'It's a wee bit old-fashioned,' Mrs Cruickshank said. 'But it's a snug wee place in the winter and the shop does a fair trade, always busy. It's a fine place for a shop, with the school just along the road so all the weans pop in and out. The women are in and out all day long and the men come in on their way to and from work for their tobacco and newspapers.'

'But I could never afford this,' Meggie said, the whole idea still seeming preposterous.

'Aye, you could. I'd not have brought you here unless I was sure of that. There'd even be some left over to buy stock for the first couple of months and a wee bit to stay in the bank.'

'I don't know. . .'

'Och, Meggie, cheer up, lass. You look scared stiff. You don't have to make your mind up right now. Mrs Binnie doesn't want to go until next year. You've plenty time to think about it, but it would be a fine way of making that money work for you.'

They went back to the shop where Mrs Binnie was occupied with another customer. 'I'll let you see the books if you're interested,' she offered. 'But I've made enough to keep myself going and save a fair bit in the bank besides.'

'Do you mind if I think about it?' Meggie asked, not wanting to disappoint this lovely old lady, but feeling rather overwhelmed by the possibilities which were suddenly opening up before her.

'Not a bit, lass. No hurry. Just let me know if you're not interested and I'll put it up for sale in a month or two.'

Meggie thanked Mrs Binnie and they left her to serve another customer.

'Do you really think I could do it?' Meggie asked, as they walked back through the town.

'Of course you can!' Mrs Cruickshank turned and faced the girl with an encouraging smile. 'You're a clever lass, Meggie, but with no school certificate you'd not get much of a job. The best you could hope for is the mill, or maybe behind the counter in someone else's shop, working for a pittance, never making anything of yourself. I know you can do better than that! Just think, with a shop of your own you'd be your own boss and there's not many women can say that. And you'd not have to think about finding somewhere to live, either.'

'I still can't believe it,' Meggie said, half to herself. Then, 'But I couldn't really, could I? I mean, I know I keep the books for you but a shop's different. What if I ordered the wrong things, or charged the wrong prices?'

'You'd need time to learn, that's all.'

'Would Mrs Binnie teach me?'

'That's what I had in mind. She's getting on in years and she's trouble with her eyes and with her joints. It's all getting a bit too much for her. Mind you, she's seventy-eight next month and you'd never have guessed that, would you?'

Meggie laughed. 'No, I wouldn't. But what will she do? Where will she go?'

'She's a son over Fife way. She's going to live with him. Aye, and that's another thing. She'd rather sell the place just as it is, furniture and everything, so you'd not need to worry about spending money on beds and chairs.'

'And you think she'd show me what to do?'

'Mrs Binnie's not planning to go until early next year. Until then you could work for your keep in the shop while she teaches you how to do things and at the same time you'd be helping her. Not that you'd need much showing, Meggie. You'd soon pick it up.'

Meggie shook her head as if to clear it. 'I still can't believe it.'

'Think it over. But,' Mrs Cruickshank warned, 'don't take too long. The board aren't happy about you still being in the workhouse when you're fit and able to do a job and look after yourself. If you don't want the shop then you'll have to find yourself a job and a place to live. On what

279

you're likely to earn you'll not be able to afford much and before you know it you'll be eating a hole in that money.'

They walked back to the workhouse in thoughtful silence, but, inside, Meggie was starting to bubble with excitement. There was nothing that could ever compensate her for the loss of her child and there was a deep, black hole of misery in her heart which would never truly heal. Meggie knew that her child was lost to her forever but was realistic enough to admit that, for her baby daughter at least, it was better this way. And perhaps, with the shop, she really could start to put the past behind her and salvage something of her own life.

Part Two

CHAPTER FIFTEEN

'My, lass, you're near run off your feet.'

Meggie looked over the waiting customers and beamed with delight. 'Mrs Cruickshank!'

The older woman made a point of calling in when she had time and Meggie was always pleased to see her. Today though, the shop was so busy that they barely had time to talk and Mrs Cruickshank finally plonked her handbag down behind the counter and helped Meggie serve. When the shop emptied at last she looked at her protégée and laughed.

'I'd hardly know the place, Meggie. What a difference you've made.' She looked round with open admiration at the tightly-packed shelves.

Meggie grinned with pleasure. 'It's thanks to you that I'm here at all.'

'But you've worked wonders. And look at all the things you sell now. Washing powder, tins of cold meat, canned fruit and even tatties.'

'I just listen to what the women want. If enough of them ask me for something I get it in.'

'And you've had new shelves put in, and is this a new counter?' She ran her hand over the highly polished surface.

'Ronnie made the shelves and extended the counter. But it was my idea to have a glass front on it, so the bairns can see to choose their sweeties. Some of them are so wee that their heads don't show over the counter,' she laughed. 'See, I've tidied everything up, to make more room. I just keep a little of everything on the shelves, where folk can see. Most of it's in the storeroom. Ronnie's put shelves in there for me, too. Look how much more space there is now everything's been sorted out.' She threw open the storeroom door, proud of the changes she had made to the shop.

'And you didn't think you'd be able to run a shop,' Bertha Cruickshank chuckled. 'I've never seen this place so busy. It was never like this in Mrs Binnie's day.'

'Mrs Binnie didn't need it to be any busier. There was no point in changing everything when she was so close to retiring. It's different for me.' Meggie leaned forward, her eyes dark and intense. 'I want to make it into a proper shop, one that sells all the weekly groceries and more besides. And then, when I've saved enough money, I'll buy another one. Just think, I might even have a big store on the High Street one day.'

Her enthusiasm was so great that Mrs Cruickshank found herself believing that she would succeed. She laughed again and said, 'Slow down, lass. You've only been running this place for six months and it looks as if you've got more than enough to cope with here.' She stepped back and waited while Meggie served two children. 'It looks to me as if you could do with some help in this shop, never mind talking about buying another one.'

Meggie weighed out sugar into pound bags, needing to make the most of every spare minute. 'It would be nice to have some help,' she admitted. 'But then half my profits would go in wages.'

Mrs Cruickshank picked up her bag and pulled on her gloves, ready to go. 'I'm right proud of you, Meggie,' she told her. 'I always knew you were special. But you can't do it all yourself, not when you're as busy as this. You'll wear yourself out.'

'I manage fine,' Meggie insisted.

Mrs Cruickshank saw the set expression on the girl's face and exclaimed, 'You should see yourself! You look just like you did when you came back to the workhouse. Aye, you're as stubborn and proud as ever, Meggie McPherson. But you take heed. Tired folk make mistakes and mistakes will cost you more money in the end than hiring someone to help you would.' She softened it by patting Meggie's hand affectionately. 'I'll call in next week.'

'Aye.' But Meggie's face was thoughtful as she watched her friend walk back towards the town.

'The *Courier*, please.' Meggie jumped. She had been so lost in thought over what Mrs Cruickshank had said that she hadn't realised there was someone waiting to be served. Hurriedly she took his money and gave him his change.

'I'll have to come here more often,' he said, holding his open palm out towards her.

Meggie looked at him blankly.

'You've given me too much change,' he explained, looking at her more closely now.

Meggie sighed. 'So I have. Thank you. I was miles away,' she admitted with a smile, taking the extra pennies and dropping them into the till.

He smiled, attracted by the heart-shaped face, the warm brown eyes and the generous curve of her mouth, unable to tear his eyes away from her. He had the ridiculous urge to lean over the counter and kiss her. Instead he said, 'Perhaps you could keep me a *Courier* every night?'

Meggie, aware of the intent way he was looking at her, blushed. Keeping her eyes lowered she nodded, 'All right.'

'Aren't you going to ask my name?' he teased.

She looked up at him now, meeting eyes almost as dark as her own, seeing the haze of stubble on a firm chin, the flash of white teeth when he smiled, the mane of thick brown hair which flopped forward over his forehead. With his olive-toned skin, his strong bone structure, widely-spaced eyes and up-turned mouth, his face was expressive, arresting and, strangely familiar. She felt a tremor of excitement run through her and, as he held her eyes with his, was aware of a hint of challenge in that look, of an almost animal attraction. Heat flooded through her and abruptly she dropped her gaze again and made a pretence of tidying the remaining papers.

'It's Oliver Laing,' he said, admiring the shiny curtain of hair which was now hiding her face. 'You'll keep me a paper tomorrow, then?'

'Yes,' she said, keeping her head down to hide the blush which was now creeping up her neck.

He turned and walked away, just as she looked up again and Meggie got a confusing glimpse of a profile that seemed to contradict the humour and mobility of his eyes and mouth when seen full face. A high, sloping forehead, a straight nose and a firm chin, all set on a head which was carried with a slight upward tilt, gave an impression of self-assurance which was accentuated both by his height and the smart cut of his dark suit. Fascinated by these contrasting impressions she watched as he strode off up the hill, his long legs making easy work of the steep gradient, one hand casually in a trouser pocket, the other tapping the rolled-up *Courier* against his leg. She was unreasonably irritated by the arrival of a customer who forced her to tear her eyes away from Oliver Laing's rapidly disappearing form. When she looked back he had gone.

It was still only half-light when she woke the next morning to the sound of heavy rain. It seemed that she had only just closed her eyes, but although her body ached and she yearned to turn over and go back to sleep she felt the now familiar tingle of pleasure with which she greeted each new day. Yawning she pulled herself from between the warm sheets and went to look out of the window. A dark vista of damp roofs and wet streets met her bleary eyes. Below her she heard the loud grind of a van and watched sleepily as it rumbled over the wet setts, its headlamps reflecting eerily on the glistening puddles. It was a full minute before the implication of that delivery van shocked her brain into full wakefulness.

Hurriedly dragging on her clothes she ran downstairs and fumbled with the locks and bolts on the shop door.

'I thought you were never going to open up.' Ronnie Sandys dragged the rain-spattered papers inside, water dripping from his light red hair and running down his round, freckled face. Ronnie, who made his living by collecting the publishers' bundles off the train and distributing them round the town's paper shops, had proved a real friend. Nursing a growing affection for Meggie he had eagerly volunteered his spare time to do the odd jobs which had helped to transform the shop.

'I overslept,' she explained unnecessarily.

'Aye, I can see that,' he laughed, looking at her tangled hair and bleary eyes. 'I bet there's no tea for me this morning, either.'

'No. I'm sorry, Ronnie. I must have slept right through the alarm.'

He dumped the last bundle and looked at her fondly. 'You're working too hard, Meggie,' he told her. 'Why don't you get someone in to help you?'

She sighed. 'My friend said the same thing yesterday.'

'Well, do it then. It's too much for one person.'

'Maybe I should.'

'Of course you should. Then you'll have time to come out with me.' His blue eyes twinkled as he spoke.

'I'll have no time for anything if I don't get these papers sorted,' she retorted.

'Aye, I'm running late, too. Tell you what, you can give me my cup of tea when I come with the evening papers.'

'All right,' she called after him, smiling as he ran through the rain apparently impervious to the weather in his collarless shirt, sleeveless pullover and comfortably baggy corduroy trousers. Turning back to the pile of papers, the first thing she did was put a copy of the *Courier* under the counter for Oliver Laing.

Meggie knew that it was nothing more than tiredness that had made her oversleep that morning. Just as it was tiredness which made it so difficult for her to concentrate on the paperwork and to be patient with the children when they took five whole minutes to choose their sweeties when there were four or five other customers waiting to be served. Success, the thing she wanted above all else, was working against her. Mrs Cruickshank and Ronnie were right. She needed help. So, that Sunday, Meggie resolutely shut the door on the paperwork which was littering her table and set out to see her friend, Sally Keir.

Meggie's business meant she couldn't see Sally as often as she would have liked, but the two girls had stayed in touch. Meggie was fond of Sally, she missed her cheerful company and would always be grateful for the kindness Mrs Keir had shown her. Remembering just how difficult life was for Sally's family, Meggie was hoping that one of Sally's sisters would like to work in the shop.

It was a blustery, November day, but not too cold to spoil

Meggie's enjoyment of the sharp clean air after the close confines of the shop. She was, she told herself, as she paused contentedly outside the shop to admire a view of the distant hills, incredibly fortunate to have been born in such a beautiful area. Inverannan was a small town, built on a loop of the river Annan near the end of its twisting journey down from the hills of Perthshire. The area of flat land which edged the river was now a magnificent park and the town spread eastwards, away from it, straggling over the hills which crept up from the greater Forth valley.

Meggie's shop was towards the top of the proud little town, looking down over the High Street, the splendid town hall, the ruined castle, the park itself and, hidden by tree tops, the little house where Sally still lived, supported by her gentleman.

It was a walk of about two miles, all downhill. Meggie made the most of her day of freedom by wrapping up well against the winter chill and window gazing at the High Street shops, taking note of what they sold and gasping at the prices. Arnotts was Inverannan's smartest store with several departments strung out along a prime position in the High Street. Various windows displayed goods as diverse as watches, garden tools, skeins of wool and evening dresses. On the other side of the road a high-class grocers, Houghs, had windows full of exotic tea, coffee beans and a hundred other things she would never be able to sell in her own modest shop. She stood back and admired the black and gold lettering above the windows, unable to make up her mind which kind of store she would most like to own. Both, she told herself, walking on with a smile which made other people smile back and go on their way feeling happier. And why not? She was young and successful. Anything was possible. In ten years' time perhaps McPhersons would be the name emblazoned above Inverannan's biggest shop.

At the bottom end of the High Street, the park gates were standing open, giving a view across tree-studded grassland to the river, glinting in the sunlight. Meggie joined the steady stream of people who had emerged from their firesides to enjoy the unexpected sunshine of this bright winter's day. Some, fresh out of the kirk, strolled through the park, carefully pacing the paths, looking stiff and uncomfortable in their Sunday best. A gang of youngsters, released from the confines of Sunday school, raced across the damp grass shrieking with laughter and drawing frowning glances of disapproval from the adults.

Meggie felt a surge of her own youthful high spirits, so long kept in check by events and responsibilities which had added years to her age. She remembered carefree days running round the Craigie countryside with Matty and felt a nostalgic longing for the innocent pleasures of childhood. She watched them for a moment longer then walked on, looking every inch the dignified young lady.

Ahead of her the park sloped towards the bottom end of the town, and she could already distinguish the house where she and Matty had lived. She quickened her pace, impatient to see Sally again.

Her old home was on the end of a block of six small houses, all divided into flats, the upstairs ones reached by way of a common path which led round the back. Meggie opened the gate and walked through, keeping her head down, unwilling to confront the memories which came flooding back. Looking forward to seeing her friend again, Meggie ran up Sally's stairs and knocked on the door. There was no answer so she knocked again, louder this time. Still no reply. She lingered at the door, disappointed and cold and wondering what to do now. It was Sunday, a day when most married men stayed dutifully at home with their wives and families, leaving their mistresses free, so it was quite possible that Sally had gone out, perhaps to visit her own family. Or maybe she was still in bed. Meggie knocked one last time, so hard that she bruised her knuckles.

'Who is it?' The voice from behind the door was muffled, unwelcoming.

'Sally? It's me, Meggie.'

'Go away, Meggie. I'm . . . I'm not well.'

Perturbed by this uncharacteristically cold welcome from her high-spirited friend, Meggie shouted, 'Sally, what's wrong? Let me in.'

'No. Just go away, Meggie.'

Seriously alarmed now, Meggie yelled, '*No!*' and hammered furiously on the door.

'What's all the bloody racket?' Someone further along the block threw open a window and yelled angrily.

Suddenly a key turned in Sally's lock and the door opened just wide enough for Meggie to squeeze inside. Once in the dark hall she could hardly see her friend, who stayed huddled behind the door. 'Did you have to make all that noise?' Sally asked.

'What's wrong?' Meggie repeated, perplexed and hurt by this cold welcome.

In the gloom, Sally's shoulders rose in a dismissive shrug. 'Nothing. What do you want?'

'I've taken a day off. I wanted to talk to you, Sal. It's a long time since I've seen you. I miss you.' It was true. Fond as she had been of Mrs Binnie and despite the friendship which had grown between her and Bertha Cruickshank, Meggie missed having someone of her own age to talk to. But this hostile, defensive creature wasn't at all like the cheerful, outspoken girl with whom Meggie had shared confidences. Tentatively she put out a hand and touched Sally's arm. To her surprise the other girl gripped her hand fiercely then threw herself into Meggie's arms. Meggie held her for a moment then gently detached herself and led the way into the sitting room.

The room was as dark as the hall, the curtains defiantly blocking out all the bright winter daylight. Meggie threw them back and was then unable to hold in a gasp of shock. Sally had always been proud of her neat little home, keeping it scrupulously clean and tidy, often shaming Meggie with her enthusiasm for having everything in its right place. But this room looked as if someone had deliberately wrecked it. Chairs were overturned, a cup lay on the floor, its spilled contents making a dark stain on the carpet and Sally's collection of sepia photographs – treasured reminders of her family – were strewn around, their frames broken, the glass in dangerous shards on the carpet. Horrified, Meggie looked at her friend who was leaning against the door-frame. What she saw there made the damage to the room fade into insignificance.

Sally's face was a mass of pulpy flesh, her eyes almost closed, her mouth swollen, her features unrecognisable. She held her arms tightly folded over her ribs and was hunched up over them as if she was in pain.

'Sally! What happened?' Meggie righted a chair, cleared the glass out of the way with her foot and helped her friend to sit down.

Sally grunted with pain as she eased her bruised body onto the chair; then, with a hint of her old humour, said, 'You've caught me at a bad time, Meggie.' But her voice was strained, distorted by her bruised mouth and tears appeared from the swollen slits of eyes.

'You just sit there,' Meggie ordered, springing into frantic action.

Sally subsided with a small sigh and sat back, closing her eyes.

In the immaculate kitchen Meggie filled a bowl with hot water from the geyser, found a piece of clean cloth and rushed back to her friend. With infinite care she bathed Sally's face, wiping smears of blood from round her nose and under an eye.

'Who did this to you, Sal?' she asked when she had finished, handing her friend a cup of hot, sweet tea.

Sally took a careful sip and seemed to revive a little. 'Who do you think?'

'Your Arthur?' Surely not. Sally's gentleman was a mild-mannered, fairly young businessman who had kept her here for almost four years now. In her wildest flights of fancy Meggie could not imagine him behaving so violently.

But Sally nodded. 'Arthur. And it's not the first time he's hit me.'

'Och, Sal . . .' Meggie drew a chair close to Sally's, took her hand and waited, biting back her anger.

'It was my own fault,' Sally said at last. 'I asked for it. I deserved it.'

'Your own fault! Don't be stupid, Sal.' Meggie was outraged. 'No one ever deserves to be beaten like this.'

'He caught me with another man,' Sal whispered.

'Another man! But I thought you were happy with Arthur?'

Sally shrugged and grimaced at the pain the slight movement caused her. 'I was. But it couldn't last forever, could it? I mean, Arthur's a married man. He could never give me anything more than this place. I want a proper home, Meggie, a husband, kids.'

293

'And you met someone else?'

'Aye.' Sally's wistful smile emerged as an ugly contortion of her swollen features. 'Douglas, his name is. Och, Meggie, he's real nice. He works at the mill. I met him one time when I went home to see my Mam. You know how Arthur never comes on a Saturday or Sunday?'

'Aye.'

'We went to the park and once to the picture house. He told me he loved me, Meggie,' she ended on a sob.

'That's wonderful, Sal.'

'No it's not! I went out with him last night. He walked me home. Huh,' she laughed, a short, acid sound. 'I asked him in. It was the first time I'd ever had anyone in the flat, apart from you. But I wanted somewhere private because I'd decided to tell him everything, Meggie. I couldn't go on seeing him unless I told him the truth.'

'What did he say?'

'I didn't get the chance to tell him,' Sally sighed. 'Arthur did that. He was waiting for me when we came in. He'd seen us in the town together.'

'Oh, no . . .'

'Douglas called me some awful names. I can't say I blame him. I should have told him before. But it was the way he looked at me, Meggie. Like I was some kind of filthy animal . . .' she sobbed again, burying her face briefly in her hands. 'Then he just walked out.'

'I'm sorry, Sal.' Meggie wished she had kept quiet, the words were so inadequate.

'As soon as he was gone Arthur started on me. I've never seen him so angry. Och, he's hit me before, but nothing like this.'

'Look, tell me where your things are and I'll pack them up. You can come home with me,' Meggie decided.

294

'I can't.'

'You can't stay here. What if he comes back?'

'He won't. Anyway, I don't think I could walk all the way to your place right now, Meggie.'

'But I can't leave you here. You need to see a doctor, Sal.'

'My mam would know what to do. Could you fetch her for me?'

Meggie was already on her feet. 'Aye. I'll go right now. Will you be all right for an hour or so?'

Sally nodded. 'Meggie,' she stopped the other girl at the door. 'Don't tell my Dad. Just my Mam.'

'Just your Mam,' Meggie promised. 'I'll not be long.'

A couple of hours later Sally was in bed and sleeping lightly. Meggie and Mrs Keir worked at tidying the sitting room.

'Och, just look at this,' Sally's mother held up a broken photograph. 'Sal will be heartbroken. She saved up for weeks so that she could have these pictures taken of us all.'

'The photograph itself looks all right,' Meggie reassured her. 'It just needs a new frame.'

'Aye.' Mrs Keir scooped broken glass into the dustpan then rose wearily to her feet. 'Poor Sal. I suppose I should be grateful there's no lasting damage done, but she'll be carrying a broken heart around with her long after those bruises have healed. She was right fond of young Douglas.'

'If he really loves her maybe he'll come back, when he's had time to get used to things,' Meggie suggested hopefully.

Mrs Keir sighed. 'Not him. I've known him since he was a wean with wet breeks. He's a nice enough lad, a decent sort, from a stern, church-going family. Och, I did warn her what would happen if he found out. But I was too late. She'd already fallen in love with him. Poor lass. Goodness knows what she'll do now. Come home, I suppose, though she

295

won't want to.' She emptied her shovel into the pail and looked round the room. 'I don't think there's much else we can do here.'

'No,' Meggie agreed. 'You go on home. I'll stay here tonight.'

'But what about your shop?'

'I'll get up early. Will you look in and see how she is tomorrow?'

'Of course I will.' Unexpectedly Mrs Keir leaned over and kissed Meggie's cheek. 'You're a good lass, Meggie. Your mother would be proud of you if she could see you now.'

Meggie watched the older woman walk carefully down the wooden stairs wishing she could have the warm, honest relationship with her own mother that Sally shared with hers. Was Mrs Keir right, she wondered? Would her Ma and Pa be proud of her now?

Meggie gave Oliver Laing his paper then followed him to the door, anxious to close up and get back to Sally.

He turned, laughter making his eyes sparkle. 'Are you coming for a walk with me, then?' he teased.

She laughed back. 'I am not. I just want to close up. I stayed open just for you.' He had been coming so regularly that they had fallen into an easy, friendly banter. But underneath it, Meggie was always aware of a thrill of excitement.

'If you're closing up we could go for a walk. If you like,' he added, his face perfectly serious now, his eyes searching hers.

'I can't,' she said, caught between dismay and relief. 'I've promised to go and see my friend. She's not well.' In her lonely bed at night she had allowed herself to dream of this moment, to imagine what it would be like to be kissed by someone as young and good-looking as Oliver Laing. But, now that her dreams were coming true, she knew it was impossible. What lies would she have to tell him about how she came to be the owner of a shop at her age? How could she explain her past? Sally's experience with Douglas had been a salutary lesson for Meggie and had convinced her that no decent man would want her, either, not when he knew the truth about her past. Better not to put herself in that position to start with.

Watching her, Oliver saw only confusion and embarrassment. But he was not a man to give up easily. 'Never mind. Another night?'

'Maybe,' she agreed, unable to keep her eyes away from him.

He walked off up the street, whistling to himself. Meggie forgot why she was standing in the doorway and watched until he reached the corner. There, as if he had been aware of her eyes on his back, he turned and waved before finally disappearing from view.

Meggie took two deep breaths to calm her thudding heart then determinedly shut the door and locked it, pulling down the blind and turning the sign round so that it read CLOSED.

'How are you feeling, Sal?' Meggie asked, walking into her friend's sitting room.

'Not too bad.' Sally smiled. 'A lot better than last night anyway.'

Meggie was relieved to find her friend sitting perkily in her favourite chair. Her face, though still sore-looking and heavily bruised, was already less swollen. Best of all, Sally seemed to have regained some of her old spirit and was much more her usual self.

'Aye, you'll be fine, lass,' Mrs Keir said, shoving her arms into her worn and scruffy coat. 'Now that Meggie's here I'll away home and see to the weans. I'll see you the morn, hen.' She bent to kiss her daughter, who reached up and hugged her warmly.

'Thanks, Mam. But you're not to come rushing down here like you did today. I'm fine and you've enough to do without running round after me.'

'Och, and what's a mother for?' Mrs Keir laughed softly and let herself out.

Meggie sighed. 'You're really lucky, Sally.'

'Lucky!'

'Aye. With your Mam. As soon as my Ma and Pa found out that a man had been keeping me they didn't want anything more to do with me. But your Mam's different. She doesn't seem to mind.'

'She keeps her feelings to herself, that's all,' Sally said. 'She didn't like it any more than your Mam. There was all hell to pay when she found out.'

'You wouldn't think it now then.'

'No. She came round in the end. She had to. It was either that or never speak to me again. She loves me too much to let that happen. She'd be the same with any of us. Doesn't mean she approves, mind.'

'I wish my parents were like that,' Meggie murmured sadly; then, fixing a smile back on her face she asked, 'What are you going to do now, Sal? You can't stay here.'

'Go back to Mam and Dad's, I suppose. Look for a job.'

'How about coming and living with me? I've got loads of room.'

'I couldn't, Meggie.'

'Why not? We're friends aren't we?'

'Aye, of course we are.'

'Well then. . .'

'Maybe after I'm better. When I've found a job.'

'But I've got a job for you. You can work with me, in the shop. I'll not pay much, mind, but there's bed and board thrown in.'

'No.'

'Sally!'

'No. Thanks, Meggie, but I'll go home. My Mam'll look after me until I get myself sorted out.' Sal raised her chin and stared straight in front of her, looking, for a minute, very like her mother. Meggie knew that it was sheer pride which was holding her back.

'You think I've made up a job, just for you, don't you?' she challenged.

'Well, haven't you?' Still Sally wouldn't look at her.

'No. But would it matter if I had? We're supposed to be friends and friends help one another, don't they?'

'This is my problem, Meggie. I got myself into it and it's not right for you to have to dig me out of it.'

'I'm not digging you out! I came to see you yesterday because I need someone to help in the shop. I wondered if one of your sisters might want to do it. But you need a job now and I'd much rather have you than one of your sisters. Too proud to know what's good for you, that's you!' Sally opened her mouth to protest, but Meggie stopped her, saying, 'Go on, say you're not being stubborn. Say you don't need a job. Go on. Say it.'

Their eyes met. For a second they glared at one another. Then Sally spluttered and collapsed into fits of laughter. 'Oh . . .' she groaned. 'My ribs.'

CHAPTER SIXTEEN

As Meggie had known they would, she and Sal settled down well together. The small compromises which were necessary for harmonious coexistence were made generously and in a spirit of true friendship, underpinned, on Sally's part, by a deep sense of gratitude. It was an indebtedness which was never allowed to cloud their relationship but which tied Sally to Meggie with strands of loyalty almost as strong as those which bound her to her own family.

Meggie revelled in having a true friend of her own age in which to confide, someone who seemed instinctively to understand her feelings. With Sally's energetic presence the little house came alive and they spent many cosy evenings, sitting in the warmth of the fireside, sharing their plans, their hopes, their disappointments.

For Meggie it was a magical time, a period of her life which she would always remember with affectionate nostalgia, the bad times all behind her, the future beckoning and full of promise. With the support of her friends – Sally's enthusiastic, impulsive nature balanced by Bertha Cruickshank's rock-like common sense – Meggie blossomed. The weight of constant worry and responsibility which had dragged her down for so long finally fell away, leaving an ambitious young woman with a lively sense of humour and a sharp, eager mind.

Sally, earning her living in a way which could cause offence to no one, knew her mother was proud of her at last. Regardless of her own impoverished circumstances, Mrs

Keir had steadfastly refused to take money from her daughter, feeling that to do so would be to condone a way of life of which she could never approve. Now, one of Sally's greatest pleasures was to hand over a few shillings of honestly earned money each week, like any dutiful daughter would do, and have it accepted easily and without comment.

Keen to prove that Meggie's faith in her had not been misplaced, Sally applied herself conscientiously and learned her job quickly. Bright, chatty and helpful, she was soon popular with the customers and was in her element serving in the shop, gossiping unashamedly with the women, joking with the children and flirting outrageously with the men. There was only one customer who seemed impervious to her various charms.

'Who *is* that?' Sally demanded, admiration plain in her voice.

'Shushh, Sal, he'll hear you.' Meggie blushed but Oliver Laing walked unconcernedly out of the shop and on up the road without once looking back. As soon as he got home he dropped the unopened *Courier* into a waste-paper basket and, calling a dutiful, 'Good evening,' to his mother, ran lightly upstairs to change for dinner. It wouldn't be long now, he told himself, before the mysterious and lovely Miss McPherson gave in and agreed to come out with him. And then he would be a very happy man indeed.

'Who *is* he, then?' Sally, like a ferret, refused to give up once her prey was in sight and resurrected the subject of Meggie's admirer over their evening meal. 'He comes in every night, regular as clockwork. And he won't let me serve him.'

Meggie sighed but, knowing she would get no peace until

Sal's curiosity was slaked, admitted defeat. 'His name's Oliver Laing. He comes in for his *Courier*, that's all.'

'And?'

'And nothing!'

'Och, come on, Meggie! I've seen youse, whispering away together. And I've seen the way he looks at you. The man's in love.' She crossed her arms over her heart and sighed dramatically.

'Don't be stupid, Sal.' But Meggie blushed faintly.

'Has he asked you out?' Sal still wasn't satisfied.

'Aye.'

'Have you been out with him?'

'No . . . No, I haven't.'

Sally saw the shadow which flickered over her friend's face and instantly dropped her teasing tone. 'Why not, Meggie? He's lovely, a real young gent. And he does like you, you can see that from the way he looks at you.'

'I know.'

'Then what's wrong?'

'You said it yourself, Sal. He's a real gent.'

'So what? You're a businesswoman now and a match for him any day.'

'Aye, but what about what I did before? What happens if he finds out the truth? It'd be just like you and Douglas.'

Sally frowned and turned away, the reminder bringing instant, raw pain.

'I'm sorry, Sal. I didn't mean to hurt you.' Meggie was appalled by her own thoughtlessness. 'But, it's true. If he found out about me, the workhouse, Wallace, the baby . . .'

'So don't tell him.'

One of the advantages of having Sally to help in the shop was that both girls could have an afternoon off every week.

302

Meggie usually spent her free time with Bertha Cruickshank.

This particular January afternoon, there had been a heavy snowfall and Inverannan's streets were three inches deep in grey slush.

'I don't particularly want to go walking about in this muck.' Mrs Cruickshank brushed at the back of her coat where a passing horse and cart had splashed her with mud. The cars were even worse, spraying unwary pedestrians from a distance of six feet away. 'Shall we have a pot of tea and a scone somewhere?'

'Good idea,' Meggie agreed readily, knowing it would be easier to hold a conversation over a teapot than while dodging the shoppers in the High Street.

There were two small tea shops in the centre of Inverannan. Both were full of cold shoppers and there were queues of people waiting for seats.

'Tell you what,' Mrs Cruickshank said. 'We'll give ourselves a wee treat. We'll go to the City.' She strode off down the High Street in the direction of the town's smartest hotel.

Meggie followed her through the City Hotel's revolving door and couldn't help smiling to herself as it spat her out in the warm foyer. As a child she had looked with longing at those rotating glass doors, yearning to pluck up the courage to try them, just once, laughing when the doorman chased wee boys who dodged past him and spun them round at frightening speed. And now, here she was, safely through those same doors and inside the hotel, a customer, with every right to be there. She straightened her shoulders, lifted her chin and followed Mrs Cruickshank into the dining room.

'A table for two. By the window,' Mrs Cruickshank

instructed the waitress in her best accent. Weaving her way between tables occupied by obviously well-heeled women, Meggie wondered if her coat was smart enough for a place like this and wished she had a hat, something small and tasteful like the ones Mrs Cruickshank and most of the other women were wearing, and perhaps a new handbag and smart shoes to replace the practical lace-ups, so necessary for the shop. But no one gave her a second glance and she settled at the table feeling more confident.

While they waited for the waitress she looked round, trying not to stare too obviously. It was a beautiful room, she thought. Although it was a dim afternoon the restaurant was lit with soft electric lights making it feel warm and comfortable. There were eight tall windows along the length of the room, curtained in a rich blue velvet to match the chairs and carpet. The tables were covered in spotless linen cloths, the very best the town's mill could offer, and each place was set with what looked like silver cutlery with an intricately folded napkin placed at the side.

'Two afternoon teas.' Mrs Cruickshank gave their order to the waitress.

Meggie had never seen such splendour. A teapot, hot water jug, milk jug and sugar bowl, all in polished silver, were delivered along with a cup, saucer and plate in china so fine that Meggie was almost frightened to touch it. An array of delicate, crustless, triangular sandwiches was placed on one side of the table and a tiered stand bearing a mouth-watering selection of cakes and scones dominated the other.

Meggie dutifully chewed her way through two sandwiches, disappointed to discover they contained nothing more exciting than a smearing of potted hough and an overpowering dredging of pepper, then gazed at the cake-stand, awed by the sheer choice. Eventually she selected a flaky pastry slice, oozing with cream. She regretted it instantly. Each time she tried to lift the cake to her mouth, dollops of cream fell back on to her plate.

'Try the fork,' Mrs Cruickshank whispered kindly, demonstrating on her own generously filled eclair.

Meggie laughed. 'I've never been anywhere like this before,' she admitted, filing away the lessons she was learning for future reference.

Manipulating the fork and cream demanded all her attention and rendered conversation impossible, so it wasn't until they were on their second cup of tea that Meggie finally plucked up the courage to ask Mrs Cruick-shank's advice.

'I like him a lot,' she said, after describing her problem with Oliver. 'He wants me to walk out with him but I can't.'

'If he really likes you, he'll understand,' Mrs Cruickshank told her, though she didn't really believe it herself.

Meggie shook her head doubtfully.

'It's up to you, lass, but you'll have this problem every time you meet someone you like. Unless you want to spend the rest of your life on your own and end up an old spinster, you'll have to face up to it sooner or later. Go out with him, Meggie. Maybe nothing will come of it.'

'I couldn't lie to him.'

'Och, lass, I really don't know what to tell you. I don't hold with dishonesty but you've had a terrible time of it and to my mind none of it was really your fault. You just got caught up in something you were too young to deal with. It would be stupid to let it ruin your life.'

'You mean not tell him?'

'You'll have to tell him some of it. But just remember that

it wasn't your fault that you ended up in the workhouse. And you've every reason to be proud of what you've achieved since.'

'What about the baby? And Wallace, and the Houlets' Nest?' Meggie dropped her voice to a barely audible whisper.

'Put it behind you, Meggie. It's the only way.'

Meggie parted from her friend feeling more confused than ever. How could she pretend that such a traumatic period of her life had never been? How could she have a loving, trusting relationship with someone if she wasn't absolutely honest about herself? And how could she hope to have any sort of relationship if she was?

She walked home deep in thought, oblivious to the slushy roads, hardly noticing that her feet were wet, her hands almost frozen.

'You look perished.' She reached the shop at exactly the same moment as Oliver Laing, who opened the door for her.

Sally, busy behind the counter, looked up and smiled, then, seeing who Meggie was with, tactfully withdrew to the storeroom.

'I'll get your paper,' Meggie mumbled, reaching over to the counter, fumbling with her numbed fingers.

Laughing, he picked up her reddened hand and cupped it in his own, raising it to his lips and blowing on it gently. Meggie's skin tingled to the warmth of his breath, the touch of his lips on her knuckles. She felt her heartbeat quickening and knew she was breathing too fast.

Oliver Laing was smitten but he didn't even understand why Meggie was so important to him. Perhaps, he thought, gazing into her velvety eyes, it was because she was so completely natural and unaffected, almost as if she was unaware of how beautiful she was; or perhaps it was the slight air of mystery which hung about her. He had watched her often, admiring the competent manner in which she dealt with her customers, the firm, skilful way in which she handled difficult people. And yet, underneath it all there was something else, something he couldn't identify, something that manifested itself whenever he spoke to her, stripping her momentarily of the veneer of assurance, making her seem incredibly young and vulnerable, and doubly desirable. All his instincts made him want to hold her, to protect her, to love her. But would she even give him the chance? Unaware that he was doing it, he tightened his grip.

'Will you come for a walk in the park with me on Sunday?' he asked.

Meggie looked into his eyes, saw something of the tenderness there and was lost.

'All right,' she whispered.

Expecting another rejection, his eyes widened with surprise. His grip loosened, he tossed the unruly fringe of hair back into place and grinned with delight, his dark eyes flashing with pleasure. 'You will?' he asked, cursing himself for sounding like a green schoolboy.

Touched by the openness of his reaction, Meggie smiled up at him, giving herself up to the sheer pleasure of the moment. 'If you want to.'

'I'll call for you. Two o'clock,' he told her, anxious to make the arrangments before she changed her mind.

'I'll be ready,' she answered, her heart hammering so fast that she felt dizzy.

He took the paper and backed out of the shop, smiling at her. 'Sunday, then?' he asked again as he went through the door.

'Sunday,' she laughed.

'That's the lot.' Ronnie tipped his flat cap back on his head and winked at Sally, who giggled. 'My cuppa ready?'

'Of course,' she said, giving him her most seductive smile. It wasn't in Sally's nature to be downcast for long. Determinedly refusing to dwell on the bruised heart which had been the result of her short liaison with Douglas, within a very few weeks of arriving at the shop, Sally had fastened her affections firmly on Ronnie Sandys. But, to her increasing frustration, despite exerting all her charms on him, Ronnie's passion remained riveted on Meggie.

'Thanks, Sal.' Ronnie followed her into the storeroom then, completely oblivious to the effect he had on her, he ruined her day by asking, 'Where's Meggie this morning?'

'Upstairs,' she answered without enthusiasm.

'How about fetching her down here? I want to ask her to come out with me,' he added conspiratorially.

Sally sighed resignedly. Life was really unfair sometimes, she thought. There was Ronnie, wasting his time over Meggie who only had eyes for Oliver Laing while she herself would give her back teeth for a chance to spend just one evening alone with Ronnie, who hardly knew she existed. But she went upstairs and fetched Meggie.

'So there you are,' Ronnie greeted Meggie cheerfully. 'I'm in a wee bit of a hurry so I'll come right out with it. Och, you know fine I like you, Meggie. I like you a lot and I was wondering if you'd come out with me. There's one of those comedy films on at the picture house. We could go there if you like.' He blurted it all out in a breathless rush then waited expectantly for her reply.

Meggie groaned. She had been expecting this, dreading it. She liked Ronnie, had been flattered by his attentions, had even thought she might like to go out with him. But that was before Oliver Laing. 'Thanks, Ronnie, but I don't think I should.'

'Why not?' The downcast look on his face might have been funny if she hadn't felt so guilty.

'I like you, Ronnie. I really do . . .'

'So, come out with me then.'

'I don't think that would be fair.'

Now he had an inkling of what was going on. 'There's someone else.' He said it in a flat, dull voice.

'I'm sorry, Ronnie.'

'Anyone I know?' He felt ashamed that he had to ask that question.

'I don't think so.'

'Och . . . well.' He shoved his cap back on his head. 'Thanks for telling me, Meggie. I would have been hurt if I'd found out from someone else.' He attempted to sound dignified but knew the words came out bitterly.

'Och, Ronnie, don't be like that,' she pleaded, knowing he was hurt. 'It's not as if we were seeing each other, is it? We're still friends, aren't we?'

'I suppose so,' he agreed grudgingly.

'I'll see you in the morning as usual then.'

It sounded like a dismissal. 'Aye.' Abruptly he stomped from the storeroom and back into the shop.

'Bloody hell, Ronnie, you look right sour-faced,' Sally commented as he emerged behind her.

'Who's this bloke Meggie's seeing then?' he asked bluntly.

'His name's Oliver Laing. Proper toff he is. Been after her for weeks. Comes in here every night for a paper and can't keep his eyes off her.'

'A toff, eh? Not much chance for the likes of me, then, is there?'

'Och, cheer up, Ronnie. She's only going for a walk with him. He's not asked her to marry him!'

He grinned ruefully. 'You think there's still some hope for me?'

'There's always hope, Ronnie,' she sighed.

Luckily the weather cleared by Sunday and although cold, it was a still, dry afternoon as Meggie and Oliver strolled through the park. For Meggie the occasion was in danger of being spoiled by her own nervousness, the ever present niggle of fear, the knowledge that an unguarded word might lead him to suspect something of her past.

'What do you do, Oliver?' she asked, to deflect his attention away from herself.

'I work for my father. The family owns the Strathannan Mining Company. My father runs it now.'

'Will you take over from him one day?'

'I doubt it. I'm not sure that I'd want to, not the way the mines are operated now.'

'My father was a miner,' the words slipped out before she could stop them.

'Really?' He looked at her in surprise. Not realising how hard Meggie was working to improve herself, he had assumed from the way she spoke and acted that she came from a much more comfortable background than a miner's pay would provide. 'Where?' he asked. 'Did he work for the company?'

'I'll tell you later,' she said hastily. 'Tell me more about you first. Won't your father be disappointed if you don't take over from him?'

'No. My oldest cousin will do that. You see, my grand-father left the company to my father and his older brother. He was killed in the war, but he left two sons. Robbie's a year older than me and at university. His younger brother, Edwin, will follow him there later this year. They'll both join the company after they graduate.'

'Did you go to university?' she asked, slightly awestruck.

'No. I'd had more than enough of school. I'm not much good at book learning,' he admitted candidly. 'I like to get involved in things, see how they work, fix things. That's what I'm really good at.'

She could see the enthusiasm in his strong face. 'Do you work at one of the mines?'

'No. I wish I could. Mother doesn't approve of me coming home covered in grease like a common workman. I'm stuck in the office. Och, it's not too bad and I owe it to Dad to help where I can. It's difficult for him. He tries to keep things going but the seams are wet and getting more and more difficult to mine. The equipment's old and unreliable. We need to open new seams, invest in new winding gear and pumps, but we can't afford it. As it is we're barely in profit and Father has an obligation to make sure there's enough money for his brother's family to live comfortably as well as keeping the miners themselves in work.'

'I always thought the mine owners were rich.' She could still remember the bitterness in her father's voice when he spoke about them.

'Some are,' Oliver admitted. 'Trouble is my grandfather wasn't much of a businessman. He wanted the profits but he wouldn't put anything back into the mines. We're paying the price for that now.'

Meggie, looking sideways at Oliver, saw a brooding,

intense young man, a very different person from the light-hearted tease who frequented the shop, and realised that there were as many different facets to him as there were to her. The thought cheered her slightly. If he cared so much about others, his family, the miners, then surely, when the time came – if it came – he would understand what had motivated her.

Catching her looking at him, he grinned suddenly. 'That's enough of that. Now it's your turn.'

She shivered suddenly. 'It's getting cold,' she muttered. 'Let's go back.'

He looked puzzled for a moment then shrugged. 'All right.' But then he stopped and looked directly at her. 'Who are you, Meggie McPherson?' he asked softly.

There was no avoiding it. And now, after one short walk through the park it would be over. But it was better this way, better to know where she stood before she let things develop too far. 'What do you want to know?' she asked dully, walking on, forcing him to run to catch up with her.

Oliver was intrigued but cautious. 'You said your father was a miner? Is he dead? Is that why you live on your own?' Hers was, he realised, a very unconventional situation and not one of which his mother would approve.

'No, he's not dead. My mother and father live near Glasgow.' She sighed. 'I'll tell you about it and I'll understand if you don't want to see me again when you know about me.'

He raised a quizzical eyebrow, a frequent gesture she already recognised. 'Now I'm really curious,' he teased.

Ignoring the cold she sat on a bench, twisting her hands nervously in her lap. He fought to resist the urge to put an arm round her shoulders, failed and was relieved when she made no attempt to move away.

312

'I used to live in the workhouse.' She said the words flatly but her face burned with shame.

'The workhouse!' His words were startled, almost indignant, and Meggie's heart sank. 'But what on earth were you doing there?'

'My parents sent me and my brother there.'

'They put their children in the workhouse?' Now there was a note of disbelief in his voice.

'Aye!' She was angry and defensive now. 'It happens sometimes. To poor folk like us. Not that you'd know anything about that, Mr Mineowner.'

'I don't own the mines, Meggie.' Now he was angry, too, hurt by something he didn't even understand. 'Is that it? Are you angry with me because of what my father is? Because your father's a collier and mine owns the Company?'

'Was a collier,' Meggie retorted. 'Was a collier. He's not now, not since the strike.' She jerked away from him.

Oliver let his arm fall to his side. 'I see.'

'No, you don't. How could you? Don't you understand, Oliver? I'm just a workhouse girl. You can't want to be seen with the likes of me.' Fear made her sound bitter.

For a moment he was silent then he asked, 'Is that why it took you so long to agree to come out with me? Did you really think I would change my mind when I found out you'd been in the workhouse?'

'Well haven't you?' she challenged, looking at him, searching for the truth in his troubled eyes.

'Of course not,' he told her. 'Meggie . . . Please, don't be angry. Lots of folk end up in the workhouse through no fault of their own. Can't you tell me about it?'

Nothing could have stopped her now.

'Pa was a miner at the Dene. We lived in Craigie.' She saw he knew the place and went on grimly. 'After the union big-

313

wigs had made their speeches, it was my Pa who went round the houses, talking to all the men, encouraging them to stay out. When it was all over they said he was a troublemaker. He lost his job and we got put out of the house. The mine manager saw to it that Pa couldn't get a job in any of the other pits. Pa's brother's a miner, through by Glasgow way, and Pa thought he'd have the chance of a job through there. So Ma and Pa, and my two younger brothers, went to stay with my uncle and aunt but there wasn't room for my brother and me. They put us in the workhouse.'

'That's awful.'

'There was nothing else they could do.'

'I don't understand why you didn't want to tell me, Meggie. It wasn't your fault. And look at you now, your own shop and everything. You should be proud, not ashamed.'

Meggie tried to find the words to tell him the rest, to spell out the depth of her disgrace, and couldn't do it, couldn't bear to see the respect die from his eyes. And then he was speaking again.

'It's unusual for a girl of your age to have a shop, isn't it? How did you manage that? Did someone help you?' He was full of admiration now.

Meggie nodded and took shelter in a half-truth. 'Mrs Cruickshank, the workhouse superintendent.'

Oliver laughed. 'That old battleaxe? Even my mother's scared of her.'

Meggie allowed herself to smile. 'She was very good to me.'

'And she helped you to buy the shop?'

'Mrs Binnie, who used to own it, is a friend of hers.'

'I'm amazed,' he chuckled. 'When I was a bairn my

314

mother used to threaten to send me to Mrs Cruickshank at the workhouse if I wasn't good. I always thought she was a witch or something.'

'She's the kindest person I've ever known.'

'She must be. Not everyone would help a girl of your age set up in business.'

Meggie knew that he wrongly assumed that Mrs Cruickshank had put up the money. She opened her mouth to correct him then shut it again. After all, she hadn't told him any lies. And surely it was easier this way. Kinder. Later, if they were still seeing one another, then she would explain. But even as she thought it, she knew she would never find the necessary courage. It was already to late for that.

'And what about your parents?' he asked. 'What happened to them?'

'Ma and Pa don't want anything to do with me now.'

'Why? Aren't they proud of you and the way you run the shop?'

'They don't know about the shop,' she sighed. 'It was because of my brother, Matty. He was in the workhouse, too. I was supposed to be looking after him. He hated it there. We ran away. Went to Glasgow to look for Ma and Pa but we couldn't find them. We had no money, nothing, so we had to come back to Inverannan.'

'Back to the workhouse?'

'In the end.'

'I didn't know you had a brother living with you. I'd like to meet him.'

'He doesn't live with me. Matty got into trouble for stealing. They sent him to a home. Ma and Pa blamed me.'

Oliver snaked an arm back round Meggie's shoulders and she sat there astonished by how easy it had been to weave a believable tale around the truth, leaving out the

315

most damning facts. She stored it away in her conscience, something else to hide, of which to be ashamed.

'It's the saddest, bravest thing I've ever heard.' He squeezed her shoulder gently. 'Thank you for telling me.'

Please, she prayed, forgive me and don't let him ever find out the truth.

'Come on, cheer up. You've told me now and it wasn't too bad, was it?' He smiled into her eyes, melting her heart.

He kissed her then, on a park bench with the winter day drawing close around them, not caring who might see.

Meggie felt his breath on her face and closed her eyes as his lips brushed hers. His tongue, sweet and gentle, probed teasingly and her mouth opened under his, drawing his tongue deeper into her, holding him close. But then, abruptly, she drew away, realising just in time that this was hardly the reaction of the untouched virgin he must think her to be.

Oliver, understanding that she was inexperienced and probably nervous, kissed her again, lightly, softly, wary of frightening her but alarmed by the strength of his own emotions. 'You're cold,' he whispered. 'If you promise to come out with me again I'll take you home.'

'I promise,' she said, glad that her shiver of excitement could be mistaken for cold. When he left her at the shop she stood for a few minutes in the dark silence at the bottom of the stairs, still feeling the heat on her lips where he had kissed her goodbye. Oliver was warm, sympathetic and so handsome that other girls had looked at her with envy on their faces. She had felt so proud to be with him but, now that he had gone, the elation began to fade, leaving her feeling guilty and uneasy. There was so much she hadn't told him, so much that was incomplete in what he did

316

know, and surely he deserved to be told the truth. But how could she do that now?

Even though she was already more than half in love with Oliver and had seen for herself what a decent, caring person he was, Meggie didn't know him well enough to trust him with the whole truth about her past. In any case, it was already too late and now she would have to live with the lies and deception. But, she told herself, as she walked slowly up the stairs, it would be worth it if it meant there was a future for her and Oliver. So long as he never found out the truth. And there was no reason for him to do that.

'How did it go?' Sally was waiting with questions as soon as Meggie opened the door.

'Fine,' Meggie said.

'Did he kiss you?'

'Mind your own business,' Meggie retorted, not wanting to share those first sweet kisses with anyone else.

'He did. I can tell,' Sally whooped with triumph.

Suddenly the shop, which had been the hub of of Meggie's life, was relegated to second place. She opened up each morning yearning for half-past six when Oliver called in on his way home from work. Though she was glad that Ronnie was still friendly, if a little more reserved, she was completely unaware of the way his eyes, filled with longing, followed her every move when he came with the papers. Her whole being was concentrated on Oliver Laing.

Every Sunday Oliver took her out. If it was fine they simply walked, sometimes in the park, other times in the High Street, peering into shop windows, pretending they had a hundred pounds to spend. On wet days they lingered over pots of cooling tea in the Pavilion tea rooms, their knees touching under the table.

Though she yearned for the natural confirmation of their love, Meggie made sure they had few opportunities to be truly alone. The best she would allow Oliver was a few stolen minutes of privacy in some not-too-secluded corner of the park, or in the shadow of the shop doorway. Her young body longed for so much more than brief kisses and fleeting caresses and to feel his own obvious arousal as he held her, to know that he was holding himself back out of respect for her, added to her torment. But she was afraid, frightened that she would betray herself, that by behaving in a way that surely no decent girl would, she would make him realise that she was vastly more experienced than he. But each time they met, the urge to offer him what he so clearly wanted was harder to deny.

Then, one Sunday in early summer, she went downstairs to meet him as usual and found him standing proudly beside a gleaming black motor car.

'Jump in,' he invited, holding the door open.

She had never been in a car before and simply stood, staring at it in amazement. 'Is this yours?' she asked at last.

'Yes,' he said settling her in the front seat and running round to sit behind the wheel.

'It's lovely. You didn't tell me you had a car.'

'I wanted to surprise you. It was a birthday present from my father.'

'Your birthday? Why didn't you tell me?' She was dismayed to have missed such an important occasion.

'It was ages ago,' he assured her cheerfully. 'Before we started going out together. Actually this used to be Father's car. He promised me I could have it for my birthday but I had to wait for his new one to be delivered. And then he wouldn't let me take it out until he was sure I could drive it safely.'

'And can you?' she asked, already nervous as the car rumbled towards the town at what seemed to be horrendous speed.

'I'm better than Father is. He should stick to horses. When he wants to stop he tries to pull back on the steering wheel as if it was a pair of reins.' He chuckled, the affection he felt for his father quite obvious. For a moment Meggie envied him.

She sat back, gradually relaxing as she saw that Oliver was in fact a skilful driver, though the speed at which they tore through corners still terrified her at times. Leaving Inverannan behind they sped effortlessly along narrow country roads, skimming the hedgerows and sending up clouds of dust behind them. They were running eastwards, parallel to the river Forth, which was widening out in a sheen of silver below them. Cultivated fields gave way to more rugged, hilly country where the only other living things were the sheep dotted across the hillsides. And then, cresting a rise, they were facing the estuary where the Forth widened and merged with the North Sea. Meggie strained forward in her seat, drinking in the magnificent view.

'It's beautiful,' she gasped.

'Haven't you been to the coast before?' he asked, glad to see such pleasure on her face.

'Once, when I was a bairn. I think it was a Sunday school outing, or a miners' trip. Something like that. We went up into the hills once, too. I don't remember seeing anything like this, though.'

As Oliver drove on the coastline slowly unravelled before them. Tiny, red-roofed villages appeared, nestling in coves, or perching on exposed headlands. Quaint harbours, busy with fishing boats, came into view, then, with the next twist of the road, disappeared again. All along the coast golden

319

ribbons of sand snaked out before them, broken here and there by rocky points or low, sandy cliffs. They wound down the windows and let the sun stream in, warming their arms, bringing tangy, salty air into the car with it. Meggie sighed contentedly, sure there could never be another day as perfect as this.

'This is my favourite place,' Oliver told her as the car rattled violently over the setts of another village. He drove down a hill and into a sort of elongated square with shops on either side and an ancient tollbooth in the middle.

The houses were quaintly old-fashioned, their roofs covered in red tiles, gulls basking on the stepped gable ends. Many of the houses were of the traditional design, the living quarters up a flight of exterior steps, or forestairs, the storeroom or workshop underneath. Even on a Sunday, men and women were sitting either at the top of the stairs or just inside the door at the bottom, working on nets, tying lines, knitting or darning, according to need.

'It's beautiful!' Meggie exclaimed. 'What's it called?'

'Kilweem. Father used to bring us here for a weekend every summer. It's got the most marvellous beach you'll ever see.'

To the consternation of another motorist, Oliver circled merrily round the tollbooth, then shot down an alarmingly steep side wynd. The setts here were ancient, smooth with use but high and irregular, making the little car jolt about violently. As they plunged downwards the wynd narrowed, twisting sharply, the forestairs of the fishermen's cottages jutting into the road. Meggie had the very odd sensation of having gone back in time and knew this place must have changed very little in the last two centuries. And then, opening up before them, was a tiny harbour, the fishing boats bobbing peacefully within an enclosing wall. With one last drop the wynd gave way to a broad, flat quayside. Grinning, Oliver parked the car so that they were looking out over the water.

'I always liked to look at the boats best,' he told her, getting out and opening her door for her.

Arm in arm, a light breeze ruffling their hair, they walked along the sea wall. Here and there, sitting on upturned crates, were groups of fishermen, some working on nets or creels, other simply enjoying the sun, all, to Meggie's amusement, wearng thick jumpers, caps and high boots.As the young couple walked past, most of them looked up and offered a short but friendly greeting.

At the end of the sea wall, Oliver and Meggie turned and looked back. The village straggled picturesquely up the hill, forming an intricate backdrop of twisting wynds, fishermen's cottages, red roofs and a church tower. Below that was the quayside with its fishermen, the clutter of crates, the spread of drying nets, creels and ropes, the ever-present smell of fish. In the foreground were the boats themselves, brightly painted in reds, greens and blues, wedged tightly round the harbour wall, rising and falling with the swell of the sea, the water lapping against them with a soothing, rhythmic slap and splash. Meggie was captivated and wished there was some way she could preserve every detail in her memory.

'There's the beach, look.' Oliver pointed to his right. On the other side of a rocky promontory was what seemed to be a never-ending, curving stretch of golden sand. 'Do you want to sit on the sand?'

'Yes.' She was already hurrying back, almost running in her eagerness to explore.

'We'll take the car to the other side. I think there's a little road somewhere that leads right on to the sand.' Oliver started the engine with the minimum of fuss and manoeuvred the car expertly so that it was facing back the way they had come.

'We'll never get it back up that hill!' Meggie cried, gripping the side of the seat.

'Oh, yes we will.' Oliver stamped his foot down and took a run at it. They made it, just, the little car crawling and spluttering back on to the main street just as the engine was on the point of dying.

Oliver drove slowly along the main road, searching for a way down to the beach. 'Ah. The Butts! This is it.' He turned the car down another setted wynd, wider this time and mercifully straight. At the bottom the setts simply disappeared into the sand. 'Perfect,' Oliver said, shutting off the engine.

Meggie ran into the sand, laughing as it seeped into her shoes and between her toes. Ahead of her the sea lapped gently up the beach, bubbling and hissing. To her right was the rocky headland. With childlike abandon she clambered over the rocks until she could see over to the harbour then scrambled down again and ran to join Oliver who was hauling a large picnic basket off the back seat of the car.

Grasping a handle each they set off along the beach, ploughing through the fine, powdery sand, then running down to the firmer stuff, making a game of dodging the incoming tide. Caught by an unexpectedly strong surge of foaming water, Meggie was left with wet, sand-caked shoes.

'Take them off,' Oliver invited.

'Turn round,' she ordered. Oliver chuckled and walked on ahead. Glancing up and down the almost deserted beach to make sure she was unobserved, Meggie kicked off her shoes then rapidly rolled down her stockings. She bundled

322

them up, caked sand and all, and stuffed them into her handbag.

'Where shall we have our picnic? On the sand or in the dunes?' Oliver asked.

'Let's try and find some shade in the dunes,' she suggested. Despite the gentle breeze riding in with the waves, the spring sunshine was almost too hot now.

Slipping in the dry sand they climbed slowly up the dunes then down into the ocean of rolling peaks and troughs which lay between the road and the beach. Finding a sheltered hollow, partially protected from the sun, Oliver spread out a rug and set out the picnic.

From the wicker basket came plates, cups, saucers, cutlery and napkins. Under them were layers of food, chicken legs, sliced ham, sandwiches, meat pies, sponge cakes, shortbread, apples and cheese. From the corners of the hamper he produced a bottle of wine, a flask of cold tea, a bottle of blackcurrant cordial and another of plain water.

'I think that's everything,' he said, lying back and stretching out, hands behind his head and squinting up at the sun.

'Everything for an army,' Meggie laughed. 'Did your mother pack this?'

'Mother!' He laughed. 'No. The girl did it, but I told her what I wanted.'

At this reminder of the social gulf between them, Meggie's pleasure faded slightly. But the day was too warm, the setting too idyllic, the company too agreeable to be easily spoiled. There were certain to be many times when she would be aware of the difference in their backgrounds and it was something she would just have to cope with, something she could learn from. Between him and Mrs Cruickshank, the films she and Sally often went to see and the magazines she sometimes flicked through, it wouldn't be long before no one would be able to tell that they weren't ideally matched.

'It's perfect,' she told him.

They ate slowly, crunching through the sand which, no matter how careful they were, seemed to work its way into every mouthful of food. Then Meggie repacked the hamper and leaned back against the slope of the dune, looking through half-closed eyes at Oliver, who was dozing contentedly in the sun.

He really was very good-looking she thought, admiring the curl of his extraordinarily long eyelashes as they rested on his cheek, hiding eyes which were a rich, chestnuty brown, speckled with green flecks. He was dark, his skin already tanning with the sun. His hair, just a shade or two lighter than her own, was thick and longer than was usual, cut so that the sheer weight of it dragged it over one eye whenever he dipped his head. When he came into the shop at night, smartly dressed in his business suit, that mane of hair looked absurdly out of place, defiant even, almost as if it was his claim to individuality, but today in a casual jacket and light flannels it looked absolutely right. His nose was fine and straight but perhaps a bit too long, she thought, enjoying her leisurely inspection. Added to his wide cheekbones and sharply-angled jaw, it gave his profile a severity which wasn't apparent face to face. From straight on you could see the good-humoured lift to his lips and the fine laughter lines, already forming down the side of his mouth and splaying out from the corners of his eyes. It was a warm face, an expressive face, but somehow still young and unfinished, as if it was waiting for the passage of time, or experience, to draw in some missing dimension.

Lazily he flicked open an eye and caught her staring at

him. Unperturbed he grinned and sat up. 'It's hot. Would you mind if I took off my jacket?'

She chuckled. 'You don't need to ask my permission not to bake yourself.'

Oliver gratefully took off his jacket, and his tie, and then loosened the top buttons of his shirt. Meggie, seeing a glimpse of paler skin, a light scattering of finest hairs, longed to run her fingers over his body and she shivered despite the heat.

'That's better. I'm near melted.' With a sigh of relief he flung himself down next to her and took her hand in a loose, friendly grip. 'Are you enjoying yourself, Meggie?' he asked, watching her just as closely as she had been looking at him.

'It's lovely,' she smiled up at him, her lips parted in deliberate invitation.

He kissed her, gently at first, his fingers playing in her hair. Her blood already warmed by the sun she rolled sideways, allowing her body to mould itself to his as he pulled her closer still, her pulse racing as she felt him grow and stiffen against her. She made no complaint when he burrowed through her clothing and released her breasts to the sun and groaned with pleasure when he lowered his head and took a nipple in his mouth, sucking and teasing, making her writhe with the need for more. Dimly she knew that, even with Wallace, it had never been like this, that Oliver was awakening something she had not known existed within her. Desperately she strained against him, abandoning herself to the desire which was building inside her, a tension that Oliver could so easily release. But then Oliver turned away for a moment to undo his own clothing and when he came back to her, his arousal nakedly obvious as he reached under her skirt, sanity returned.

'No,' she said gently, catching his hand, pushing him back.

'Meggie!' It was an agonised plea. She saw the longing in his face, the passion in his eyes and knew she was right. She had to stop this now.

'I'm sorry, Oliver. I can't,' she whispered, hanging her head from the shame of leading him so far only to deny him at the last moment. She had wanted him so much, too much. Surely he would know about her now, would realise that she was not what he thought her to be. But how, she sobbed suddenly, could she face him with the truth? To see the revulsion, the condemnation in his eyes would be the end of her. Why had she ever let it go this far? Why hadn't she stopped it long ago, before she had fallen in love with him?

Oliver wiped sweat from his face then turned round and silently adjusted his clothing. When he looked back at her he saw she was crying.

'Meggie.' He was on his knees in the sand beside her. 'I'm sorry. Please I know I shouldn't have . . . It's just that I love you so much.' He put his arms round her and she rested her head on his bare shoulder, breathing in the smell of him. 'I'm sorry,' he repeated. 'I didn't mean to frighten you.'

'It's not that . . .' She raised huge, round eyes and looked directly at him. 'I'm not frightened and it's me who should be sorry.'

He smiled, not understanding, still angry with himself. 'You've nothing to be sorry for, Meggie.'

'I have.' Her voice was sharp now. 'I should have stopped you earlier. But I couldn't. I wanted you as much as you wanted me,' she admitted finally.

He stared at her for a moment, slightly shocked by such frankness but then everything about Meggie McPherson was unusual; it was one of the things he liked about her. 'You did?' he asked.

She wiped her eyes and grinned lopsidedly. 'Of course I did. But we can't.'

Impulsively he threw his arms round her and drew her into a tight hug. 'Then we'll wait,' he told her, pausing a little for effect before adding, 'until after we're married.'

'Married?' Meggie's heart soared then plummeted to the ground in the space of two seconds. So many difficulties the dark, secret side of her insisted; so much happiness the other, more positive side countered.

'I love you, Meggie,' Oliver whispered into her ear. 'I love you.'

'I love you, too,' she told him, knowing it was true, that she would never love anyone as she loved him.

'Will you marry me, Meggie?' he asked.

She nodded. 'Yes,' she croaked. *Oh, please,* she prayed behind closed eyes, *make it be all right.*

CHAPTER SEVENTEEN

'Congratulations!' Sally, who was the first person they told, grabbed the astonished Oliver, whirled him round the room in an impromptu polka, then capped it with a kiss, darting her tongue quickly into and around his soft mouth before twirling away and enclosing her friend in a suffocating hug.

'When? Have youse set a date? Which kirk are you having? Who will you ask to the wedding? Where will youse live?' The questions tumbled out with breathless enthusiasm.

'Slow down, Sal. We're not even officially engaged yet.' But Meggie was infected with Sally's excitement and laughed with her high-spirited friend.

'What did your mum and dad say?' Sally asked Oliver. The light in Oliver's eyes snapped out. 'I haven't told them yet,' he admitted gruffly.

Meggie felt as if someone had doused her in cold water, sluicing her dream of happiness away and leaving only bleak reality. She dropped listlessly into a chair. 'They'll never agree, Oliver,' she said, understanding only too clearly how Oliver's parents would view his engagement to a girl of her background.

Sally was dismayed. 'I'm sorry, Meggie. That was a really stupid thing to go and say. Look, I'll away to bed, get out of your way. Leave youse to talk things through.' Ignoring their protests she fled, leaving Meggie and Oliver alone in the sitting room.

'Your parents'll never agree to us getting married,' Meggie repeated sadly as soon as the door closed.

'Of course they will!' Oliver had recovered himself enough to sound convincing. And, in fact, though the unavoidable interview with his parents would be uncomfortable, he had absolutely no doubt of his ability to win their support. And even if they weren't entirely convinced, they had only to meet Meggie to understand how he felt.

'Not when they know where I came from,' she insisted. 'Miners' daughters don't marry the mine owner's son. Nor do girls from the workhouse.'

'This is 1931, Meggie. Things are different now. Anyway, we're both of age so there's nothing they can do to stop us. Not that it'll come to that,' he added hastily.

'Oliver,' she asked. 'Do your parents know anything about me at all?'

'They know I'm seeing you; know you own the shop. . .'

'But nothing about my background?'

'No. Why should they? Let them judge you for what you are, Meggie,' he said, putting an arm round her. 'They're bound to say all the usual things about me being too young and not having enough money, but they'll come round in the end. Once they're used to the idea they'll want to meet you.'

She pulled a face. 'I'm already dreading it.'

He laughed and kissed her on the end of her nose. 'Don't worry. They'll love you. Anyway, it'll be worse for me, meeting your parents. They've no reason to be grateful to my family, have they? But I'd like to start off the right way, do it properly and ask your father if I can marry you.'

'You don't have to ask my father anything,' she told him firmly.

'Meggie,' he said thoughtfully. 'Don't you think this

would be a good time to try and make things right with your parents?'

'I don't even know their address,' she admitted, then feeling his insistent gaze on her, added, 'I suppose I could ask Mrs Cruickshank. It's probably in the workhouse records.'

'Ask her for it, Meggie,' he said, taking her in his arms and kissing her gently. 'Please. For me.'

There was nothing she wouldn't do for him. 'All right,' she agreed. 'For you.'

Oliver toyed with the food on his plate, feeling the tension round the dinner table rise with every passing second.

'She lives on her own? A girl of that age?' Elsie Laing sniffed her disapproval.

'Meggie's done very well for herself, Mother,' he insisted, knowing that there was nothing to gain by losing his temper. 'I've asked her to marry me.'

'Married! To someone we've never even met?' Elsie's fork clattered on to her plate. 'And what about Emily Sutherland? We all thought that you and Emily. . .'

'Mother . . .' Oliver sighed. The Sutherlands – wealthy owners of the Nethertown Mill – and the Laings were the burgh's most influential families. Elsie had long ago seen in the pretty but vacuous Emily, not only the malleable daughter-in-law who would have insufficient strength of character to withstand her own forceful personality, but also the means of bolstering the Strathannan Mining Company's flagging finances. So remorselessly had she thrown the two young people together that they could no longer stand the sight of one another. Fortunately for Oliver, all this had had no effect on his relationship with Emily's brother, Iain, who had been his best friend since

330

they had been packed off to school together as frightened and homesick eight-year-olds.

'I will never be able to face Mildred Sutherland again,' Elsie declared. 'To think that you could prefer a shop girl . . . a shop girl . . . to Emily. The disgrace! We'll never live it down.' She glared at her son, her anger rising even furher when he stared silently ahead, refusing to be drawn into an argument. Recognising that white-faced, thin-lipped stubbornness, a trait he had inherited from her own father, Elsie knew Oliver would be impossible to reason with now that he had made up his mind. Instead, she rounded on her husband. 'Wallace. You speak to him. This girl cannot possibly be suitable.' Flinging her screwed-up napkin on to the table, she flounced from the room, leaving her son and husband alone.

Wallace Laing's face bore an expression of open relief as he watched the door slam after his wife. As in so many other things he didn't share her views on the subject of his son's marriage and was infinitely grateful that he was not to have the empty-headed, vain and probably extravagant Emily foisted on to his family. He turned to Oliver and said, 'If you're sure you're making the right choice, Oliver, then you'll have my support. But I do think you could have taken the trouble to introduce us before things got to this stage.'

Oliver smiled at his father and half raised an eloquent eyebrow. 'You know why I didn't, Father.'

'Och, your mother'll come round. It doesn't matter a damn what she thinks anyway.' Wallace dismissed his wife's views as casually as he sometimes booted the cat through the back door. He poured brandy into each of their glasses, lit a cigar, settled comfortably in his chair and asked, 'So, tell me about her, Oliver. I must say she sounds as if she's a strong-minded woman. A shop of her own, eh?'

331

'That's what I like about her, Father. Meggie's got a mind of her own, and she's not afraid to use it.'

'Good for her.' But Wallace had a fleeting image of his own wife who was a little too fond of using her own mind, and tongue. 'Meggie you say? What's her family name?'

'McPherson. Meggie McPherson.'

The glass fell from Wallace's hand. The delicate balloon shattered, scattering hundreds of tiny shards over the tablecloth. Wallace watched the brandy stain work its way over the pristine crispness of the white linen, feeling the blood rush from his head then surge back again, pounding under his temples.

'Father! Are you all right?' Oliver was on his feet instantly.

Wallace recovered his wits sufficiently to shake his head and start coughing. 'Don't fuss,' he spluttered 'Brandy went back the wrong way, that's all. Fetch me a glass of water will you?'

While Oliver hurried to comply, Wallace Laing battled to overcome the devastating shock which his son had so innocently delivered. Meggie McPherson. His lovely little Meggie. But surely not. McPherson was a common enough name. Very likely it was a simple coincidence. But he knew that wasn't so. Meggie, his Meggie, had bought herself a shop with the money he had given her, he knew that much from Mrs Cruickshank, though to save himself from further torment and inevitable temptation he had never asked for more than the barest details. With an enduring fondness for the girl who had given him so much pleasure, he had sincerely hoped that she would find happiness. But with his own son? Even before the sweat of shock had dried on his face Wallace knew he had to put a stop to this.

Oliver brought a glass of freshly drawn water and offered

332

it to his father, concerned to see the hectic colour on his face, the way his breath was coming in shallow, panting gasps. 'Are you sure you're all right, Father?'

'Aye, aye.' Wallace waved him away irritably.

Oliver sat down and took a gulp of his own drink. 'I should like to bring Meggie back here for tea on Sunday, Father, if that's all right.'

Wallace was more in command of himself now. 'No. Not this Sunday. Give it a couple of weeks. Let your mother calm down a bit first.' Give himself time to think, time to see her for himself, warn her off. Whatever happened she couldn't be allowed to come to this house.

Oliver frowned, sensing the shift in his father's mood. 'If you think that's for the best,' he said, his voice stiff with disappointment.

'I do. Now I'm going to bed. Good night, Oliver.'

'Morning, sir, What can I get you?' Sally asked, looking up from the block of butter she was carefully cutting and wrapping. She recognised Meggie's Mr Wallace instantly and, for once bereft of speech, just stared.

'I want to speak to Miss McPherson,' he said, his tall, grey-haired figure seeming to fill and dominate the shop.

'She's not here, sir,' Sally answered politely. 'Can I help?'

'When will she be back?'

'I'm not right sure. She's gone to see her Ma and Pa, through by Glasgow. She'll be a day or two I should think.'

'Damn!' Wallace's gloved hand thumped against the counter. His head began to pound ominously and there was the familiar tight feeling in his chest. Whatever happened he had to see Meggie before Oliver could speak to her again, warn her away, make her understand that marriage to his son was quite impossible. Perhaps he should follow her to Glasgow. 'Where in Glasgow?' he demanded.

Sally scowled, irritated by his arrogant manner. 'I'm afraid I don't know, sir.'

Wallace levelled his most intimidating glare at her. Sally met it calmly, even allowing a small, defiant smile to ripple her well-shaped lips.

Abruptly Wallace reached into his inner pocket. Extracting a printed card he thrust it at her. 'Give this to Miss McPherson the minute she gets back. Tell her I called. It is very important. Do you understand?' He spoke to her as if she was a particularly dense eight-year-old.

'Yes, sir.' Sally took the card, laid it casually at the side of the till and went back to cutting butter.

Wallace stomped out of the shop.

As soon as the door crashed closed behind him, causing the little bell above it to jangle wildly, Sally picked up the card again and read it carefully. Provost Wallace Laing. So that's who Meggie's Mr Wallace was. No wonder he had dumped her the minute he found out about the baby. A man in his position wouldn't want to risk any scandal. But what did he want with her now? Intrigued, Sally edged the card carefully into the till drawer where it wouldn't be overlooked, but seconds later she snatched it out again and stood peering at it, lost in thought, a worried frown puckering her brow.

Meggie approached the tenement building which was now her parents' home at a brisk, determined pace. A small boy ran past, leaving the unmistakable smell of unwashed body lingering in the air behind him. There seemed to be children everywhere, running up and down the pavement, clustered

334

in the close and huddled on the stairs. Without exception they were barefooted, poorly-dressed and grubby, their faces streaked with dirt, their hair matted and tangled. The close smelt of damp, of rotting rubbish and urine.

Meggie was appalled. Could this really be where her country-loving mother was living? She checked the piece of paper which she held clasped in her hand. Mrs Cruickshank's writing was clear. There was no mistake.

Encouraged by Oliver, Meggie had come to Lairdstoun full of hope, believing that the news of her forthcoming wedding provided her with the perfect opportunity to make peace with her family. It would give her the chance to talk to them, to make them understand. But now that she was only minutes away from meeting them her confidence deserted her and she had a sudden, brutal recollection of the contempt on her father's face the last time she had seen him. Her stomach contracted tightly and, feeling faintly sick, she hesitated at the close entrance, half-tempted to turn and run, to catch the first train home to Inverannan. But if she did that she would never pluck up the courage to come here again.

She forced herself to go inside and found herself in a dreary hallway with sludge-coloured paint peeling from the walls. According to the address her father had given to the workhouse, they lived at number five. Meggie found it on the first-floor landing. Resolutely she stepped up to the door and knocked. Behind her she heard another door click open and turned round in time to catch a glimpse of a white face before the door closed again. As it did so her parents' door opened and a familiar face peered out at her.

There was a moment's stunned silence, then, 'Hello, Ma.'

'Meggie!' Netta made no attempt to invite her daughter

inside, nor was there a smile of welcome on her careworn face, just a shocked stare.

'What are you doing here?' Netta's voice was harsh and hostile and she cast a wary look at her neighbours' doors, knowing that sharp ears would be listening, ready to relay anything of interest to the whole close.

'I just wanted to see you, Ma.' Meggie tried unsuccessfully to meet her mother's eyes. 'Can I come in?'

Netta stepped back silently, allowing Meggie inside. Meggie followed her, then stood in the middle of the floor, not sure what to do or say next. Netta, equally confused, took refuge in familiar tasks, setting the blackened kettle back on the hob and rattling around with cups and spoons.

This, Meggie knew, was what was called a room and kitchen. The kitchen was a sizeable room and it needed to be for this was where the routine of daily life took place. The first half housed the sink, a small range, a scrubbed table and a cabinet. At the back, grouped round the fireplace, were two easy chairs. A drop-leaf table and a couple of upright chairs sat by the single window. Against the wall was a box-bed and, underneath it, a cupboard, half open to show the coal which was stored there. The door to the second room was open and Meggie could see a metal-framed bed which took up most of the available space. It wasn't that different, she thought, to the miner's cottage in Craigie. In fact, it was better, because here there was gas and running water. Even so, it was a depressing place.

The open window let in gusts of air which were tainted with the same foul stench as the close and there was a constant din, the gangs of children yelling and screaming, the shouts of the barrows boys, the clop of the horses pulling carts which rattled and bumped over the setts, the roar of motor cars and trucks. A heavy-footed neighbour clumped overhead making the whole room vibrate. Instinctively, Meggie knew how much her mother must hate living here.

'Now you're here you'd best sit down.' Netta carried cups of tea to the table and they sat silently on either side of it, staring out of the window down to the busy street below.

'Where's Pa and the boys?' Meggie asked, desperate to break through the defensive wall her mother seemed to have build round herself.

'Your Pa's at work. So's Perce. Bertie's off out somewhere. They'll be back for their tea.'

They sat on in tense silence, one not wanting to talk, the other not knowing how to begin, until Meggie suddenly remembered her basket. 'I brought you some things,' she said, picking it up and pushing it across the table.

Netta seemed reluctant but finally removed the cloth from the top. Meggie had raided the shop, filling the basket until it was so heavy she could hardly lift it. There were sweeties for the boys, tobacco and cigarette papers for her father, chocolate for Netta, a packet of tea, butter, cheese, tins of meat and much more. At the bottom, carefully wrapped in paper, was a lump of beef, specially bought from the fleshers first thing that morning. Netta, who had never, in all her married life, been able to afford such a thing, simply gaped at it.

Slowly she raised her eyes and stared at her daughter, obviously not liking what she saw. A thin hand went out and fingered the good wool of Meggie's black coat disdainfully. Abruptly she repacked the basket and shoved it back at Meggie. 'I don't need this. Take it away with you.'

'Ma! It's just a wee present. I couldn't come with nothing, could I?' There was a pleading note in her voice.

'Look at you! All dressed up like it's somebody's funeral.

And this!' She prodded the basket. 'Och, I know fine how you got the money to pay for fancy things like this, Margaret McPherson. And I want none of it.'

'I earned this through honest, hard work.' Meggie's temper flared.

'Aye, the sort of work you do lying on your back!' Netta was on her feet now, her pale eyes blazing. 'I never thought a daughter of mine could sink so low. You and that brother of yours. One a thief, the other a whore. I'm that ashamed of both of youse.' She covered her face with her hands and looked away in real distress.

'I am not a whore.' The words were clipped, tremulous with the effort of control.

Netta shook her head.

'Listen to me, Ma.' Meggie ran to her mother, grabbed her by the shoulder and spun her round, knowing she would never get another chance to explain. 'I am not a whore.'

'Wheesht! Keep your voice down. Do you think I want all the neighbours knowing about you? I'd never be able to hold my head up round here again.'

'To hell with the neighbours,' Meggie shouted, then, lowering her voice, 'Ma, won't you just listen to me, please?'

Netta looked at this daughter who had changed so completely from the fun-loving child she still remembered, seeing her for the first time as the strong-willed determined young woman she now was. And there was something burning in those deep, dark eyes, something which compelled Netta to sink back into her chair and wait.

Slowly, Meggie told her story, or almost all of her story. The child, the baby daughter she had given away, was locked in her heart, her secret grief, too raw, too terrible to be shared.

'Are you telling me the truth, Meggie?' Netta asked, but she already knew she was, it was there, in the pain in Meggie's eyes, in the tight lines of tension in her face as she spoke.

'Aye.'

'Matty was telling lies?'

'Och, Ma, don't blame Matty. He got in with a bad crowd. I didn't send him out to steal for me but I wasn't strict enough. I couldn't control him, Ma. I love him so much and I really tried my best for him. But it all went wrong.'

'Och, lass . . .' Netta's hands wound themselves together as love for her daughter fought with everything she had ever been taught about right and wrong. 'But to go with men. . .'

'I told you how it was, Ma. I didn't mean to do it but there was no other way.'

'And this man, the one . . .' She couldn't bring herself to put the rest into words.

'Mr Wallace. His name was Mr Wallace. And he was a kind, gentle man, Ma. He looked after me, and Matty.'

'He gave you the money for the shop?' It seemed almost unbelievable.

Meggie nodded.

'You should never have taken it. It isn't right, Meggie.'

'Would it have been better for me to be back on the streets? Or in some factory, if I was lucky, because that was all I could have hoped for without his help. He really cared for me, Ma, and I cared for him. It was just his way of making sure I was all right.'

Netta rubbed a hand over her aching head. When she looked up at her daughter again there were tears in her eyes. 'If only we'd never sent youse to the workhouse.'

Meggie had no wish to add to her mother's obvious

unhappiness. 'It's all in the past now, Ma. And I've got some special news for you.' Meggie covered her mother's roughened hand with her own and was relieved to feel a slight, answering pressure.

After a second, Netta withdrew her hand, wiped her eyes on her apron and did her best to smile. 'What is it, lass?'

'I'm going to be married, Ma.' Meggie couldn't keep the high note of elation from her voice.

At last Netta's pale eyes lost their guarded, suspicious look and met those of her daughter with open delight. 'Och, Meggie, but that's just grand!' To have her daughter a respectable, married woman, someone she could boast to the neighbours about, would do much to put things right and might even persuade Tam to relax his harsh, unforgiving attitude.

'You'll like him, Ma. I want you and Pa to meet him.'

'Tell me all about him.' Netta sat forward eagerly.

'His name's Oliver, Ma. He's tall, got dark hair and, och . . .' She spread her hands expressively. 'He's just wonderful.'

Behind them the door opened. The smile died from Netta's face and she jumped guiltily to her feet.

'Tam . . . Tam, it's our Meggie.'

Tam, tired and dirty after a full day at the steelworks, eyed his daughter coldly. 'I can see that. Well, there's nothing for the likes of her in this house. Tell her to get on her way.'

'Tam, please, hear what she has to say.' She went to her husband's side and plucked at his sleeve. 'Please listen to her.'

When Tam made no further comment, Netta turned to Meggie and pleaded, 'Go on, lass. Tell your Pa what you've just told me.'

For the second time that day, Meggie related her story. Tam made no move towards her but stood stiffly just inside the door, his face grim and unresponsive.

'Och, Tam, don't you see? She did it all for Matty.'

'That doesn't make it right!' he spat. 'Any decent lass would have stayed in the workhouse rather than sell herself the way she did.' He stared at his daughter, his eyes burning into hers as he spoke.

'Pa . . .' Meggie was appalled by the depth of hatred in his voice.

'She's getting married, Tam. She wants to bring her young man here to meet us.' Netta raced on, trying to ignore the fury she felt building in her husband. 'What's his name, Meggie?'

'Oliver. Oliver Laing.' Meggie's voice was dull and flat. She already knew there was nothing she could say or do to win back her father's love.

'And what does he do?' Netta glanced nervously at her husband who was now washing himself at the sink.

'His father owns the Strathannan Mining Company. Oliver works in the offices.' Meggie made an effort to sound happy, determined not to let her father destroy this fragile new relationship with her mother. But, to her dismay, Netta gave a small gasp and took a pace backwards. Tam growled, threw the bar of soap into the sink and turned round to face his daughter. 'You are going to marry Oliver Laing?'

'Aye.'

'It was thanks to his father that I lost my job, my house, and three of my children. He was to blame for everything that happened. It was all that bastard's fault!' Tam was angrier than Meggie had ever seen him. Flecks of spittle flew from the corners of his mouth, his eyes bulged and a vein pulsed alarmingly at his temple.

'It wasn't Oliver's fault!' Meggie backed away, moving closer to her mother as her father bore down on her.

'And what sort of man would marry the likes of you?' asked, his face level with hers. 'I'll tell you, shall I. No one! No decent man would want you. Never mind someone like Wallace Laing's son. Or haven't you told him about yourself?'

Meggie flushed and looked away.

'Tam!' Netta gasped. 'Surely there's no need . . .'

'There's every need. Coming here flaunting her fancy clothes and baskets of charity. All bought with dirty money. And then she rubs our faces in the muck by telling me she's going to marry the son of the bastard who caused all this in the first place. Go back to Inverannan. Ask Oliver Laing about all the men who died in his father's pits because he was too greedy for profits to pay to have the place made safe. Ask him what it's like to have a murderer for a father.' Tam swept the basket off the table, sending the contents rolling across the floor. In his fury he picked them up and tossed them, one by one, through the still open window.

All hope destroyed, Meggie ran for the door.

'Meggie!' Netta caught up with her on the landing in full view of the avid gaggle of neighbours who had gathered there, shamelessly eavesdropping.

'Netta, get back in here!' Tam roared. Faced with an impossible choice, Netta started to back towards the door.

Meggie turned away and ran blindly down the stairs, passing two long-legged youths on their way up.

'Who was that, Ma?' asked the taller one of the two.

Netta took one last look at her daughter's retreating

fiigure, hesitated for a moment, then said, 'No one. No one at all. . .'

'I'm sorry it didn't work out,' Oliver sympathised. Really nothing was going right.

Oliver had called in at the shop on his way to work this morning, not seriously expecting Meggie to be home and knowing, as soon as he saw her, that things had gone badly wrong. 'Still,' he reassured her, 'we've got one another and that's all that matters.'

Meggie smiled for the first time since coming home, though her red-rimmed eyes still bore evidence of the tears she had shed last night. 'Aye,' she agreed, her heart full of love for him. 'That's all that matters.'

Seeing the shop was still empty he stole a gentle kiss. Then glancing at the counter he picked up a copy of the *Inverannan Press*, the burgh's weekly paper. 'Better not forget this. Father asked me to pick him up a copy. His picture's in it.' He laughed. 'He cuts them all out and sticks them in a scrapbook. For posterity, he says. Vanity more like.' He folded the paper and jammed it in his pocket. 'Sunday, then?'

She nodded. 'Sunday.'

The shop was relentlessly busy that morning and it was after ten before there was a lull long enough for Meggie to pick up a copy of the *Press* and leaf through it. It was just idle curiosity really, the urge to see a picture of Oliver's father before she met him in the flesh.

The large, half-page photo of Wallace, shaking hands with a visiting MP, halted her. She stared, looking with fondness at the man who had treated her so generously. It was only when she saw the chain of office round his neck that she looked down at the caption describing the meeting.

343

'Wallace Laing, Provost of Inverannan welcoming Milton Buchannan, MP for Western Strathannan.' She must have read it wrongly, or perhaps the paper had made a mistake, she thought, feeling sick and faint as the full implication of that picture sank in.

She was still there, leaning weakly on the counter, staring at the paper when Sally, who had been stacking a delivery in the storeroom, came into the shop. Her habitually cheery greeting died on her lips when she peered over Meggie's shoulder.

At that point a customer came into the shop. Finding herself ignored by both of the young women behind the counter, she coughed and said, 'Well, if youse don't want my custom. . .'

Meggie didn't move.

'Yes, Mrs McElwain? What can I get you?' Sally asked, plastering a smile on her face.

Mrs McElwain offered a lengthy list and waited while Sally rushed around assembling the goods on the counter-top, piling them round Meggie.

'Och my, lass. You've a miserable face on you the day,' the woman joked. Then, getting no response, asked, 'Is there something the matter, hen?'

'Meggie's got a sore head, Mrs McElwain.'

'Och, there's a lot of the 'flu about just now. My neighbour's got a right bad dose. Not half as bad as I was last year, mind. Doctor Gillies said he'd never heard a chest like mine,' Mrs McElwain informed her trapped audience proudly. 'Now, my Ronnie, he's bothered by his bowels. Wind! Och, you've never heard the likes. Many's the time he's given me a right red face I can tell youse. Still, you know what they say. "Where e'er you be, let the wind blow free." ' She chortled horribly, rammed her groceries into a

fraying string bag and whispered, with a hint of embarrassment, 'Just put it in the book, hen.'

Sally waited until Mrs McElwain was safely out of the
shop before reaching into the till and handing Meggie the
card Wallace had left for her.

'He was here,' she said. 'Yesterday. Asking to see you.'

'I never knew,' Meggie whispered hoarsely. 'I never
knew. And he lied to me. Telling me his name was Mr
Wallace.' She brought her hand down on the picture so hard
that it stung, bringing tears of pain to her bleak eyes.

'They all do it, Meggie,' Sally told her. 'It's just a way of
protecting themselves.'

'Oliver . . .' Meggie breathed. 'We would have been so
happy.'

'You still will be,' Sally insisted briskly.

'How can we?' Meggie demanded. 'I've given birth to
Oliver's half-sister! His father's child. How can we get
married now?'

'What's wrong, Meggie?' Oliver asked. He had called at the
shop for her as usual on Sunday but instead of her normal,
happy smile, she had greeted him with a terse nod and
walked out on to the rainy street ahead of him, obviously
angry about something. He offered his arm but she ignored
it and even moved away from him a little so that they
walked towards the town as if they were strangers.

Meggie looked at him, pain slicing through her soul when
she saw the confusion on his face. She loved him so much
that her own heart had already broken. She could see his
love for her plain in his soft eyes but for how much longer
would it be there? The minute she told him about herself,
that love would turn to hate. There was no other way in
which he could possibly react. Dread making her voice

sound cold, she said, 'I need to talk to you. Can we go somewhere quiet?'

'We'll need to get out of the rain,' he said coolly, wondering what on earth he could have done to make her so angry with him. There was nothing that he could think of. 'What about the Pavilion Tea Rooms?'

'No. There'll be too many folk there.'

'But it's pouring with rain. We're already soaked. We need to get indoors.'

'The hothouses. They'll be quiet on a day like this.'

He shrugged. 'All right.'

The hothouses were four huge glass and metal constructions on the east side of the park, quite near the castle ruins. Although the tea rooms were fairly busy, Meggie's guess that the hothouses would be almost deserted proved to be correct. Oliver inserted two pennies into the turnstile and led the way towards an overpowering mass of greenery. It was dark, the overcast sky blocking out the light, and the rain beating on the glass roof made the place seem even more gloomy and oppressive. Silently they walked through the first two houses, passing only one other couple, and found a seat in a private corner, almost completely surrounded by exotic foliage. It was warm, the humidity adding to the sheen of fear already dampening her face.

'Are you going to tell me what's wrong?' Oliver asked impatiently, taking off his wet coat and sitting beside her.

'Afternoon, sir. Miss. Horrible day.' A park-keeper peered round the foliage at them and touched his cap respectfully.

'Yes,' Oliver agreed tersely. He detested the greenhouses, even on a sunny day, and this afternoon they were doubly depressing.

'Aye, well, enjoy your visit.' The park-keeper, satisfied

that there was nothing untoward taking place among his plants, sauntered off. But he would be back, just to keep an eye on the young couple. They wouldn't be the first to try take advantage of this secluded little corner and he didn't hold with that sort of thing, not at all.

'Are you going to tell me what's going on, Meggie?' Thoroughly disgruntled now, Oliver faced her angrily.

'I'm sorry,' she muttered, not noticing the rain which had dripped down her neck and was soaking her back.

'Sorry for what?'

'I don't want to get married, Oliver,' she whispered.

'What?' Surely he hadn't heard her correctly.

'I don't want to get married,' she repeated, unable to look at him.

Oliver watched her closely, saw the bleached white of her face, the puffiness around her eyes, the way her mouth trembled when she spoke. 'Och, Meggie, it's all right,' he said, taking her cold hands in his. 'I understand. But your parents will come round, I'm sure they will. And so will mine.'

She yanked her hands away and shoved them deep into her coat pockets. 'It's nothing to do with my parents.'

'Then what is it? Would you rather wait a year or so? It's all right if you do. It'll give me time to get some money together and find somewhere for us to live.' Oliver did his best to hide his disappointment. But, he told himself, Meggie was very young and probably scared of making such a big commitment. For her he was prepared to wait, indefinitely if necessary.

'You don't understand,' she cried. 'I don't want to get married to you, Oliver, not ever.' It was cruel and she knew it. His face seemed to set in an expression of hurt surprise. 'I'm sorry.'

'But why?'

'I just can't.'

The fringe of hair fell forward over his face, making him look boyish and softening the misleadingly hard profile. Meggie longed to lean over, to hold him and comfort him but knew she couldn't bear to touch him. She got up and began to walk away. 'I'm really sorry, Oliver.'

Oliver stared at her for a second, then lunged forward and grabbed her arm. 'Oh no you don't,' he snapped. 'You can't just tell me it's over and then calmly walk away.'

She looked down at the hand which was holding her arm so painfully tight. 'Let go of me.'

'Not until you sit down and tell me the truth.'

'There's nothing to tell.'

'I love you, Meggie,' he exploded. 'I want to marry you. I thought you loved me. You can't do this to me.' He ran his fingers through his hair, then looked into her eyes. 'Don't you love me, Meggie? Is that it?'

Meggie couldn't bear the anguish she read in his eyes. She sank down beside him knowing she had to end this, and do it without involving Wallace, do it in some way which would leave Oliver free to love someone else. There was only one way she could achieve that. 'I can't marry you, Oliver, because I haven't told you the truth. Your parents would never forgive you if we went ahead.'

'My parents aren't important, Meggie. You're the only person in the whole world who matters to me,' he told her, meaning every word.

'You won't say that when you know about me, Oliver. You'll hate me.'

He laughed uneasily. 'Don't be stupid, Meggie. Nothing can change the way I feel about you.'

'I told you that Matty and me ran away to Glasgow to

look for Ma and Pa?' she began, sliding along the seat so that she was as far away from him as possible.

'Yes.' He tried to take her hand but she pulled away from him.

'And I told you we came back to Inverannan?'

'Back to the workhouse,' he said impatiently. 'And I told you that didn't matter.'

'Not back to the workhouse. That came later. I went to live at the Houlets' Nest.' She looked at his face to see if he understood what she was saying but he was expressionless, listening. 'It's a brothel.'

Still he said nothing though she saw the way his eyes blinked rapidly, saw the way the little muscle at the angle of his jaw twitched as he clenched his teeth together.

'I didn't know what it was at first, but I soon found out. I worked there. As one of the girls. Going with men, Oliver. For money,' she added to be sure he understood precisely what she meant. 'I was trying to save enough for Matty and me to rent a place of our own.' Even now she couldn't bear for Oliver to think the absolute worst of her, had to try and justify herself to him.

Oliver sat so stiffly, so still, that it was almost as if he had stopped breathing. His face was a ghastly grey, making the faint haze of beard seem blue on his chin. His eyes were fixed and unblinking. But then he seemed to regain control of himself. 'Why didn't you tell me before?' he croaked, staring blindly in front of him

'I couldn't,' she whispered. 'I was so ashamed.'

'Meggie, Meggie . . .' he groaned. His voice seemed to break and he coughed to try and clear the tight lump from his throat.

Meggie fought the tears which were flooding her eyes. He was too good for her, she could see that clearly now. And still she had to hurt him, to put herself beyond his reach, to save him from the even greater pain of knowing his father's part in all this.

'That's not all,' she said.

'No, Meggie. You don't need to tell me anything else.' But they both knew he was frightened to hear what she had to say.

'A man took me out of the Houlets' Nest,' she went on ruthlessly. 'He set me up in a wee flat. I was his mistress, Oliver.'

He was almost relieved. 'Were you fond of him?' he managed to stammer out. He needed to know that there had been some emotion involved, that it hadn't been just for the money.

'Aye. I was. He was a good man.' Just like his son. Why hadn't she seen the likeness before? It was so obvious now. The same nose, the same shaped ears . . . 'I had his baby,' she blurted out suddenly. 'A little girl. She was adopted.'

He seemed to crumple before her. 'A child? You've had a child?' It was as if night had fallen and he was wading around in a sea of darkness. His head span.

'I'm sorry, Oliver.' How many times had she said that? 'But now you see why we can't get married.' She got up wearily, knowing that she had succeeded at last.

Oliver sank his face into his hands and couldn't look up, even when he heard her walking away from him.

'Good afternoon, miss. Looks like the rain's off,' the park-keeper said as she passed him. Meggie walked on, seeming not to have heard, all her concentration focused on getting to the privacy of her own home before she broke down.

'Stuck-up little madam,' the park-keeper sniffed, walking on up the hothouse.

'Still here, sir?' he asked cheerfully, seeing Oliver still sitting on the bench, leaning forward, his head in his hands. Bored by the never-ending perambulation of his territory, the keeper moved closer, hoping for a few minutes of conversation to break the tedium of his day. 'Looks like it's clearing up, sir. Nice bit of blue sky out there now.'

When the young gentleman remained silent the park-keeper scowled. Another toff who thought he was above talking to an ordinary working man, he thought bitterly. He was about to move on when he saw Oliver's shoulders heave, heard a strangled, choking noise from the man on the bench. For another minute he stood there, fascinated by the appalling spectacle of a grown man's tears.

'Bloody disgrace,' he muttered to himself when he finally moved away.

CHAPTER EIGHTEEN

'**H**e's here.' Sally ran to the window and waved vigorously at Ronnie who was standing in the street below, smiling up at her.

'You go, Sal. I'm not really in the mood,' Meggie said.

'Get your coat on,' Sally ordered. 'It's a lovely day and a run out'll do you good.'

'I've got a wee bit of a sore head. I'd be better to stay here.'

'Och, will you stop making excuses, Meggie! If you won't go then neither will I.' Sally took off her coat and plumped down into a chair.

'But Sal, you like Ronnie, I know you do. If I come I'll just be in the way.'

Sally kicked off her shoes and folded her arms.

'Go on, Sal, please. Enjoy yourself,' Meggie pleaded.

'Meggie McPherson! How much longer are you going to keep this up for? It's near three months now since I've seen you smile. You can't go on moping for ever. You'll just have to get on with life without Oliver, like I had to do after Douglas. You never saw me making everyone else around me miserable.'

'Now you're making me feel guilty.'

'Good, because to be honest you're being a right pain in the bum and I'm fed up with it.' She saw her friend's face fall and went on. 'Anyway, it's you, not me, that Ronnie's interested in and fine you know it.'

'But I'm not ready to get involved with anyone else. I still love Oliver.'

'Oliver's gone and the sooner you face that the better. And Ronnie's only trying to help.' She smiled at her friend and started to put her shoes back on. 'Come on. What harm can a day out do? And if you're worried about Ronnie, well, I'll be there, too, so nothing's going to happen, is it?'

'I suppose not.'

Sally flung Meggie's coat at her. 'Hurry up. He'll be wondering what's taking us so long.'

'All right,' Meggie agreed at last. 'And Sal?'

'What now?'

'Thanks.' To Sally's astonishment, Meggie kissed her.

A couple of minutes later they were all squashing into the front of Ronnie's van.

'Comfortable, ladies?' he asked, as they drove away.

'Och, aye.' Sally, who was in the middle, giggled and snuggled up against him.

He grinned. 'Watch it Sal, I might get the wrong idea.'

'I wish you would,' she said wistfully and even Meggie laughed.

It was a patchy sort of day, the sun doing its best to break through scudding clouds which had been delivering sharp showers all through the early morning. But the further they drove the brighter it became. The early autumn countryside looked beautifully mellow, the leaves at their greenest, just before they started to turn, the fields full of burnt stubble.

'I thought we'd go down to the coast,' Ronnie suggested. 'There's some bonny wee fishing villages there and we could have a picnic on a beach somewhere.'

'Sounds great,' Sally agreed enthusiastically.

'No!' Meggie shouted it and they both looked at her in amazement.

'Why ever not?' Sally asked.

Meggie shrugged. 'I'm not keen on the seaside. Anyway, it's too windy, the beach will be cold.'

'I thought you liked the sea?' Sally said. 'Didn't you go to one of the villages with Oliver . . . Ah . . .' She grimaced. 'Sorry, Meggie.'

'Meggie's right,' Ronnie rescued her quickly. 'The seaside can be cold at this time of year. Tell you what, we'll go into the hills. How about that?'

'Wonderful,' Sally agreed.

'I'd like that,' Meggie said softly.

'Och, isn't it beautiful?' Sally sighed as they drove through the strath an hour later, purple-hued hills making a stunning backdrop to the village they were approaching.

They drove over an ancient, hump-backed bridge which spanned the fast-flowing upper reaches of the Annan, and into the village – Pitochrie according to the sign. It was nothing more than a main street with a line of houses on either side, a church, a shop and a school, though there were glimpses of farms and other, larger houses set back from the road. On their right the hills rose steeply, their velvety slopes broken by a series of rugged glens and gullies. High above the village they could just make out the form of a shepherd and his dog, driving the sheep down from the upper slopes, his whistle and the dog's energetic barking echoing round the strath below. On their left, seeming to come right up to the backs of the houses, was a dense wood.

'How about having our picnic here?' Ronnie asked. 'We could go into the woods there, or, if youse like, we could walk up the hills a wee way. I bet there's a smashing view from up there.'

'The woods look a bit dark,' Sal commented. 'Can we get on to the hills?'

'We can if you don't mind walking,' Ronnie decided.

'Look, there's a track. It looks as if it goes to that cottage up there.' He squinted against the sun and pointed to where the ribbon of a rough track wound up the hillside.

Sally tucked one hand through Meggie's arm, took one handle of the picnic basket with the other, sharing the heavy load with Ronnie, and they started the long climb.

An hour later, red-faced, warm and ready to rest they found the perfect spot for their picnic.

A few feet from the track a clear mountain stream rushed to join up with the Annan in the valley below. It tumbled over huge rocks in a series of roaring, foaming falls, stilling temporarily in deep, calm pools before swirling on to the next silvered cascade.

'Perfect,' Ronnie declared, climbing clumsily onto a rocky outcrop which looked down on the water and helping the girls up beside him.

They ate a picnic of fresh bread, cheese, tomatoes and apples, then sat contentedly in the afternoon sun, sheltered from the breeze by the rocks.

'That water is just too tempting.' Sally, who could never be still for more than a few minutes at a time, jumped down from the rock.

'Where are you going?' Meggie called, then laughed as Sal reappeared, her legs bared, her skirt hitched up between her legs.

'Och, but it's cold!' Sally shrieked, plunging into the icy water and splashing with the inhibition of a child. 'Come on, Meggie. The water's lovely.'

Meggie hesitated for just a second then clambered down to remove her own stockings behind the rock where Ronnie couldn't see her. The water was beautiful, but so cold that after five minutes neither girl could feel her toes. Reluctantly they pulled their stockings over damp legs and scrambled back onto the rock where Ronnie had fallen asleep.

Meggie sat with her knees under her chin, gazing down at the valley below. 'Isn't this the most perfect place?'

'It's a bit remote. It's all right for a day out but I wouldn't like to have to live here. I mean, imagine what it must be like in winter. And what is there to do?' A town girl through and through, Sally recoiled from the isolation of a village so deep in the countryside.

'It must be beautiful with snow on the hills,' Meggie said wistfully, her imagination cloaking the slopes in crisp whiteness.

'And bloody cold,' the ever pragmatic Sally retorted. 'And look at that wee cottage up there. It must be awful living somewhere like that. They're miles from anyone else. It must take them two hours just to get to the village shop and back.'

Meggie squinted in the direction of Sally's pointing finger. There, a little higher up the hillside, nestling in a natural hollow beside a single rowan tree, was a tiny cottage. As they looked, the shepherd, his dog circling round his feet, came down off the hills and walked towards the house. Seeming to sense the presence of strangers, the dog barked. The shepherd glanced up, saw them, waved and disappeared inside.

They sat on in companionble silence for another half an hour before Ronnie stirred and decided it was time to start off for home.

Sally laughingly unembarrassed, decided she had to answer an urgent call of nature and went off to look for a suitably private place, leaving Meggie alone with Ronnie.

'I've had a wonderful time,' she told him, helping to repack the hamper.

'Me too,' he said seriously. 'We could do it again next Sunday if you like. Just the two of us.'

Meggie looked away. 'I don't know, Ronnie.'

He reached for her hand, and she didn't have the heart to pull it away. 'I know you're still hurting, Meggie, so I won't put any pressure on you. But we can still be friends, can't we? Where's the harm in a day out together?'

'I . . .' she started.

'Tell you what,' he interrupted her before she could frame a suitable excuse. 'If it's nice next Sunday, I'll take you up to St Andrews. It's a smashing wee town.'

'I don't think. . .'

'Ask Sally to come, too, if you like,' he offered anxiously.

She laughed. 'All right. You win.'

'Braw!'

By the time they got back to Inverannan, it was almost dark. The rain which had managed to hold off for their day out began to fall as if making up for lost time. The pavements were shiny with water, the streets eerily dark and deserted. As they drove up the hill towards the shop, Meggie thought she saw a shadowy figure by the door but, at the sound of the approaching van, it turned briefly then hurried away.

'Did you see someone then?' she asked.

'Where?' Sally, who had been dozing, roused herself and looked round blearily.

'In the shop doorway.'

'I didn't see anything,' Ronnie said, but he had been concentrating on the road. 'Are you sure there was someone there?'

'I think so.'

'Probably someone run out of sugar. You know what they're like,' Sally suggested.

357

'Aye. I suppose so.' It was true that they were frequently disturbed on Sundays by emergency requests but surely anyone wanting to buy something would have waited until the van drew up.

'Give me your keys and wait here. I'll just have a wee look before you go in.' Ronnie turned his collar up against the rain and disappeared round the back of the shop. 'Everything's fine,' he announced, five minutes later. 'Probably just someone sheltering from the rain.'

They thanked Ronnie again – Sally even gave him a friendly kiss on the cheek – then, with a toot on his horn he drove away and the girls ran indoors.

'Aren't you glad you decided to come?' Sally asked, sinking wearily into a chair and kicking off her shoes.

'Aye. I really enjoyed myself,' Meggie admitted, realising with a small shock that she had hardly thought of Oliver all day.

'All that walking's tired me out,' Sally yawned, laying back and closing her eyes. A full day of watching Ronnie looking at Meggie had left her feeling unusually dispirited. Life was so unfair, she thought, indulging in a rare moment of self-pity.

Meggie too was tired, her legs aching from the long climb up the hill and back, her eyes heavy from the sharp country air. Sighing contentedly she relaxed in a chair, closing her eyes and reviewing the day.

She felt happier tonight than she had done for a long time and much of it, she knew, was thanks to Ronnie Sandys. Lacking the social polish and urbane confidence conferred by Oliver's more affluent background, Ronnie looked exactly what he was – a working man – but he was well-mannered, gentle and unfailingly good-humoured. She also knew that he was hard-working and generous with his time.

In fact, she couldn't think of anything she didn't like about him. He was even quite good-looking, though in a very different way to Oliver. Where Oliver was slim, his features quite sharply cut, Ronnie was more heavily built, his upper body well developed by the constant lifting his job entailed. His face was rounder, his features – taken separately – coarser, and his gingery hair was already receding a little, making his brow seem disproportionately high.

But the overall effect was a perfect reflection of his personality – kind, witty, even-tempered and reliable. And he had been so patient, overcoming his disappointment when she became involved with Oliver and making sure he stayed on friendly terms with her. Always hoping, she realised now, for another opportunity. She couldn't let him down, not again, so she would go out with him on Sunday. But beyond that she simply couldn't think.

True to his promise, Ronnie took Meggie – alone because Sally insisted she had to go and visit her family – to St Andrews the following Sunday. He was an undemanding but entertaining companion, making it easy for Meggie to relax and enjoy a second day out.

They roamed around the historic old burgh, looking in at the colleges, walking round the abbey and castle ruins and even had a quick look at the famous golf club before finding a pleasant restaurant for high tea. Realising he would need to tread very carefully indeed if he was to have the remotest chance of building a relationship with Meggie, Ronnie was a model of decorum. When he delivered her home that evening he contented himself with simply pecking her cheek. She, equally cautious, was relieved when he didn't linger, so solving the problem of whether she should ask him upstairs for supper.

Rather than negotiating the boxes and crates which were stacked in the backyard, Meggie let herself in through the shop, struggling with the triple locks in the dark. Humming to herself she went slowly upstairs and into the sitting room, walking over to switch on the standard lamp.

'Hello, Meggie.' The soft, low, male voice was so unexpected that she screamed, dropped her bag and backed towards the door, her heart pounding in fear.

In the shadows of the room a dark figure detached itself from a chair and walked towards her. 'Don't be frightened, Meggie,' it said, the smooth, almost laughing tone sounding infinitely threatening.

'Get away from me,' she screamed, feeling for the door.

But still he came towards her, reaching out and grabbing her wrist before she could get to the door handle. Sure her last moment had come she opened her mouth to scream again but the sound was stifled by a calloused hand, which clamped itself over her face. Even as she sank her teeth into it, he reached out and flicked on the main light.

She blinked and stared up into the grinning face of a young man.

'That's not a very friendly way to welcome your brother,' he said, rubbing his damaged hand.

'Matty?' She could still hardly believe it. 'Matty, is it really you?'

He grinned a familiar, cheeky smile, threw himself back into the chair, took out a packet of cigarettes, lit one and took a deep, appreciative draw before answering her. 'Don't tell me you don't recognise me,' he drawled in his newly deepened voice.

'Of course I do.' She came nearer to him now, studying him closely.

He had changed, she saw that right away. Like her he had

grown up. Though smaller than her he was stockily built and powerful. His face was leaner, harder looking and the untidy hair and the dark stubble on his unshaven chin gave him a scruffy appearance, as did his shabby clothes. But his eyes were the same as she remembered them, dark, heavy-lidded and secretive. She felt stangely uncomfortable under his amused gaze.

'Well, big sister, you seem to have done very well for yourself,' he said. 'A shop and wee house all of your own. And nice clothes, too.' His eyes raked her and she felt self-conscious about her stylish dress and fashionable shoes. 'The business must be doing well.'

'I work hard for what I've got, Matty,' she told him, sounding defensive.

'I never said you didn't. It's good to know that someone in the family is getting on in life.' He sounded bitter and Meggie was shocked to realise that she didn't much like this new version of her brother. But, she told herself, almost as soon as the thought surfaced, Matty had had a difficult time of it, and that was partly her fault.

'How did you know where to find me?' she asked, sitting down opposite him because her legs felt so shaky.

He shrugged. 'I asked around.'

'What about . . . I mean when did you get out of the. . .'

'Reformatory,' he supplied. 'That's what it was, Meggie. A reformatory for difficult boys. A year or so ago. It was a bad place, Meggie. Worse than the workhouse. I wish you hadn't let me go there.'

'Matty! There was nothing I could do,' she cried.

'I was just a wee lad, Meggie. You were supposed to be looking after me,' he accused, those unnervingly intense eyes seeming to bore into her.

'Aye. And I was just a young girl. I did terrible, awful

things to try and provide a home for you, Matty. So don't you dare try to make me feel worse than I already do about what happened. I've suffered, too, you know.' She glared at him angrily.

'It wasn't my fault,' he whined, with a confusing return to the little boy she remembered. 'Don't be angry with me, Meggie.'

She sighed. 'I'm not. It was just such a shock seeing you here. But I am glad you've come.'

'Are you?' he asked.

'Of course I am. You're my brother. Now then, tell me what you've been doing.'

'This and that.' He was deliberately vague. 'I stayed in Glasgow, slept rough for a while.'

'You were on the streets?' She was horrified.

'Aye. I was looking for Ma and Pa. I found them in the end but they wouldn't let me stay. That's when I decided to come here.'

'I went to see them too,' she said sadly. 'I think Ma was pleased to see me but Pa'll never forgive us, either of us. I write to her but she's never written back.'

'Too bad. They don't matter any more. You and me have always been a pair. We belong together, Meggie. You won't let me down again, will you?' he added slyly.

'No, of course I won't, she told him, deliberately ignoring the unease his sudden reappearance was causing her.

'Can I stay here, then?'

'Well . . . I . . . that is, there's no spare bed.'

'So who's living with you?'

'Sally.'

'That little cow who lived next door?'

'Matty! Sally's my best friend.'

'Sorry.' He held up his hands. 'I didn't mean anything.

362

It's just the way everyone talks, at the home, on the streets. I'll soon get out of it now I'm with you.'

'You'd better.' But she made herself smile at him. 'But we really don't have a spare bed.'

'Doesn't matter. I can sleep on the sofa. Even the floor would be better than what I've been used to.'

'I suppose so,' she said uncertainly, wondering what Sally's reaction would be.

'Look, if you don't want me to stay, just say so and I'll go. I've slept rough before you know. I won't even notice the rain.' He coughed, thumping at his chest. 'I've a wee bit of a cold, but no matter. I'll go if you don't want me here.'

Meggie knew she was being manipulated but some part of her felt she owed him something. 'You can have my room. I'll sleep on the sofa.'

'There's no need for that.'

'You can't sleep out here, Matty. We both get up early in the morning. We'd wake you up and you'd be in the way.'

'All right.'

'I'll just go and get some of my things out.' In truth she needed some time to get her jumbled thoughts in order. She rummaged in her wardrobe, her mind only half on her task. What was it about Matty that disturbed her so much? Why did she feel so uncomfortable with him? He was still recognisably her brother but he felt like a stranger, a hostile, threatening intruder. But she was being unfair. Of course he had changed, but so had she. They would both need to get to know one another again. And it was obvious that he had been very unhappy. No one had come along to help him the way Wallace and Mrs Cruickshank had helped her. So, she told herself, gathering up enough clothes for tomorrow, it was up to her to make him feel wanted again. He was right, he was her brother. They belonged together.

'There. I'll have to leave the rest of my things in there but the wardrobe's quite big. There'll be room for your stuff, too.'

'I haven't got any stuff.'

'What, nothing at all?'

'Just what I'm wearing. No money, no clothes. Nothing.'

'Oh, Matty . . .' She reached for her purse and handed him a ten-shilling note. 'Here.'

'Och, I can't,' he said, pocketing it quickly.

'Tell me when you need some more.'

'Thanks. I'll pay you back as soon as I get a job. If I could just stay here until then?'

'Aye. That'll be fine,' she said, relieved to know this wasn't going to be a permanent arrangement. Then a disturbing thought occurred to her and she looked at him suddenly, her expression puzzled. 'How did you get in here?'

'Through the door,' he laughed.

'The back door?'

'Aye.'

'Did Sally let you in?'

'No. It was open.'

'It can't have been. We're always careful to lock it behind us.'

'Are you calling me a liar?' he demanded, his dark face ugly with anger.

'No . . . no, of course not. But I'm sure Sally wouldn't forget something like that.'

'Well, she must have, mustn't she?'

'I suppose so,' she allowed reluctantly.

At that point Sally herself burst into the room, talking even before she came through the door.

'Did you have a good time, Meggie? Where did he take

you? St Andrews was ... Oh!' She stopped in obvious confusion.

'Sally, this is my brother, Matty. You remember him?'

'Aye. Of course I do,' Sally smiled at him cheerfully. 'Nice to see you again, Matty.'

Matty allowed his eyes to travel the length of her body, lingering obviously on her full breasts. 'And you,' he said, the innuendo plain.

Sally flushed angrily. 'Your manners haven't improved I see,' she snapped back. 'You always were an ignorant little sod.'

'Sally! Matty!' Meggie cried in dismay.

Matty shrugged. 'Every woman likes to be appreciated. That right, Sal?'

'Not by kids like you, I don't,' she retorted.

'Sorry, I'm sure. But if you don't want to be looked at, wear a decent dress,' he sneered, resting his gaze again on her well-displayed cleavage.

Sally's face burned scarlet and for once she was speechless.

'I'll get off to bed then.' Matty uncoiled himself from the chair and sauntered through to the bedroom, leaving his aghast sister staring after him.

'Oh, Sal, I'm sorry,' she said, turning to her friend.

'It's not your fault,' Sally said, but Meggie knew she was very angry. 'What's he doing here anyway?'

'He's staying here until he gets a job.'

'That'll be a treat for us, won't it?' was Sally's acid comment.

'He is my brother, Sal.'

'Och, I know. Don't worry, I'll soon sort him out.' She turned and grinned suddenly, her good humour restored. 'Forget about him for now. Tell me about you and Ronnie.'

'There's nothing to tell.'

Sally sighed dramatically. 'I can see I'll have to have a good talk with Mr Sandys.'

'You will not!' Meggie shouted her alarm, quite ready to believe that Sally would do exactly that.

'Keep your breeks on! I was only kidding,' Sally chuckled. 'You will be seeing him again though?'

'Of course I will.'

'Thank goodness.'

'Tomorrow, when he brings the papers.'

'Meggie!'

'Just give up, Sal, will you?' she laughed.

'All right.' Sally yawned widely. 'Think I'll go to bed.' She gathered her things and, still yawning, made for her bedroom.

'Sal,' Meggie spoke just as she started to close the door. 'Did you lock the back door when you went out?'

'Aye. I always do.'

'Are you sure?'

'Aye. You know how the door's warped? I had to give it a good jerk to shut it. I thought the key would be hard to turn but it locked easily. I was surprised. That's why I remember. Why?'

'Matty said it was open.'

'Well, it wasn't.'

'Then how did he get in?'

Sally snorted. 'It's easy if you know how. I'll get my dad to come and show you, shall I? He's an expert in getting into places without a key.'

'Oh no, . . .'

'Too late to worry about it now, Meggie,' Sally advised with her usual practicality. 'Now I am off to bed. Good-night.'

'Night, Sal.'

It wasn't the lumpiness of the sofa that kept Meggie awake well into the small hours that night.

CHAPTER NINETEEN

The atmosphere in the house was never quite the same again. Matty had brought something bitter and unpleasant with him and it tainted everyone around him.

'I don't know what to do about him,' Meggie confided in Bertha Cruickshank one afternoon. 'He and Sally don't get on at all. He stays in bed till midday then, when he does get up, he goes out and stays out until all hours of the night. I'm worried that he's getting into bad company but he gets angry when I ask him where he's been. I feel like I'm letting him down all over again.'

Mrs Cruickshank, who had her own low opinion of Matty McPherson, wasn't inclined to be sympathetic. 'You're too soft with him, Meggie. He made his own trouble and the sooner you stop blaming yourself, the better you'll be. You don't owe him anything. Is he not having any luck finding work? That's what he needs. A good hard job.'

'There's not a lot of work about and no one's going to employ someone with his record. To be honest I don't think he's even trying. Ronnie says he sees him hanging round the town most days. It's not good for him having all that time on his hands.'

'If you want to keep him occupied why not make him work for you? You're giving him money anyway, you might as well make him earn it.'

'I'm not sure Sally would be happy having him around the shop all day.'

'Didn't you say you were thinking about taking on a delivery boy?'

'Aye.' Meggie's eyes lit up with enthusiasm. 'All the town centre grocers have a delivery service. I've been looking into it and I know I can do the same thing, but more cheaply. I'm sure to get a lot more business if I can deliver the same range of goods with a reliable and friendly service. I've talked it over with Ronnie and he thinks it's a good idea.'

Bertha Cruickshank smiled. Ronnie's name was a regular feature in Meggie's conversation and it was obvious that the pair were becoming close. 'Well then, there's your answer. Buy a bicycle, stick a basket on it and send Matty off delivering things for you. He won't be hanging round the shop and at least you'll know what he's up to all day.'

'I suppose I could,' Meggie said thoughtfully. The idea had already occurred to her but she had shied away from it, not at all sure that Matty would be reliable enough.

'Right, that's quite enough about that brother of yours. Now tell me about you and Ronnie Sandys. I've seen him around the town and folk speak highly of him.'

Meggie giggled. 'You've been checking up on him!'

'No ...! Well, maybe just asking a few folk,' Bertha admitted with a laugh. 'It was a shame about his father, wasn't it?'

'Yes. But old Mr Sandys had been ill for a long time. Ronnie was expecting it but he was very upset. It had just been him and his Dad for so long I think he's finding it hard living on his own now.'

'Do you see a lot of him?'

'Twice a day when he comes with the papers. And we usually go out on Sundays.'

'Does he get on with Matty?'

369

'Ronnie gets on with everyone. I think he makes a special effort with Matty for my sake.'

'It sounds as if he's serious about you, lass.'

Meggie looked uncomfortable. 'He is.'

'But?'

'Och, I don't know. I am fond of Ronnie, very fond of him. I'd hate to lose him. But it's not the same as it was with Oliver.' But Meggie knew what the problem really was. Deep down she was scared. Frightened that honest, gentle Ronnie would one day find out the truth about her. And like Oliver, he would reject her. What decent man wouldn't?

Bertha smiled and patted her hand. 'Maybe you don't feel as strongly about him as you did about Oliver but, you know, that kind of love doesn't last more than a year, two if you're lucky. It's the sort of steady affection and respect that you feel for Ronnie that's really important. Ronnie Sandys sounds as if he's got all the qualities to make a good husband. He's hard-working, kind and trustworthy and those are the things that really count. And it's not as if he's got a mother and father who are going to ask a lot of awkward questions, is it?' As always she understood the real reason for Meggie's doubts.

'No . . . And I know he loves me.'

'Well, then. You could do an awful lot worse, Meggie. If Ronnie pops the question, you think hard about what *you* want before you turn him down.'

'Here's the list. You'll get two boxes in the basket at a time. The orders are made up and stacked against the wall. Start at the far end and work your way back.'

'I'll be bloody knackered by the time I've delivered that lot,' Matty complained.

'I need the help and you need the job. It'll be good for you. It's time you were earning your keep.'

'If you don't want me here you've just got to say so, Meggie,' he said petulantly. 'Not that I can afford to live anywhere else on what you're paying me.'

'You're getting a fair rate for the job. Now just go and get on with it,' she snapped, weary of his idleness, his sullen temper, the bad atmosphere which pervaded the place whenever he and Sally were together.

'You've turned into a right bitch, Meggie,' was his parting shot as he jumped on the bike and pedalled unsteadily down the hill.

'Bravo,' Sally cheered, as Meggie came back into the shop. 'It's time you were standing up to him. Honestly, it's hard to realise you two are actually related. How come he's so horrible and you're so nice?'

'Don't you start, Sally. There's folk waiting to be served. Go and see to them.' For once Sally failed to bring a smile to her friend's strained face.

'He's doing fine,' Meggie, stirring a pan of rich gravy, said in answer to Ronnie's question. 'And when he's finished the deliveries he even comes and helps out in the shop.' She couldn't quite keep the note of wonder out of her voice. Matty had astounded her by working with a degree of diligence of which no one had thought him capable. The deliveries were made promptly, accurately and, judging from the complimentary remarks from satisfied customers, politely. 'You should see him serving the women,' she added, laughing now. 'A proper charmer, he is.'

'I can imagine,' Ronnie said wryly, his face creased in concentration as he carved the joint of beef ready for Sunday lunch. 'Still, I'm glad he's pulling his weight.' For

Meggie's sake he tried hard to sound pleased, but there was something unpredictable about Matty's character that made him uneasy. One moment he would be quite deliberately charming, adopting a smooth, urbane manner which completely belied his background and gave him an aura of maturity and sophistication that, together with his brooding good looks, drew the women customers to him like flies to sticky paper. The next minute, however, that same dark face could assume the churlish sullenness of a difficult adolescent while he whined and sulked like a thwarted infant.

To Ronnie it was perfectly obvious that Matty was shamelessly exploiting the obligation Meggie felt towards her brother. He ached to put the lad right – a hefty kick up his lazy backside would do him the power of good – but Ronnie knew Meggie well enough to understand that he couldn't criticise her brother without very good reason, certainly not on something as nebulous as this gut feeling that the lad was a right bad lot. But, if everything went as well as he hoped it would, he would soon be in a position to offer Meggie some real protection and sort out young Matty in the process.

'Will youse come to the table please.' Meggie called Matty and Sally from their respective rooms as she set plates brimming with beef, vegetables and roast potatoes on the table, feeling proud of her efforts. Since his father's death, Ronnie often joined them for Sunday lunch and she relished the opportunity to display her domestic skills. She felt easier about inviting Ronnie upstairs now that Matty was living with them. His very presence defused the gossips' tongues and gave the little household a respectability that two girls living on thir own couldn't hope to achieve. Meggie loved it when they all gathered to sit round the table for a formal meal, discussing the past week, almost as if they were a real family. And today there was an extra gleam of excitement in her eyes as she took her place opposite Ronnie, who smiled back at her, his own eyes mirroring her pleasure.

'What's this then?' Sally asked, fingering the wine glass by her plate and looking at Meggie, already suspecting what was coming.

Ronnie finally won his battle with the cork and, with a flourish, placed the bottle of wine in the centre of the table. 'It's a celebration,' he told her.

They waited while he filled each glass with ruby-coloured liquid.

'Hurry up,' Matty complained. 'The dinner's getting cold.'

'A toast,' Ronnie announced importantly. 'To Meggie, who has agreed to be my wife.' He raised his glass in her direction.

Sally ignored her wine and shoved her chair back so suddenly that it toppled over. She hopped over it and ran round the table to embrace her friend. 'That's wonderful,' she cried, kissing Meggie warmly. 'I'm right pleased for you.'

'What about me then?' Ronnie teased.

Sally turned more slowly to Ronnie. If there was a germ of regret in her heart she refused to let it show on this of all days. 'Congratulations, Ronnie,' she said, her voice soft and sincere.

He held out his arms to her. 'Thanks, Sally.' He held her close for a minute, understanding how difficult this must be for her. She had never made a secret of how she felt about him but, in typically generous fashion, had accepted that he could not return her feelings, even finding room in her heart to be happy for Meggie. It was a situation which might have destroyed a lesser friendship. The fact that it hadn't was almost entirely due to Sally's unselfish attitude and her place in Ronnie's affections was second only to Meggie herself.

She looked up at him now, a suggestion of moisture in her eyes. 'I know you'll be happy. You're just perfect for each other.'

Over Sally's head, Ronnie smiled at Meggie who was dabbing surreptitiously at her own eyes.

'Can we get on with the meal?' Matty asked, instantly dispelling the emotion.

'Aren't you going to congratulate us, Matty?' Meggie frowned.

There was an uncomfortable pause before Matty said, 'I suppose so.' He picked up his glass and drained it in one gulp. 'Congratulations. I hope youse'll be very happy.' But it was said without warmth and he started on his dinner without waiting for the others, his expression preoccupied.

A wedding between Ronnie and Meggie would ruin all Matty's plans and was not something he felt inclined to celebrate. He had worked harder during the last four months than he had ever worked in his life. Not because he got any particular satisfaction from a good day's work but because Meggie had a thriving little business here and he meant to have a part of it for himself. But first he had to make her trust him, show her that he could work hard and be relied upon. No easy task given his past record but one made easier than it should have been by Meggie's strong sense of loyalty, something he played on craftily, reminding her frequently and with apparent innocence, of the hardships he had suffered on her behalf, of how she had let him down, repeating time and time again that they were family, that they belonged together.

He stuffed his mouth full of meat and glared at Ronnie from under lowering brows, then shifted his gaze to take in Sally, too. If either of them had happened to look up just then they would have been shocked to see the hatred in the black depths of his eyes.

Meggie, glancing up and catching her brother's bitter expression, felt her heart turn over and was aware of how precariously balanced her happiness was. One careless word from Matty could ruin everything and, just for a moment, the hostility in his face when he looked at Ronnie had been frighteningly obvious. But, she asked herself, what reason could Matty possibly have for wanting to destroy them? Unless he thought that there would be no place for him here once she and Ronnie were married? Yes, she decided, that was the most likely explanation and something she should have anticipated.

After all, she knew how insecure Matty was. Time and time again he had reminded her that she was all he had, that they belonged together. It had been stupid to announce her wedding plans so suddenly, without first warning him. Though he had the body and manner of a grown man, in many ways he was still immature, reacting with instinctive, childish spitefulness whenever he felt threatened. Goodness knows what he might do or say if he thought she was going to let him down again. She would have to talk to him, tonight, make him understand that he would always have a home with her, make him see that his future, as much as hers, depended on keeping shameful secrets from the kind and honest man who was going to be her husband.

Determined to stay as near to the truth as possible and so minimise the risk of some casual remark exposing her, she had already told Ronnie an edited version of the past. He knew about the workhouse, and that she had worked at a public house – but as a barmaid. He had accepted that she had earned enough money to rent a small flat at the bottom of the town and had sympathised when she described how everything had gone wrong when Matty was arrested for stealing. He already knew that Mrs Cruickshank had helped her to buy the shop and, like Oliver, wrongly assumed that the help had been financial. Meggie could not correct him.

It was a credible enough story and Ronnie, who was not suspicious by nature, never saw any reason to doubt any of what Meggie told him. Meggie despised herself for deceiving him, but for his sake she hoped that the truth would always remain buried.

She loved Ronnie, Meggie knew that now, though not in the same, intense way that she had loved Oliver. What she felt for Ronnie had grown gradually as their friendship deepened, strengthening week by week as they got to know one another better, until there came the time when she simply couldn't imagine life without him. When he asked her to marry him it seemed the natural thing to do, the next logical step in their relationship and, putting aside her guilt about her past, she had been glad to accept. Ronnie would give her the respectability and security under which her shame could stay hidden. It was her second chance for happiness and she had learnt her lesson the first time. She wasn't going to throw it all away by telling Ronnie things which could only hurt him and ruin both their lives.

After dinner, as Meggie had known she would, Sally had gone to visit her family. Matty, too, had disappeared and was unlikely to return until late evening.

In the sitting room, comfortably arranged on the sofa, Ronnie wasted no time in pulling Meggie close to him.

'Happy?' he asked, having kissed her thoroughly.

She nodded. 'Aye. I am happy, Ronnie.'

He looked at her thoughtfully. 'You went very quiet over dinner. I wondered if you were having second thoughts.' When she didn't say anything he went on. 'I'm not like Oliver Laing, Meggie. I couldn't care less about you being in the workhouse, if that's what's bothering you. To my mind everyone's the same whether they're born rich or poor.' He understood that, because of her background, she had been badly let down by Oliver Laing, but was hurt that she didn't seem to trust him completely either. 'I love you, Meggie, and I always will.'

'I know. And I love you, too, Ronnie.' But there was so much she couldn't put into words.

'And you haven't changed your mind?'

'Of course not.' She smiled at him now and reached up, covering his mouth with her own.

Ronnie responded instantly, holding her to him and easing her down into the cushions. Meggie wound her arms round his neck, gasping with pleasure as his hands found their way under her blouse and grasped a nipple, gently teasing it to hardness. Their tongues met, intertwining briefly, then he plunged into her mouth, his desire hard and urgent against her groin. She responded instantly, pressing herself into him, a tremor of excitement running through her at this tantalising taste of what was to come. But, then, desperate though he was to make love with her, though his body ached with denial, Ronnie pulled away and sat up, as she had known he would.

'I want you so much, Meggie,' he groaned, the repeated frustration getting harder to bear.

She cradled his head. 'I know. I know.'

He kissed her again, his hand sliding back to her firm breasts where the nipples were still hard with need. 'Next September we'll be married,' he told her by way of consolation, then groaned. 'It's such a long time. . .'

'Ronnie, if you really want to . . . you don't need to wait,' she offered softly, her own need as urgent as his.

But Ronnie's beliefs were too deeply embedded for that. 'No, lass. It wouldn't be right. You wouldn't think much of me afterwards if I let you take a risk like that.' He took her face between his hands and kissed her lightly. 'I know you really want to keep yourself for our wedding night and I respect you for that, Meggie. I really do. It'll be all the more special because we've waited.'

'There you are, Mrs Penman. Here, let me open the door for you.' Matty rushed round the counter and held the door open for the plump, middle-aged woman in her everyday shawl and old shoes. She simpered like a sixteen-year-old and flashed a ridiculously coquettish smile at him as she went out. 'Och, that bag looks right heavy. I'll carry it home for you. It'll only take a minute.' Matty winked at his sister, offered his free arm to Mrs Penman and escorted her to her house, just across the road.

'If he carries on like that they'll all expect to have their messages taken home for nothing,' Sally complained.

'Stop picking fault with him, Sally. He's just trying to help.' Meggie defended her brother vigorously.

'He gets under my feet in the shop all day,' Sally said. 'It was better when he was on the delivery round.'

The delivery service had been an unqualified success, so much so that simply making up the orders was almost a full-time job. At Matty's suggestion Meggie had taken on a young lad to make the deliveries while Matty himself assembled the orders and prepared the accounts, helping out in the shop when his own jobs were done.

'Och, Sally, I know you and Matty don't get on but can't you see how hard he's been working lately? You should be glad there's someone else to help.'

'He only works if you're here,' Sally retorted angrily. 'And how come he gets to serve in the shop while I have to restock the shelves and mess around in the storeroom? It's not fair, Meggie. I've been here longer than he has but he's getting all the good jobs.'

'Sally!' Meggie, who tried to be scrupulously fair, was appalled. 'That's not true. We all do a bit of everything. Anyway Matty's good with the customers. They like him.'

'He makes too many mistakes. The till's never right any more and he gives the wrong change, charges the wrong prices. Mrs McNaughton was in here this morning complaining that he shortchanged her yesterday.'

'She took her time coming back about it then!'

'You know she can't walk far. And she wouldn't say she was shortchanged if she wasn't.'

'She might have made a mistake.'

'It was Matty who made the mistake, Meggie.'

'Well, what if he did? Even you make mistakes sometimes, Sally.'

'Not as many as he does,' Sally said darkly.

'What are you suggesting?' Meggie asked furiously.

'Och, Meggie, why do you always have to stick up for him, even when you know he's in the wrong?'

'He's my brother!'

'So that makes it all right for him to help himself to cash from the till, does it?'

379

Meggie looked away from her friend's challenging stare. 'If he needs it, yes.'

'I give up!' Sally threw the weights back beside the scales and stormed off upstairs.

'I'm sorry about yesterday,' Sally said the next morning, when the two girls were working together in the shop and Matty was in the storeroom.

'Me, too,' Meggie said quickly. 'And I will have a word with Matty about what you said.'

'All right,' Sally smiled in relief. She hated it when they argued, a rare occurrence in the past but something which was happening more frequently now that Matty was living and working with them.

'Have a word with me about what?' Matty, who had been listening gave Sally a venomous look as he came into the shop then beamed at his sister.

'I'll leave you to it.' Sally disappeared upstairs.

'She doesn't like me,' Matty got in first.

'Sally's my friend, Matty. Couldn't you try to get along with her, for my sake?'

'I have tried, Meggie. She's the awkward one. Why is everything always my fault?' he retorted, turning his back on her.

'I want to talk to you about something else, Matty.' She stopped him as he went back into the storeroom.

He shrugged and waited impatiently while she served a customer.

'Matty . . .' she began awkwardly, not quite knowing how to say what had to be said without making it sound like an accusation. 'I've noticed that the takings are down some nights. Have you been borrowing money from the till?'

380

'Who says? Sally? And you believe her, I suppose?'

'Sally didn't have to say anything, Matty. It's my shop. I know when the takings are down.'

'Well, it's not me. If anyone's stealing it must be Sally.'

'Matty! Sally is my best friend. She has never stolen anything in her life.'

'How do you know?' he challenged. 'You think that just because I stole things when I was a bairn – to help you, mind – you think that if anything goes missing it must be me who took it. It'll always be like that, won't it? You'll never really trust me, Meggie, will you?'

'Of course I will. . .'

'Then why are you accusing me of stealing from the till?'

'I asked if you had borrowed some money, Matty. There's a difference.'

'I borrowed ten shillings on Thursday. You weren't here to ask. I didn't think you'd mind. I put it back on Friday when I got paid.'

'You should have told me.'

'I didn't think it was important. I'm sorry,' he said sullenly.

'It's all right. Just tell me next time.'

'What did he say?' Sally asked later.

'He borrowed ten shillings on Thursday and put it back on Friday.'

'And you believed him?'

'Of course I did,' Meggie insisted.

'Och, well, it's your shop, your profit. Why should I care?'

It was Meggie's day off and Sally was in the storeroom, dragging a sack of potatoes towards the shop.

381

'Give me a hand, will you?' she called to Matty, who was setting up the orders ready for the lad to deliver.

He looked round slowly and then ambled casually towards her, a sneer making his dark face ugly. 'You managed before I came here, didn't you?' he asked, leaning against the wall and watching her.

'Forget it,' she spat back at him, heaving the sack into the shop and slamming the door on him.

After the orders were finished, Matty served in the shop as normal, making a great fuss over the women customers. Sally, still furiously angry, busied herself with the routine chores he habitually avoided, weighing flour, cutting butter and cheese, and did her best to stay well away from him.

'Eh . . . I'm sorry but I don't think this is right.' A harassed young mother, struggling to control three active children, stared at the change in her hand and spoke hesitantly.

'Oh! Well, then, let's have a look.' Matty, all concern, made a great deal of counting up the cost of her messages again. 'I'm not right good at figuring,' he admitted with the false smile Sally hated. 'I've likely made a mistake.' He grinned winningly and winked at the two women waiting to be served. They smiled back and waited patiently.

'There, I've written it down for you. It adds up to three shillings and fourpence. Isn't that what I charged you?'

The young woman nodded uncertainly. 'Aye . . . but. . .'

'And that makes six shillings and eight pence change.' Matty reached over and unfolded her hand then counted out the money onto the counter. 'Six shillings and eight pence there right enough, hen.' He smiled at her. 'Shall I count it again for you?'

'But I gave you a pound note, Mr McPherson. I'm sure I did.'

Matty scratched his head in a display of perplexity. 'Och . . . I don't think so . . .' He turned to the other women. 'Did youse see what she gave me?'

They shook their heads. 'Sorry. . .'

'But I'm sure it was a pound note. It was my last one. It's all I had till payday,' she pleaded desperately.

'Och, I know!' He grinned triumphantly. 'Whatever you gave me it'll be the top one in the till drawer. Let's have a wee look.' He pulled the drawer out with a flourish and there, on top of the pile of notes, was a limp ten shilling note. He pulled it out and waved it at the woman. 'I'm sorry, hen.'

'I know it was a pound note,' she cried. 'How will I feed the weans till Friday on six shillings and eight pence?'

'Sally! Serve these other ladies, will you,' he ordered imperiously.

With exceedingly bad grace Sally did as he asked, one ear straining to hear what he was now saying to the distraught woman.

'It was a pound note,' she insisted. 'I wouldn't make a mistake like that.'

'I'm right sorry, hen, but you saw for yourself. It was a ten shilling note on top. Look, if you're short of cash, let me put ten shillings in the book, as a special favour. I'll give you ten shillings from the till and you can pay me back when you can.'

'Och, I don't know. That's an awful lot of money to be owing. I couldn't give it all back to you on payday.' But the tears had gone from her eyes now.

'Not to worry. Bit by bit will be fine.' He took the ten shilling note from the till again and handed it to her. 'Now then, what's your name and I'll mark it in the book?' He drew the book from the shelf and waited.

'Mrs Semple,' she whispered, flushing scarlet with embarrassment and shooting an agonised look at the other customers, who were pretending not to have noticed anything amiss.

'Mrs Semple,' he repeated, too loudly. 'There we are. I'll just add the ten bob on so that'll make . . . fourteen shillings and seven pence you owe.' He beamed at her and Sally cringed inside for the poor woman who grabbed her children and scuttled from the shop with her head down.

'That woman'll be too affronted ever to come back in here,' Sally hissed when the other women had gone. 'You never bring that book out in front of other customers.'

Matty laughed. 'If they want credit. . .'

'And what about her money, Matty? Are you sure she didn't give you a pound?'

'You saw the ten shilling note. It was on top.'

'Of course it was! The larger notes go to the bottom, the ten shilling ones on top. Always. You know that.'

'Aye, but she gave me ten shillings. She made a mistake, Sally. And I helped her out, didn't I?'

'Did you? I don't expect she thinks so.'

'Fucking hell,' he swore. 'Bugger off, Sally. Leave me alone. Mind your own business and don't you ever dare to query anything I do again. This is my sister's shop and when she's not here, I'm in charge. You're just a skivvy, paid to do what you're told.' He brought his face close to hers and she backed off, scared of the violence she sensed in him.

Surreptitiously, Sally kept an eye on Matty for the rest of the day, but he was painstakingly and obviously accurate in everything he did. Until it was time to close up. Sally, whose job it was to empty the till each night, turned away from the counter to pick up the cash bag, a large canvas sack in which she carried the money upstairs. From the corner of her eye she saw Matty serve a late customer with twenty cigarettes and then palm a ten shilling note as he put the payment in the till. What she didn't realise was that Matty knew she had seen him.

'I saw you!' Sally shouted.

'You know the trouble with you, don't you?' Matty countered with cold fury. 'You're jealous. You never wanted me here and now you're trying to get rid of me. But it won't work. Meggie's my sister. She knows I wouldn't steal from her. Don't you, Meggie?'

'I don't know what to believe,' Meggie sighed.

'I'm telling you. I didn't steal anything from the till. And that stupid woman . . . what's her name. . .?'

'Helen Semple,' Sally supplied the name quickly. 'You know her, Meggie? She's a sweet wee thing, gey quiet with three weans all under five and a husband who blacks her eye for her every Saturday night. She's as honest as my Mam and she pays off what she owes every week, regular as clockwork.'

'Helen Semple? I can't see her making a mistake with money,' Meggie admitted. 'She's to count every penny.'

'Aye, and this week she was a wee bit short and decided to try and get it out of us. If one of youse had served her she'd never have tried it, I bet,' Matty raged. 'She thought she could take advantage of me.'

'The other way round more like,' Sally insisted. 'Anyway, how do you explain the till always being short, Meggie? It never used to be. It's only since Matty came here. And we're short on cigarettes. I've seen you helping yourself to those, too, Matty.'

'I sometimes take a packet of fags. So what? It's only

twenty or so a week and I gave Meggie the money for them last week, didn't I?' He turned to his sister for confirmation.

'You paid me for twenty on payday,' she agreed uneasily.

'Twenty!' Sally sneered. 'Two hundred would be nearer the mark.'

'I pay for everything I take from the shop and if there's money going missing from the till it's you taking it, not me,' he bellowed at her. 'You're doing it deliberately, trying to make Meggie think I'm stealing from her. I've seen you, putting money in your apron pocket.'

Sally's face froze, the sheer absurdity of the accusation temporarily robbing her of the power of speech.

'Matty!' Meggie was astounded. 'How can you say things like that?'

'Because it's true. I didn't like to say anything before, Meggie, because I know she's your friend. But I've seen her.'

'Meggie . . .' Sally appealed to her friend.

'Look in her pocket if you don't believe me. There's a pound note in there now. I saw her take it from the till when she emptied the money into the cash bag.'

'Liar!' Sally was on her feet, eyes blazing, looking for all the world as if she were about to strike him.

'I'll show you, shall I?' Matty made towards the door where both Sally and Meggie hung their work overalls.

'No. I'll show you,' Sally cried, shoving past him, grabbing her overall from the hook and throwing it at Meggie. 'Go on. Look in the pockets. There's nothing there.'

Meggie stared helplessly at the overall. 'I believe you,' she said. 'I don't need to look in your pockets, Sal.'

'She knows you'd say that! Look in her pocket, Meggie, and settle this once and for all.'

'Aye, Meggie,' Sally insisted.

Reluctantly, Meggie slipped her hand into a pocket. She came away with a handful of the little bits of paper, covered in pencil figures, which Sally used to add up the bills. Sally, hands on ample hips, waited, her temper simmering dangerously. Matty distributed his stocky limbs calmly over a chair and examined his nails. Meggie plunged her hand into the other pocket and closed it round the same collection of rubbish. She pulled her hand out and stared. There, perfectly obvious, was a grubby pound note.

'There! What did I tell you?' Matty surged to his feet, a gloating expression on his face.

Aghast, Meggie looked up at her friend and actually saw the blood fade from her face. Sally clutched at the back of a chair for support. 'I didn't take it,' she mumbled, then recovering quickly, rounded on Matty. 'I did not steal that money. Someone else must have put it in my pocket.' Her voice was low and icily controlled now.

'I hope you're not saying it was me?' Matty hissed.

'Stop it! Stop it, both of you,' Meggie begged, clamping her hands over her ears. 'Please, stop yelling at each other and listen to me.'

Matty sank back into his chair while Sally remained standing, seeming defensive and unhappy, the fight drained from her.

Meggie got up and put an arm round her shoulders. 'I know you didn't steal anything, Sal,' she said softly. 'I don't know how that money got there but I know you didn't take it.'

Sal whispered, 'Thanks, Meggie.'

'Then you think it was me? Do you think I put it there?' Matty asked coldly.

That was precisely what Meggie did think. 'I don't know

what to think, Matty.' She looked at him coldly. 'All I am sure of is that Sally would never steal anything from me.'

'If you don't trust me, Meggie, I won't stay here. I'll go and pack my things.' Matty got up and took a step towards his room.

'Good!' Sally faced him, hands on hips, her eyes blazing.

Suddenly Meggie screwed up the pound note and hurled it viciously at the door. 'Stop it!' she yelled. 'Both of you. Matty, come back here.'

Matty turned and shrugged, a faint grin lifting his mouth, his eyes cold and calculating. 'There's not room for all of us, Meggie. Not in the house and not in the shop. If you don't believe Sally is stealing from you then it stands to reason that you think I am. One of us has to go, Meggie. It's your shop. You choose.' He gave her an impossible choice.

'Sally isn't stealing and I won't ask her to go.'

'Then I'll go.'

'Where would you go, Matty? Be sensible. There's no need for this. You can both stay.' Meggie had sometimes longed for Matty to find a room of his own so that she and Sally could return to the happy atmosphere they had enjoyed before his arrival, but she couldn't let him leave like this. To send him out with nowhere to sleep, no job and little money would be failing him again, would be yet another weight on her conscience.

'Matty's right about one thing, Meggie. One of us has to go,' Sally said sadly.

In an abrupt change of attitude Matty flung himself into the chair again. 'Well, I don't see why it should be me. After all, I've done nothing wrong and I'm Meggie's brother. I've got a right to be here. Besides, Meggie's right, I've nowhere to go.'

'I'm sorry, Meggie, but I can't stay here with him.' Sally was almost in tears now.

'No! Sal, you can't go. I need you. Please,' Meggie begged.

'I'll be at my Mam's if you need me for anything, Meggie,' Sal said. 'I'll come back for my things tomorrow.' She flung on her coat and marched to the door.

Matty sniggered.

'Sal! Wait!' Meggie pounded down the stairs after her. 'Sal. Please stay. I know you'd never steal anything from me. Don't go. You're my best friend. I need you here.'

'I know,' Sal looked at Meggie sadly. 'But I can't stay, Meggie. It would never stop. In the end you wouldn't know who to believe. I couldn't bear it if you really thought I'd steal from you. This way you'll see for yourself. He won't be able to stop himself just because I've gone. It's too easy for him. He'll ruin you if you don't stand up to him, Meggie.'

'I've never thought a bad thing about you, Sally,' Meggie sobbed. 'But Matty's my brother. I've got to look after him.'

'I know that, too.' Sally leaned over and kissed her friend. 'Goodbye, Meggie.'

'Can we still be friends?' Meggie whispered.

'I'll always be your friend and you know where to find me.' Sally let herself out and walked away down the dark street.

From the upstairs window, Matty watched the first obstacle to his ambition walk away in defeat, a thin smile curling his mouth.

CHAPTER TWENTY

'Twenty of the usual, please, hen.'

Meggie reached up to the cigarettes. 'Och, there's none left. I'll just fetch some from the storeroom, Mr Stewart. I'll not be a second.'

There had been deliveries from three different wholesalers in the past two days but, with Sally gone, they had been too busy to tidy everything away and the room was piled high with boxes, crates and cartons. Meggie picked her way towards the cupboard where the cigarettes were stacked and found the familiar Players carton on the bottom of the heap. She extricated it carefully and looked vainly round for another one. Frowning, she made her way back to the shop, served her customer, then picked up the delivery note from the shelf under the till. It had her brother's signature on the bottom.

Later, when Matty had finished making up the orders, she made a physical count of the cigarette and tobacco delivery.

'Matty,' she asked. 'Did you check the cigarettes when they were delivered?'

'I didn't have time. I just put them straight in the cupboard. Why?'

'We're about four hundred cigarettes short.'

'Well, that's not my fault. I can't serve in the shop, make up the orders and check deliveries all at the same time, can I?'

'And I can't afford to lose four hundred cigarettes,' she retorted.

He merely shrugged and turned away. Meggie was prevented from giving vent to her anger by the arrival of a customer.

'Morning, Meggie,' she called cheerfully.

'Morning, Mrs Haddow.' Putting the missing cigarettes to the back of her mind, Meggie welcomed one of her best customers. 'What can I get you the day?'

'Nothing, hen. I've just popped in to pay off what I owe,' the older woman whispered, checking to make sure there was no one else in the shop. 'It's five shillings and eleven pence I think.' She slid a ten shilling note across the counter top. 'I'm away to my sister's in Ayr for a week and I want to clear everything afore I go.'

'It's braw weather for a holiday,' Meggie said, reaching under the counter for the book.

'Aye. Let's hope it's like this for your wedding, hen. Going away for your honeymoon, are you?'

'We're going to the Trossachs for the week,' Meggie answered, flicking through the pages. 'I just hope it doesn't rain.'

'It's fair braw over there. The lochs are just lovely and the weather can be grand at that time of year,' Mrs Haddow assured her. 'Have you got your dress and everything all sorted out?'

'I've asked Moira Nairn to make it for me.'

'Moira made wee Susan McBain's dress. A right good job she made of it, too. She's a fine hand with the needle has Moira.' Mrs Haddow nodded her approval. 'You know, lass, I wouldn't want you to think I was interfering, but I know find you've no mother to help you out so if you need anything doing you've only to ask. Even if it's only washing dishes after the reception. I'd be pleased to roll up my sleeves for youse.'

Meggie smiled. This was by no means the only offer of help which had been made in the last month or so and she was genuinely warmed by the generosity of her customers. 'Thank you, Mrs Haddow, that's right kind of you. We're having the reception in the Co-operative Hall and we'd be right happy for you and Mr Haddow to come but there's no need to worry about dishes,' she laughed.

'Och, Ronnie's doing you proud, lass.' Mrs Haddow's voice was full of admiration.

'Aye, he is that,' Meggie agreed proudly. 'Ronnie's organising everything and it's a good job because I never seem to have a minute to spare these days.'

'Missing Sally, are you?' Mrs Haddow probed eagerly. Sally had been popular with the customers and her sudden departure had been the cause of much speculation, most of it revolving around Sally's assumed relationship with Meggie's good-looking brother. 'Did youse two have a falling out? I always thought youse were right good friends.'

'We didn't fall out, Mrs Haddow,' Meggie insisted.

'Then why did she go? She never even said goodbye.'

'She went back to live with her mam and dad, that's all.'

Mrs Haddow nodded knowingly and looked pointedly at Matty, who was lounging indolently against the lower end of the counter, reading a paper. 'Aye, well, it wasn't right, a single lass like Sally in the same house as a fine-looking man like your Matthew.' She looked back at Meggie for some titbit of information to take back to her friends but the girl was frowning at the book and didn't seem to have heard.

'How much did you say you owed, Mrs Haddow?' Meggie asked.

'Five and eleven, lass.'

'Are you sure?'

'Well, I may be a penny or two out.'

'According to this there's eleven shillings and five pence outstanding.'

'Eleven shillings! No!' Mrs Haddow's voice rose to a shocked shriek. Remembering where she was, she looked round quickly, only going on when she was sure there was still no one else in the shop. 'I've never owed that much, not in my whole life!'

'It is a lot,' Meggie conceded uneasily. 'I wonder if there's been a mistake.' She ran a finger down the page. 'Two shillings added yesterday, one and six on Wednesday, two and five on Tuesday. Added to the five shillings and six pence from the week before, that makes eleven shillings and five pence.'

'That's where you've gone wrong, lass,' Mrs Haddow sighed in mighty relief. 'You've forgotten to mark the book when I paid you last Friday. I cleared off that five and six, like I do every week.'

'It's not marked down here,' Meggie shook her head in perplexity. 'I'm very sorry, Mrs Haddow. It won't happen again. I'm usually so careful to make a note of what folk pay me. I don't know what I can have been thinking of.' Not for one minute did she doubt that Mrs Haddow was telling her the truth.

'It wasn't you, lass. It was your brother I paid.' They both looked across at Matty in time to see him slip quietly through the storeroom door. 'Och, don't fret yourself over it, lass. It's sorted out now and that's the main thing.' She patted Meggie's hand kindly. 'It gave my old heart a right shock though, I can tell you,' she laughed again. 'Best tell that brother of yours to be more careful in future.'

'I will. And I really am sorry, Mrs Haddow.'

'Och, away with you, lass! We both know it was nothing more than a wee mistake. I know fine you wouldn't try and diddle me.'

'Matty,' Meggie called as soon as Mrs Haddow was safely out of range. 'Come here a wee minute.'

'What?' he asked, a picture of innocence.

'Did Mrs Haddow come in last Friday?'

'How should I remember? She's in and out all the time.'

'She paid off her account.'

'She might have done.'

'Why didn't you mark it in the book?' Meggie demanded furiously.

'If she paid, I marked it down.'

'No you didn't.'

'Maybe I forgot,' he shrugged carelessly.

'And maybe you didn't,' she challenged him coldly.

'That's not fair! It's always the same. Every time something goes missing, you blame me. First the cigarettes and now this. Once a thief, always a thief, that's what you think, isn't it? You think I'm stealing from you, don't you?' He turned the accusation on her, facing her with a convincing combination of anger and hurt.

'*Are* you stealing from me, Matty?' she asked, watching him carefully.

'*No!*' His dark eyes bore into hers, his gaze never flickering.

Meggie met his stare with equal determination. Everything pointed to Matty helping himself, both from the till and from the storeroom. But would he be able to meet her eyes so steadily if he was lying? And perhaps he was right, perhaps she was jumping to conclusions, judging him on his past record. Just like her mother and father were judging her. Surely her own brother deserved better from her? And it was easy to make mistakes when the shop was so busy. Her gaze wavered then fell. 'Good, then there's no more to be said,' she told him briskly. 'Just be more careful in future.'

She watched him stomp off to the storeroom, but still in the back of her mind was the uncomfortable niggle of doubt.

'What did the tobacco wholesaler say?' Sally asked when Meggie described the incidents to her. The question was superfluous. Sally had instantly known who was responsible.

'They swore they'd delivered the right amount of cigarettes.'

'Aye and young Bert Brown, their delivery man, he's as straight as they come.' Sally wanted to make sure that no one else was being blamed for Matty's duplicity. As always she was brutally honest. 'If you want the truth, I think it was Matty.'

Meggie sighed. 'Aye, probably. He's so careless sometimes. It was just a mistake.'

Sally caught the lack of conviction in her friend's voice and pressed on. 'Aye, and a gey expensive one. You can't afford to let mistakes like that happen very often, Meggie.'

'I'll just have to check everything myself from now on.'

'Why don't you ask Ronnie to speak to him?' Sally suggested.

Meggie flushed. 'I don't want to tell Ronnie,' she admitted.

'Bloody hell!' Sally swore, thoroughly exasperated. 'Why on earth not?'

Meggie shrugged and looked uncomfortable. 'I don't want any bad feeling between them.' The truth was that she had become aware of a tenseness in the atmosphere whenever the two men met and the last thing she wanted was to precipitate an open disagreement. 'Anyway,' she went on, 'the real trouble is that we're run off our feet without you. That's why neither of us had time to check the delivery. I do wish you'd come back, Sal. It's not the same without you.'

'Och, Meggie. I do miss you, and the shop. You know I do. But I won't come back, not while Matty's there. Anyway, you and Ronnie will be married soon. He's moving in with you, isn't he?'

'Aye. He can run his business just as easily from my place as from his, and there's no point in paying rent on his house when there's plenty of room with me.'

'So I would have had to move out anyway,' Sally pointed out reasonably.

'You could still work in the shop.'

'Not with Matty I couldn't, Meggie. It would just cause trouble and you'd be caught in the middle of it again.' Sally caught her friend's hand. 'Don't worry, Meggie. I'm all right. I've got another job and I'm happy enough back with Mam and Dad.'

Although she was smiling, Sally was seriously disturbed when she waved goodbye to her friend a few minutes later. Matty McPherson was nothing but trouble and Meggie's loyalty to him was apparently unshakeable. But what, Sally wondered, would happen after the wedding? If Meggie continued to protect her brother she would be risking her relationship with Ronnie who certainly wasn't the type to stand idly by and let Matty help himself to the shop's profits. Sally was frightened that unless someone did something to stop him, Matty would destroy the happiness of her two dearest friends. So, if Meggie couldn't, or wouldn't, help herself, then it was up to the people who loved her to do it for her.

Even so, it was only after a great deal of soul-searching that Sally finally had a few private words with her father, a man who moved in rather shady company.

A day or so later, Ronnie was surprised to get a visit from Sally's unkempt father. It was as a result of that visit that he found himself in one of Inverannan's most disreputable public houses on Wednesday night, keeping Harry Keir supplied with pints of best heavy.

'I'll have another when you're ready, Ronnie lad.' Harry belched softly and wiped his mouth with the back of his hand.

Ronnie shoved his way through the crowd at the bar and returned bearing two brimming pint glasses. He placed them both in front of Harry and sat nursing his own half-finished beer. Ronnie's drinking was usually confined to a single pint at his comfortable local on a Friday night. Within an hour of arriving here tonight, Harry Keir had sunk four pints and was looking for a fifth, all without noticeable effect. Ronnie had rapidly abandoned any attempt to keep up with him. Tonight he needed to have his wits about him.

'Are you not a drinking man yourself, then?' Harry asked with a touch of derision in his voice.

'I like a pint or two,' Ronnie said, nearly heaving when a man at the next table turned and spat copiously into the shallow metal tray placed strategically on the floor for just that purpose.

'There's your man,' Harry hissed and nodded over the froth on his pint.

Ronnie turned round in time to catch a glimpse of Matty McPherson, pushing his way through to the bar. From the way he was greeted it was plain that he was a regular customer.

Ronnie felt a tightening in his stomach. 'You know what to do?'

Harry nodded and held out his hand. Ronnie placed a small roll of pound notes in it.

While Harry made his way directly towards Matty, Ronnie eased his way to the bar, finally standing about six feet from Meggie's brother. He was careful to keep his back to him. With an old cap stuck on his head and one of his father's threadbare jackets on, Ronnie was fairly confident that Matty wouldn't notice him, especially not in this crowd.

'Are you in business the night, Jimmy?' he heard Harry address Matty.

'Might be.'

'Only I've a fair bit of cash on me. I'd take as many cigarettes as you've got, for a reasonable price like.' He looked pointedly at the bundle Matty was carrying inside his jacket.

'Not seen you in here before.' Matty eyed him suspiciously.

'Not my usual place. But you did a deal with my good pal Jocky last week. Two hundred Players at half shop price. He said to mention his name.'

'Jocky from Cairnsbank?' Matty asked warily.

'No. Jocky Robertson from Netherton. We're neighbours.'

Matty relaxed. 'Right.' He looked round quickly and eased himself out of the crowd and into a quieter corner where they were less likely to be overheard. Not that he felt he had anything to fear in this particular pub, not from the law at least. 'Let's see your money first.'

Harry waved the roll of notes under Matty's nose.

Matty took it, counted some off and handed the rest back to Harry. 'That'll buy you six hundred. Half shop price.'

'It's a deal.' Harry accepted the bundle Matty handed him, peered inside to check the contents and nodded, well satisfied. 'The same next week?' he asked hopefully, thinking of the profit to be made by reselling these to his own cronies.

Matty sucked air through his teeth and shook his head. 'No. Too risky. Be in here in a month or so. I might have something for you then. And,' he lunged forward suddenly and grasped Harry by the lapels, lifting him off his feet and snarling into his face. 'Keep your bloody mouth shut. Right?'

Harry nodded vehemently.

'I don't know you and you don't know me. You tell anyone where you got those and you'll wake up dead one morning. Got it?' He dropped the smaller man back on to his feet.

'Aye.' Harry brushed himself down. 'No need to be like that,' he complained.

'Just so's you understand,' Matty warned him, walking away and ordering himself a whisky from the bar.

'Bloody hell,' Harry swore when he met Ronnie outside the pub a few minutes later. 'I wouldn't like to cross that bastard. Right evil look about him, he has. Don't you go dropping me in it with him.'

'Don't you worry your head about him, Harry, lad. I'll keep your name out of it. I just needed to be sure of what he was doing, that's all.' Ronnie was more than satisfied with his night's work.

'Well, here's the fags. You paid for them.' Reluctantly, Harry offered the package to Ronnie.

'I've no use for them, Harry. Keep them.'

'Shouldn't they go back to our Sally's friend?'

Ronnie shook his head. 'No. There's no point.' To offer Meggie such hard proof of Matty's dishonesty would break her heart and Ronnie was sure she wouldn't thank him for shattering her illusions. No, all he wanted to do was get rid of Matty. After he had confronted him with what he knew, threatened him with the police if necessary, he was confident that the younger man would be persuaded to take himself off somewhere well away from Inverannan and Meggie.

'Do you want me to wait with you?'

'No.' Ronnie gave a grim laugh. 'This is something I'm looking forward to doing all on my own.'

It was a full hour before Ronnie, partly hidden in a doorway, saw Matty emerge from the pub. He let him walk a little way up the road before running up behind him and tapping him lightly on the shoulder.

'It's a braw evening, is it not?' he asked, seeming his normal, cheerful self.

Matty wheeled round, instantly defensive, then relaxed when he saw it was only Ronnie. 'Aye. It is that,' he agreed, walking on again.

'A braw night for a bit of business.'

Matty tensed visibly and lengthened his stride.

'Meggie would be right upset to know you're flogging her stock round the pubs,' Ronnie said in a matter-of-fact tone. 'Aye, and the polis would be interested, too.'

Matty stopped and turned round to face Ronnie, his face contorted by an angry scowl, his fists drawn back, ready to strike.

Ronnie didn't move. 'Och, I wouldn't try that, if I were

you, Matty. I'm not stupid enough to come after you without telling someone else what I'm up to. Someone else who saw what you were selling in that pub. Bit of luck that we just happened to be in there tonight, wasn't it?'

Matty lowered his fists, breathing heavily but just controlling his fury. 'You saw nothing!'

Ronnie smiled. 'I saw everything. Six hundred you sold him. Cigarettes you stole from Meggie's shop. And not for the first time either.'

'You can prove nothing.' But there was a wary look in Matty's eyes now.

'I've got witnesses. You've been caught, lad. Don't bother to deny it.'

Ronnie took a step closer to Matty. He towered over the younger man but, of the two, it was Matty who seemed the more menacing, his face dark with anger, his whole body tense, ready to strike. But Ronnie, confident in the greater bulk of his own powerful body and convinced that he had succeeded in trapping the other man, was not easily intimidated. 'If you don't want Meggie to find out about this, if you don't want to find yourself in jail, then you'd better listen to what I am going to say.' Ronnie was actually enjoying this feeling of power.

'I'm listening.'

'Get out of here, Matty. Leave Inverannan. Make some excuse, any excuse, and go. Anywhere, so long as it's away from Meggie. Do that and I'll not tell her what I saw the night.'

'She's my sister. We belong together.'

'You belong in the bloody jail,' Ronnie retorted. 'Get the hell out of her life and don't ever think about coming back or you'll have me to deal with.'

'Och, I'm terrified,' Matty sneered with such contempt in his voice that Ronnie took an involuntary step backwards.

'You little bastard,' Ronnie growled. 'After all the hard work Meggie's put into that business, you're ruining her. Don't you think she deserves better than that?'

'You don't know my sister very well, do you?' Matty asked, making it sound like any ordinary conversation. 'Perhaps you and I should have a wee talk, Ronnie.' He slung his arm round the other man's shoulders and attempted to draw him to the side of the pavement.

Ronnie knocked Matty's arm away. 'There is nothing you can say that I want to hear.'

'Ah, but there is,' Matty assured him with a chilling grin. 'You see, my sister isn't the wonderful, innocent lass you think she is.'

'I won't listen to this,' Ronnie said, trying to walk away, understanding that somehow Matty had contrived to get the better of him.

'Ah, but you will,' Matty insisted, grabbing Ronnie's arm and holding it with force enough to leave bruises, even through his clothing. 'I've been meaning to have this wee talk with you for a long while, Ronnie.'

'Take your fucking hands off me or I will go to the police,' Ronnie roared.

'You do and I'll make sure that certain things about Meggie get spread around the district. Things that will shock all those strait-laced old wifies who come into the shop. She'll be ruined inside a month.'

'You'd spread lies about your own sister?'

'Not lies, Ronnie. The truth.' He stared at the older man, his dark eyes seeming to bore into his head. The confidence drained from Ronnie's face and suddenly he looked away. Satisfied, Matty turned and walked back to the pub where

402

he found seats at a table at the back of the room. After half a minute Ronnie followed him.

'Here, I've a feeling you're going to need this.' Matty shoved a large whisky at him.

'I'll not drink with you, Matty McPherson. Just say what you have to say and get out.'

Matty shrugged, his arrogance adding to Ronnie's disquiet. 'Suit yourself.'

'Well?' Ronnie demanded.

'Och, you know it pains me to have to do this to an honest, upright sort of man like yourself, Ronnie. Aye, it does that. Mind you, you've brought it on yourself. If you'd kept your fat nose out of my business it would never have come to this. Only got yourself to blame.'

'Get on with it!' Ronnie snarled through clenched teeth, wanting nothing more than to bury his fist in that confidently grinning mouth.

'Did you know,' Matty asked conversationally, 'that it was Meggie who sent me out stealing? Did she ever explain that to you, Ronnie? Did she ever tell you that it was her fault that I ended up in the jail?'

'Liar!' Ronnie slammed the palms of his hands on the table and stood up.

Matty calmly placed a hand on each of Ronnie's shoulders and pushed him back into his seat. 'Aye, you can call me what you want, but listen to what I've got to say and then ask Meggie whether it's true or not. That's the one sure way to find out, isn't it?'

Ronnie glared at him, the muscles on his face working in agitation, but he said nothing more.

'Aye,' Matty went on, leaning back in his seat. 'Like I said, Meggie sent me out stealing. Not that there was any choice, not to start with. We'd run away from the

403

workhouse see, to try and find our ma and pa. We'd no money so I had to steal food. It was that or starve.'

Ronnie actually felt his heart blip with relief. 'I know about the workhouse and if you had to steal to stay alive, that's different. I'm sure Meggie would have told me about that herself one day.'

'Maybe she would have,' Matty agreed easily. 'But I wonder if she would have told you the rest of it? That's why Oliver Laing left her, you know, when he found out the truth about her.' He was enjoying himself now, deliberately drawing it out, tormenting the other man.

'Any man who can walk out on a woman like Meggie just because she'd been in the workhouse doesn't deserve to be happy,' Ronnie proclaimed.

'Is that what she told you?' Matty asked. 'Well, I can't say I blame her for that, either.' He drained his glass and sauntered up to the bar, leaving Ronnie fretting but unable to walk away now. 'Did she tell you about the Houlets' Nest?' he asked as he sat down again. 'Och, that was a terrible place to take a young lad like me. But the money was good. Meggie's always been one for the money, Ronnie.'

'The Houlets' Nest?' Even Ronnie, with his relatively sheltered life, had heard of the Houlets' Nest. The blood left his face and he wiped sweat from the back of his neck. 'She was a barmaid. She told me that.' But had never mentioned that it was the Houlets' Nest she had worked in.

'Aye. Of sorts. A barmaid who offered ... other services.'

Without warning Ronnie lunged across the table, making a grab for Matty's throat. Matty simply swung back on his chair then, with the swiftness of a snake, reached over and got hold of a handful of Ronnie's hair, twisting it cruelly

404

and forcing the other man close to him. One or two people turned towards the source of the commotion but then shrugged and went back to their own business. Arguments were commonplace enough to cause little comment.

'Don't try that again,' Matty snarled. 'You hit me and I've got friends in this town who will make you very, very sorry. Now,' he pushed Ronnie away, 'Sit there until I've finished.'

Ronnie groped for the whisky glass and drained it in one mouthful, coughing slightly as the coarse liquid caught at the back of his throat.

'I'll spell it out for you shall I, Ronnie?' Matty asked, his eyes dark and unreadable. 'My sister was a whore.'

Ronnie groaned audibly. 'No . . . I don't believe it.'

'Like I said, all you've got to do is ask her,' Matty said. 'Still, that's not the end of it. There was this old man who took a fancy to her. He set her up in a wee flat. Made her his mistress, I suppose you'd call it. Aye, he was a right tight-fisted old bastard, though. Never gave her enough money to feed us both so that's when she sent me out stealing for her again. I nicked things from the shops, things I could sell easily to make a shilling or two. 'Course, I got caught in the end. I got sent to a home for bad boys,' he chuckled. 'Meggie? Well, the police came to the flat and discovered she was under-age and put her back in the workhouse. She had the baby there.' He dropped the bomb with stunning accuracy, then waited, a smirk on his face.

Ronnie sagged in his seat, his heart seemed to have stopped, the people round him had frozen. Nothing was real. Nothing except Matty McPherson's grinning face. 'Meggie had a baby?' he asked, his voice a choked whisper.

'Aye. A girl it was. I don't know what happened to it.' Matty gazed at the shattered man opposite him and knew he had said enough. 'You do understand, don't you?' he asked, when Ronnie stumbled to his feet. 'That if there's any trouble about the cigarettes I'll have to tell everyone what I've just told you. It's up to you, of course.' He smiled at Ronnie as if they had been indulging in nothing more than a casual, friendly chat. 'Oh, one more thing. Don't tell her I told you Ronnie.' Although his voice remained bland there was a thinly-veiled menace in his expression. 'Me and my friends, we wouldn't like you to do that.'

Ronnie simply stared in front of him, his face set in an expression of blank shock, his skin so bleached of colour that the growth of stubble on his chin contrasted against the pallor of his cheeks like black against white. Then, slowly, silently, he rose from his seat and shambled out of the pub, a broken man.

At five-thirty the next morning, Meggie put the kettle on then went to unlock the shop door ready for Ronnie. She was startled to see the morning papers stacked on the pavement, exposed to the drizzling rain. Puzzled, she dragged them into the shop and examined them carefully. There wasn't even a note.

The shop, as usual, was so busy that Meggie didn't have many free minutes in which to ponder Ronnie's odd behaviour. He would be back with the evening papers later in the afternoon and she would see him then. She would need to remind him to check the arrangements with the Co-operative Hall for the reception and he should go and pick up his suit, make sure it fitted properly. On Sunday morning she would go and see Bertha Cruickshank and keep her up to date with all her plans, and Mrs Cruickshank would know whether Mrs Binnie would be well enough to come to the wedding. Four weeks tomorrow and she would be Mrs

Ronnie Sandys. She could hardly bear to wait. She smiled, a bubble of excitement welling inside her.

'You look happy, Meggie.'

Meggie looked up and directed her beaming smile at her brother, who had gone out of his way to be helpful and pleasant today. 'I am,' she sang. 'As happy as it is possible to be.'

'I'm glad.' He kissed her cheek, an event so rare that she stared at him in astonishment.

'Och, don't I get to be happy for you, too?' he teased.

'Aye. You do,' she laughed, hugging him.

The bell over the shop door tinkled and she looked up, her face still alight with happiness.

'Ronnie! What are you doing here at this time of the day?' she asked delightedly. 'What happened to you this morning?' The smile on her face faded as she realised there was no answering one from Ronnie. 'What's wrong?' she asked, reaching up to kiss his cheek as she usually did if there were no customers in the shop. To her dismay he pushed her away, roughly.

'I want to talk to you,' he said, his voice dull and flat, his eyes looking anywhere but at her face.

Meggie felt the first warnings of disaster in her stomach, which tightened and lurched queasily. 'All right.' She tried to keep smiling.

'Upstairs. In private.'

'You go on, Meggie. I'll look after things here,' Matty offered, squeezing her shoulder supportively.

'Thanks, Matty.' Meggie led the way up to her cosy little sitting room. 'You look terrible, Ronnie,' she said, worried by his white face and heavily circled eyes. 'Shall I make you a cup of tea?'

'I want you to answer one question,' he rasped, his voice

hoarse. 'Just one and I want you to swear that you'll answer me honestly.' At last he looked at her and she flinched away from what she read in his bloodshot eyes.

'I swear,' she whispered, her heart beating so wildly that he could see the soft pulse at the base of her throat.

Ronnie struggled to get the words out, knowing that if he asked her this terrible question, even if the answer was no, it was over between them. What girl could accept that sort of insult from a man who was supposed to love her? He looked at her, seeing the soft innocence of her heart-shaped face, the velvety softness of those dark brown eyes, the youthful firmness of her shapely body. Could it really be true that other men had seen and done what he hadn't, that her chasteness was nothing more than a vile deception? Taking a deep breath he asked, 'Is it true that you were a whore, Meggie?'

Even though she had been expecting them, the words hit her like an open-handed blow, driving the breath from her body, making her head spin and her stomach contract.

'Aye.' There was no possibility of lying to him. She looked into his eyes, pleading silently for him to understand, for the chance to explain the events which had shaped that dreadful period of her life. But there was nothing there but pain, pain which forced her to look away in shame and stare miserably at the floor. She didn't even look up when he walked past her and out of her life.

CHAPTER TWENTY-ONE

In the lonely weeks that followed, Meggie came to appreciate the little community of Inverannan streets of which she was now a part. Although she had only been able to bring herself to tell her closest friends Sally and Mrs Cruickshank that the wedding had been cancelled, she soon realised that, somehow, word had spread round her customers. Although Meggie knew they must surely gossip and speculate among themselves, not even the nosiest of them asked her an intrusive question. Instead, they made time to stay and chat for a minute or two longer than usual, involving her in the minutiae of their own lives, asking her for small favours which were calculated to fill the long, empty hours after the shop closed.

Meggie suddenly found herself in demand as a babysitter, had several invitations to share a meal with one or other of the families and was even asked to help one woman pack up her household, ready for flitting. Their unspoken support was like a protective blanket, making it possible for her to face each new day.

'I'm just needing four ounces of cheese, lass,' Mrs Haddow said as she bustled into the shop. 'I'm glad to see you looking better, at last, hen. There's colour in your face the day.'

'It's the cold.' Meggie smiled back at a woman of whom she had grown fond. Of all her customers, Mrs Haddow had been the kindest, the most concerned.

'It's gey icy the morn, right enough. But we can't complain. We've been lucky. This is the first cold snap we've had this year and it's almost Christmas.' She waited while Meggie weighed and wrapped the cheese.

'Anything else, Mrs Haddow?'

'No, lass.' The stoutly-built, grey-haired woman glanced quickly behind her and said, 'Just put it in the book, Meggie. You know,' she went on, 'I didn't like to say anything to you before but I'm glad you're starting to cheer up, lass. I'm right sorry things didn't work out for you and Ronnie Sandys but these things happen and no man's worth making yourself ill over.'

Meggie smiled ruefully. 'I'm all right now.'

'Good. See you stay that way. You're a bonny-looking lass, Meggie, and there's plenty fine young men out there who would be proud to have you on their arms. You'll find the right one soon, you'll see.'

It was kindly meant but Meggie flinched and lost some of her newly emerging colour. 'I don't think so,' she said, so quietly that Mrs Haddow barely caught the words.

'Och, lass, of course you will!' Mrs Haddow exclaimed. 'And you'll not be sitting here on your own over Christmas and New Year either. You can come to us for your dinner on Christmas Day and we always have a wee party on Hogmanay.'

'Thank you, Mrs Haddow. I'd like that, but I promised Matty I'd cook his Christmas dinner for him here.'

'That's fine, lass. So long as you're not on your own. But call in for a wee drink at the New Year. Matty too. You'll both be welcome.' Mrs Haddow picked up her cheese and hurried from the shop.

New Year was the traditional time for adult celebration in Strathannan with Christmas being given over to the children. Few families could afford to put two fancy meals on the table in such a short space of time so the festive feast was generally saved for New Year's Day, when every woman did her best to have the traditional steak pie ready to help her man recover from the excesses of the night before.

To make this year special, Meggie was determined to give Matty and herself a Christmas and New Year to remember and that included cooking Matty a real Christmas dinner. She was up early on Christmas morning to prepare the plump chicken, vegetables and stuffing. As she set the rich pudding steaming over a saucepan of boiling water she felt the first real surge of pleasure she had known since Ronnie walked out of her life.

Last week she had withdrawn some of her savings from the bank and gone to Craig and Lockie, Inverannan's finest jewellers. After lengthy deliberation she had chosen a handsome wristwatch for Matty, to replace the tarnished old fob watch which he had somehow acquired but which no longer kept good time. She would give it to him when they had eaten their meal. In the afternoon the Netherton Mill band was playing carols in the park, then it would be time for tea and the rich, iced cake she had made specially. After that they could listen to the wireless and play cards until bedtime. It would, she thought with a small sigh of satisfaction, be one of the best Christmases they had ever had. And next week there would be the New Year to celebrate. Anxious to put the events of the last months behind her, 1933 was a year that Meggie was especially eager to welcome in.

Meggie had assumed that Mrs Cruickshank would see in the New Year with her, as she had in previous years, and had been dismayed to learn that, following the closure of the Inverannan workhouse, the superintendent had decided to retire rather than seek another post. She had already gone to Glasgow to live with her widowed sister. Meggie had parted from her friend with tears in her eyes, promising to visit as soon as she could. Now it would be just herself and Matty. But at least that would give them the opportunity to join their neighbours and, judging by the singing and laughter which had echoed down the normally quiet street last year, it was something to which they should look forward. On New Year's Day itself, when Matty would undoubtedly have friends of his own to visit, she would go and see Sally.

Meggie checked the water under the pudding and frowned at the thought of her best friend, trying to remember the last time they had met for a proper chat. It must have been two or three months ago, soon after she and Ronnie had broken up. Somehow they hadn't seen much of one another since then. But Mrs Keir had told Meggie that Sally had a new boyfriend, which probably explained why she had been out every time Meggie called. She was surprised, and a little bit hurt, to think that Sally hadn't made the effort to come and tell her about him herself. But, Meggie thought, their friendship was far too precious to be allowed to lapse just because of a few bruised feelings and they would have the chance to catch up on all their news on New Year's Day.

Her musings were interrupted at that point by Matty who emerged from his bedroom looking heavy-eyed and irritable – the predictable result of an early celebration with his friends.

'Happy Christmas, Matty,' she said, reaching up to kiss his unshaven cheek.

For a moment he looked surprised, as if he had forgotten what day it was, then he grinned and planted a reciprocal kiss on her cheek. 'Aye, Happy Christmas, Meggie,' he said, sinking down on to an easy chair. 'Smells good.' He sniffed the air appreciatively. 'Make us some breakfast, hen.'

'It's after one o'clock! If you have breakfast now you'll never manage your dinner. You can have a cup of tea and a slice of toast. That's all.'

He gave an exaggerated sigh. 'All right,' then settled back in the chair and closed his eyes.

Meggie smiled at him with tolerant affection. By the look of him he had had too much to drink last night, not that that was unusual. She felt the familiar tremor of unease about his wild behaviour, but to challenge him about it now would send him into a sulk and ruin the atmosphere for the rest of the day. Sitting there, his hair uncombed, his shirt unevenly buttoned, the immature stubble, patchy and soft on his pale cheeks, the cynicism which habitually twisted his mouth forgotten in this unguarded moment, Matty looked almost childish again.

It was only rarely now that she glimpsed this side of her brother. He worked so hard at his tough, grown-up image, cultivating a deep voice, adopting an aggressive manner, mixing with men much older than himself, haunting the rougher bars, smoking, drinking and, she suspected, picking up women, that it was almost impossible to believe that he was still only seventeen; harder still to realise that she, at twenty, was a mere three years older than him. There were times when Matty was secretive and sly, others when he was intimidating, frightening even, giving the impression of barely suppressed violence; too many occasions when he treated her with open hostility, reminding her that he still remembered how badly she had let him down. But, underneath the complicated layers of his personality was the Matty only she knew and loved, the hurt and rejected child, the little boy who had had to be tough to survive, the lad who, despite the façade of maturity and confidence, still relied on his older sister to take care of him.

Sensing her eyes on him he looked up and winked. Laughing, she turned away to pour his tea and butter his toast.

Matty ate his scanty breakfast, then stood up, gazing round the room she had decorated while he was out the previous night.

'You've made a braw job of the room, Meggie,' he praised her, bringing a flush of pleased colour to her cheeks. He stood there, beaming like an overgrown child at the paper chains and holly which were festooning the ceiling and walls. But, when his gaze rested on the table, already set for dinner, his smile faded. There, on a snowy tablecloth, set beside his own knife and fork, was a small, brightly wrapped parcel.

'I wanted to make it special,' she told him. 'I know there's just the two of us and we're not bairns any more but there's no reason why we shouldn't still enjoy Christmas, is there?'

'No. None at all,' he told her, edging towards the door. 'When's dinner?'

'Matty, you're not going out? Not on Christmas Day?' she cried.

'Don't worry yourself, hen,' he laughed. 'I'm just going to clear my head after last night, so's I can enjoy my dinner.'

'All right,' she conceded. 'But be back by half-past two.'

'You sound just like Ma,' he teased, slipping out of the door, leaving her half-amused, half-exasperated.

Seeing his own gift so conspicuously placed, Matty had panicked. Now he rushed from the house, desperately wondering how, on Christmas Day itself, he could put his hands on anything even remotely suitable for Meggie. If he couldn't come up with something, Meggie would be deeply hurt. But, he thought sourly, that would be her own fault for making such a fuss about Christmas. He might even be able to turn it to his own advantage by telling her he couldn't afford to buy her anything. Make her feel guilty for paying him such low wages while stashing away all the profit in her own bank account. Still, he mused, after all the trouble he had gone to to get rid of Ronnie Sandys, it would be a shame to spoil his own chances of getting a share of the shop over something as stupid as a Christmas gift.

He wandered down to the park and examined the hothouses, wondering if he could force a way in and help himself to an exotic plant, but the doors were securely locked. The only way in was to break one of the huge panes of glass and Matty didn't want to risk hurting himself. Meggie would just have to make do with half a pound of sweeties from the shop. Feeling disgruntled he threw a stone at a lurking cat which yelped in pain and crashed off through the bushes. Matty watched it, lobbing another stone after it for good measure, then, his face suddenly breaking out in a wide smile, he stuck his hands in his pockets and, with a marked air of purpose, strode back towards the town.

Meggie, who had almost convinced herself that she had seen the last of Matty for that day, jumped up in relief when she heard his footsteps on the stairs and busied herself with the final touches to their meal. Matty rushed in and went straight to his bedroom. He emerged, washed and tidied, in time to accept the task of carving the chicken.

'That was braw,' he told her, half an hour later, patting his full stomach. 'The best meal I've ever had. You made a right good job of that, our Meggie.'

She blushed with pleasure, then asked, 'Aren't you going to open your present?'

'Can I?' he asked, a gleam of excitement in his dark eyes as he picked up the red-wrapped package and shook it gently.

'Aye,' she laughed, enjoying this as much as him and longing to see his reaction to her gift.

'Och, Meggie . . .' He withdrew the wristwatch from its case and looked at it with unconcealed delight. 'It's smashing, really braw,' he beamed at her, reminding her yet again of the affectionate youngster to whom she had been so close. Grinning widely he fastened the thick leather strap round his wrist, then set the time from his old pocket watch. He admired his newly adorned arm for a few more seconds, then looked up at Meggie. 'I didn't expect anything like this,' he told her, his face settling into more serious lines. 'I've nothing as braw for you.'

'Whatever you've got me, I'll be right happy with it,' she assured him happily.

'I've got you two things,' he said grandly.

'Two?' She couldn't resist looking round the room trying to discover where his present to her was hidden.

'Aye. Here's the first one.' With a flourish he produced a brown paper bag from his pocket.

'What's this?' she asked, taking it from him.

'Look and see.'

Meggie peered into the bag and just managed to hide her disappointment at the selection of loose sweeties from the shop. 'Thanks, Matty. They're my favourites,' she told him.

'I know,' he said. 'And now just sit there until I get the other present. It's in my room.'

He rushed off to his own bedroom and Meggie was mystified to hear a series of bumps, what sounded like a string of swear words and a yelp of pain. When he reappeared, he was clutching something which writhed and hissed inside his jacket.

'What on earth have you got there?' she asked.

'Here. It's for you. Take it.' Matty thrust a spitting bundle of black and white fur at her.

'A cat?' Meggie put out her arms to take her reluctant new pet and was rewarded by a swiping blow that left three deep scratches down the back of her hand.

'Little sod!' Matty swore, dropping the creature when it turned its fury on him and aiding its terrified retreat towards the back of the sofa with a sharp prod from his booted foot.

'Matty!' Meggie laughed. 'Leave him.' She dropped on to her knees and peered behind the sofa to be met with the baleful gaze of two huge green eyes. 'Och, the poor wee thing's terrified.'

'He's a bloody monster!' Matty sucked at the blood welling from his deeply scored hand.

'He's just a baby,' Meggie insisted. 'Where did you get him?'

'A friend of mine. His cat had kittens at the back end of the summer. He's been keeping this one for me. It'll be about three months old now,' he lied glibly, relieved that his rather desperate, last-minute gift was an apparent success.

Inspiration had come to him in the park, where the unfortunate cat had reminded him of a feral colony which prowled the back streets near his favourite public house, always on the lookout for titbits. It had been simplicity itself to lure them to him using the still pungent and greasy newspapers from someone's fish supper which he had retrieved from a rubbish bin.

'Thanks, Matty. He's lovely.'

417

'You'd best give him a good clean,' he warned, as the kitten scratched its left ear vigorously.

'He needs a good feed first,' Meggie decided, hurrying to the larder for a few shreds of cooling chicken. 'Come on, then,' she tempted the tiny creature, dangling the succulent meat tantalisingly close to its pink nose. A needle-tipped claw flashed out, making her jump back but she laughed and waved the meat again. Eventually hunger overcame caution and the little animal emerged and gobbled the meat hungrily. Meggie fed him some more and ran her hand along the side of the cat's face, smiling as it nuzzled into her, purring loudly.

'He likes you,' Matty said, keeping well out of the way.

'Aye. And I like him. You're a sweet wee thing, aren't you?' she said lifting the kitten up and sitting down with it in her lap where it got up and turned around three times before finally curling up and falling instantly asleep, still purring.

'You'll have to think of a name for him,' Matty said, slipping his jacket on quietly while Meggie was still preoccupied with the cat.

'Domino,' she decided quickly. 'Because he's black and white.' She tickled the animal between its ears and it purred even louder. 'Poor wee thing. He doesn't look as if he's been very well cared for. He looks more like one of those wild cats that used to live round the pit.'

'If you don't want him I can take him back,' he offered sharply, ready to take umbrage.

'Och, don't be so daft. Of course I want him.' She looked over at her brother, but her smile faded when she realised he had his jacket on. 'You're not going out, Matty?'

'Aye.'

'But it's Christmas Day!'

'So what?'

'I thought we could go to see the band in the park. They're playing carols this afternoon.'

'Nothing to stop you going.'

'On my own?'

'Well, stay here and play with that bloody cat then.'

Determined not to let his mercurial temper spoil the day, she swallowed the angry retort which rose to her lips and asked instead, 'Where are you going?'

'That's none of your bloody business, Meggie.' The pleasant mood of the past hour dissolved as if it had never been. 'Bloody hell, you'd think you were my effing mother the way you carry on.'

Meggie looked away, not wanting him to see the pain his harsh words had caused. She heard the door slam as he went out.

Gently she shifted the cat from her lap and set about clearing away the remains of their meal. That done she set the table again, placing the large, iced Christmas cake in the centre, cutting sandwiches of cold chicken and covering it all with a damp cloth, ready for Matty when he came home. Domino mewed faintly, stretched and curled up again, perfectly content to sleep the afternoon away. Meggie sighed and walked over to the window, looking down on the street below. From a house further up the road a family emerged, all dressed up in their Sunday best, the two children laughing happily and clutching what were obviously new toys. Hand in hand they set off down the hill. Meggie stood for a few moments more, feeling lonely and wondering how to fill the rest of the afternoon. Then, moving quickly she put on her coat and good shoes and went downstairs. It was Christmas Day, she told herself, a time for enjoyment. If Matty wouldn't go to the park with her then she would go on her own.

From the park gates it seemed that half the population of Inverannan had wrapped themselves up in heavy coats and scarves and come to sing carols round the bandstand. Walking slowly she hovered on the edge of the crowd, feeling conspicuous and lonely among so many happy couples and family groups.

'Merry Christmas!' A man, well-swathed in a long muffler, passed her a printed sheet of carols.

'Thanks. Happy Christmas to you, too,' she responded with forced gaiety.

While the others sang, abandoning themselves to the festive atmosphere, Meggie looked round, searching for familiar faces. She quickly identified several women she knew but they were all with their families and she didn't like to impose herself on them. And then, no more than twenty feet away, almost in the centre of the crowd she spotted Sally.

The carol ended and the crowd shifted slightly, hiding her friend from view again. Meggie pushed her way forward, a smile of excitement lighting her face as the next song began. Again she got a glimpse of Sally's dark hair, still nine or ten feet away from her. 'Sally!' she called, muttering an apology and pushing forward again. 'Sallee!' A pause between verses allowed the word to carry clearly.

Hearing her name, Sally looked up, but, when she saw Meggie, her expression froze. For a moment she simply stared, her eyes wide with shock then, instead of the smile of greeting which Meggie was expecting, Sally looked round at someone just behind her, hidden from sight. With a desperate, apologetic look at Meggie, Sally turned and vanished into the throng of people. Meggie pressed on through the crowd, fighting her way towards the outer edges and emerged just in time to see Sally, her arm tucked through that of a man's, disappearing rapidly over a grassy crest. Meggie stood perfectly still and stared after them. She had only had the briefest glimpse of Sally's companion but it had been more than enough for her to recognise Ronnie Sandys.

'Oliver!' Elsie Laing snapped at her son, who had forgotten to turn the carol sheet they were sharing.

'. . . What?' he asked, sounding half dazed. 'Oh . . . Sorry.' Rapidly he flipped the page and winced as his mother's shrill voice picked up in the middle of 'Silent Night', half a beat behind everyone else.

He looked again at the throng of people on the far side of the bandstand, his eyes raking the crowd. A disturbance, a milling and parting of the crowd, had attracted his attention and he had watched helplessly as Meggie McPherson, as beautiful as ever, briefly appeared, only to be swallowed up again. Though he scanned the crowd, pushing forward and standing on his toes to peer over heads, attracting a loud rebuke from his mother, he failed to find her again. In vain he tried to put his mind back to the music but that one fleeting glimpse of the woman he loved had ruined the day.

'Slow down, Ronnie,' Sally gasped, almost running to keep up with him.

'Sorry.' The apology was gruff, but his steps slowed.

Slipping her arm possessively through his, Sally walked beside him, her brow furrowed, her expression apprehensive. They were almost at the park gates before she gathered her courage and said what was on her mind. 'I would have liked to see Meggie.'

Ronnie stayed silent and strode determinedly on.

'Ronnie! Did you hear what I said?'

'Aye,' he admitted. 'I heard you, Sally.'

'Well?'

'Sally, I've no mind to argue with you today of all days.'

'But we need to talk about this, Ronnie. Meggie's my best friend.'

He sighed, stopped and looked at her for a moment, then steered her towards one of the sheltered seats near the memorial to the great war, just inside the park gates. 'I don't know what there is to talk about, Sal. You know how I feel about Meggie.'

'Aye.' She sank down beside him. 'I think you still love her, Ronnie.' It was what she had always been afraid of. The pernicious fear that Ronnie had turned to her on the rebound, that he really did still love Meggie, that one day he would return to her, haunted Sally, spoiling her pleasure in an otherwise contented relationship.

How many times recently had she let her mind wander back to that August evening when Ronnie, distraught and emotional, had appeared on her doorstep, desperate for a sympathetic ear? Her father, drunk on the money from the sale of cigarettes, had already retired unsteadily to bed and her mother, ever tactful had followed him, leaving them alone. Ronnie had cried that evening, the first time Sally had ever seen a grown man reduced to tears, and her generous heart had bled for the pain he was feeling. In the bare front room of her parents' house she had held him to her, soothing him, listening as he poured out his soul. It had seemed quite natural, in the heavily charged and highly emotional atmosphere, to kiss his face and absolutely right to allow him to slide his mouth round to meet hers, telling herself that she was doing nothing more than offering

422

comfort. But, with that first kiss, Sally unleashed something wild and uncontrollable. She had loved Ronnie from the very beginning, had felt a tremor of desire whenever she was close to him and had kept her pain tightly within herself when she saw him drawn, not to her, but to her best friend. Now, when his embrace became more passionate, when she felt his firm, hard body thrusting towards her, she could not find the strength to reject him and answered his frenzied demands generously, her desire fired by the love she had carried inside herself for so long. When he pushed her down on to her bed in the corner of the room, she made no attempt to stop what she knew was going to happen but wrapped herself round him, urging him on. Driven only by instinct, by the compulsion to somehow rid himself of his pain, Ronnie plunged into her, unknowingly fulfilling her most private fantasy. Then he closed his eyes, shuddered and groaned as the frustrations imposed by his chaste relationship with Meggie exploded hotly into Sally.

'I'm sorry, Sal,' he muttered shamefacedly afterwards.

She smiled gently and said, 'I'm not,' aware, even as she spoke, of the shocked expression on his face. 'Don't look at me like that, Ronnie,' she chided him gently. 'I'm not ashamed of what we did. I love you. I've loved you from the first day we met.'

'But I shouldn't have . . .' he stammered, his mind reeling with confusion. Only an hour ago he had thought there was nothing left to make his life worthwhile yet now he had forced himself on another woman, a woman who was now saying she loved him.

Sally saw the bewilderment on his face and, with a sharp pang of fear, understood that she had not won him yet, that she would never have another chance, that if she didn't bind him to her tonight he would walk out of her life and be too ashamed to face her again. Slowly, deliberately, she kissed him again, darting her tongue between his lips, sliding her hands sensuously over his sweating body, and was gratified to feel him stir anew.

'Yes, you should,' she told him, dropping her hand to where he was hardening again.

Pushing him back, she straddled him, taking him deep inside her again, using all her skills to excite him. Ronnie, inexperienced as he was, caught her by the arms, held her back and resisted while his eyes sought hers. For a moment they waited, unmoving, their eyes locked. Then almost violently he closed his arms round her and pulled her underneath him where his own urgent rhythm was matched by the rise and fall of her hips. Sally shuddered, crying out his name. Ronnie groaned and sank his face to her breasts before stiffening and then gradually relaxing in her arms.

Later, while they lay sated and exhausted, their limbs heavy and still entangled, he stirred and looked down at her flushed face, feeling slightly awed by what they had unleashed in each other. He drew a finger gently over her naked breasts and she opened sleepy eyes and smiled at him. But then she frowned and sat up abruptly, jerking the sheet up over her shoulders.

'Sally?' He was confused by this sudden change, worried that he had read her wrongly after all, that she was now regretting what had happened. Instantly, he sought to reassure her. 'You mustn't worry Sal, if anything happens because of tonight, I'll not let you down.' Suddenly it was vitally important that she thought well of him.

Sally squeezed his hand briefly. 'I know you won't,' she told him. 'But there's something I have to tell you, Ronnie. Now, before things get more complicated for us.'

'What?'

'You're not the first,' she told him, knowing she had to say this while he was still vulnerable.

She waited then, knowing that he might simply walk out of her life too, just as he had walked out of Meggie's. But he didn't. He lay there, silently, his face expressionless as she explained why she had allowed an older man to keep her, swearing that he had been the only one and admitting that she had thought she had been in love with him. 'It was a mistake,' she ended, watching Ronnie closely.

Ronnie closed his eyes, his head swimming. So much had happened, and too fast for him to have assimilated it all. Strangely he didn't feel disgusted by Sally's admission. And that was because Sally had been honest and open from the start. If he was to believe what she had told him – and he did – hers had been a serious relationship and very different from the blatant prostitution which had been Meggie's trade. The love he had felt for Meggie McPherson had died, driven out by a wave of nauseating disgust, the instant he read the truth in her eyes. But with Sally he felt only sympathy, the need to protect her, the desire to have that wonderful body under his again and again.

'We all make mistakes, Sally,' he told her sadly, stroking her hair. 'Mine was Meggie.'

She knew then that it would be all right.

Over the next weeks, Sally took Meggie's place in Ronnie's life, so efficiently that in less than a month she had claimed his heart. So deeply did he love Sally now that he sometimes wondered how he could ever have imagined himself to be in love with Meggie McPherson. For her, a woman who had deceived him so wickedly, he could feel only bitterness. A bare two months after his parting from Meggie, Ronnie asked Sally to marry him. The decision made, his proposal accepted, he had never regretted it.

Sitting beside Sally now, in the freezing afternoon air on Christmas Day, Ronnie saw the unusual strain round her mouth, felt the tension of her body and suddenly remembered her last words.

'I don't love Meggie, Sal,' he told her, cupping her face in his hands. 'I used to think I did. But not anymore. Not now I've got you.'

Sally took a deep breath, gathering her courage. But, she told herself, she had to know, had to be sure. 'I'm not that different to Meggie,' she told him, so quietly he had to strain to catch the words. 'You know I've been with a man before. I'm scared, Ronnie. Scared that one day you'll hate me for it.'

'Och, Sally,' he breathed. 'I could never hate you.' He kissed her gently and smiled into her troubled eyes. 'Can't you see how different it was?'

'I'm not sure if you do, Ronnie.'

'You were honest with me, Sal. You never let me think you were something you weren't. That was the awful thing. That, and . . . well, it was different. Meggie was a common prostitute, selling herself to half a dozen different men every night.' The thought made his stomach churn. He swallowed the sudden threatening rush of moisture and waited a second before he felt able to go on. 'It makes me feel sick, Sal. Really sick. With you it was different.'

'Do you really mean that, Ronnie?' she asked, clutching his hand so tightly that it hurt.

'Aye, I do. I swear I do.'

Looking into his eyes she believed him. For the first time in their relationship her mind was truly at rest. 'Thank you,' she whispered, kissing him softly. Then, becoming thoughtful again, she said, 'Don't think too badly of Meggie, Ronnie. She's not as wicked as you think she is. Everything

426

she did, she did for Matty, to try and give him a decent home.'

'Aye, and a right little bastard he is too. They're out of the same mould those two, Sally, and I don't want you having anything to do with either of them.'

Sally knew then that she had a choice. She could be loyal to the friend who had given her a job and a home, given her back her self-respect, or she could marry Ronnie. She could not have both. But if she chose Meggie, what other chance would she have of happiness? What other man would love her the way Ronnie did? If she wasn't careful she would let her past destroy her, just as Meggie's had.

'All right,' she agreed firmly. 'I won't try to see Meggie again.'

Ronnie grinned suddenly. 'Right then, that's that all cleared up. Now let's get off home to your Mam and Dad's and tell them we're getting wed at Easter.'

'My Mam'll be right relieved,' she joked. 'She thought she was going to be stuck with me under her feet forever.'

'No chance of that, lass,' he told her, linking her arm through his. 'No chance of that at all.'

They walked happily up the road, oblivious to the increasing winter chill. But Sally couldn't help looking back, just once, to see if she could catch a glimpse of her friend.

It was a cold and miserable Meggie who trailed back up the hill to the darkened house. In her mind she could still see Sally, her arm tucked through Ronnie's. She quickened her pace, deliberately denying the bitterness which was threatening to overwhelm her. Even in her distress she knew that it wasn't fair to blame Sally for what had obviously happened. She had always known that Sally was sweet on

Ronnie, known too that he liked Sally in return, so it was only natural that he should have turned to her when things went wrong. Really, she told herself, she should be glad they had found happiness together. Nothing of what had happened had been Ronnie's fault and she was generous enough to acknowledge that he deserved happiness. And Sally, too. In fact, she decided with a small sigh, they were perfectly matched. But somehow all her rationalisation failed to bring her any comfort. Instead she was even more deeply aware of how badly wrong her own life had gone.

By the time she got home the short winter day had faded and there was already a touch of frost in the air. The houses she passed all had their curtains drawn but from behind them came the warm yellow glow of lights and occasional sounds of laughter.

In contrast, her own home was dark and unwelcoming. Inside the fire had almost gone out and it was bitterly cold. She prodded it with the poker, coaxing it back to reluctant life and threw on some coal. Domino stretched, digging his claws into the sofa and allowed her to pick him up. Meggie stroked his fur, glad of the warmth of his little body, and was irrationally hurt when he twisted out of her arms and stalked disdainfully to the fireside rug where he curled up in the warmth of the fire's flickering glow.

She sank on to the sofa, shivering in the chilly room and waited in the darkness, counting the chimes on the town clock until after ten o'clock. Still Matty hadn't come home.

Finally, stiff, cold and miserable, she uncovered the drying sandwiches and scraped the chicken filling into a dish. Domino, opening one lazy eye and twitching his nose, stretched again before greedily devouring the remains of the Christmas tea. He showed his appreciation by purring happily and wrapping himself round her legs, his back arched, his tail in the air. Then, duty done, he took himself over to the door and sat there, mewing loudly. Meggie wrapped herself in her coat, took him downstairs to the back yard and watched helplessly as he leapt across the crates stored there, up on to the wall and finally jumped down to the street. By the time she wrestled the back gate open he had vanished. For more than an hour she walked up and down the street, calling his name. In the end, defeated by the bitter cold, she went indoors to bed.

CHAPTER TWENTY-TWO

'Are you sure you will be able to manage on your own?' Meggie asked.

Matty glared at her. 'If you can't trust me to look after the shop for a couple of days after all this time . . .'

'Aye, I suppose you're right,' she murmured. She had no doubt at all that Matty was perfectly capable of coping alone. What she was less certain about was his trustworthiness. 'You'll be run off your feet tomorrow, though. Fridays and Saturdays are aye busy, even for the two of us. As soon as I get back from visiting Mrs Cruickshank I'm going to advertise for someone to help out.' It was something she should have done over a year ago but had kept putting it off, always clinging to the hope that Sally would come back. There was no hope of that now that Sally and Ronnie were married.

'Why waste money?' Matty asked, unwilling to have anyone else in the shop who might soon realise just how much of the takings ended up in his pocket. 'We manage fine just the two of us.'

'We don't manage fine, Matty,' she argued. 'I can't remember the last time I had a day off.'

Matty knew his sister well enough to understand that further argument was pointless. His face dark with anger he glared at her for a moment, then turned his back and didn't even look round when she picked up her small overnight bag and walked out of the shop.

On the train to Glasgow, Meggie had plenty of time to think about her brother's attitude. She had to admit that he worked hard enough, though he insisted on a half day off each week and flatly refused to get up in time to help with the morning papers. But what really bothered her were the frequent shortfalls in the till, the discrepancies in the stock. The individual amounts were not large but added together over the course of a month the total was enough to make a noticeable difference to her profits. When challenged, Matty readily admitted making mistakes, attributing his shortcomings to his lack of education. Meggie had seen for herself how careless he could be in totalling bills and giving change but, despite watching him closely, had never caught him in anything other than what appeared to be a genuine error. Rather than risk her relationship with him she had decided to give him the benefit of the doubt. Nevertheless she was uneasy.

At the station, determined not to let her doubts about his honesty spoil her weekend, Meggie put her brother firmly out of her mind and consulted the directions Mrs Cruickshank had sent with her last letter. She found the tramstop her friend mentioned easily enough and within a minute or two the right tram came along, its trolley sparking on the overhead lines. She sat near the door, counting the stops and peering at street names, frightened that she might get lost in such a vast city. She need not have worried.

'Your stop next, hen,' the friendly conductor shouted back to her.

Meggie got off the tram and found herself in the middle of a busy road, vehicles streaming by in both directions. Clutching her small case she dodged round the back of a lorry, then stood on the pavement, slightly awed by the sheer volume of traffic.

'Meggie! Meggie, lass. Over here.'

Meggie turned and there, sheltering from the drizzle in

the doorway of a small Co-operative store, was Mrs Cruickshank. 'I was wondering whether this was the right stop,' Meggie laughed, hurrying to embrace her old friend warmly. 'Thanks for coming to meet me. How did you know what time I'd get here?'

'It was just a guess. I'd to come out for the messages and I thought I'd just wait for a wee while and hope you arrived while I was here. I knew fine you'd not be sure which way to go when you got off the tram. Now then, it's not far and we'd best hurry if we don't want a good soaking.'

They set off along a road of tenement houses then turned, going down a slight hill. The tenements ended abruptly, given way to a piece of poorly kept parkland with swings and a lopsided roundabout.

'It's quicker through here.' Mrs Cruickshank led the way through a gap in the rusting railings. A few minutes later they emerged on to a quiet suburban road, as different to the street of tenements as it was possible to be. Instead of cobbles, the road surface was smooth and the pavements were lined with trees. The houses themselves were recently built, and in pairs, each smartly painted and with a small square of fenced garden between it and the pavement.

'In here, lass.'

Meggie followed her friend up a flower-edged path and into a hallway which smelt of lavender polish.

'Come right on through.' Mrs Cruickshank drew aside a heavy curtain which gave added protection from the fierce winter draughts and Meggie found herself in a cosily furnished sitting room. Despite the fact that it was summer, a healthy fire crackled in the hearth and, in the chair nearest to it, her legs covered by a thick rug, sat an elderly lady.

'Och, Winnie's asleep. We'll not disturb her. Come on

through to the kitchen and we'll have a cup of tea and a good chat.'

'Have you settled down in Glasgow, then?' Meggie asked, as soon as she was seated at the small wooden table.

'Och, aye. I suppose so. It's different from a wee town like Inverannan right enough, but the folk are all friendly.' She frowned and looked at Meggie sadly. 'I can't say I'd have chosen to come here, mind. It was a big wrench, leaving all my friends behind.'

'Why didn't you stay in Inverannan?' Meggie asked. 'I've often wondered.'

'I didn't have any choice in the end. Winnie had just lost her husband. She can't manage on her own. I had to come and look after her.'

'Bertha? Is that you?' A tremulous voice came from the sitting room.

'That's her had her wee nap. Come and meet my sister, Meggie. Och, and do you not think it's time you called me by my given name? Bertha sounds much more friendly than Mrs Cruickshank, doesn't it?' she laughed.

'I'll try,' Meggie agreed. 'But it might take me a wee while to get used to it.'

'I'm needing a cup of tea, Bertha,' the voice called again, impatiently now.

Puzzled, Meggie followed her friend back into the sitting room. 'Winnie, this is my friend, Meggie McPherson. Do you remember me telling you she was coming to stay for the weekend?' There was patience and affection in Bertha Cruickshank's voice as she leaned over the older woman, tucking in the blanket and speaking slowly and clearly, as if to a child. 'Meggie, this is my sister, Mrs Winifred Hendrie.'

Meggie stepped forward with a smile. What she saw explained why Bertha had felt obliged to come to Glasgow and also accounted for the way the other woman had shouted for attention. Winnie Hendrie was obviously many years older than her sister and extremely frail, a fact emphasied by the wheelchair which stood behind the door. Her hair, controlled by a hairnet, was sparse and white, her pale eyes were milky looking, her face was an intricate web of lines. The hands which rested on the arms of the chair trembled and were twisted and deformed with arthritis.

'Of course I mind of you telling me!' Winnie replied, peering in Meggie's direction. 'You'll need to come closer than that if I'm to get a good look at you, hen,' she commanded in a surprisingly firm voice.

Meggie stepped forward again and gently took the talon-like hand which was waving hopefully in front of her. 'I'm pleased to meet you, Mrs Hendrie.'

'And I'm pleased to meet you, too, lass. Now then, I can't stay round here chatting all day. The bairns'll be hungry and my man'll be coming in for his dinner in an hour or so, so I'd better away hame and peel the tatties.' She struggled vainly to get out of her chair. 'Where's my hat and coat?' she asked. 'What have you done with my good coat, Bertha?'

'It's upstairs on the bed, Winnie,' Bertha replied easily. 'I'll away and get it for you. You just sit there by the fire for a minute or so longer.'

'Don't you be long or I'll never have the dinner ready on time.'

Bertha tucked the rug more firmly round her sister's legs and then went back to the kitchen, shutting the door softly behind them. 'She's nearly eighty,' she told Meggie by way of explanation. 'Her mind wanders, poor thing. Aye, it's no joke, getting old. May I be forgiven for even thinking it but there are times when I'm grateful that she can't walk. I'd

434

spend half the day looking for her if she could. She led Frank – he was her husband – a right merry dance for the last year or so before he died. Wore him out, poor soul.'

'So long as you don't wear yourself out, too,' Meggie said, realising now that her friend looked tired.

'Och, I'm right enough. And there's no help for it anyway. I'm the only one left to care for her. She's my oldest sister. There were four of us, but Jess and Mona died years since. I'm the youngest. An afterthought I was and nearly twenty years younger than Winnie. When we were weans she was like a mother to me, lass. I couldn't let her down now. She never asked anything of me before and it's the least I can do for her. I'd not see her put away into one of those homes.'

'It must be hard work, though.'

'No more than I'm used to,' Bertha insisted. 'No more than I'm used to. Now, tell me about yourself, Meggie.'

Over tea and freshly baked scones, while Winnie slumbered in front of the fire, Meggie brought her friend up to date with all that had happened.

'I'm happy for Sally. She was a good-hearted lassie, though it must have hurt you to see her marrying Ronnie. It's a shame you're not friends any more, though. You need friends, Meggie,' Mrs Cruickshank commented.

'I keep in touch with Sally's mum. She says it's Ronnie who won't let Sally see me. I suppose I can understand why. I do miss her, though.'

'And have you not found yourself another young man yet?' Bertha's tone was teasing but her eyes were alert as she watched Meggie's face.

'No.'

'Because of Ronnie? Do you still love him, Meggie?

Because if you do, you're only making things worse for yourself. You've got to forget him.'

Meggie laughed sharply. 'That's the funny thing. I was hurt but later, when I began to get over it I realised that I didn't really love Ronnie. Not like I loved Oliver. I was marrying him for the wrong reasons. I just wanted to be like everyone else . . .'

'Is that really what you want, Meggie? Do you want to be tied down with kids and a husband? What about the shop?'

'Why can't I have both?' Meggie demanded.

Mrs Cruickshank laughed. 'Aye! Why not indeed.'

On Saturday afternoon, leaving Winnie in the care of a neighbour, Bertha took Meggie to the city centre where they spent a glorious two hours in the Sauchiehall Street shops. Meggie bought a pretty scarf for Bertha and a smart new pullover for Matty. But all too soon, it was Sunday afternoon and time for her to start for home.

'Come and see me again, lass,' Bertha begged, as she saw Meggie on to the tram.

'Why don't you come and stay with me next time?'

'Och, it's just too difficult. I can't leave Winnie for that length of time and I certainly can't bring her with me. I'm sorry, Meggie, I'd like to see Inverannan again but it's impossible.'

'Then I'll just have to come to you again.'

'Any time, lass. Just pack a bag and come. I'll always be right glad to see you.'

On impulse, Meggie stepped back off the tram step and planted a kiss on her friend's cheek. 'Thanks for having me, Bertha.'

'Are you getting on or no?' the driver demanded.

'Aye,' Meggie chuckled, and jumped back on board,

waving vigorously until a bend in the road hid her friend from sight.

'Did you have a good time, then?' Matty asked when she arrived home later that evening.

'Wonderful,' she replied, realising that the break had done her good. She felt rested, more relaxed and happier than she had done for a long time. 'How did things go here? Everything all right?'

'Of course!' He feigned indignation. 'Make us something to eat, will you, Meggie. I'm fair starving.'

The benefit Meggie had derived from her weekend in Glasgow lasted only until the following Friday. The shop was so busy that Meggie didn't notice the uniformed lad who pushed his way to the front of the queue.

'Is there anything else, Mrs Haddow?'

'No, lass.'

'That's three and eightpence then, please.'

'Right, lass.' Mrs Haddow winked then handed over a crisp ten-shilling note. Meggie raked in the cash drawer and gave back the full ten shillings in change, pausing to make a discreet pencil note at the side of the till before turning to the next customer.

'You Miss Margaret McPherson?' a male voice asked.

'Och, Meggie, it's a telegram boy!' the next customer exclaimed worriedly. In their world a telegram inevitably brought bad news and still sent a chill shiver of fear through those folk who remembered the great war.

The lad handed over the envelope then turned round and, conscious of every eye following him, marched smartly from the shop.

'Who is it from, lass?'

'Och, I hope it's not bad news.'

'Do you want to sit down before you open it?'

The customers clustered round, ready to offer help, advice or support if necessary.

Shaking slightly Meggie slit the envelope and pulled out the single sheet of paper.

'It's from my Ma,' she told her audience, knowing that there was no way she could hope to keep this to herself. 'My Pa's very ill. She wants me to go and see him.'

'Och,' someone said gloomily. 'It sounds bad. She wouldn't have sent for you if there was any hope for him.'

'Aye.' Everyone seemed to agree.

'What's going on?' Matty, who had been working in the storeroom came into the shop and surveyed the silent crowd.

'It's your pa,' someone told him. 'He's been taken poorly. It must be bad. Your ma's sent a telegram.'

Meggie held out the piece of paper and he read it quickly. 'What am I going to do?' she asked faintly.

'Serve these folks to start with,' he said, taking control and turning to the waiting customers. Disappointed, they muttered among themselves.

Meggie was so familiar with the shop and all it sold that she worked quite automatically until the last customer was served.

'We'll have to go and see him,' she decided, addressing Matty who was busy restocking the shelves.

'I'm going nowhere,' he told her flatly.

'Matty! Pa's ill. We must go and see him. For all we know he might be dying.'

'He never did anything to help me. Why should I go and see him now?' Matty's voice was bitter and the expression on his face was so loaded with malice that Meggie shivered.

'He didn't understand, Matty. That's all. We should go and make things right with them both. Before it's too late.'

'You can bloody well go if you want. But I'm staying here.'

'Matty, please . . .'

'No! Anyway,' he added, 'we can't both go and you know that fine. One of us has to stay and keep the shop open. We can't just close down whenever it suits us. Folk round here depend on us.'

Meggie had no answer to that. 'Then I'll go on my own,' she decided, but she was talking to the air. Matty had gone.

Once again Meggie found herself on a Glasgow-bound train, but there was no pleasure in the journey this time. Her stomach felt queasy and there was a tight band of tension round her head, making it ache dully.

The front door of her parents' house stood ajar slightly. Meggie knocked but, getting no response, pushed it open and walked inside. It was a different house, three or four closes further up the street from the one they had been living in the last time she had come to see them. Like many tenement families, the McPhersons flitted to better accommodation as their circumstances allowed it. With Tam and both boys now working Netta had seized the chance, less than two months ago, to move to a better close, one which had the attraction of a concreted back court, a tiled stairway and a toilet on each landing. Here, too, they had the advantage of their own tiny hall with a large room on either side of it. Now, Meggie stood in the hall, wondering which of the two doors she should open first. Taking a guess she went through the one on the left.

She saw her mother right away. Netta was on her hands and knees, a tin of blacklead at her side, furiously buffing the range to a satin sheen. The steelies already shone. Behind her the rest of the room sparkled, every surface newly polished, the rugs freshly beaten, the windows washed.

Meggie felt herself go weak with relief. For the four hours it had taken her to get here she had been consumed by the fear that she would be too late, that her father might have died. But here was her mother going about her regular chores, so absorbed in what she was doing that she obviously hadn't heard her daughter come in.

'Hello, Ma,' Meggie said softly.

Netta jumped and swung round, pulling herself painfully up from her knees. 'So you came?' Meggie didn't miss the glance that was directed over her shoulder. 'Is our Matty there, too?'

'No, Ma. Matty couldn't come. He stayed to watch the shop.'

Meggie saw that her mother wasn't deceived and looked away from those piercingly direct eyes, feeling shame on her brother's behalf. 'Och, well, if he had more important things to do there's no more to be said.' Meggie, who had been expecting a warmer welcome was dismayed by the coolness of her mother's tone.

'How's Pa?' Meggie asked, dropping her case on a chair.

'Don't go leaving that there. Take it away ben the wee room,' Netta ordered impatiently.

Like the other house, this one had a tiny room leading off the kitchen. Shrugging, Meggie picked up her case and laid it on the double mattress which filled the whole, windowless space. Obviously this was where her brothers slept. Her Ma and Pa would sleep in the warmth of the bed recess in the kitchen, which meant that the room on the other side of the hall was the 'best' room, probably only used for special visitors, like the minister, and at Hogmanay. It was quite an improvement over the house they had been living in last time Meggie had come to see them and she was pleased that their circumstances were easier.

'Now then, Bertie and Perce will be in from their work the now,' Netta said briskly. 'I've a right load of baking to do for there'll be plenty folk in and out of here over the next few days. I'll get busy with that and you can peel the tatties.'

Meggie was completely bemused. 'What about Pa? What happened, Ma? Where is he?' she asked, forced to speak to her mother's back as Netta took flour and eggs out of her cupboards.

'T'damn! I'm needing sugar and there's not enough margarine either,' Netta hissed to herself. 'Meggie, run down to the Co-op and fetch some. And you'd better bring three pounds of flour too. The book's on the shelf. Just hand it in and they'll mark it up.'

'Ma! Tell me what happened to Pa,' Meggie demanded angrily.

Netta seemed to freeze for a moment, then turned round very slowly and faced her daughter. 'Your Pa's in the best room,' she said coldly, nodding towards the room on the other side of the hall. 'You can go and see him if you like.' Then she turned back to her cupboard.

Furiously, Meggie stormed across the tiny hall and into the other room. A wall of solid darkness hit her and she stood just inside the doorway, disorientated and confused. Like the main room it smelt of furniture polish but underneath it all was the faint musty dampness associated with a room which is seldom used. As her eyes grew accustomed to the gloom, Meggie made out the lighter square where the window must be. She edged her way towards it, grunting with pain as she banged into something

441

with a sharp edge, and threw back the curtains. The view over the enclosed back court was especially grey and sombre on this overcast day. Steam, issuing from the wash-house as some housewife took her turn with the boiler, drifted up past the window, bring the familiar smells of boiling water and soda, adding to the feeling of dampness. Half expecting to find her father asleep in a chair, Meggie turned round. What she actually saw made her scream and clutch wildly at the arm of a chair for support. There, supported by a trestle of planks across three upright chairs, was an open coffin. And in it was Tam McPherson.

Meggie, the sheer horror of the situation making her head reel, backed away towards the window then collapsed weakly against the wall and slid to the floor. It was many minutes before she was able to force herself to stand up. Her legs trembling, her stomach churning, she walked slowly back across the room, hanging on to the furniture as she went. She stopped by the coffin, deliberately making herself look down on the grey-tinged face which was all that was visible of Tam McPherson. His hair was grey, she thought, making him look older, and his nose looked bigger. The pennies over his eyes and the unnatural colour of his skin made him seem unreal.

Slowly she reached out a hand, letting the tips of her fingers brush against his skin. She had expected it to be stiff but it was soft and incredibly cold. Shivering she withdrew her hand but the faint movement must have been enough to disturb one of the pennies because it slid down his cheek and lost itself in the lining of the coffin. Horrified, Meggie was unable to look away from the one blind eye that stared so relentlessly at the ceiling. Her own mouth opened and, without realising it, she screamed.

Somehow she got herself back to the kitchen, though

afterwards she couldn't recall doing so. The sight of her mother, placidly dropping pancake mixture on to the hot griddle, brought her back to her senses.

'Why didn't you tell me?' she demanded, grabbing her mother by her shoulders and roughly forcing her to turn round. To her dismay she saw that there were streams of silent tears flowing over her mother's lined cheeks. Perhaps it was simply shock which had made her act so strangely. 'What happened, Ma?' she asked, more softly, her voice trembling. The answer made her reel.

'You killed him. That's what happened.' Despite the tears which still flowed, Netta's voice was steady, cold and flat.

'Ma!'

'Aye. You and Matty. As surely as if you'd pushed him under the cart yourselves.' She waited, but when Meggie was unable to do anything more than gape at her, she went on relentlessly. 'He was never the same. After he found out about you and Matty he changed. Blamed himself for the way youse turned out. That man in there . . . he isn't the man I married. The Tam McPherson I married was a kind, caring man who never touched a drop of strong drink. I never once saw him drunk, not even on Hogmanay. Not like that one in there! If I didn't get his pay on a Friday night he'd have drunk the most of it by Monday morning. Every night the same. Coming in stotting drunk at ten or eleven o'clock and all the neighbours peering round their doors at him. Aye, he was killing himself anyway. Falling under the coal cart just finished him off a bit earlier, that's all. They say he was too drunk to ken what hit him but it still took him three days in the hospital to die. They brought him home this morning. The funeral's on Monday and there's a lot to be done afore then.' She turned back to her baking.

443

Meggie groaned in anguish and collapsed on to a chair, fighting to hang on to her self-control.

The pancakes were cooling under a damp towel, a pot of mince was simmering on the hob and two rounds of shortbread were sitting on the table when Meggie next became aware of her surroundings. She had no memory of her mother making these things but knew it must have taken her well over an hour. While she still sat in the chair, ignored by her mother and wrapped in angry misery, the door opened and two young men walked in. Seeing her they stopped and stared.

'It's your sister.' Netta, still at her mixing bowl, greeted them without warmth.

'Our Meggie?' The taller of the two, a dark-haired, black-eyed lad, didn't bother to hide his astonishment. He was, she thought, very like Matty, only taller and without the sullen sneer which so often marred Matty's face. His features were a little softer, too – more open.

His brother, slightly shorter but more heavily built and with a strong resemblance to the way their father had once looked, wore a more suspicious expression. Though Meggie tried desperately to sort out which one was Perce and which Bertie, she failed.

As if reading her mind the taller one said, 'I'm Perce. He's Bertie. Come to see Pa, have you? You can come to hospital with us the night but I doubt he'll recognise you.'

Bertie, who had been staring at her with something close to hostility, now turned to his mother and asked, 'What the hell's she doing here, Ma?'

Meggie couldn't stand any more. She stood up and shouted, 'Tell them, Ma. Tell them.'

Netta carefully transferred the cake tin from the table to the oven then straightened up and wiped her hands on her apron. 'Come with me, lads. There's something I have to tell you.'

They knew. Meggie could see it in her brothers' eyes as they followed their mother out of the room. She remembered the displaced penny and wished she had been courageous enough to put it back.

The custom in the closes was for the dead to be laid out in an open coffin for all to see. Though the McPhersons had lived in this particular close for such a short time a steady stream of neighbours, the very young and the very old included, came to pay their respects. At some point in the evening, unnoticed by Meggie, Perce and Bertie disappeared but, through it all, Netta dispensed tea and freshly-baked cakes with a frightening degree of calm. Not once did she make any attempt to introduce her daughter, though many an enquiring eye was turned Meggie's way.

It was gone eleven before the last neighbour went home. Shortly after that the boys came back and, after Bertie had silently dumped Meggie's suitcase on the floor of the main room, took themselves straight to bed. The look he gave her turned her stomach and made her wonder exactly what her brothers had been told about her. She longed to talk to them, to try and explain that she wasn't the evil person they obviously thought her to be, but now wasn't the right time. After the funeral, she promised herself. She would make time to speak to them then.

Bone-tired now, Meggie longed for the oblivion of sleep. 'Am I sleeping with you, Ma?' she asked, looking at the bed recess with its double mattress still hidden behind drawn curtains.

'In your father's place!' Netta was affronted by the

suggestion. 'You can have the sofa. There's blankets in the hall press.'

Meggie hauled sheets, pillows and a couple of blankets out of the cupboard, her heart so tight with grief and hurt that she longed for the gas light to be extinguished and the protective privacy of darkness.

'You'll not be needing these.' To Meggie's astonishment, Netta grabbed the sheets and took them back to the cupboard. 'It's not worth dirtying a pair of my good sheets just for one night,' she said coming back and pulling aside the curtains to the bed recess. 'I've better things to do with my time than wash sheets for the likes of you.'

Meggie's head throbbed sickeningly. What had been a dull, nagging ache, exploded into full-blown pain. 'Three nights, Ma. Didn't you say the funeral was on Monday?'

'Aye. But you'll not be wanting to stay for that.'

'Of course I want to stay.' Meggie was appalled.

'I don't want you to.' It was totally without emotion, absolutely chilling in its certainty.

'You don't want me at my own father's funeral?' Meggie's voice was hushed, incredulous.

'No.'

'You've no right!' Meggie yelled the words as anger surged from her stomach, seeming to rebound off her aching head, making her feel nauseous and dizzy with pain.

'I've every right.' Still that frighteningly flat tone.

'I'm going to the funeral, Ma. You can't stop me.'

'No, neither I can,' Netta agreed. 'But you'll not be going from this house. Not with this family.'

Meggie's anger dissipated under the confusion in her mind. When she spoke again she sounded bewildered. 'I don't understand, Ma. Why did you send for me, if you don't want me here?'

446

At last there was some reaction. Netta flung aside her hairbrush and came to face her daughter. Gone was the vagueness which had clouded her eyes and in its place was naked hatred. 'I wanted you, and that brother of yours, to see what you had done. I wanted you to understand that you killed him. It's just a pity you didn't think it was important enough to come as soon as you got the telegram. If you had done you would have seen the way he was in that hospital, could have seen for yourself that he blames you, too. He wouldn't want youse at his funeral, neither of youse. He'd be affronted to have a whore at his graveside.' She waited, staring at her daughter, refusing to look away until, beaten and unbearably sad, Meggie lowered her own eyes.

Satisfied that she had inflicted as much pain as she possible could, Netta climbed into her bed and yanked the curtains shut, making an unbreachable barrier between herself and her daughter.

It was barely light the next morning when Meggie struggled from the uncomfortable sofa. Her head still pounded and her eyes felt gritty, her mouth sour. Quietly she dressed and, taking her case, slipped out of the house.

It was still only a few minutes after seven when one of the early morning trams deposited her in another tenement-lined street. Walking like someone in a trance she turned at the Temperance Hotel and made her way down the hill. The little park was empty, the grass long, and heavy with morning dew. Unheeding she waded through it and sat on a swing where, finally, the tears fell, coursing down her cheeks and dripping unheeded on to the shoulders of her coat.

'Maybe she's no weel?' a young voice suggested, worming its way into the edges of her mind.

'Or aff her heed,' another one said, bringing an outburst of sniggering.

'Hey, Missus, gie's oor swing.' A louder, more aggressive voice this time which succeeded in breaking through Meggie's shocked state.

Slowly, wondering where she was, she looked up, squinting through swollen eyes.

'Cripes! Did sumwan thump ye?' a braver soul asked, stepping forward and peering into her face.

Meggie, her head swimming, saw that she was surrounded by half a dozen urchins, their bare legs already grubby, their mouths bearing sticky traces of the jelly pieces which had been their breakfasts, their eyes agog with curiosity.

She jumped up so sharply that the swing seat jerked back and returned to hit her viciously below the knees, tearing her stockings. She gasped, then shoved her way through the diminutive crowd, almost running in her haste to get away from them. Their taunts carried through the clear, morning air behind her.

'Heed case.'

'Nutter.'

Meggie ran down the narrow lane and emerged on to the street of neat little semis. Ignoring the startled glances from two housewives, setting out for their messages, she tore up the front garden path and hammered on the door.

Footsteps sounded in the hallway and the door was flung open.

'Meggie!' Bertha Cruickshank was too shocked to do anything more than stare for the first few seconds. Meggie's hair straggled, tangled and untidy, over her shoulders with tendrils clinging damply to her blotched face and her eyes were so swollen that they were barely open. Her coat was unevenly buttoned, drawing the eye to the torn stockings and waterlogged shoes. 'Meggie,' she repeated, holding out her arms. 'What in the name has happened to you?'

Meggie choked on a sob and stepped into the comforting circle of those warm arms and laid her hot head on the firmly padded shoulder. 'I'm sorry,' she muttered.

'Sorry? Och, no, Meggie, you've never any need to be sorry when you come here. Come on inside, lass.' Gently she drew the girl inside the house and slammed the door on the neighbours who were peeking out from behind their curtains.

An hour later Bertha Cruickshank was tucking Meggie up in her own, still warm bed. When she went back downstairs to tend to her sister she had to pause to wipe away traces of tears from her own eyes, appalled that the girl's mother could treat her so harshly. Well, she thought, she would just fill the emotional gap in Meggie's life herself. Meggie was like a daughter to her already and, even if Mrs McPherson wouldn't recognise the many good qualities in her own child, she certainly could and would be proud to take that woman's place.

CHAPTER TWENTY-THREE

Doctor Galloway put his stethoscope back in his cavernous leather bag and snapped it shut.

'Well?' Wallace Laing's voice still had its customary snap of impatience.

Galloway sighed. Wallace and he were of an age. When he had come to Inverannan, more than forty years ago now, newly qualified and proud to have been able to buy into an established practice, Wallace had been one of his first patients. Wallace himself, until recently, had been blessed with remarkably robust health and had had little cause for professional consultations. His wife, however, was another matter. Elsie Laing had at her disposal a whole repertoire of ailments, most of them imaginary.

Only last month she had called him out in the middle of his dinner because of one of her migraine headaches, headaches which he firmly believed were caused by her own acidly unattractive personality. As usual a small phial of harmless tablets and ten minutes of listening to her incredibly broad spectrum of complaints had sufficed to effect an immediate improvement.

But this time he was here to see Wallace and there were no easy remedies for what was wrong with him. The inevitable outcome was something Galloway viewed with great sadness.

'Well?' Wallace barked again. 'Come on, Douggie, don't mess me about. I asked you a question and I want to know the bloody answer.'

'Aye, well, get yourself all steamed up and you won't be around long enough to hear it!' Douglas Galloway retorted, knowing his old friend would find it difficult to deal with a more sympathetic approach.

There was a moment's pause before Wallace coughed and asked, 'As bad as that, then?'

'Not good, Wallace. Not good, my friend.'

'I will get better, this time?'

'Och, aye, I daresay. But it's no good you thinking you can jump out of that bed and get back to work in a hurry, mind.'

'How long?'

'As long as it takes!' was the unhelpful reply.

'Bloody hell, Douggie. I can't stay here, wasting time laying on my behind when there's work to be done.'

Galloway shrugged. 'Fine, go back to work as soon as you feel better. I can't stop you. But I'm warning you, Wallace, you'll not see your next birthday, if you do.'

Wallace sank back on to the pillows, seeming defeated. 'All right. You've made your point. What do I have to do?'

Galloway allowed himself a small smile. 'Wallace, do I have to spell it out for you? You had your second heart attack in six months less than three weeks ago. You were lucky again this time. Next time you won't be. That much I can guarantee. There's not a lot more I can do for you apart from prescribing tablets for the angina. After that it's up to you. You will have to accept certain limitations.'

'Humph . . .'

'Rest. Cut back on the whisky. No cigars. Keep away from the office. Eat less. Gentle exercise. No excitement.'

'Might as well turn up my toes now and be done with it!'

'You'll do that soon enough, my friend, if you don't take my advice.'

'Bloody hell!' Wallace hissed again. 'The company won't run itself, Douggie. I'm needed there.'

'It's your choice. I've given you the benefit of my professional expertise. Take it or leave it.' Galloway got up and glanced at his watch, conscious of other patients still to be visited. When he reached the door he looked back and said, 'Let that son of yours take over from you now, Wallace. You've surely earned the right to retirement at your age.'

'Oliver? He works hard, but his heart's not in it. Go on, get off on your rounds. You're just making me bloody miserable. Call in the night for a wee half. I've a bottle of fine malt just waiting for an appreciative palate like yours.'

Galloway muttered an oath. 'Have you not heard a word I've said?'

'Aye. Every blasted one of them. That's why that bottle's still there. I'm not able to drink it so you better had, before the temptation gets too much for me.'

'In that case I would be neglecting my duty if I refused your generous offer.' Galloway closed the door and went downstairs laughing. His jolly mood vanished the moment he saw Elsie Laing waiting for him in her sitting-room doorway.

'A word, Doctor, if you please.'

'Just a minute or two, Mrs Laing ... other calls you know.' Funny, he mused, how he had never felt tempted to call Wallace's wife by her given name, but then she was a woman who did not inspire friendship, let alone affection. Fleetingly he wondered what Wallace had ever seen in her. To his mind Elsie Laing looked exactly what she was, a thin streak of misery.

'I'm surprised you find anything to laugh at in my

452

husband's condition,' she attacked him as soon as the door was closed.

'A private joke, Mrs Laing, nothing more.' Galloway pointedly checked his watch. 'What was it you wanted, Mrs Laing?'

'I want to know when Wallace will be fit to go back to the office.'

He shook his head. 'I have been trying to persuade him that he should never go back.'

'Never go back!' The tone of voice and the furious expression would have thoroughly intimidated a meeker man. Douglas Galloway managed to convey his contempt by the coolness of his stare.

'That is what I said.'

'Doctor Galloway, you obviously do not understand the position. The company needs Wallace. He is the only one capable of running it. Without him things will begin to slacken off. If he is not there every day, people will take advantage. Things will not be done as they should be done. We will start to lose money, Doctor Galloway.'

Galloway clenched his back teeth. 'Mrs Laing! Your husband is a very sick man. He was fortunate to have survived that last attack. He will not live though another one. At best I give him a year. If you allow him to go back to work, he will not last the month.' He was gratified to see her pale.

'A year?' It was an appalled whisper.

'Of course Wallace does not yet appreciate how serious his condition is, though I am sure he will suspect when he begins to see how many things he can no longer do.'

'He is an . . . an invalid?'

'I think we can say that, yes. Any exertion, any excitement could very well precipitate a fatal attack. He must accept his limitations. In fact he will have no choice. I am sorry.'

'Sorry!' The venom in that one word startled him. 'Sorry? What use is sorry? Sorry won't keep the company going. Sorry doesn't put money in the bank, Doctor Galloway.'

He gaped at her, his professional manner deserting him.

'I am not satisfied, Doctor Galloway. You are nothing more than a small-town doctor. I am sure that a more eminent man would be able to do something to help my husband.'

'You are, of course, at liberty to ask for a second opinion,' he said coldly.

'And I will, Doctor Galloway. Indeed I will.'

Galloway picked up his bag and rammed his hat back on his head. 'I'll bid you good day, Mrs Laing. Please don't bother to see me out.' He brushed past the startled maid and let himself out into the fresh air, only resisting the temptation to slam the door by reminding himself of Wallace in the bedroom above.

'Dad?' Oliver put his head round the edge of his father's door and spoke in a whisper.

'Oliver? Come in, lad. Come on in.' Wallace hitched himself into a sitting position. As he did so a pile of papers slid off the bed.

'Did I wake you?' Oliver still whispered and had difficulty seeing his father's face in the stuffy, darkened room.

'Speak up, Oliver. I'm not in the funeral parlour yet. And open those bloody curtains.'

Oliver grinned and did as he was told. 'Were you asleep?' he asked, bending to gather the papers. Nestling between them was a delicate bracelet, its fine gold links studded with

454

jet and diamonds. 'I've not seen this before,' he said, looping it round his fingers and examining it closely, admiring the fine workmanship.

Wallace lurched forward and grabbed it from his hand. 'Just a trinket,' he snapped. 'Hand me that box,' he ordered, pointing at the lockable box in which he kept his personal papers and small items of value like his own father's gold watch and signet ring. Quickly he stuffed the papers and the bracelet into it and slammed the lid shut. 'I've been sorting through my things, making sure everything's in order,' he explained. 'The bracelet was your grandmother's. Your mother never liked it.'

'Sorting through your papers! You're supposed to be resting.' Oliver put the box back on the bedside table and promptly forgot about the bracelet.

'I've done enough resting to last me a lifetime. I'm so bloody bored! Your mother won't even let me have a paper to read in case it excites me. Can you believe that?'

'Aye. I can. And maybe she's right. I've often seen you working yourself into a rage over some politician or other.'

'If that's the best you can do, you'd better go back downstairs.' But Wallace grinned when he said it.

Oliver dragged a chair to the side of the bed, aware as he did so of the frightening change in his father. Always a big man, Wallace had visibly shrunk over the past three weeks. His face was gaunt with terrible hollows under his cheekbones and black circles around his eyes. The tendons on his neck no longer seemed a sign of strength but looked scrawny, the skin loose and crêpey. The hands which fiddled endlessly with the bedspread were the hands of an old man, knobbled and freckled, the nails horny. Overcome by a sense of impending loss, Oliver looked away, fighting

455

the grief which was closing his throat. 'I'll see you get the paper,' he choked. 'And a pack of cards, too, if you like.'

'You expect me to play bloody patience?'

'Aye, bloody patience,' Oliver agreed, responding to his father's determined stoicism and managing a normal grin.

Wallace sighed. 'It's doing me no good being cooped up in here all day, you know. I'm stiffening up. I'd be better off downstairs.'

'Dad! You promised to stay here until the end of the week.'

'It's your mother, she's fussing round me like a demented chicken. I'll be a mental case long before my heart gives up.'

'She's only looking after you.'

'Och, aye, she's looking after me all right. I've never known the like. Ever since Galloway told her I'd be dead inside the year. Gave her the fright of her life, it did. Wonderful what the thought of losing her income can do for a woman, lad.' He tried to make it sound like a joke but Oliver was aware of the underlying bitterness.

Oliver squeezed his father's hand, unable to trust himself to speak.

'Aye, well, that's enough of that morbid talk. What's happening at the office?'

'Nothing for you to concern yourself about. Everything's ticking along perfectly smoothly, Dad. You know, I'm quite capable of running things there now.'

Wallace sighed heavily. 'Aye, son. I know that fine. You'll make a first-class job of it; better than me, if you want the truth. You've a fine mind for detail and a good memory. You're sharp. Aye, that's the word, sharp. And not weighed down by the old way of doing things or unduly taken with these newfangled ideas. It's people like you, young blood, that's what the industry needs.'

Oliver had never before heard himself praised so fulsomely. He was both flattered and uncomfortable. 'I'm just doing my best.'

'Aye. You always do and I'm right proud of you for buckling down to it for I know it's not what you'd have chosen to do.'

'You'd be surprised.'

'Would I? You've never made a secret of not being entirely happy there.'

Oliver grinned. 'It's different now. I'm more involved. I'm honestly enjoying it.' And, much to his own surprise, he was. In his father's absence he was effectively in control and knew he was doing a good job.

'Can't wait to get your backside in my chair, eh?'

'No,' Oliver laughed. 'But when you do come back, don't expect me to slip quietly back to my old position.'

Wallace looked speculatively at his son. There was no doubt that Oliver had matured in the last months. But still he felt that there was something far wrong. It was as if Oliver was immersing himself in work to compensate for something else. And Wallace knew what, or to be precise, who, that somebody was. 'And what happens when the cousins are ready to take over? It's not long now.'

'Then I'll bow out gracefully. I've a mind to try my luck overseas. Australia maybe. Or South Africa. There's plenty of opportunities there.'

'So far away, Oliver? Do you dislike Scotland so much?'

'No.'

'You're going to let a failed love affair ruin your life, drive you away from your home and family?' Wallace spoke with his customary bluntness and, seeing his son flinch, knew he had struck home. 'Forget her, Oliver. It's

457

over. Find yourself another lass. Settle down and have a family.'

'I will. But not here.'

Wallace leaned back against his pillows with a grunt. 'I know why you want to leave, Oliver. I may be old but I'm not blind. And I'm your father. You may not like to think so but we're alike, you and me. You've never got over Meggie McPherson. You don't want to stay around a town where you're constantly reminded of her.' Wallace spoke from a deeper understanding than Oliver could ever know. How many times had he seen a dark-haired lass and felt his heart beating fast with anticipation, only to have it plummet when the girl turned out to be someone else? How many times had he been tempted to call in at the shop, just to see the lass who had given him so many happy memories?

'That's true,' Oliver admitted it slowly. 'But there's more to it than that.'

'Aye, lad. Pride.'

'Pride?'

'Aye. Like I said, you and me, we're a lot alike. I wouldn't care to see the company being taken over by someone else after I'd put so much hard work into it, either, not at your age.'

Oliver seemed to consider it for a moment then acknowledged defeat with a wry smile. 'Aye, it will be a bit of a kick in the teeth, but Robbie's the eldest, he'll be in charge. Och, I don't really grudge him it, Dad. I like him, we've always got on well, but he's got his own ideas, he'll want to do things his way. And you know I've always wanted to try my hand at something else, see other places. When Robbie joins the company it'll give me the opportunity to do just that.'

'You'll be doing nothing more than running away. And

you know it as well as I do. You'll never feel settled until you put that girl out of your mind once and for all.'

'I have been trying.'

'Oliver.' Suddenly Wallace grasped his son's hand and sat up.

'What is it?' Oliver sprang up, alarmed.

'I want you to promise me one thing.' Wallace's breathing was fast and uneven.

'Anything. What is it, Dad?'

'Promise me you'll not just up and go as soon as I'm in my grave. Your cousins will need you, Oliver. Need you to steer them away from trouble. Make sure they're capable of taking over, lad.'

Oliver hesitated. It could mean as much as five more years before his cousins had the experience fully to control the Strathannan Mining Company. As if sensing his unwillingness to commit himself, Wallace gripped his son's hand. 'Promise me, Oliver. You're the only one with the know-how to keep the thing afloat. If you don't, then everything I've worked for will be wasted. Forty-odd bloody years for nothing.'

Oliver had a gut-wrenching glimpse of what it must be like to have worked so hard and so long only to see everything fall at the last minute because of a quirk of fate. He was beaten. 'Don't worry, Dad. I know my duty. But that's not why I'll do it. I'll do it because I love you, Dad.' How long was it since he had told his father that? Had he ever said it before? He wished he had, and often, because now it was almost too late.

'I'm proud of you, Oliver. Right proud.' The deep voice was slurred and weary now. Apparently satisfied, Wallace settled back and closed his eyes.

* * *

459

'Doctor Galloway, Mrs Laing.' The young maid announced the visitor with her habitual nervousness.

'What does he want?' Elsie demanded angrily.

'I . . . I don't know,' the girl stammered nervously. Mrs Laing terrified her. Never in her eighteen years had she been so miserable. She hadn't wanted to go into service. No one did these days when there were better paying jobs in offices, shops and mills, but her mother, who had been a parlour maid on the Earl of Strathannan's estate before she got married, had insisted on her taking this job.

'Didn't you ask, you stupid girl?'

'Please, Mrs Laing, he just said he'd come to see Mr Laing.'

'Well, tell him he can't.'

'Yes, Mrs Laing.' The girl disappeared then came back a minute later, this time looking frankly scared. 'I'm sorry, Mrs Laing. Doctor Galloway has already gone up to Mr Laing's room.'

'What? Upstairs? Why didn't you stop him? Go. Go at once and tell him to leave. What do you think you are doing letting people wander around the house.'

'It wasn't my fault. I asked him to wait.'

'Of course it was your fault!' She would have said more but the maid was rescued by the timely appearance of Oliver, who came into the room looking far from pleased.

'What on earth's going on?' he demanded, looking from the tearful maid to his enraged mother.

'This stupid girl let Douglas Galloway upstairs to visit your father.'

'I didn't. I left him . . .'

'I took Doctor Galloway upstairs, Mother,' he explained, smiling at the maid.

'That will be all, Vera,' Elsie thundered, further incensed

by the way the girl was preening herself in front of Oliver. 'Oh, and I want you to sweep my bedroom carpet before I retire for the night. It's covered in powder.'

'But I did it this afternoon!'

'Then you will have to do it again.'

'It's my evening off, Mrs Laing,' the girl insisted bravely.

'Evenings off are a privilege to be earned, Vera.'

'But I'm going out!'

'I think not, Vera.'

Now there was open defiance in the girl's voice and rebellion in her eyes. 'I've already made my arrangements, Mrs Laing. It's too late to cancel them.'

'You will do as you are told!' Elsie's voice rose to a shriek.

'That's not fair!'

'Vera!' Oliver hissed a warning.

'If you think I am treating you unfairly then I am sure you would prefer not to work for me,' Elsie said, smiling.

It was a ploy she had used on several previous occasions and she waited smugly, expecting the girl to grovel and apologise. She was disappointed.

'No.'

'Then go and clean the bedroom carpet.'

'I mean *no*, I would prefer not to work for you any more, Mrs Laing.' Vera's face was as white as her ridiculously frilled cap but she spoke up clearly. 'I want to give you one month's notice.'

Elsie flushed and very nearly told the girl to pack her bags and get out that night. What stopped her was the realisation that she would then be obliged to perform all the household tasks herself. These days many girls considered domestic jobs to be beneath them and even with a month's notice, she would be lucky to find a suitable replacement. 'One month,' she agreed sourly.

Trembling slightly, Vera turned to go, already dreading what she was going to tell her mother.

'Well, I can't say I'm sorry,' Elsie declared, sinking into her chair. 'That girl is absolutely useless. She does nothing right. Nothing at all. And to speak to me like that! Just who does she think she is?'

'A human being, Mother,' Oliver muttered darkly.

'What did you say, Oliver?'

'I'll see you in the morning. Don't wait up.' He left her fuming like a well-stoked boiler, knowing, even as he escaped into the fresh air, that she would feed her fury and vent her spleen on him over breakfast the next morning. Perhaps a few drinks with his best friend, Iain Sutherland, would have improved his own temper before then.

By the time Oliver returned home, sometime after eleven o'clock, his mood had been only slightly mellowed by two large malt whiskies and the determinedly cheerful company of his friend. Although the disagreement with his mother had already receded into the back of his mind, he was still depressed by his earlier conversation with his father.

Oliver had always held his father in great affection. Where his mother had been impossibly demanding and bad-tempered, giving the younger Oliver the very clear impression that she didn't like him very much, and frequently leaving him smarting with outrage and frustration after some unearned criticism, his father had been unfailingly fair. It was his father to whom he had turned with the inevitable childish difficulties; his father who had praised his school reports, giving him the confidence to work to the upper limit of his abilities; his father who had secretly provided the new blazer when Oliver's orginal one had been wrecked in a fight with a bigger lad. And his father who had thrashed him soundly when, at the age of twelve, he had come home drunk and reeking of cigarette smoke after an evening raiding the Sutherlands' drinks cabinet.

The bond between them had been strong enough to survive Oliver's marked reluctance to enter the family business. In the end, it had been loyalty to his father that had taken him to the company's offices, where he had worked long and hard to learn the intricacies of the business on the understanding that he would remain there only until such time as his cousins came to relieve him. But, much to Oliver's surprise, as his understanding grew, he found he was actually enjoying the challenge of keeping the business viable. By the time he met Meggie he had almost decided to stay on, to make his career permanently with the company. But breaking up with her had changed all that. All he wanted to do now was get as far away from Inverannan as possible, away from the ever present possibility of bumping into her in the small town, away from the memories which seemed to linger in every street they had ever walked together.

His father's illness had made such a course of action impossible. The promise Oliver had just made would tie him to the company for several more years.

As he let himself into the house that night his brain was reeling with confusion. The conflicting emotions of love, grief and resentment all battled in his head. Sleep was obviously going to be impossible, he thought, hanging his coat and hat on the hall stand. What he needed now was a cup of tea and half an hour with his head in a good book, something to clear his brain.

He peered into the sitting room, relieved to see that his

mother had retired for the night, then made his way to the bookshelves. He ran his eye over the familiar volumes with a frown of irritation, seeing nothing he particularly wanted to read. He dismissed his father's Dickens collection along with novels by Somerset Maugham, H. G. Wells and D. H. Lawrence. His mother's selection of Agatha Christie and Dorothy Sayers held little appeal, nor did a collection of poems by Robert Burns. But then, just as he was about to give up and resort to the daily paper where the news was all depressing stuff about the unrest in Germany and the World Economic Conference in London, he spotted a new book, wedged hard against the very side of the bottom shelf. The books were so tightly jammed in that he extracted it only with difficulty. Oliver examined the cover of Huxley's *Brave New World*, then smiled slowly. Someone else's vision of the future might be just the thing to take his mind off his own problems for a little while. Tucking the book under his arm he made his way to the back of the house, meaning to make himself a hot drink and then take it, and the book, up to bed with him.

The kitchen was in darkness, and, on this mid-July night, surprisingly cold. Oliver shivered and fumbled for the light switch. A bright yellow glow flooded over the wooden table, which was situated in the centre of the room, causing the figure who was hunched over it to start and sit up.

'Mr Oliver!'

'Vera!' To his horror he saw she was crying. Her eyes were red and her whole face was bloated with misery. Her woebegone appearance was exacerbated by her cap, a starched band of white, lace-trimmed material, tied at the back of her head by four white tapes, which had slipped down over her eyebrows.

464

'I'm sorry, Mr Oliver.' She sank her head on to the table and collapsed in a flood of helpless sobs.

Embarrassed, Oliver began to back out of the room. It had been a long, worrying day and he felt incapable of dealing with even the simplest problem. He would certainly be out of his depth with this overwrought female.

He was almost in the doorway when she looked up at him with watery blue eyes. 'I shouldn't have done it, Mr Oliver,' she sniffed, rubbing ineffectually at her waterlogged face.

Oliver, stifled a sigh. 'Shouldn't have done what?' he asked, resigning himself to a difficult few minutes.

'I shouldn't have given my notice. My Mam's right angry with me. She says there's no jobs going anywhere in Inverannan and she can't afford to have me back at home unless I can pay for my keep.'

Oliver raked his mind for some suitably optimistic reply. 'You've got a whole month to find something else. I'm sure you'll be all right. Folks are always looking for good domestic help,' he offered at last.

'Not without a reference,' she said, sounding angry now. Oliver groaned inwardly. 'Ah . . .'

'Mrs Laing said if any employer wrote to her about me she would feel it was her duty to warn them that I'm lazy and insolent.' She sobbed hugely. 'But I'm not, Mr Oliver. Honest I'm not. I always work hard and I'm polite, too. Usually,' she added dully.

Oliver was aware of the injustice of it but knew he could not interfere in domestic matters. 'I wish there was something I could do, Vera,' he said awkwardly. 'Look, if I happen to hear of anything I'll let you know, I promise you that.' It was a futile gesture. The chances of him hearing about the sort of job which would suit a girl like Vera were extremely remote. 'Now make yourself a cup of tea and get away to bed. I daresay you've to be up early in the morning and it wouldn't do for you to get into worse bother by sleeping in, would it?'

'No, sir.'

'And remember what I said. If there is anything . . .'

'Aye.' She seemed to brighten a little. 'Thank you, sir.'

'Good night, Vera.'

'Good night, Mr Oliver.'

What a day, he thought, trailing wearily up to bed.

CHAPTER TWENTY-FOUR

Oliver gave little thought to Vera over the next three weeks. His father, thank goodness, was beginning to recover and was itching to get back to work. Only the combined pressure of Doctor Galloway, Mr Finch, the eminent Edinburgh physician who had been called in by Elsie, and Oliver himself, had persuaded him to remain at home for a month or two longer.

Oliver revelled in the continuing responsibility but, after dinner each evening, his father demanded a detailed run-down on the day's business. As he came through the front door that evening Oliver's mind was on the disappointing coal sales. It was a result of the depression and wouldn't pick up again until industry began to recover, as the national government promised it would. His father knew that as well as he did, but even so, Oliver realised the news would cause his father the kind of stress he needed to avoid. The evening ahead would be a difficult one.

He was right. Concerned by the sales figures, Wallace detained Oliver for almost three hours. Oliver, seeing his hopes of meeting Iain for a quiet drink receding with every passing minute, managed to give the outward appearance of patience. His father was already red-faced and irritable. To enter into an argument could only make matters worse.

'Well, I suppose we'll ride it out. Pity though. I was hoping things would start picking up before this. Still, they wouldn't have been any better if I'd been there so don't go blaming yourself, Oliver,' Wallace eventually conceded.

'I'm not.'

Wallace grunted. 'I can see I'll need to get back to work soon, before you decide you can manage without me.'

Oliver stood up. 'I refuse to argue with you about that.'

'That's half the trouble,' Wallace admitted morosely. 'I can't get anyone to have a good argument with me. Even Douggie Galloway's treating me like a maiden aunt. I am so bloody fed up, Oliver.'

'I know it's difficult for you, Dad. Just try to be patient.' Oliver gathered his papers together. 'Can I get you anything before I go upstairs?'

'Aye, ask that lass to bring me something to drink, will you?'

'Can you take Father's supper in, Vera?' Oliver poked his head round the kitchen door.

'Aye. It's all ready. Poor Mr Laing. He hates these but the doctor says that's all he's to have at this time of night.' She put two dry biscuits on a tray with a pot of tea and turned to face him. 'I was wondering if I could have a wee word with you, sir.'

'What about?'

'Well.' She seemed hesitant now. 'You remember you said to let you know if there was anything you could do for me . . .?'

'Yeees . . .' he said, sensing he was about to regret that rash promise.

She heard the wariness in his voice but rushed on desperately, determined to hold him to his word. 'Well. I've seen a job. In a shop. I went to see them and they say I can start on Monday next. But they want references.'

'I see.'

'I was wondering if you could go in and have a word with them. They'll know something's wrong if I don't have a reference from Mrs Laing. If I try and explain it'll just

468

sound like I'm making excuses. But if you could tell them I'm honest and hardworking, well I'm sure they'd believe you.'

'I don't think . . .'

'You did promise, sir,' she reminded him boldly.

Guilt brought a wry smile to his face. 'Yes, I did, didn't I?'

She gave him no chance to change his mind. 'Thank you, Mr Oliver,' she beamed, picking up the tray and making quickly for the door. 'I'd better be taking Mr Laing his supper.'

'You've forgotten something.'

'What?' She put the tray down and examined it. 'Milk, teaspoon . . . no, I think it's all there.'

'The address,' Oliver chuckled, knowing he had been out-manoeuvred. 'Where am I supposed to go to give you this wonderful reference?'

'McPherson's. That wee shop on the corner, halfway down the hill. Do you know it?'

'I . . . I . . .' No, he couldn't do this. Not actually go into Meggie's shop and speak to her.

'It's the general store. Och, you must know it!' Vera misinterpreted his confusion.

'Yes,' he managed at last. 'Of course I know it.'

'Maybe the morn? On your way home from work. I think they stay open quite late.'

'Tomorrow,' he agreed. Having made her a promise he couldn't go back on it. 'Don't worry. I'll go there tomorrow.'

Oliver walked very slowly up the hill. He could see the shop ahead of him but the closer he got to it, the more slowly his legs moved. 'You're being ridiculous,' he said to himself, aloud, causing the small boy and girl who were passing to look up at him in astonishment before running off down the road, giggling together. Oliver looked after them and grinned, feeling foolish. What on earth was he frightened of? he asked himself. His task was a simple one, furthermore he was honour-bound to do it. And had it been any other shop, any other establishment in the whole of Scotland, he would have been pleased to do Vera this small favour. But this was Meggie McPherson's shop and the thought of seeing her again had reduced him to the sort of nerves he had only ever experienced before in the dentist's waiting room.

This was just stupidity, he told himself, deliberately forcing his pace. It was probable that Meggie would hardly remember him, and, even more likely, she was almost certainly married, perhaps with a young family of her own by this time. After all, it was more than two years . . .

The shop door gaped in front of him. Oliver straightened his tie, ran a hand through his hair, then walked firmly inside, hoping he looked a lot more collected than he felt. To his immense relief a young man was serving behind the counter and there was no sign of Meggie.

'Yes?' Matty handed his previous customer her change and turned to Oliver.

'You were advertising for an assistant?'

'Aye?' Matty's eyes raked the smart, confident young man in front of him. Surely he wasn't after the job. Even his accent marked him out as a member of a different strata of society.

'Our maid, Miss Vera Mackay, applied for it. She asked me to supply a reference.'

Matty didn't bother to hide the sneer of contempt that curled his lip. He had no time for the type of people who

470

employed maids. Again he let his eyes travel insolently over Oliver's obviously expensive suit, his gaze coming to rest on the fingers which were drumming impatiently on the countertop. That heavy gold signet ring was probably worth more than he earned in a whole year.

Oliver bridled, feeling the other man's hostility. 'Do you know anything about it?' he demanded.

'No.' Matty was dismissive.

Oliver's temper rose, banishing his nerves. 'Then who would?'

Matty ignored him and served another customer. Oliver drummed his fingers more loudly and glared at the younger man.

Taking his time, Matty dispatched the woman and ambled back to Oliver. 'My sister dealt with it,' he said, opening a paper.

'Then I would like to speak with her.' The anger was obvious now.

'Why didn't you say so before?' Matty closed the paper and went to the storeroom door. 'Meggie. Someone to see you about the job.'

'I'll be there in just a wee minute,' she called, her voice jolting Oliver so badly that he walked away and pretended deep interest in the display of household cleansers on one side of the shop.

'Will you finish tidying up in there for me please, Matty?' Meggie asked, coming into the shop, untying her dusty apron as she did so.

Matty sloped off, nodding towards Oliver's back as he went.

'I'm terribly sorry, sir,' Meggie said, as she walked towards him, 'but I have promisd the position to a young woman and . . .' the words petered out to a small gasp as Oliver turned round.

'Hello, Meggie.' She was even more beautiful than he remembered. The intervening years had changed her. The heart-shaped, once urchin-like face had matured so that the underlying bone structure was displayed. High cheekbones, wide-set eyes, a firm chin, a generous, expressive mouth and flawless skin combined to give a perfect, faintly exotic whole. Tall and slim, but with undeniably feminine curves, the sight of her stunned him into tongue-tied silence. When he should have simply explained what he wanted, he could only stand and gape. Somewhere, his mind registered that he was making a complete fool of himself, but he seemed incapable of making any sensible move.

Meggie was so astounded to find Oliver in her shop that she noticed nothing strange in his manner. She also found herself staring. The misleading severity of his profile which was still such a surprising contrast to the sensitivity of his whole face, the strong jawline, the mouth which seemed always on the point of smiling, the warmth in his deep eyes, the hair worn longer than fashion dictated. It was all still there, just as she remembered it. Meggie knew that if she stretched a hand out and touched the blue-tinged stubble on Oliver's chin, she would find it unexpectedly soft. The temptation was almost too great and she actually had to restrain herself from doing just that. And then, catching her completely off-guard, came the small *frisson* of excitement, the shiver which started deep inside her and spread through her like an electric current, causing a disturbing throb between her legs and making her nipples harden and tingle.

Shocked and embarrassed by her own involuntary re-action to him, Meggie flushed and fled to the other side of the counter, seeking refuge in her official position. Oliver stood on the other side and tried to think of anything but her.

'You came about the job?' What a ridiculous thing to say, she cursed herself silently. Obviously he didn't want to work here.

He chuckled as the humour in the situation struck him, and the tension was broken. 'You interviewed our maid, Miss Vera Mackay,' he said, glad to get to the point of his visit.

A customer came into the shop. Meggie called Matty, then was distracted again as two more women came in, both calling a cheerful greeting to her.

She laughed. 'We're not going to get any peace here. Come on upstairs.'

The sitting room over the shop was where she had interviewed all the applicants. She spoke without thinking and, having issued the invitation, it was now too late to withdraw it. Uneasily, still unsettled by the emotions which had crackled through her just minutes earlier, she led the way. Once in the little room she nodded him towards a chair and settled herself in another, not too close to him.

'Miss Mackay told me she worked for your mother. The job's hers as soon as she brings her references for me to see. Is there some problem, Oliver? Is that why you're here?' Meggie sincerely hoped not. She had liked Vera Mackay on sight and had believed they could work together well.

'Well . . . yes and no.' He wondered how he could put this without seeming to betray his own family. He couldn't avoid it, he realised, not if he wanted to be fair to Vera, which he certainly had to be.

'Och . . .' Meggie sighed her frustration. 'I suppose I'll have to put the card back in the window. It's a pity though. I thought Miss Mackay seemed a straightforward, honest girl. I liked her.'

'No!' he spoke more loudly than he intended, then grinned again. 'Sorry. It's just that I don't know quite how to put this.'

'Put what?' Now she was intrigued. 'Either you can recommend her or you can't.'

'I can,' he told her quickly, impressed by her authoritative manner. 'Wholeheartedly. But my mother has refused to give her a reference.'

'I see . . .' But she sounded doubtful.

'No, you don't. Look, I suppose I'd better be honest with you.'

'I suppose you had,' she agreed.

'Vera is a smashing girl. She works hard, she's honest, she's polite and tidy . . . everything, really. But my mother was dreadfully unfair to her. In the end Vera handed in her notice. Goodness knows how she stuck it out as long as she did. Mother knows she'll never find anyone half as good, certainly not before Vera leaves. But it's her own fault, really. It happens with all the girls who work for us. Most of them stick it out for about six months, then off they go and work for someone else. I've lost count of the number of maids we've had. Anyway, that's what upset Mother and that's why she won't give her a reference. It really is most unfair, Meggie. Vera deserves a chance and you'll not regret employing her.'

Meggie regarded him dubiously. It was a very strange situation for the son of the household to come pleading on behalf of the maid. The unwelcome suspicion that there might be more to it, that there might be some personal involvement, was hard to ignore.

474

'I don't know, Oliver. It's all very . . . unusual, to say the least.'

Suddenly Oliver realised what she must be thinking. The thought made his eyes sparkle with laughter. 'Meggie McPherson. You haven't believed a word I've said,' he accused her bluntly, making her blush. 'I know what you're wondering and you are absolutely wrong. Vera Mackay is a nice girl but it's certainly not a case of the young man of the house having wicked designs on the maid.'

His openness disarmed her. 'I didn't, for a minute, think . . . ,' she began.

'Yes, you did! Poor Vera. If only she knew, she'd be affronted. Anyway,' he added, 'she's not to my taste, Meggie. Nobody's been to my taste since you.' He groaned inwardly as soon as he heard the words emerge from his own lips. What an inane thing to say. He closed his eyes briefly, wishing with all his heart that he could cancel the last minute. But when he risked looking back at her, expecting to see anger in her face, he was relieved to see nothing more than faint surprise.

Under her calm exterior, Meggie's heart was thumping painfully. His words had astounded her, causing a brief flare of hope which was instantly extinguished by the knowledge that any relationship with Oliver was as doomed now as it had been two years ago. She forced herself to sound businesslike.

'Well, I suppose I should take your word for it. I liked Vera and it really wouldn't be fair to turn her down if what happened wasn't her fault.' She stood up and moved towards the door, clearly terminating the interview.

Oliver took his cue from her. 'It wasn't. Can I tell her you will be in touch?'

'She can start on the Monday, as arranged. On one

month's trial. Ask her to pop in one day this week and we'll sort out the final details.'

'Right.' He followed her downstairs and back into the shop where she turned and offered her hand. 'Thank you for coming, Oliver.'

'It was nice to see you again, Meggie.' So formal, he thought sadly, walking quickly out of the shop.

Vera duly arrived on the following Monday morning and it was quickly obvious that Oliver had spoken nothing less than the truth. Within four weeks Meggie was pleased to offer her a permanent job and even happier to realise that she and Vera were going to be good friends. Spending ten hours a day together it was inevitable that Vera would tell Meggie something about her time with the Laing household. Meggie, with Oliver Laing still very much on her mind, knew she shouldn't encourage gossip but couldn't stop herself from listening, always hoping for some mention of him.

'That Mrs Laing! I don't know how Mr Laing and Mr Oliver put up with her,' Vera said one afternoon, during a short lull in trade. 'She's the most horrible woman you could imagine. I've never heard anyone complain like she did. It was awful. No matter what I did, it wasn't right. I wouldn't have minded if I was lazy or careless but I'm not. It really got me down in the end.'

Meggie had had her own proof of Vera's efficiency, so much so that the girl could already be trusted to look after the shop in her or Matty's absence. 'She sounds a terrible person to work for. I wonder if she's found anyone else for your job.'

'I don't know.'

'You've not been back then?'

Vera laughed. 'I wouldn't dare.'

Still Meggie probed. 'I thought it was very nice of Oliver Laing to come and see me about you. You must have got on well with him.' As she said it she was ashamed to recognise a pang of jealousy.

Vera nodded enthusiastically. 'Och, he's a really nice man.' Then seeing the way Meggie was looking at her with one finely arched eyebrow expressively raised, she giggled. 'It was nothing like that. I don't think he even noticed me until the night I gave in my notice. More's the pity.' She sighed dramatically. 'He's so handsome and a proper gent. Just like Mr Laing. They say Mr Oliver had a bad experience,' she confided in a whisper. 'His young lady let him down. She can't have been right in the head, that's all I can say!'

Meggie swallowed hard, but an answer was expected. 'That's sad,' she murmured.

'Mind you, I wouldn't want Mrs Laing as a mother-in-law. Horrible, she is. Mr Laing's lovely, though. Proper nice manners. It's a shame about him.'

Meggie looked up sharply. 'A shame? Why?'

'Och, he's proper poorly. His heart. Had a right bad do a couple of months back. Doesn't look like he'll last long. Like an old man he is now.'

Vera moved away to serve a customer. Glad of the interruption, Meggie leaned against the counter, her mind reeling. The unexpected news about Wallace had shocked her deeply. She had never loved him as she loved his son but she would always remember him with gratitude and affection. It was impossible to think of a strong, active man like Wallace being ill. She couldn't bear to think of him dying and hated herself for the possibilities which that eventuality had immediately suggested to her.

* * *

'A *Courier*, please.'

Meggie smiled at Oliver and handed over the paper. It had become a habit again, this calling in on his way home from work each evening, just before the shop closed, when Matty and Vera had both finished work. She lived each day in a state of brittle, expectant tension, just waiting for the moment when the man she still loved would walk through the door, yet dreading it, terrified of where this was leading them. If it was leading them anywhere. Despite the almost electric tension that crackled between them, Oliver had said nothing more, done nothing to make Meggie think this was anything other than a genuine purchase and her shop was simply the most convenient one for him to call at.

'How's your father?' she asked him now, playing the charade of making casual conversation as she would with any other regular customer, though all the time her heart was banging painfully under her ribs.

He frowned. 'As stubborn as ever. Insisting he's coming back to work. I don't know how much longer I can keep him away from the place, but frankly I'm scared to let him come back. The way he is now it will be too much for him, I know it will.'

'It must be hard for a man like that to sit around at home all day,' she commented softly.

Oliver looked at her curiously. 'I didn't realise you knew my father. I never introduced you, did I?'

'Oh . . . No . . .' she covered her guilty confusion quickly. 'But you used to talk about him such a lot that I almost felt I knew him and I could always see how fond you are of him. Vera told me he was ill.'

'Ah! I'd forgotten about Vera.'

'She's wonderful. I can't think how we managed without

478

her.' Meggie grasped at the chance to change the subject. 'Did your mother find someone to replace her?'

'Eventually. This time it's a woman who comes in every day. She's older, not afraid to speak her mind,' he laughed. 'Mother might have met her match at last.' He stepped back, allowing another customer up to the counter. 'See you tomorrow,' he called as he left the shop.

And that was how it went on for more than three months. Three months of unsatisfactory conversations, snatched between customers, as Oliver, sensing a reserve in her manner, fearing another, final rejection, fought to disguise the depth of his love for her, and tried desperately to build a foundation for their relationship.

When the change came, neither of them was prepared for it.

'You do know I never read this blasted paper?' he said bad-temperedly, brushing sleet from his coat. He was cold, tired, worried about the company's finances and, most of all, longing to hold the woman he loved in his arms again.

'So why buy it?' she asked, aware of the strange intensity of his eyes.

'You know why!' he snapped. 'Because it's the only way I can see you.'

'Oliver . . .'

'Meggie,' he spoke over her objection. 'I still love you. I've always loved you. Can't we try again?'

'Nothing's changed, Oliver.' How those words seemed to choke her. 'My past hasn't altered.'

'I don't give a damn about your past!' He hissed over the counter at her. 'I'd have made that clear two years ago if you'd given me the chance.'

'No, Oliver. It would never work. I'd always be scared of

479

meeting someone who recognised me. Think how ashamed you'd feel then.'

'I will never be ashamed of you, Meggie. And I'll thrash anyone who dares to say a single bad word against you, and that's a promise.'

'Please, Oliver, don't do this.' There was genuine distress in her eyes now. With every cell of her being she longed to tell him how much she still loved him. But what then? How could she ever let Oliver Laing take her home to meet his parents?

'Why not?' he demanded. 'Tell me why not, Meggie? Don't you love me any more, is that it?' She shook her head, too choked to speak. 'Then you've found someone else?' Again that tense shake of the head. 'Then why? For pity's sake, Meggie. Why?'

She had to say something and grasped at the only fragile straw available to her. 'Don't you see how much your parents would be against it? What will you tell them when they ask about my family?'

'I'll tell them the truth. I've told you before, I'm not ashamed of you, Meggie.'

'But you couldn't tell them the whole truth?' she persisted.

'Would you want me to?' he countered, glaring at her.

'No,' she admitted.

'So we won't tell them anything yet. But, let's not throw this chance away too, Meggie. Let me at least spend some time with you. Please.'

She closed her eyes, fighting to keep control of her emotions, which were urging her to throw herself into his arms, to allow him to kiss her, to feel his strong hands on her body again. She shivered suddenly, dizzy with longing, and opened her eyes to smile at him. But, as she looked at him, she recognised that physical likeness which marked him as his father's son; Wallace's son; Wallace, the father of her child. The shudder that passed through her body then was one of despair.

'No.' Her voice was deliberately cold. 'I'm sorry, Oliver. No.'

Shattered, Oliver saw the passage of emotions over her face and knew his own impatience had lost him the only woman he had ever cared about. Incapable of speech he turned away and walked from the shop before she could see how badly he was hurting.

Matty, who, having come to see why she was so late in making his dinner, had been watching from behind the half-open storeroom door, turned and ran lightly up the stairs before Meggie could notice him. His face was twisted in a venomous smile.

CHAPTER TWENTY-FIVE

Wallace Laing walked slowly through the town, even though it tired him to do so. It was one of his better days and he had the imperative urge to see his home town just once more. He knew he was saying goodbye, that there were many places he would never see again. But there was one person he must see, one last task to perform.

Again there was that tight feeling in his chest, the familiar sensation of impotent anger against a fate which had decided to send him this terrible illness now, when the Strathannan Mining Company needed someone firm at the helm. His nephews were bright enough, but they lacked the experience needed to keep a concern like that ticking over.

And now Oliver, the one person who had the understanding, the experience and the business acumen necessary to steer the company through increasingly turbulent waters, was again talking about throwing it all up and trying his luck abroad.

Wallace paused for breath at the bottom of the hill, leaning heavily on the stick which he insisted he didn't really need. When, three months ago, Oliver had first mentioned meeting Meggie McPherson again, he had been horrified; the possibility of Oliver being involved with the woman who had borne his own father's child was as obscene now as it had been two years ago.

Then, relief had rapidly turned to despair when Oliver, in an emotional reaction to Meggie's refusal to become involved with him, had admitted to his father just how much he loved her, how hurt he had been and, crucially, how determined he now was to leave Inverannan. Wallace suspected that, despite his earlier promise, as soon as he had been put in the ground, Oliver would be off, leaving the company to his cousins. His priorities altered by an awareness of his own mortality, Wallace had begun to wonder whether it was right to let his son's happiness, the future of the company and everything he had ever cared about be destroyed by his own past mistakes when in a few months' time it would no longer be of any concern to him anyway.

Wallace grunted, mildly surprised that he could think of the time when he would no longer be alive with such equanimity. He leaned more heavily on his stick, aware of the warning sounded by his labouring heart. Aye, a few more months were all he could hope for. The time had come to be done with the past, to make things tidy in preparation for the inevitable.

Breathing more easily now that the decision was finally made, Wallace continued on his way up the hill. Outside the general store he stopped again. Then, straightening his back, swinging his stick as if it were ornament and not necessity, he stepped inside.

The shop was busy, seeming to be crammed with customers. Above the steady din of conversation came the occasional clunk of the scales and the chink of money. Wallace lingered in the cool shadows by the door, waiting for the crowd to thin, but his eyes strained to catch a glimpse of the girls working behind the counter. A woman, her shopping bag full, the weight of it dragging at her shoulder, making her walk with a lopsided gait, cleared a path through the waiting customers as she left the shop. Before the gap closed, Wallace caught a glimpse of a white-aproned girl. He stepped forwards then back again, surprised and disappointed to recognise Vera's auburn curls. The other assistant was still hidden by the milling women.

Wallace hovered by the doorway, waiting impatiently as the queue of women gradually reduced. Then, as another customer left, he caught his first glimpse of Meggie. His heart, labouring inside his chest, increased its beat, responding to a surge of remembered pleasure. Unnoticed, Wallace allowed himself to stare at her, drinking in the sight of her smooth, dark hair, her creamy skin, her heart-shaped face and those incredibly beautiful eyes. When she turned away and reached up to lift something from an upper shelf, the bodice of her dress tightened, outlining the curves of her shapely body.

Wallace was aware of the fleeting, unsustainable pulse of desire in his groin, of the uneven racing of his heart and a faint dizziness. It seemed to him that the passing years had ripened her, given her poise and assurance, emphasising her essential femininity, while cruelly draining him of his vitality. He had a vivid picture of himself as she would see him. No longer the proud, vigorous man who had shared hours of pleasure in her bed, but a frail, trembling invalid. He turned, leaning heavily on his stick again, desperate to escape, but as he moved the last customer also turned, banging into him, sending his stick sliding over the floor and forcing him to grab hold of the counter for support.

'Och . . .' The woman's impatient reproof died on her tongue. 'I'm right sorry. I didn't see you there. Are you all right?' She took his arm, steadied him and tried to steer him to the wooden chair, gratefully used by many of the women as they waited for their messages to be assembled. 'Just have a wee seat.'

Wallace hung on stubbornly to the counter, his legs as

weak as an infant taking its first steps, humiliated to be fussed over by a woman who looked older than he was. 'If you would just retrieve my walking stick,' he suggested, his authoritative tone immediately marking him out as a man of some importance.

'Wallace!'

'Mr Laing!'

Vera and Meggie spoke in unison, then both rushed round the counter, arriving in front of Wallace just as the customer handed him his walking stick.

'I'm right sorry,' she repeated, handing it to him. 'I didn't know you were so close behind me. Are you sure you're all right?'

'Of course I'm all right.' He was so upset to have made such a fool of himself that his good manners deserted him, making him bark the words.

'Well! There's no need to take that tone of voice. And it was as much your fault as mine.' She glared at him, affronted, and marched out of the shop.

'Mr Laing. Can I get you a drink of water?' Vera asked, her concern obvious.

Although he was careful to look at Vera, Wallace was aware only of Meggie's eyes watching him. From deep inside himself, he summoned up great reserves of strength. He pulled himself upright, straightened his back and raised his head, ignoring the frantic beating of his heart, the familiar rise of tightness and pain in his chest. Taking his stick he tapped it sharply on the floor and smiled, mustering all his old charm. 'I am perfectly all right, thank you, Vera. I lost my balance for a second, that is all.'

Relieved, she smiled back.

'Wallace?' Meggie overcame her shock at his appearance and stepped closer. Was this elderly and obviously ill gentleman the same man who had awakened her own body? She closed her eyes, unable to reconcile the slight, wasted figure before her with the energetic and demanding lover who had given her so much.

Wallace saw the shock on her face and was overcome with sadness. 'It was you I came to see, Meggie,' he said. 'Can we talk somewhere private?'

So that's why he was here, come to warn her off again. Well, she should have expected it.

The bell over the door pinged and another customer came in, calling out her order as she walked towards the counter. Meggie's face creased with exasperation. Wallace looked determined to have his say and she simply couldn't risk letting anything slip in front of a customer or Vera, and especially not in front of Matty, who might come back at any second.

'All right. Five minutes. Come upstairs.' She hurried round the counter and into the storeroom, not waiting for him.

Wallace followed slowly, pausing at the bottom of the stairs to take a small pill from the tin box he always carried in his waistcoat pocket and slip it under his tongue. The relief was almost immediate. The pain in his chest eased and he took a deep breath, steadying himself for the climb upstairs. Despite that, he was white-faced, clammy and gasping for breath when he finally came into her sitting room.

Meggie, waiting impatiently by the fireplace, was frightened by Wallace's ghastly appearance. The respect and affection she still had for him quickly overcame the resentment she had been feeling at this renewed interference. 'Wallace. Please, sit down.' She took his arm and guided him to the most comfortable chair. He offered no

486

resistance and collapsed gratefully into its welcoming softness. 'Can I get you anything?' she asked.

'No, lass. Just give me a minute to get my breath back,' he said, with the ghost of a wry smile. 'Those stairs of yours are gey steep.'

Meggie waited patiently, relaxing a little as his skin lost its waxy whiteness.

A tall, proud man whose strong features were disturbingly like Oliver's and a fair reflection of his determined personality, Wallace had always seemed indestructible to her. It was as if he had shrunk, his cheeks were hollow, his eyes, so like his son's, were sunk in blackened caverns and his once thick hair was thin and dry looking. His lips, which had once travelled her body, were tinged with blue.

As if aware of her horrified scrutiny, he opened his eyes and smiled at her. 'You're wondering what on earth you ever saw in an old man like me,' he said with devastating directness.

'No . . .' She denied it instinctively.

'Stop hovering over me, lass. Sit down and listen to what I've got to say.'

'You don't have to say anything, Wallace. I know why you're here.'

'Do you?' he asked, raising one eyebrow in a gesture so like Oliver's that she felt her stomach contract in pain.

'It's about me and Oliver. Well, you're too late. I've already told him I don't want to see him again.'

'Just listen to me, Meggie, will you?'

'Wallace,' she refused to let him go on. 'I know it was wrong. I know nothing can ever come of it.' Her mouth trembled as she spoke, her emotions raw and exposed.

'Do you love him so very much then, lass?' he asked gently.

'Aye. Very much,' she admitted, the catch in her voice betraying her. But then she looked directly at him, her eyes moist but defiant. 'You didn't need to come here and tell me what to do, Wallace. I know the difference between right and wrong. I won't see Oliver again.'

He sighed. 'Such a bloody mess . . . To think that you and Oliver . . . Not that I blame him, mind. You're a fine young woman, Meggie. If I'd been a younger man myself, if I'd been free . . .' He shook himself. 'I never regretted it . . . you and I . . . until now.' He reached out and took her hand. 'You're wrong, you know, about why I came here.'

'I don't understand.' She was confused now, the deep love she had for his son, her disappointment, her anger, her resentment, her shame, all tangling inside her. 'Then why are you here?'

'I am here because I love my son and it hurts me more than I can say to see him so utterly miserable.' Only as he said it, did he recognise it as the truth. It wasn't the Strathannan Mining Company that mattered, but Oliver.

Meggie turned away to hide the fresh flood of tears. 'Not as miserable as I am,' she mumbled.

'I can see that, lass. That's why I had to come. To try and put things right.'

'You want me to go away.' It was a flat statement of the obvious solution. With her gone Oliver would have a better chance of forgetting her, of finding someone else.

'Would that make either of you happy? I don't think so.'

'Then what?' she cried, sounding angry now.

'Meggie, I'm an old man. I've not many more months left to me. I'd like to see my only son happy again before I die and there's only one person who can make that happen. You.'

488

Meggie shook her head, weeping openly now. 'How can I?'

'Because of what happened between us?'

She nodded, scrubbing tears from her face with an inadequate, white hanky. 'Because I had your child.' It was a tormented, anguished wail.

'Does he really have to know about that?' Wallace asked.

Meggie stared, her mouth gaping open. 'I thought you would tell him.'

'There was a time when I might have done,' he admitted. 'But knowing your days are nearly up has a way of making you see what's really important. And what's not.'

'Can you really want your son to marry a woman who was once your mistress?'

'No.' It was cruelly blunt. 'Let's be honest with each other, Meggie. I would have wished for Oliver to fall in love with someone else. Anyone else. I couldn't ever accept you as my daughter-in-law, not after what there was between us. You know that.'

'So what do you want?' she asked dully.

'I told you. I want Oliver to be happy. Nothing else is important.'

'I don't understand,' she cried.

'Meggie. I couldn't allow you to marry Oliver. Not while I'm alive.' He stressed the last word, then paused, watching her carefully.

Meggie understood at last. Appalled, she simply stared at him.

'You see, you do understand.' He smiled at her now. 'It's not that I don't approve of you, Meggie. I never did think of you as being the same as those other girls. You were always different, special. But how could I have you in my family, knowing you the way I do? We would never be able to look at one another without guilt, without embarrassment. I'd never be able to see you without wanting you for myself, without remembering. Do you think Oliver wouldn't sense that something was wrong?'

'Of course he would,' she said sadly.

'But, after I'm dead, it will be different.'

'No!' Horrified, she denied the inevitable. 'Please, Wallace, don't . . .'

'Meggie. Look at me.'

Slowly she raised her head and did as he ordered.

'Do you truly love my son?' he asked, already knowing the answer.

'Yes,' she replied, meeting his eyes steadily. 'More than anything.'

'And he loves you. So, is it right that something that happened between us should be allowed to ruin both your lives?'

'I was a whore, Wallace. Your mistress.'

'You were never a whore, Meggie. You were just a young lass doing her best to look after her brother.'

'Your mistress,' she repeated.

'Aye. And you made me a happy man, Meggie. You gave me something fine to remember and you shouldn't be ashamed of that. If anyone's to blame, I am.'

She smiled now. 'You were always so good to me.'

'Other folk wouldn't see it that way. They would say I was evil, that what we shared was bad.'

'It wasn't. It was the first good thing that happened to me. If it hadn't been for you I might still be at the Houlets' Nest.'

'So you see, you know it was right, and I know it was right. So long as we know that then there's nothing for either of us to be ashamed of. It's just other folk who make it bad. Folk who don't understand.'

'Would Oliver understand?' she asked.

'I don't know,' he admitted. 'Have you told him anything about yourself?'

She nodded. 'I've been as honest as I could. He knows everything about me except the name of the man who kept me. He never asked. And I didn't tell him.'

'And he still wants you, knowing what he does?'

'Aye.'

'Then you must know he really loves you, Meggie Go back to him, lass. Tell him you'll marry him. Just leave it until after I'm gone.'

'I'd have to tell him the truth, Wallace. I couldn't keep any more secrets. They destroy you in the end.'

'No. Please, lass . . . If you still feel anything at all for me, don't tell him. I love my son; he respects me. Even after I'm dead I'd like to think that respect remained. I'm asking you to do this one thing for me, Meggie. If you can do that then you and Oliver have my blessing.'

She shook her head violently as if trying to clear it then rubbed her fingers into her aching temples. 'You mean I can marry Oliver?' she asked, almost unable to make herself believe what he had said.

'Just promise me you won't tell him about us. For me, Meggie, for my son's peace of mind, keep it locked in your heart.'

'I won't tell him,' she promised.

'And you'll contact him, make it right between you?' He was pleading with her now, his eyes desperate.

'I don't know . . .' But she did know . . . she did know.

'I've not long to go, lass. All I ask is that you keep away from my home until after . . . after I'm gone. Then marry my son and be happy, both of you.' And keep him here, with the company, he added to himself, satisfied with the way things had gone. He struggled to his feet, feeling utterly drained. Then, thrusting his hand into his inside pocket, drew out a small suede case. 'This is yours, Meggie. I'd like you to keep it.'

Meggie ran a finger over the velvety material, then opened the case to reveal the exquisite gold bracelet, the diamonds sparkling against the black jet. 'I can't . . .' she stammered.

'To remember me by, Meggie.'

Meggie stood, her head lowered, tears flowing freely down her face. 'Thank you, Wallace,' she choked.

He leaned over and kissed her cheek gently. 'Aye,' he said, walking slowly to the door. 'If only I'd been a younger man, Meggie McPherson.'

Oliver, white and strained-looking, put a supporting arm round his mother, who was weeping copiously into a lace-edged handkerchief, and led her away from the graveside. He had been touched and astounded by the sheer number of people who had attended the funeral. Wallace had died peacefully in his sleep the night after arriving home exhausted from a walk around the town. Oliver had dealt with his mother, who had abandoned herself to the role of grieving widow, and the necessary arrangements with a composure of which his Wallace would have been proud but which gave him little chance to mourn the father he had loved. He had got himself through the well-attended service with no outward sign of his overwhelming grief but was now nearing the end of his endurance.

Meggie, who had been standing with Bertha Cruickshank at the back of the crowd of mourners, stepped aside to let him pass and, for a fleeting moment, their eyes locked. Meggie, looking at the man she loved, was stunned by the blankness in his expression. She yearned to put out her arms to him, to hold him and comfort him but here, in such solemn surroundings, she could do nothing more than smile gently. Then, just for a moment, something stirred within him. But it was the wrong place, the wrong time, his mind was still reeling with grief. Seeing Meggie so unexpectedly threatened to destroy Oliver's precarious self-control. His jaw tightened, his lips closed in a tight, unsmiling line. He was thankful for the distraction of yet another mourner who wished to offer personal sympathy and turned away gladly. To Meggie's dismay she thought she saw antipathy in Oliver's face.

That one, cold look told her all she needed to know and released her from her promise to Wallace. Oliver no longer loved her. She too turned away, thankful that in these sombre surroundings, no one would think it strange to see tears on her face. Taking Bertha's arm, Meggie hurried from the cemetery, walking blindly across the grass, hardly caring which direction she was going in, desperate to get as far away from him as possible. By the time Oliver looked up again, his emotions more controlled now, his eyes soft and troubled, she had disappeared.

Beside him, Elsie stuffed the saturated handkerchief back in her handbag and looked at her son through eyes which showed no trace of recent tears.

'If your father had only done as he was told, this need not have happened,' she declared. 'Walking round the town indeed! And where does that leave me, I ask you?'

'Mother, not now,' Oliver begged, a rough edge of anger in his voice.

Elsie shot him a suitably injured look, then stepped into the car and prepared herself for a further show of grief for the benefit of the relatives who would be gathering at the house for the funeral tea.

The afternoon dragged. To Oliver's jaundiced eye his father's real friends, people such as Mr Sutherland and Doctor Galloway, all lingered long enough to show respect but had the decency to remove themselves before their presence became an intrusion. Others, like Mr Carlyle, Bill Knight and the mine officals, ate and drank their fill and generally carried on as though, the dead safely buried, they were free to put morbid thoughts from their minds and thoroughly enjoy themselves at his widow's expense. After an hour, Oliver dispatched his mother upstairs to the weeping comfort of his aunt and loitered in the hallway, less than willing to face the crowd which still thronged the drawing room.

'How much longer is this likely to go on?' a not-unsympathetic voice drawled.

Oliver turned with a tired shrug. 'Until the whisky runs out,' he suggested cynically.

Robert Laing, his elegant eldest cousin, raised himself languidly from the bottom stair and clapped a hand round Oliver's shoulders. 'Let's get some fresh air, Oliver. I've been waiting to catch you. We need to talk.'

'Now, Robbie?' Oliver asked wearily. Much as he liked his cousin, all he wanted at this particular moment was a few minutes to himself.

Robbie grimaced apologetically. 'I know this isn't the best of times but I have to be away from here tonight and this really shouldn't wait.'

'All right,' Oliver conceded without enthusiasm. 'We'll go outside.'

The garden was long and behind the formal lawn and flower beds, all now crisp with frost and the remains of an early snowfall, was a vegetable garden complete with greenhouse and tool shed. Between the shed and the rear wall of the garden, a small patch of rough grass, completely hidden from the house, offered perfect seclusion.

'This do?' Oliver threw himself down on the damp grass.

'Perfect.' Robbie shivered, but folded his long limbs and sank down beside Oliver. He lit a cigarette and gazed up at the incredibly blue sky. 'It doesn't seem right somehow,' he murmured, half to himself.

'What doesn't?' Oliver asked.

'To have a funeral on such a beautiful winter's day. It should be dull, raining.' Robbie's bright eyes clouded and he looked at his cousin. 'I am sorry, Oliver. I was very fond of Uncle Wallace. All this must be awful for you.' The words were quite genuine, spoken with real affection for the man who had done his best to make up for the loss of his father.

'I'll be glad when it's over,' Oliver admitted. 'There's been so much to do, so many people to see, things to arrange. I've hardly had time to come to terms with it myself. And then there's the business . . .'

'It's the business I want to talk to you about,' Robbie said, looking uncomfortable. 'I feel guilty about landing you with this now, Oliver but I think it's only fair to tell you my plans.'

'You'll be joining us later this year?' The understanding had always been that Robbie and his brother Edwin would take their places in the company as soon as they graduated.

'No.'

Oliver turned to look at his cousin properly. 'No?'

Robbie smiled. 'I'm getting married instead.'

'Instead!' Oliver spluttered. 'Instead of working? Don't be ridiculous, Robbie. If you're going to have a wife to support, that's all the more reason to get your feet under the desk and start learning the business. Who's the lucky girl?'

'Dorothy Williams.'

'Dorothy Williams,' Oliver repeated. 'Do I know her?'

'Unlikely. She's Welsh. You remember me talking about my friend, Simon Matthews? You met him once. Tall lad with dark, very curly hair. He and I shared lodgings during our second year at varsity.'

'I remember.'

'He's a neighbour of Dorothy's. I met her last year when I went home with him one weekend. I've been seeing her ever since.'

'Which explains why you hardly ever came back to Strathannan,' Oliver teased him gently.

Robbie laughed. 'Well, Wales seemed a lot more inviting,' he admitted.

'So, congratulations, Robbie. When's the wedding to be?'

'Ten months yet. October.'

'So, what will you do? Does Dorothy get on with your mother? Will you all share the same house or will you look for a place of your own?'

'Ah . . . that's the difficult bit.'

Oliver cocked an eyebrow at his cousin. 'Oh?'

'Well, the thing is, Dorothy's an only child. Her father owns three slate mines in North Wales. The plan is for me to go in with him and, eventually, take over the business.'

'I see,' Oliver said thoughtfully. 'And is that what you want to do, Robbie?'

'Yes,' Robbie answered with typical honesty. 'And I want to take Edwin with me.'

'And what about the Strathannan Mining Company?' Oliver asked quietly.

'That's rather up to you. You're running it now. Why not

496

carry on? I'm sure you didn't really want me and Edwin coming in and interfering,' he laughed.

'The company belongs to all three of us, Robbie. Equal shares.' Oliver felt as if a steel trap were closing on him.

'Yes, equal shares. But as I see it this is the ideal way to get the company back on to a solid footing. You see, Edwin and I won't need to rely on the company for our living. We'll get that, quite comfortably, from the Williams' mines. I'm proposing that you stay on, in overall control, drawing a salary to reflect that responsibility. Any profit after that should be re-invested. I've listened to you and Wallace often enough to know that one of the reasons we aren't making decent profits is that the machinery and gear are hopelessly outdated.'

'You're talking about huge amounts of money.'

'Look at how much we spent on repairs and maintenance last year! Look at how much work we lost because of breakdowns,' Robbie insisted. 'What we need to do is invest as much as possible over the next ten or fifteen years. By then the pits will be as efficient as any other and we'll be truly competitive again. You have to take the long term view, Oliver.' Robbie's eyes sparkled with enthusiasm.

'So it's not that you're not interested in the company?'

'Far from it. But I am realistic enough to know that if we let it limp along the way it has been doing, one of these days it'll just collapse under us. You've seen for yourself how much it costs to mine a ton of coal, and how much we then sell it for.'

'There were times last year when we were making a loss,' Oliver admitted.

'So. What do you think?'

'I think it's a good idea, in principle, and I'd be more than

497

happy to stay on, on the understanding that I make the operational decisions,' Oliver said thoughtfully.

'But?'

'But, we hardly make enough money to keep ourselves. If I'm going to be paid a regular salary, there won't be enough left for the sort of massive investment you're talking about.'

'I know, and I've got the answer to that, too.' Robbie beamed.

'I thought you might have.'

'The three of us now hold equal shares of the company.'

Oliver nodded. 'More or less. Edwin and I have thirty-three per cent. You, as the oldest, have thirty-four.'

'Well, I propose that we each sell eight per cent. It still gives us the controlling interest and it will raise enough money for us to buy some essential new equipment. Exactly what will be up to you.'

'Sell!' Oliver was horrified. 'My father could have done that years ago. He didn't because he was determined that the company should stay with the family.'

'It will be in the family,' Robbie chuckled. 'Dorothy has a nice little fortune stashed away, just waiting for a worthy cause. She'll buy the shares.'

'Does she know about this?' Oliver asked.

'Not yet. But don't worry about her, she'll do anything to please me.'

Oliver shook his head in amazement. 'Poor girl. I hope you're not just marrying her for her money, Robbie.'

There were very few people who could have made such a remark and escape with nothing more than the scathing glare which Robbie levelled on his cousin.

Oliver held his hands up. 'Sorry.'

'But,' Robbie grinned easily and went on, 'I'd be stupid not to see the advantages in the situation. This is our chance to really make something of the company, Oliver. In ten, maybe fifteen years' time, we could all be rich men. And when that happens we'll buy the shares back so that we all three get the benefit of the increased dividends.'

Oliver leaned back, looking up at the clear sky, lost in thought. Robbie lit another cigarette and waited.

'I'll have overall control?' Oliver asked at last.

'Yes. You're the one with the expertise.'

'And a decent salary?'

'A very decent salary.'

'And Edwin agrees?'

'He does.'

'Then,' said Oliver, springing to his feet and offering a hand to his cousin, 'I think it's a damned good idea.'

Robbie pumped Oliver's hand enthusiastically. 'We'll get a solicitor to sort out the details. In the meantime, it's all yours.' Shoving his hands deep into his pockets he strolled back towards the house.

CHAPTER TWENTY-SIX

At this time of the evening the shop was quiet, a brief lull before the customary rush of men on their way home from work, all impatient to collect their cigarettes or papers at the end of a long day.

Meggie cast an experienced eye over her shelves and turned to her assistant. 'Vera, fetch some cigarettes through, will you please. We're running low.'

She was surprised to have to remind the girl ten minutes later. 'Don't forget those cigarettes,' she said, starting to count the day's takings.

'I've not finished cutting the cheese.' Vera concentrated fiercely on the cheese cutter, drawing the wire deftly through a chunk of golden cheddar. It was a job she did every night, weighing cheese, sugar and flour ready for the morning.

Meggie looked at the pile of wrapped cheese and laughed. 'There's enough there for the next week.'

'I'd better just weigh out some more sugar. We aye sell a lot of that on Friday mornings.' Vera plunged the scoop into the sack. 'And there's hardly any tea ready and then the floor needs a good sweep.'

'All right.' Puzzled, Meggie went to fetch the cigarettes herself. Vera was usually bright, cheerful and willing, eagerly turning her hand to any task but, come to think of it, Meggie mused, Vera had seemed rather subdued all week. Perhaps she wasn't feeling well.

'Is everything all right, Vera?' she asked as the girl put on her coat, ready to go home.

'Aye. Why?' she asked, concentrating on her buttons.

'I just thought you looked a bit pale and you've been very quiet today.'

'Och, I've got a wee bit of a sore head,' she excused herself.

'Why didn't you say something?' Meggie asked. 'You could have had an Askit powder or something. Go on home then and I hope you feel better in the morning.'

'Good night, Vera,' called Matty, coming through from the storeroom at that moment, but Vera ignored him and hurried away.

Meggie shovelled the last of the cash into the bag, ready to be banked the next morning. 'Do you think Vera's been acting strangely today?' she asked her brother as they made their way upstairs. 'I hope she's not coming down with something.'

Matty shrugged. 'She seemed all right to me. Och, I nearly forgot.' Matty took two letters from his pocket and handed them to his sister.

Meggie hung up her overall and kicked off her shoes before examining the envelopes; one in a large, unfamiliar hand, probably a bill, the other in Bertha Cruickshank's distinctive script. These regular letters from her friend were something to which Meggie looked forward, though she hadn't expected to get one so soon after seeing her for Wallace's funeral. But the news in it was sad.

'Another funeral,' she sighed, putting the closely written sheet back in its envelope. 'Bertha's sister has died.'

'Well, that'll be a relief,' Matty said callously.

'Matty! She was the only relative Mrs Cruickshank had left.'

'I thought you said the old woman was crippled and not right in the head?'

'Aye . . .'

'Well, then, she's better off dead.'

Meggie bit back her angry words, knowing they would have no effect on her brother. 'Well, I think it's sad,' she insisted. 'She'll be all on her own now.'

'If you're worried about her, why not go and see her?' Matty suggested with unusual generosity. 'Take a day off and go tomorrow.' He was always glad to get the shop to himself and he had a particular reason for wanting to get her out of the way now.

'Would you mind if I left you to manage on your own?'

''Course not. And Vera will be here.'

'Sure?'

'Just go, Meggie. I've managed here without you plenty of times before.'

'Maybe I will, then.' Her mind more than half on her plans for the coming day, Meggie opened the next envelope, frowned, then concentrated and read it through again.

'It's from our Perce!' she exclaimed.

'Perce? Why's he writing to you? He's never bothered about us before.'

'He says he's getting married on the first of next month to a lassie called Moira McSweeney. They've got a single end in Springburn and he's got a job in the engine works there. He's sent his address.' Meggie felt quite excited by this obvious olive branch.

'Likely wants you to send him a wedding present. They'll think you're rich what with a shop of your own and all.'

'Why are you so horrible about everyone, Matty?' she demanded angrily. 'Perce and Bertie were just children when we left home. They're not to blame for what happened.'

'They're not children now though, are they? They could

502

have come and seen us ages ago. They didn't even make you welcome when Dad died.'

'Perhaps that's it! Maybe things will be different now,' Meggie speculated hopefully.

'He's just trying it on,' Matty scoffed. 'Seeing what he can get out of you, you'll see.'

'If I'm going to Glasgow to see Mrs Cruickshank anyway, I might as well call in and see Mam and the boys, too. It would be nice to be friends again, wouldn't it, Matty? They are our family, after all.'

'More fool you if that's what you think. Still, you go ahead if you really want to. Why don't you make a weekend of it?'

Meggie looked thoughtful. 'I suppose I could.'

'Of course you could,' he encouraged her.

'I will,' she decided, hanging her apron on the back of the door. 'I'll go tomorrow and come back on Sunday. And you wait and see, Matty, Perce just wants us all to be family again. I know he does.'

'Crap,' he muttered.

'Meggie! Och, I was hoping you'd come and see me.' Bertha Cruickshank drew her young friend inside the house and kissed her on the cheek.

'I'm sorry about your sister,' Meggie said, kissing her back. 'You must miss her.'

'Aye I do, though there was many a time I could cheerfully have strangled her. Still, at least it didn't come as a shock, and she went peacefully, in her sleep. I'm grateful for that. I knew, when I came to Wallace Laing's funeral, that Winnie would be next. I didn't expect it to be just two days later, though.' For a moment her eyes misted and her mouth trembled. 'I just wish I hadn't left her to come to Inverannan.'

'You were only gone for a few hours, Bertha, and you did make sure there was someone with her. And it's the only time you've left her.' Meggie did her best to offer consolation.

'Aye,' Bertha gathered herself and smiled weakly. 'And it's not as if she knew where she was. She didn't even recognise me for the last month or so.'

'I'm sorry I missed the funeral.' In truth Meggie felt she'd let her friend down. 'By the time I got your letter it was too late.'

'I know. Funerals are no places for young things like you, Meggie. There was enough to do, making the arrangements, to keep me occupied. I'd much rather have your company now it's all over.' She put her arm round Meggie's shoulders and drew her inside.

'These scones are yesterday's but they'll still be fresh enough,' she said, ten minutes later, emerging from the kitchen with a laden tray. 'I baked and baked for the funeral but in the end only three people came and they were all neighbours. I've enough scones and sausage rolls to last a month.'

'Have you decided what you're going to do now?' Meggie asked later. 'Will you come back to Inverannan?'

'No, lass. I don't think so.'

Meggie couldn't hide her disappointment. 'I was hoping you would.'

'Och, I'm too old to be wanting to flit again.'

'You can live with me. You know you can.'

'Aye. I knew you'd say that, but we'd soon drive each other round the bend,' she laughed. 'I'm set in my ways and

I like this house with its wee bit of garden. Better than that back yard of yours!'

'You could stay with me until you found a house of your own. I could help you look.'

'No. To tell the truth, Meggie, I'm settled here. The house is mine now and it's a cosy enough wee place. The neighbours are good-hearted folk and I've made friends at the kirk. If I moved back to Inverannan it would be like starting all over again. I can't say I like living on my own, but I daresay I'll get used to it in time.'

'Do you think Matty's right about Perce?' Meggie asked, later that evening after telling Bertha about her brother's unexpected letter.

'He might be. It is strange that he's contacted you after so long. And Matty is right about one thing.'

'What?' asked Meggie, astounded at hearing any word of praise for Matty from one of his fiercest detractors.

'Well, you saw both of your brothers when your Pa died. If they had wanted to be friends, why didn't they make a move then? From what you said they were very cruel in the way they treated you.'

'They were shocked by Pa's death. It wasn't the right time, especially the way Ma was.'

'Do you think she'll be any different this time?' Bertha asked gently.

In the soft golden light of the lamps, Meggie's face looked older, sadder than Mrs Cruickshank had ever seen it.

'I don't know,' Meggie admitted. 'And, to tell the truth, I'm a bit scared to find out.'

'You don't have to go, lass. Why not wait until after the wedding and go and see Perce then, in his new home. It might be easier that way.'

'No,' Meggie said, and Mrs Cruickshank recognised the

look of stubborn determination on her face. 'I'll go and see them tomorrow and find out one way or the other. Anyway, I've bought Perce a wedding present and I'll have to give it to him now.' She paused, then said, 'Why don't you come with me? I could do with a bit of support.'

Bertha grimaced, clearly unwilling, but then said, 'Well . . . I suppose it might help, having me there. Your mother'll not want to show herself up in front of a stranger. She'll have to mind her tongue, if I'm there. It might make all the difference.'

'Aye,' Meggie agreed eagerly. 'It might.'

'Right then, that's settled.' Mrs Cruickshank got up and gathered the used cups. 'You away to your bed, lass. I'll wrap up a few of those cakes and sausage rolls to take to your mother. A peace offering,' she chuckled.

Meggie and Mrs Cruickshank got off the Lairdstoun tram in a wind-driven, sleety downpour and dashed across the road to shelter in the doorway of the nearest shop.

Above them the sky was an unrelenting, metallic grey, heavy with the threat of snow. The streets were cold and dismal, folk hurried by, heads bent against the wind, anxious only to get home. 'That's the worst of it past. We'd best make a run for it before it starts again,' Bertha decided, struggling to get her umbrella up. As soon as she did so the wind caught it, turning it inside out. 'We'll just have to get wet. Come on.'

'This is it.' Meggie led the way into the tenement building as the rain turned to hail, the stones stinging her face.

Dripping water, their shoulders and hair white with hailstones, they stood outside the McPhersons' front door. The wind blasted down the close, whipping street litter with it, rattling windows and thumping against the tenement walls. It was as if the very building shook.

'Go on, lass,' Bertha said. 'Knock on the door. I've not come all this way to stand in a draughty hallway.'

Nervously Meggie tapped on the door.

'They'll not have heard that,' Mrs Cruickshank said, raising her own fist and thumping vigorously.

'Hold your horses,' came the plaintive cry from inside. 'I heard you the first time.'

Meggie frowned. 'That's Ma,' she explained, unnecessarily.

The door was flung open. 'Hello, Ma.' Meggie spoke out immediately, sounding much too bright in her effort to overcome her nerves.

Netta gaped, then glared.

Seeing the anger on the other woman's face, the disappointment on Meggie's, Mrs Cruickshank stepped forward and offered her hand. 'Mrs McPherson. I'm so pleased to meet you at last. My name is Mrs Bertha Cruickshank, I'm a friend of your daughter's. When Meggie said she was coming to see you today I asked if I could come and meet you. I do hope you don't mind?' The hand stayed stubbornly outstretched.

Netta looked from her daughter to the imposing figure of Mrs Cruickshank, her confusion plain. For a moment the door moved forward and it seemed that she was going to slam it in their faces, but then good manners won and Netta stepped back.

'You'd best come along in,' she muttered.

In any other house in Glasgow, social callers, even unwelcome ones, would hve been given a cup of tea. Netta, standing defiantly in front of the fireplace, didn't even offer them a seat. Undeterred, Mrs Cruickshank divested herself of her damp hat and coat, hung it calmly on the back of the door and made herself comfortable in one of the two fireside chairs, holding out her hands to the heat. 'My and it's terrible out there,' she said, drawing back a little as the wind sent a draught of smoky air down the chimney.

Netta, aghast at this display of bad manners from a woman she had never met before, stared at her, outraged, but was met only by a sweet smile.

'I do hope you don't mind me coming,' Mrs Cruickshank said when it was obvious that no one else was going to speak. 'But Meggie's told me so much about her family that I was keen to meet you all. Especially as you're from Strathannan. I am too and, och, I do miss the place. Glasgow's just not the same, is it? Do you ever wish you could go back there, Mrs McPherson?'

Netta flopped down on the other chair and pulled herself together sufficiently to murmur, 'Sometimes.'

'Och, before I forget . . .' Mrs Cruickshank hoisted her bag on to her lap and rummaged around in it, finally withdrawing two sizeable parcels. 'I brought these for you, Mrs McPherson. Just a few homemade cakes and scones. And there's sausage rolls in here too. Mind you, Meggie says my pancakes are not a patch on the ones you used to make when she was a bairn.'

'Thank you.' Netta accepted the gift gracefully. 'I'll just make a wee drink of tea. The kettle's already on the boil.' Bemused, she was glad to be able to turn her back on her visitors.

Mrs Cruickshank looked across at Meggie and winked.

Behind them Netta hunted her cupboards for unchipped china. Whatever else this woman was, she would be used to the best, that was obvious from the good quality of her clothes.

'I'll help you, Ma,' Meggie offered.

Netta instinctively started to refuse, then changed her mind and muttered, 'Put the scones on a plate.' Waiting for the tea to brew, she gave herself enough time to regain her composure. Then, holding her head high, her eyes cold and determined, she poured tea and handed it round.

'Now then, Meggie. If Mrs Cruickshank here is such a good friend of yours she'll surely know that you and me don't get along. Or haven't you told her about yourself?'

Meggie flinched. 'Ma, please.'

'We've never met, Mrs McPherson,' Bertha Cruickshank said, 'but I did have the pleasure of meeting your husband. You see, I was the women's superintendent at the Inverannan workhouse. I was on duty the day your husband brought Meggie and Matty to us. Meggie and I have been friends ever since. She's a wonderful young woman, Mrs McPherson, and you should be proud of her.' There was the slightest note of censure in her voice now.

'Proud!' Netta screeched, incensed to be invaded and then criticised by a total stranger. 'How can a mother be proud of a daughter who lived as a . . a prostitute?'

Meggie blanched and started to get up. 'There's no point, Bertha. Let's just go home.'

'Aye,' Netta agreed instantly. 'I don't know why you came here again. You're not welcome. I thought I'd made that plain.'

The sheer hostility of it gave Meggie the strength to answer back, knowing there was nothing to be lost now. 'I came because I love you, Ma. I always have. I hoped we might try and understand each other, especially after Perce wrote to me. I've brought him a wedding present.' She bent down and lifted the heavy parcel which she had placed on the table.

'Trying to buy your way back?' Netta asked nastily.

'No!'

'Look.' Seeing the momentary uncertainty on Netta's face, Mrs Cruickshank quickly imposed herself between them. 'This isn't right,' she told them both sternly. 'You should be ashamed of yourselves. A mother and her daughter shouldn't be fighting like this. Now you are together, the least you can do is sit down and talk to each other.'

'There is nothing to say that hasn't already been said,' Netta insisted.

'Can I at least stay and see Perce?' Meggie asked bitterly. 'Surely I've got the right to see my own brother.'

Netta shrugged. 'He works until twelve. He'll be home any time now.'

They waited in silence, each one counting the minutes on the clock over the fireplace. At last, quick footsteps sounded on the stairs and the door burst open.

'It's bitter out there, Ma,' Perce said, shaking water from his hair and hanging his coat with the others on the back of the door. Then, alerted by the silence which greeted him, he turned round slowly. 'Meggie?'

'Hello, Perce.' She got up and stepped towards him. Embarrassed he moved away and looked agitatedly at his mother.

'You've been writing letters to her,' she accused him furiously.

'Aye,' he admitted. 'But I never expected her to turn up here.'

'I came to bring you a wedding present from me and Matty,' Meggie explained. 'Here.' She offered him the parcel.

510

'You didn't need to buy us anything,' he muttered. 'That's not why I wrote.'

'Why did you write to her?' Netta demanded. 'It's just causing more trouble . . . as if we haven't got enough already.'

'I'd like to hear about your fiancée and your wedding plans, Perce,' Meggie said firmly, ignoring her mother. 'Is there somewhere we can talk?'

'I suppose we can use the front room,' he suggested.

'No!' Meggie still remembered the shock of finding her father's coffined body in that room. 'If the rain's stopped I'd rather go outside.'

'What about your dinner?' Netta asked, rounding on her son angrily.

'Put it in the oven, Ma. Perce can get it later.' Meggie was already shrugging herself back into her wet coat. With a worried glance at his mother's angry face, Perce did the same.

'We'll not be long,' he said, following his sister out of the door, leaving Netta and Bertha facing each other in uneasy silence.

'Well,' Bertha said, smiling at her reluctant hostess. 'I think I owe you an apology, Mrs McPherson. I don't know what I was thinking of, coming here when you don't even know me. I hope I'm not putting you to any bother.'

'I . . no, of course not.' Embarrassed to have had the family discord exposed before this self-assured, rather bossy woman, Netta answered with a frosty smile.

'You see,' Bertha confided. 'I thought it might be easier for both of you to make up your differences with a stranger looking on. I can see I was wrong. You must think me very ill-mannered.'

Astounded by this abrupt change of manner, Netta was

prepared to be polite. 'I daresay you did what you thought was best, Mrs Cruickshank,' she said stiffly. 'But you don't know Meggie like I do.' With the anger gone, Netta McPherson was a sad, disappointed woman.

'I think I probably know more about Meggie than you do.'

'I doubt it,' Netta retorted, pouring fresh tea and handing Bertha a cup.

'Your son's a fine young man,' Bertha said changing the subject. 'You must be very proud of him.'

'Aye.' Netta allowed herself to sit at the table, opposite Bertha. 'Perce is a hard worker, like his father.'

'Mr McPherson was a miner, wasn't he? From Craigie? My father was a miner too. In Fife.' Bertha established another link. 'Tell me, Mrs McPherson. What brought you to live in Lairdstoun?'

Slowly, patiently, Bertha set out to win the other woman over. In the course of an hour she had the story of the McPhersons' removal to Glasgow, of the fight to raise a family on low wages and of Tam's death.

'You must miss your husband, Mrs McPherson. It's gey hard for a woman on her own. But at least you've got a family. I've no one of my own now. I lost my sister, just last week,' Bertha confided, tears misting her eyes and, touched, Netta reached over the table and patted the other woman's hand comfortingly. 'She was a poor soul before she died, but I miss her so much. If it wasn't for Meggie I'd be absolutely alone. She's like a daughter to me, Mrs McPherson. And such a brave girl, so honest. I do wish you could see how hard she's tried to overcome the mistakes she made when she was just a bairn.'

'Mistakes!' Netta withdrew her hand.

'Mrs McPherson, she was a child, and a child from a

512

good, God-fearing home. She'd not the experience to know what she'd got herself into until it was too late. And all because she felt responsible for her brother. You could say she sacrificed herself to look after him. Surely you can't blame her for that?'

Mellowed by company which she had found unexpectedly warm and sympathetic, Netta's answer was less harsh than Bertha had anticipated. 'I suppose I shouldn't, but it's hard, Mrs Cruickshank. Tam never forgave her, so how can I? I'd feel ... I'd feel as if I was letting him down.'

'I'm not asking you to pretend nothing's happened, but can't you just give yourself the chance to get to know her again?'

'Did you say you're a widow, Mrs Cruickshank?' Netta asked.

'The war.'

'I can tell you this, then, you being a widow woman yourself, and knowing about such things, but when me and Tam got wed, I didn't even know what to do. Och! And what a shock I got. I mean ... nobody spoke about such things. I thought you fell for a bairn by kissing! I was that feart of getting in trouble that I wouldn't do more than hold Tam's hand afore the wedding. And the boys, well they respected you for that. I wanted Meggie to be the same! I brought her up to be respectable. And that wasn't easy, Mrs Cruickshank, not in a place like Craigie. And look what she did! She broke her father's heart, so she did. And mine, too.'

'Broken hearts can be mended, Mrs McPherson. I wish I'd been fortunate enough to have a daughter like Meggie. It's been a great sadness to me that I never had a family of my own.'

Netta sighed, feeling warmer towards the other woman now. 'I'll think about what you've said, Mrs Cruickshank.

Now then, tell me about your husband. Had youse been married long when he died?'

Satisfied for now, Bertha gave herself up to reminiscences. 'Just two years.'

And they sat on, the teapot emptying slowly, a tentative friendship beginning to form between them.

The skies were even darker. Driven by a biting wind, huge drops of icy rain splattered the puddled pavements, soaked through the heaviest of coats and blinded the few folk who had cause to be out in such diabolical conditions.

'We can't walk about in this,' Meggie complained. 'We'll catch our deaths. Isn't there a teashop or something?'

'Round here?' Perce scoffed. 'Who do you think can afford to sit in teashops round here?'

She reddened slightly, aware that she was making a poor start. 'Anywhere, then, just so long as it's out of the rain.'

'There's a chippy on Cumnock Road with a sit-in service.'

'That'll do.' She followed him through sheeting rain, dodging through the pools which had formed round the tram lines, water saturating her hair, oily splashes splattering the backs of her legs.

The chip shop was small, brightly lit and redolent of frying fish. The half-dozen tables crammed into the back half were empty.

'Bloody weather's keeping everyone indoors.' A man, his face red from the heat of the fryers, greeted them as they went in. 'What's it to be?'

Meggie, her stomach alerted to hunger by the glorious smell, said, 'A fish supper for me, please.' She was aware of Perce surreptitiously counting his change and silently cursed herself for being so insensitive. 'Och, no,' she changed her mind quickly, knowing it would be unforgivable to offer him money. 'I had all those scones and sausage rolls just an hour ago. I'd better just have chips.'

'Me, too. To eat in,' Perce said.

'There's plenty room.' The man waved a hand at his empty café. 'Find yourselves a seat and I'll bring it over to you.'

They sat opposite each other, feeling awkward and embarrassed, neither knowing quite what to say. Meggie found it hard to believe that this tall, unfriendly stranger was her brother.

They ate in uncomfortable silence for a minute or two before Meggie, knowing one of them had to broach the subject sooner or later, said, 'Thanks for writing to me, Perce.'

He fiddled with a greasy chip. 'I would have written before but I knew Mam wouldn't like it.' He subsided into silence again.

'Tell me about your fiancée, Perce,' she prompted him gently.

'Her name's Moira McSweeney. I told you that in the letter, didn't I?'

She laughed. 'Aye. But what's she like? Does she come from round here? How did you meet her?'

Perce toyed some more with his food, still strangely reluctant to talk. 'She comes from Springburn. I met her at a dance and she's wee with dark hair,' he told her at last.

'And you've got a house and a job in Springburn?'

'Aye, just a single end to start with, but that's all we'll need at first. I've a job at the engine works, starting in a fortnight. The pay's not much but there's prospects.'

'That's good, Perce.' She waited for him to go on, perhaps to ask her something about herself or Matty. When

515

he sat in complete silence, staring at the congealing remains on his plate, she asked, 'How's Bertie?'

He shrugged. 'He got married three months ago.'

'Married? Och, I wish I'd known.'

'Got the lassie in trouble.'

'Oh . . . But where is he living?'

'With her folks. Five of them in a room and kitchen. Irish, they are. Left footers and all.' The prejudice of generations hardened his words.

'Poor Bertie,' Meggie murmured.

'Stupid bastard. It was his own fault,' was Perce's harsh comment and for a moment he reminded Meggie of Matty in one of his nastier moods.

This wasn't going at all as she had hoped it would. No matter how hard she tried, despite what he had said earlier, she felt she wasn't reaching Perce. He offered little information, except in response to a direct question, and then his answers were clipped and brief, almost as if he resented having to tell her anything. But, she wondered, why had he gone to the trouble of writing to her if it hadn't been a first move towards some sort of friendship?

'Ma's going to have quite a problem,' he said suddenly, breaking into her thoughts.

'Ma? Why?' she asked.

'Well, Bertie's already gone. In another couple of weeks I'll have left home, too.'

'She'll miss you,' she said.

'Aye. And she can't afford the rent without us to help her.'

Meggie froze as understanding swamped her. 'Is that why you wrote to me?' she asked quietly.

Still he didn't look at her. 'She's too stubborn to ask for help herself.'

'But why didn't you just say so, Perce?' She was angry now, her voice loud enough to carry to the proprietor who lounged against the counter, reading the papers in which he would wrap the chips. 'You let me think you were ready to be friends, but all you really wanted was for me to take care of Ma.' She glared at him, but he refused to look up. 'That's right, isn't it, Perce? You're not interested in me or Matty. All you want is to get rid of your responsibility for Ma.'

'I can't afford to get married and have a place of my own and pay the rent for Ma. And neither can Bertie. So it's up to you. And don't say you can't afford it. We know all about you and that shop. Look at you!' He spat the words at her, his fury increasing by the second. 'Coming here with your fancy clothes, your posh accent, rubbing our noses in it. And don't think I don't know where you got the money to buy the shop. Pa told us all about you, Meggie.'

So, Matty had been right after all, she thought bitterly. Silently, her anger betrayed only by the slight tremor of her hand as she fastened her coat, she got up and walked out of the café.

Outside, on the rain-drenched pavement she stopped, looking wildly from left to right, trying to remember which way she had come. On the other side of the road, she recognised a barrow selling secondhand clothes which were now nothing more than a sodden mass. Running, she darted through the traffic, past the barrow and on up the road to her mother's house. She pounded up the tenement stairs, ignoring the astonished glances from two women who were gossiping on the landing, and burst through the front door.

'Ma . . .' she started, but then stood still, silenced by the unexpected sound of laughter.

'Meggie!' Netta greeted her daughter with fresh surprise, as if she had forgotten she was there.

517

'Netta and I have had a nice wee chat,' Bertha Cruickshank said, smiling.

Meggie gawped, recognising the warmth between the two women, and felt excluded, betrayed.

'Did you have a nice talk with your brother?' Bertha asked cheerfully.

'No.' Meggie's face was uncompromisingly grim. 'Matty was right. He warned me about coming here.'

'Och, sit down lass.' Bertha put a strong arm round Meggie's shoulders and drew her into an empty chair. 'Now, tell us what happened.'

'I thought Perce really wanted to be friends,' Meggie said, tension making her words clipped. 'But all he wanted was for me to pay the rent on this place after he's married. He's not interested in me. He hates me. All he wants is the money he thinks I've got.'

Netta gasped. 'He had no right! No right to go talking about me behind my back.'

'Is it true, Ma?' Meggie asked tersely. 'Was he right about the rent? Can you afford to pay it?'

Netta lifted her chin and spoke firmly, 'No, I cannot. But that is no concern of yours. I'll do what other women do. I'll find myself a wee single end. Och, and what would I need with a big place like this when it's just myself?'

'You don't have to do that. I'll pay the rent for you,' Meggie told her flatly.

Netta got to her feet, smoothed her rumpled apron and faced her daughter with icy dignity. 'Thank you, Meggie but I have managed without your help for all these years and I will go on managing. Perce had no right, no right at all.'

Meggie realised that this last opportunity to make things right between herself and her mother was in danger of collapsing because of her own anger with Perce. 'I'm not offering because of what Perce said, Ma. I'm offering because I'd like to help.'

'Why?' Netta asked. 'Why do you want to help me, Meggie?'

'You're my mother,' Meggie answered simply.

'It's been a long time since I thought I had a daughter,' Netta murmured.

'Now, now, Netta, remember what we said,' Bertha Cruickshank soothed. 'Don't be too hard on the lass.'

Netta allowed herself a stiff smile. 'Aye, Meggie, you can't be all bad if a woman like Mrs Cruickshank here is willing to speak out on your behalf and maybe, well, maybe one day I'll be able to understand why you did what you did. But not yet. And I couldn't take money from you, Meggie. Not ever.'

Meggie turned away, unable to hide the pain which was contorting her face.

'Perhaps you could come and visit your Ma more often,' Bertha suggested softly. 'Could she do that, Netta?'

'If she wants to.' It was almost careless, but a very long way from the outright rejection Meggie had expected.

Meggie gazed out at the sodden streets, at the dull grey of the tenements, at her mother's tight face, and longed to be back in her own home, the curtains closed, the world locked out. 'Goodbye, Ma,' she said, sounding infinitely weary.

'Goodbye, Netta,' Bertha smiled warmly at her new friend. 'And you won't forget to come and pay me a visit, will you? You know the way?'

'Aye. I know the way,' Netta replied, her own face lighting in a brief smile. 'Next Friday?'

'Next Friday,' Bertha confirmed, as they emerged on to the landing.

Outside, the rain had finally stopped and the pavements were filling with women anxious to get their shopping done. Meggie dodged through them, striding ahead, Mrs Cruickshank hurrying behind, the silence between them so heavy that Bertha felt it crushing her.

'Slow down, lass. My old legs can't keep up with your young ones.'

But Meggie strode on, oblivious to anything but her own misery. Bertha forced herself to trot alongside her, but finally, her lungs almost bursting, she caught at Meggie's sleeve and jerked her forcibly to a stop. 'Now then,' she gasped. 'That's enough of this nonsense. What on earth's wrong with you?'

Meggie kept her back towards her old friend and Bertha put her hands on the younger woman's shoulders and made her turn round. To her horror, tears of despair were streaming down Meggie's face, her misery so intense that for a long moment Mrs Cruickshank didn't know what to do. But, as Meggie stood there, sobbing convulsively, tears dripping down her face, her shoulders hunched, her head bowed, instinct took over. Bertha Cruickshank opened her arms and pulled Meggie into them, laying her head on her shoulder and stroking it as if she were a child. Around them the crowd divided and folk flowed past as if they didn't exist.

When Meggie's sobs had calmed to an occasional hiccough, Bertha drew her into the shelter of a close. 'Now then, lass. What was that all about?' she asked.

'Everything,' Meggie muttered. 'Everything. Ma, and Perce, and now you.'

'Aye, well I can understand you being upset with your Perce. That was an underhanded thing to do, but it all worked out for the best in the end, didn't it?'

Meggie stared at her. 'For the best? Och, aye, I suppose you would think that seeing as you're such good friends with my Ma.'

'So that's it.' Mrs Cruickshank sighed.

'You're supposed to be my friend!' Meggie cried. 'The only real friend I had left.'

'I am still your friend, Meggie.'

'You're my mother's friend,' Meggie accused her coldly.

Mrs Cruickshank, who knew Meggie so well, saw through the bitterness of those words to the girl's underlying pain and refused to be offended.

'I am your friend, Meggie and I hope you are still mine. I told your mother that you were like a daughter to me and I meant it. I think she's been a very foolish woman, setting herself against you. But she's also a decent woman, Meggie, and in the end she'll come round. She needs time, time to get to know you again.'

Meggie choked back more tears and rubbed at her wet face with the sleeve of her coat. 'She hates me. They all do.'

'No, lass. No one who knows you could hate you.'

At last there was the glimmer of a smile. 'But you've asked her to come and see you.'

'Aye. We'll be friends, your Ma and me. She'll come and visit me and, in a wee while, you can come, too. You can both visit together.' She looked at Meggie closely, forcing the girl to meet her shrewd eyes. 'Now do you understand?'

Meggie looked back, her face stubborn, but at last she nodded. 'Aye.'

'It's a start, lass. You and your Ma will never be close. It's too late for that, but you could be friends, if you'll both just give me a chance to help.'

'Oh, Bertha, I'm sorry.' Meggie felt deeply ashamed.

Mrs Cruickshank smiled. 'I did take a liking to your Ma,'

she said, pushing Meggie's saturated hair away from her face. 'And how could I not when there's so much of her in you. I'm the lucky one today, lass, for I've made another friend. You just be patient and you'll have one, too.'

Drained by the events of the weekend, Meggie slept on the train back to Inverannan. Bleary-eyed and heavy-headed she went straight home and, glad to find Matty out, tumbled into bed. In the morning she was white-faced and fighting a thumping headache.

'How did it go?' Matty asked, when he appeared in the shop, a full hour after her.

Careful to keep her face averted, Meggie said, as casually as she could, 'You were right about Perce. He wasn't interested in me, only in the money he thinks I've got.'

'I warned you,' he said triumphantly.

'Aye. You did. I should have listened.'

'Aye,' he agreed smugly, relieved that he had no rivals for his sister's loyalty.

'So,' she said, having no wish to discuss her fragile hopes for a future reconciliation with her mother, knowing that Matty would only pour scorn on the idea. 'Is everything all right here?' She looked up at the clock and frowned. 'Where's Vera? She should have been here fifteen minutes ago. She's not ill, is she? I thought she seemed a bit off-colour last week.'

'Vera's left.'

'Left?' she repeated, shoving a morning paper at a regular customer and throwing the money in the till without even counting it. 'How can she have left?'

'Don't ask me.' Matty hurried to attend to another customer.

'Who else would I ask?' Meggie snapped, her aching head

getting worse by the second. 'Why did she leave, Matty? What happened?'

'She said she didn't like working with me, if you must know. She thought it was just going to be you and her working in the shop.' He laughed scornfully. 'She's a wee bit old-fashioned, doesn't think it's right to be left alone with a man all day. Said it made her uncomfortable and her Ma didn't approve.'

He lied so glibly that it didn't occur to Meggie to doubt him. 'I never even thought of that,' she said. 'Och, stupid girl. Why didn't she say something to me?'

'There wouldn't have been any point, would there?' Matty asked. 'After all, I'm your brother. You can't get rid of me. If she wasn't happy, she was the one who had to go. Anyway,' he added quickly. 'We're better on our own. We don't need anyone else.'

Meggie sighed, rubbed her aching head and turned her attention to her customers.

CHAPTER TWENTY-SEVEN

Oliver Laing had been staring at the papers in front of him for the past hour. He had absolutely no idea of their content. Sighing, he shoved them away and got up to stare out of the window. The view was magnificent. Away in the distance, over the grey slate roofs of the town, the river Forth sparkled in the sunlight, and it was possible to trace the course of the smaller Annan as it twisted through green fields and low hills to meet it. Oliver absorbed no more of it than he had the papers on his desk. Although he was over the first shock of grief at losing his father, Oliver was acutely aware of the huge void his father's death had left. But, despite his sorrow, he was confident enough of his own judgement to know he could take the company forward without his father's guiding hand, especially under the terms proposed by his cousin.

The challenge was one which should have shaken him out of this terrible lethargy and given him something positive on which to focus. Even as he stared so blankly from the window, Oliver's innate honesty forced him to realise that this paralysing inability to concentrate was not due to his father's death. The unpleasant truth was that this extended wallowing in grief was an excuse, a way of avoiding another unhappy issue.

In the three weeks since Wallace's death, Oliver had made no attempt to see Meggie. His emotions were too raw. To deliberately seek her out, to expose himself to further rejection, would be like pouring acid into an open wound. But he loved her, had never stopped loving her, and, deep down, he suspected that she loved him too, that her repeated refusal to become involved was because of a genuine fear of hurting him. Why wouldn't she see that this way the pain was so much worse? The one thing Oliver was sure of was that he would get no peace of mind while there was the faintest hope of winning her back. Turning back to his desk he bundled the papers untidily together, dropped them back on to the top of his overflowing tray and strode purposefully from the office.

For the next hour, Oliver skulked on the opposite side of the road, like a schoolboy looking for a chance to scrump a few apples, waiting until the shop emptied and Meggie, who usually closed up herself, was on her own. Oliver's agitation grew by the minute as his watch inched its way towards seven o'clock. At one minute to, a late customer ran into the shop, then out again. From his vantage point Oliver saw Meggie come from behind the counter and start to walk towards the door, ready to lock up for the night.

Oliver dashed across the road, narrowly avoiding a cyclist who braked violently and cursed him in language which made the children playing on the pavement turn and gape in astonishment. Ignoring them all, Oliver swerved round the bike and crashed into the shop, coming face to face with Meggie.

'Oliver!'

Feeling extremely foolish, he ran a hand through his hair which had flopped over one eye, straightened his jacket and tried to gather his wits and his courage. 'I just want a *Courier*,' he said.

Meggie turned back to the counter and handed him the one remaining copy with a hand that trembled visibly.

'Thought I was going to be too late,' he muttered, handing her the money.

'Then you should have come in before instead of hanging around on the corner.'

'You saw me?' He was horrified and not encouraged by the grim expression on her face.

'Of course I did,' she said softly, her heart melting just at the sight of him. 'Did you think I wouldn't recognise you, Oliver?' When every small detail was burned into her mind?

'I wasn't sure if you'd want to see me,' he admitted, the uncertainty still making his voice sound harsh.

'I came to see you! At the funeral. You didn't even speak to me.' Even as she said it, Meggie knew how stupid she had been to seek him out there, in the midst of such sorrow, understood that what she had seen in his eyes had not been hatred, but grief and shock. But she forced herself to stand still, made herself resist the urge to throw herself into his arms while all the old doubts returned to assail her. And love, love so strong that it hurt, making her heart hammer painfully against her ribs, causing her to breathe so rapidly that she felt dizzy.

But still she made no move towards him. The responsibility was hers. There would be no more chances for her and Oliver. Whatever decision she came to this time, it had to be the right one. The dying vestiges of her conscience flared one last time to remind her that this was Wallace's son. The likeness was unavoidable. Wallace lived on in Oliver's eyes, in his full-lipped mouth, in a hundred little gestures and expressions. Was this, she wondered, what Wallace had been like as a young man? As she stood there, looking into Oliver's eyes with frightening intensity, it was as if it was Wallace himself who stood before her, smiling in that half-teasing way she remembered so well, encouraging her, telling her again what he had told her on that last day of his life, assuring her that their secret would never be revealed.

Oliver saw nothing of those thoughts in Meggie's solemn face. 'Meggie . . .' he pleaded, taking a single step forward, his hand outstretched. 'Don't you know how much I love you?' He had prepared himself to come into the shop, to have a short conversation with Meggie, casually to suggest a walk on Sunday afternoon and to stroll away as if it was of no consequence if she turned him down, his hopes in tatters, his pride intact. But here he was, spilling his heart out to her like a romantic film hero. Ashamed, convinced that he had lost her forever, he turned away. He would go home now and write to Robbie, tell him that he had changed his mind, that he couldn't stay in Inverannan. Let his cousins make what they could of the Strathannan Mining Company. He would take his share and try his luck elsewhere – Australia, Canada. Anywhere, as long as it was a million miles from Meggie McPherson.

'Oliver.'

He hesitated at the door, unwilling to turn round and let her see the unmanly tears which were glistening in his eyes.

'Oliver. Please don't go.' There was such a note of desperation in her voice that, despite himself, he turned towards her, hope flaring.

It was Meggie's turn to step towards him, but then she stopped, unsure of what she saw in his face. Was it pain, or simply anger? But then she noticed the unnatural brightness of his eyes and the tautness which held him motionless, his hands clenched, his jaw so tense that it altered the shape of his face. 'Oliver, I'm sorry,' she whispered, hearing the catch in her own voice.

It was as if he melted before her. On a long, exhaled breath his shoulders fell, the set lines of his face relaxed, his hands lifted towards her and he smiled, a faint, almost disbelieving smile.

Meggie needed no further invitation. She flew across the five feet of emptiness which separated them and into his arms. Oliver buried his face in her neck, then lifted her off her feet, raising her until her face was level with his. Meggie bent forward, brushed his lips with hers and gasped as he crushed her to him. Her arms when round his neck, holding him while he kissed her, sliding his tongue into her mouth, raising prickles of naked desire wherever his body touched hers. 'I'm sorry, Oliver,' she repeated.

Slowly he put her back on her feet and put a hand up to her face. 'I love you,' he told her simply.

'And I love you,' she replied.

'Don't ever doubt me again, Meggie,' he warned her softly. 'There is nothing anyone could ever tell me about you that would make me feel differently. I love you. I'll always love you.'

'I know. I know.' She clung to him, feeling him hard against her, wanting him more than she had ever wanted anything in her whole life.

'I've missed you so much,' he rasped. 'I won't let you go again, Meggie.'

'I won't ever want to go,' she answered, the words muffled as his lips found hers again.

It was minutes later before they pulled apart, their clothes dishevelled, their pulses racing.

Gently he placed a hand on each of her shoulders and held her at arm's length, his eyes boring into hers. 'Marry me, Meggie?' he asked softly.

She didn't even have to think about her answer. 'Yes,' she told him, the love she felt shining from her eyes, which gleamed even in the half-darkness of the silent shop.

He pulled her back to him, the motion so violent that she almost fell, but was saved by the wall of his chest, the closing of his arms around her. Once more his mouth found hers and she surrendered to its greed eagerly.

'Meggie! What the hell are you doing?' Matty's impatient voice, coming from upstairs, made them jump guiltily apart.

Meggie frantically patted her hair back into place then poked her head round the storeroom door and shouted, breathlessly, 'I'm just coming, Matty.' She turned back to Oliver and admitted, 'I forgot about Matty.'

'You mean he was upstairs all the time?' Oliver asked.

She nodded and they stared at each other aghast, until Oliver laughed suddenly and she began to giggle, desperately trying to stifle the noise.

And then the moment passed and they were composed again, and facing each other more seriously. 'I do love you,' he told her again, claiming a last, tender kiss. 'Never forget that, Meggie.'

Quietly, she let him out of the shop and watched, her heart bursting with joy, as he strode off up the hill. Sensing that Meggie was still standing in the doorway, watching him, Oliver turned and waved. Meggie lifted an arm in response.

In the window above her, the curtain moved and a figure stepped quickly back into the shadows of the room behind. Scowling, Matty watched until Oliver Laing had disappeared from sight.

Nothing could mar Meggie's happiness, not Matty's open hostility, nor Mrs Laing's obvious disapproval.

Sure that not even his mother could fail to be charmed by Meggie, Oliver took them both to dinner in the City Hotel. Elsie Laing, knowing little beyond the facts that Meggie's father had been a miner, that she had spent some time in the workhouse, and that she now owned her own shop, was surprised to meet a stunningly beautiful, impeccably dressed, softly spoken and intelligent young woman. But, a woman of many petty prejudices, Mrs Laing clung stubbornly to her original opinion, that Meggie McPherson was not good enough for her son. She told him so, later, in several different, forthright ways and was dismayed to realise that nothing she said was having the slightest effect on her son, who was displaying the same, stubborn characteristics as her husband had often done.

Having said her piece she knew there was nothing more she could do to influence him without running the risk of alienating him completely. Growing daily more bitter and resentful, she subsided into silence and contemplated her own future with considerable disquiet.

'Don't take it personally,' Oliver advised Meggie. 'Mother's just a bit put out because we got engaged so soon after Father died.' This wasn't the absolute truth, but he had no intention of repeating exactly what his mother had had to say about his intended bride.

Meggie, who knew exactly why Mrs Laing disliked her, simply shrugged. She had no more intention of being the cause of trouble between her fiancé and his mother than she had of allowing Matty's openly hostile attitude to have any effect on her. She was determined that neither he nor Mrs Laing were going to be allowed to come between her and Oliver.

'I wish you'd make an effort to be pleasant to Oliver,' she told him one night when he had tried, in vain, to provoke Oliver into an argument.

'Oliver, Oliver. Bloody Oliver. That's all I get from you these days,' he fumed.

'I love him, Matty. Can't you just be glad for me?'

'I don't know what the hell you see in him. Ponce, that he is.'

'Matty!'

'Well, so he is,' he went on, too bitter to mind his words. 'Look at the way he dresses, shiny shoes, fancy suits and flashy tie pins. And he talks like his nose is sewn together.'

'It's the way he was brought up to speak. I think it sounds nice,' Meggie defended him loyally.

'Aye, you would. You're even starting to sound like him yourself. Putting on airs and graces. It won't do any good, Meggie. Underneath, you're just a common little tramp. And he knows it. It'll never work. Never.'

Meggie's cheeks flamed scarlet with rage. 'Don't you speak to me like that,' she hissed. 'This is my house, Matty and you'd better not forget it. If you don't like what I am then you'd better get out.' Defiantly she faced him, waiting for his reaction. Meggie's resurgent affair with Oliver had seemed to bring out the very worst in Matty, almost as if he was putting her loyalty to some sort of test, and even she had, at last, started seeing Matty through less tolerant eyes.

She deeply resented the way he demanded to know where she had been every time she went out with Oliver, loathed the way he ordered her about in the shop, in front of customers, as if he, not she, owned it. She was increasingly suspicious too of a new spate of discrepancies in till and stock, and, occasionally, in her purse. He was acting, she thought, with a touch of disdain, like an overgrown, spoilt and jealous child. But Matty was capable of looking after himself now and, if he didn't have a rapid change of heart, that was exactly what he would be doing. Faintly surprised by the strength of her own feelings, she waited.

Matty stared at her, expecting the easy capitulation that any argument with Meggie usually brought. To his dismay

531

she glared back at him, refusing to back down. 'Well?' she snapped.

'Och, Meggie,' he whined. 'Where would I go? I've no job, no money. You couldn't put me out. I'm your brother.'

'You are not a child any more, Matty. It's time you stopped depending on me. And I'm warning you now, I won't let you spoil things for me and Oliver.'

'It's him that's spoiling things for me,' he retorted. 'Why can't we just go on as we were? What do you want to marry him for? Why can't it just be the two of us, Meggie?'

'Och, Matty,' she sighed. 'We've each got our own lives to live. And my life is with Oliver.'

'And what about me?' he roared. 'You're getting married. He'll not want his wife working in a shop, will he? He'll make you sell up and put the money into his precious mining company. And where will that leave me Meggie? I'll be out of a job and out of a place to live then anyway. You might as well throw me out now and be done with it.'

'Do you really think I'd do that to you, Matty?' she asked sadly.

'You're getting married, aren't you? You'll have to do what he tells you then. He'll make you sell the shop and he'll take all the money for himself.'

'Oliver's not like that, Matty.'

'Huh . . .'

'I'm keeping the shop. We've already discussed it. Oliver thinks I should keep some sort of independence. You'll still have your job and a place to live. Later, when we have children, you can take over as manager. Isn't that what you want?'

'What I want doesn't matter to you any more, Meggie. Not now you've got Oliver Laing.'

When Oliver called for Meggie an hour later, Matty

watched from his bedroom window as they went up the road, their arms linked, and felt nothing but consuming jealousy. He wasn't fooled, not for one minute. He would never get his hands on the business now. Oliver Laing would see to that. His face contorted by hatred, he flung his jacket on and went to drown his bitterness in drink.

'Och, what a lovely ring!' Bertha Cruickshank enthused on her doorstep that Sunday when Oliver and Meggie went to see her. Smiling, a hint of tears in her eyes, she embraced Meggie, then, to Oliver's bemusement, turned to him and clasped him to her well-braced bosom. 'I always knew you two were right for each other,' she told them. 'I just know youse'll be happy.' Smiling, she drew them into the house. 'Look who's here,' she announced, leading them into the sitting room.

'Ma!' Meggie went towards Netta eagerly, then froze as she recognised the familiar, cold expression on her mother's face.

'Hello, Meggie,' Netta nodded, as if to a mere acquaintance.

'I told Netta you were coming to see me,' Bertha confided in a whisper. 'I thought it would be a good opportunity for her to meet Oliver, too.'

Meggie introduced Oliver, sure that her mother could not fail to like him.

'So you are in charge of the Strathannan Mining Company now?' Netta asked.

'Yes. My father died two months ago,' Oliver answered politely.

'My husband worked for the Strathannan Mining Company for twenty years,' Netta informed him stiffly. 'Started as a lad of fourteen. Never a day off sick in all those years.

After the strike in 'twenty-six your father paid him off and made sure he couldn't get a job in any other pit. Tam was never the same after that. Aye, we've a lot to remember the Strathannan Mining Company for.'

'Ma!' Meggie was horrified. 'That wasn't Oliver's fault.'

'Now then, Netta,' Bertha intervened. 'That's all water under the bridge. Times have changed and Oliver and Meggie are getting married. See the lovely ring she's wearing. And I've baked a special cake to celebrate.'

Netta grudgingly admired the ring and, over tea and cakes, helped along by Oliver who stolidly refused to take offence at her opening remarks, actually seemed to thaw a little.

'I'm glad for you, Meggie,' she said. 'You've done well for yourself, but remember, a good marriage is built on honesty. It's no use keeping secrets from each other. You'll be found out in the end.'

Meggie blanched, her mind filling with images of Wallace Laing. But how could her mother possibly know about that? Even Matty had never discovered who Oliver's father was. And Mrs Cruickshank would never divulge anything of such a confidential nature. She felt Oliver's hand covering her own, squeezing it gently. Reassured, she turned to her mother and said, 'Oliver knows what I did, Ma. I told him a long time ago.'

Netta shot a look of sheer disbelief at her daughter, then looked away again, obviously not convinced.

'Meggie told me everything, Mrs McPherson,' Oliver said firmly. 'That was why we broke up the first time. She couldn't believe that I could still love her. She was wrong.'

Netta seemed lost in thought for a moment, but then she looked at Meggie and her smile was the warmest Meggie had seen since she was a child. 'Well, lass, maybe I've been too harsh on you. Telling Oliver was a brave thing to do. But the right thing.' Maybe, just maybe, this handsome young man was in a different mould from his father, she thought, warming to him despite her determination not to. And then there was Meggie herself. Her new friend, Bertha Cruickshank, had nothing but praise for the girl and Bertha was a stern, upright sort of woman and a good judge of character. More like a mother to Meggie than she was herself. Perhaps Bertha was right there too. It could be that she was only hurting herself by refusing to let Meggie back into her life. Especially now that Bertie and Perce had got married and left home, seldom even bothering to call in for a visit.

'Will you come to the wedding, please, Ma?' Meggie begged, her mother's attendance suddenly very important to her.

'Of course you will, won't you, Netta?' Bertha Cruickshank answered for her. 'No woman would want to miss her daughter's wedding day. We'll come together. And you'll have a job telling which one of us is proudest.'

'Aye,' Netta said, smiling at her friend. 'I'll be there, lass. If you want me.'

'Of course I want you, Ma.' Impulsively she leant over and hugged her mother. Netta stiffened, but then she put her arms round her daughter and said, 'Give me time, lass. There's too much happened for it to be forgotten overnight, but I will try.'

'I don't want you to forget, Ma. I never will. All I want is for you to understand.'

Netta pulled away and dabbed at her eyes. 'I'll try,' she promised.

'Och, this is supposed to be a celebration,' Bertha said. 'And here we all are with watery eyes and runny noses. Tell

Meggie your own good news, Netta. That should cheer us all up.'

But Netta shook her head. Accustomed to having first a husband to lean on and then two strong sons, she was happier these days when someone else took the initiative. One of the reasons for her unexpectedly flourishing friendship with Mrs Cruickshank was that Bertha liked nothing better than to be in charge, while Netta was content to be organised. Each filled a need in the other's life and, in addition to that, they genuinely liked and respected one another.

'Netta's coming to live with me,' Bertha announced happily.

'I can't afford to stay on in the close now that the boys have left home.' Netta felt some explanation was due to her daughter. 'Bertha kindly offered to let me move in with her.'

'Och, it was nothing to do with kindness,' Bertha insisted. 'It's just common sense really. We get along just fine and neither of us likes living on our own. Two old wifies together,' she laughed and Netta laughed with her.

Watching them now, Meggie felt a small twinge of jealousy, recognising that the nature of her own friendship with Bertha Cruickshank had subtly altered. Her own mother now filled her role as close friend, while she was more like a favourite niece. But, she realised, the envy disappearing as quickly as it had come, she had Oliver while her mother and Bertha were both on their own. All in all, everything was working out for the best.

'It's a grand idea,' she laughed. 'Now I can see you both in one visit.'

'Thank goodness that's over,' Oliver sighed when they were back in his car, driving home again. 'At least your mother seems to have accepted the idea of us getting married. From what you said I was expecting a much harder time.'

'Bertha's been working on her,' Meggie said, with a wry smile.

'Perhaps we should get Bertha to have a word with my mother too,' he suggested. Then, with a small laugh, he added, 'No, on second thoughts, maybe not.'

'Definitely not,' Meggie said. 'But I do wish your mother liked me. It makes things so difficult for you.'

'To hell with her,' Oliver decided, pulling the car off the road and reaching for Meggie. 'To hell with the lot of them.'

Meggie's answer was stifled by the soft pressure of his mouth.

CHAPTER TWENTY-EIGHT

Meggie heard the knock on the back door and looked frantically at her watch. 'That's Oliver,' she cried. 'And I'm not near ready.' She peered at her still-damp hair in the mirror over the fireplace and sighed dramatically. 'I can't let him see me in this mess.'

Matty chuckled. 'Och, calm yourself, Meggie. Finish drying your hair and I'll let him in. I'll make him wait in the shop. Come down when you're ready.'

'Thanks, Matty,' Meggie smiled at her brother. Matty was trying so hard to be nice to her that it was almost irritating, but it did show that he had taken what she said to heart. Humming happily to herself she went back to rubbing her hair dry with a towel.

Matty kept the smile on his own face until he had closed the door on his sister. Then he hurried downstairs and opened the back door of the storeroom.

'She's not ready yet,' he said off-handedly. 'You'd better come in and wait.'

Oliver nodded and turned to go up the stairs.

'No,' Matty stopped him. 'She's running round half-dressed with her hair still wet. She wants you to wait down here.'

Oliver thought that Meggie, semi-clad, sounded a very inviting proposition but followed Matty through to the shop.

Matty stationed himself silently behind the counter and fixed Oliver with a hostile stare. Oliver decided against trying to make conversation and, helping himself to a paper from the counter, leant nonchalantly against the shelves and started to read it.

'This isn't your property yet, you know,' Matty said nastily.

'Sorry?' Oliver looked over the top of the paper.

'I said . . .'

'I heard what you said.' Oliver smiled with deceptive calm. 'I'm just not clear about what you meant.'

'I mean that you haven't got the right to help yourself to anything you fancy. If you want a paper, bloody well pay for it like anyone else.'

Oliver shrugged and tossed a handful of coins across the countertop. Matty pocketed them. Oliver watched him with narrowed eyes for a moment, then went back to his paper.

Matty let a full two minutes pass and then said, 'She doesn't really love you, you know.'

Oliver's jaw tightened and his eyes flashed dangerously. Flinging the paper to one side he marched over to Matty. 'What did you say?' he demanded.

'You heard. Meggie doesn't love you. It's your money she's after. And respectability.'

Oliver's temper sizzled, his hands itched, but, aware that Meggie might walk in on them at any moment, he controlled himself. 'If you're trying to make trouble between Meggie and me, it won't work,' he snarled. 'You're a nasty little shit, Matty. Why don't you just keep that filthy mouth of yours closed?'

Matty shrugged and grinned, infuriating Oliver even further. 'If you like. But there's things you should know about Meggie.'

'I don't want to hear anything from you.'

'Don't you even want to know that your sweet little

fiiancée is a whore? Do you think you're the first man she's been with?' He chortled and took a step back as Oliver lunged over the counter. 'Och, aye, I know what goes on down here when you come back at night. I've seen youse . . .'

'You filthy little . . .' Oliver leapt over the counter.

Matty dodged away. 'Aye, a whore, that's what my sister is. Trained at the Houlets' Nest school of prostitution. Right popular she was too.' Steadily backing away from the enraged Oliver he went on recklessly, 'Lived with an old man after that. Right little scrubber, my sister. Not the right sort of girl for a man like you, Mister Laing.'

Oliver threw himself at Matty, knocking him sideways and driving his fist into the younger man's face.

Matty immediately subsided into a snivelling heap on the floor. 'I'm telling you the truth,' he whined. 'I thought you should know. It's only right.' He brought an arm up to shield his face.

Oliver stood over him, shaking with rage. He drew his arm back, ready to strike again but Matty scuttled across the floor on his hands and knees. Slowly the red mist cleared from Oliver's eyes. Contemptuously he bent down, grabbed Matty by his collar and hauled him upright, slamming him against the shelves.

'It's true,' Matty pleaded cravenly. 'I'm not lying. Ask her yourself.' What had been such a successful ploy with Ronnie Sandys was turning out very differently with Oliver Laing. Matty realised that he had made a terrible misjudgement of this man.

'I don't need to ask her,' Oliver spat. 'Meggie has told me everything herself.'

Matty gagged as Oliver's forearm pinned his neck against the shelf. 'I was only trying to help.'

'You were trying to make trouble, you bastard,' Oliver swore, crashing Matty's head against a metal upright. 'If you ever say another bad word against Meggie I'll shove your filthy mouth up your backside, where it belongs,' he promised, banging Matty's head back again.

'I've got friends,' Matty threatened, attempting to twist away. 'You touch me and you'll be sorry.'

'I'm already sorry,' Oliver retorted, slamming Matty's head back again, crashing it against a metal support. 'Sorry that scum like you are allowed to live.'

'You can't talk to me like that. I'm Meggie's brother.'

Oliver jammed his forearm against Matty's throat. Matty coughed, then started to turn red. 'I want you out of here, Matty,' he said, coldly controlled.

Matty's eyes bulged, his mouth gaped soundlessly. Oliver took his arm away. Matty gasped, then retched, fear-laden sweat drenching his face.

Upstairs a door banged and they both heard Meggie's light footsteps on the stairs.

The two men glared at each other for another second or two then Oliver grabbed Matty by the lapels and flung him heavily to the floor.

'What's going on?' Meggie stared at her brother's sprawled form.

Oliver dragged up a strained laugh. 'Slipped up,' he said.

'Aye.' Matty pulled himself to his feet, but avoided looking at anyone. 'Caught my heel in the sugar sack.'

'Idiot,' Meggie chuckled.

'Come on, he's all right. If we're going to catch the film we'd better get a move on.' Oliver was already stepping into the storeroom, heading for the back door.

Meggie gave her brother a searching look which he avoided then, puzzled, she hurried after Oliver.

* * *

541

Sally Keir's father, Harry, was enjoying his usual cool pint of heavy in the bar of the 'Netherton Bridge'. Fortunate enough to have been taken on as general handyman at the Netherton Mill, he felt he was entitled to this half hour of relaxation each night before returning home.

Lounging against the sticky bar, he watched with interest as Matty McPherson walked in and joined two other men at the far end of the narrow room. Nodding amiably at Matty, who had already-seen him, Harry ambled casually to a small, round table, close to where Matty was standing. Taking the evening paper from his pocket he immersed himself in it, seemingly oblivious to everyone and everything around him.

Ten minutes later, he folded the paper, shoved it back in his pocket, and strolled away. Matty saw him go but, dismissing him as unimportant, immediately forgot him and turned back to his companions. Five minutes later he too was on his way home.

'I've just seen that little bastard, Matty McPherson in the Netherton,' Harry told his wife, sitting himself at the table and waiting for his dinner to be put in front of him. 'With the Drummond brothers.'

'I thought they were still in the jail?'

'No. Got out a couple of weeks back.'

'There'll be more trouble, then,' she predicted sagely.

'Och, aye. You can count on that. Whenever the Drummonds turn up, there's trouble not far behind them. And Matty McPherson's up to no good either. I didn't catch who they were talking about but some poor sod's got it coming to him.'

'Aye, well, you stay out of it, Harry. Do you hear me? We've had enough trouble in this house without you setting

542

your nose in someone else's business. You've a job now and money coming in. Let's keep it that way.'

'Och, will you not nag. Have I not turned over a new leaf?' he asked her innocently.

'Aye. And I'm the King's auntie,' she retorted, slapping a plate of stew in front of him.

Now that his personal life was so happily arranged, Oliver found himself able to put his full attention to the problem of revitalising the Strathannan Mining Company, a task which made the working day too short and frequently kept him at his desk until well after nine at night.

On this particular evening he was astounded to realise that it was already after nine-thirty. His mother had been expecting him home for dinner at eight and would have worked herself up to a fine frenzy of fury by this time. Bundling his papers away he made the rounds of the building, checking everything was secure, then let himself out of the back door, locking it behind him. He shivered, rammed his hat down firmly on his head and pulled up his collar. Sometime during the day, unnoticed by him, the pleasant, early spring weather had been ousted by gusty winds and sheeting rain. The narrow wynd which ran along the back of the building was pitch black and puddled – he discovered as he plunged a foot into an unexpected hole – with oily water. Cursing he picked his way cautiously towards the main street, a hundred yards away, concentrating on avoiding further mishaps.

When three men appeared round the corner, Oliver barely glanced up, noticing only that, like him, they were huddled deep in their coats as protection against the weather. As they neared him they split apart, as if they were intending to pass on either side of him. But the two on his right held too far over, forcing him to stop. Too late he understood his danger. Without warning, one of the men turned. In that split second Oliver thought there was something vaguely familiar about him but in their uniform of dark trousers and heavy jackets, their hats well down over faces which were wrapped in thick mufflers, there was nothing to help him identify his assailants.

Even as he thrashed around, desperately trying to break away, a fist caught him full beneath the ribs. He heard his attacker grunt with the force of the blow before he felt the pain of it through his own body. He doubled up but was hauled upright and held, defenceless and vulnerable, by a man on either side of him. The third man hit him again, lower this time, in the softness of his abdomen and again, just under his ribs. Oliver sagged and retched violently, over and over again, gasping for breath, dizzy with pain. He was still heaving when a blow from behind hit him in the kidneys and sent him face down into his own vomit. No one was holding him now. There was no need. He couldn't escape, couldn't even raise his head. He didn't want to. They were kicking him, again and again, raining blow after blow on his unprotected body. And then he was aware of something else. Of a scraping, metallic sound, and excruciating pain in his leg as an iron bar smashed into it. It seemed to go on for ever, the grunt of effort as the bar was lifted, the dull thud as it thumped into his broken limb. Oliver groaned, prayed to lose consciousness but stayed agonisingly awake, aware of every destructive blow.

They stopped. Oliver waited, half-expecting it to start again. But then he heard footsteps, close at first then fading away in the distance. It was over. He shifted his head. Pain seared through his skull bringing flashing lights and rushing nausea. His eyes refused to focus. Everything was revolving

at frightening speed. With a small sigh he let his head loll
forward in the mud, welcoming the darkness of oblivion.

'What in the name . . .?' Meggie looked at Matty in horror.
'What on earth happened to you. You're covered in mud.
And what's wrong with your hand? It's bleeding.' She
examined the skinned and bruised knuckles anxiously.
'What have you been doing?'

Matty tore his hand away. 'Och, nothing. Young Billy
had a wee bit too much to drink. I was helping him home.
You know what it's like. He was all over the bloody place.
He went his length and took me with him. In the back lane
behind his house it was. Got covered in mud and grazed my
hand. And I'm sure I've got a bruise on my knee.' The lies
were absolutely plausible.

She laughed, relieved. Her first suspicion had been that he
had been fighting. 'Away and clean yourself up. I'll make
you a cup of tea.'

'Don't bother. I'm fair knackered. I'll away to my bed.'

'Morning, hen.' Agnes Telfer bustled into the shop and
dumped her shopping basket on the counter.

Meggie smiled. 'Morning, Mrs Telfer. What can I get
you?' Meggie thought the older woman looked at her
oddly. 'I've a nice bit of bacon this morning. Best Ayrshire.
And not too fatty.'

'Well, I must say you're taking it well, lass,' Mrs Telfer
said, turning to nod to another woman who had followed
her in.

'Taking what well?' Meggie asked.

'It must've been a terrible shock. And him such a nice-
looking fellow and all.'

'Aye,' the other woman agreed. 'Will this mean you have to put the wedding back, hen, or is it too soon to tell yet?'

Meggie felt the blood drain from her cheeks. 'What are you talking about?' she asked.

'Och, don't say you didn't know? Och . . .' Mrs Telfer turned circles in distress.

'Maybe you should sit down, Meggie,' the other woman, Phyllis Storar, suggested, hurrying to the other side of the counter.

'Just tell me what you're talking about.' She nearly screamed it at them. 'Is it Oliver? Has something happened to Oliver?'

'Have you not seen the paper?' Mrs Storar asked gently.

'No.' Meggie shook her head and grabbed a copy of the *Courier*, a paper she seldom had time to read before evening.

'There, hen, at the bottom,' Mrs Telfer turned to the first page.

Meggie read the words, feeling fear clutching at her stomach, then sat and stared blankly at the page.

'Attacked, it says,' Mrs Storar said. 'Now who'd want to do a thing like that? In the hospital. Seriously ill. And you didn't know?' She turned wide eyes on Meggie.

'When?' Meggie pulled the paper back towards her and scanned the paragraph frantically.

'The night before last. Tuesday,' Mrs Telfer said. 'Thought you'd have known by now.'

'Matty!' Meggie yelled, tearing her apron off.

'What?' He had been waiting for this for the last twenty-four hours.

'Look after the shop,' she ordered, running to the door.

'Why?' he shouted after her, but she was already gone.

'Look at the paper,' the two women spoke in unison.

'It's Meggie's Oliver,' Mrs Telfer said. 'Terrible, so it is.'

Matty followed the newspaper story with a swollen forefinger, then looked up with a smile. 'Now then ladies, what can I get you?' he asked brightly.

Meggie hammered on the Laing's door, then, losing patience, opened it and walked into the tiled hallway where she was met by the astonished maid.

'Is Mrs Laing in?' Meggie asked.

'Yes, miss, but . . .'

'Where?' Meggie demanded. 'Where is she?'

'In her sitting room, miss, but she's got a bad head and doesn't want to be disturbed.'

'Which room?' Meggie gazed helplessly at the five closed doors, then, when the maid, thinking of her mistress's displeasure, still failed to move, she started flinging them open, one door after the other. On her third attempt she found Oliver's mother.

Elsie Laing, who had heard the disturbance in her hall, was reclining on her sofa, a damp cloth on her forehead. When the door opened she looked up with exaggerated weakness.

Meggie was in no state to feel sympathy. 'Where is Oliver? How is he? Why didn't you tell me?' she cried.

Wearily, Elsie pulled herself upright. 'Oliver is in hospital, here in Inverannan. He is extremely ill. I didn't tell you because he is only allowed to have members of the family to visit him. Me, Miss McPherson. And only me.'

Meggie ignored the barb. 'Extremely ill? Please, Mrs Laing, tell me what happened to him. Is he going to be all right?'

'He will live, if that is what you mean.'

Meggie gasped and sank into a chair, feeling her head begin to spin.

'Oh, for goodness' sake!' Elsie snapped her irritation and rang vigorously at her little handbell.

The maid, expecting a reprimand, came in timidly and was surprise to be asked only for a pot of tea.

'For goodness' sake, girl, pull yourself together,' Elsie ordered Meggie with considerable acerbity.

The maid, who had used her initiative and prepared tea as soon as Meggie had burst into Mrs Laing's sitting room, returned with the tray. Elsie rapidly poured a cup and handed it to Meggie, whose hand trembled so violently that the cup rattled furiously in its saucer.

'Hold that saucer firmly. I don't want you breaking my good china.'

'How can you be worried about your stupid china when Oliver's so ill?' Meggie retaliated angrily, crashing the cup and saucer down on a low table and standing up. 'You should have told me,' she said facing her future mother-in-law coldly. 'Oliver and I are engaged to be married. I had a right to know.'

'Well, everything's changed now, of course.'

'Changed?'

'Miss McPherson, Oliver has lost a leg. He will be crippled. I can see that you would not want to marry him under these circumstances. You do not need to feel any obligation. I have already explained the situation to Oliver. He understands.'

'You told him I don't want to marry him?' Meggie knew her mouth was open. 'You had no right! I love him.'

'You love what you thought he could give you. A house, a good income, status.' Mrs Laing stirred her tea with grim satisfaction.

'I'm sorry for you, Mrs Laing.' Meggie looked at her future mother-in-law with barely-concealed contempt. 'You've obviously never loved anyone the way I love Oliver. If you had you would know that I could never give him up. Don't bother to see me out.'

'But I'm Mr Laing's fiancée,' Meggie pleaded with the pleasant but determined nurse who barred her way.

'I'm sorry but the doctor's orders are quite clear. Mr Laing is very ill. We can't risk having him upset. Perhaps in a week or two?'

Meggie gave an unladylike screech of sheer frustration then turned on her heel and marched back along the corridor. The nurse watched for a second or two then returned to her duties. Thirty feet further on Meggie stopped and glanced back over her shoulder. When she was quite sure the nurse had gone she carefully retraced her steps to Oliver's ward.

Cautiously she opened the double outer doors and poked her head into the narrow corridor which led to the main ward. Seeing no one, she edged her way down the passage past a linen store, kitchen and sluice. The last four rooms were all side wards, a single patient in each. Meggie saw a man, his arm swathed in bandages, and another who was asleep, propped high on pillows. The third room was empty. The nurse had told her that Oliver was in a room of his own so Meggie knew the last door had to be his. She now had a clear view of the main ward. Several nurses were working with the patients, moving from one bed to the next and, even as she watched, one came towards her, pushing a trolley laden with sheets. Their eyes met, the nurse frowned and hastened her step. Maggie dashed across the corridor and into the room she prayed would hold Oliver. She heard the nurse call, 'Sister. Sister.'

Dreading what she would see, Meggie turned round. Oliver was lying on snow-white pillows, his eyes closed. His face, half-turned away from her, was grey with pain. One arm was caught in a sling, high on his chest, the other lay loosely on the bedspread. Further down the ominous hump of a cage kept the weight of the bedclothes off his damaged body. He looked incredibly young and defenceless. Meggie's eyes misted with tears and her chest tightened with love. She longed to reach out and touch him but was frightened she might hurt him. Instead she simply stood and looked at him, willing him to open his eyes, to get better, to understand that she would always love him.

So intense was her concentration that she forgot everything but her concern for Oliver. When the door opened behind her she jumped and looked round guiltily to find herself facing the nurse who had refused to allow her in less than ten minute before.

'I told you that no visitors were allowed,' she hissed angrily.

'I had to see him,' Meggie pleaded. 'I couldn't go without seeing him.'

'This man is seriously ill! How dare you . . .'

'Meggie?'

Meggie spun round, her eyes burning. 'Oliver?' His eyes were only half open but she could see the confusion, the hurt in them. She sank to her knees at the side of the bed and grasped his good hand. 'I didn't know,' she told him. 'I didn't know you'd been hurt.'

'I thought . . .'

'I must insist that you leave.' The nurse was speaking again. 'Mr Laing is to have absolute peace and rest.'

'Just five minutes, nurse. Please. I promise I won't upset him,' Meggie begged, her anguish touching the heart of even this seasoned nurse.

'I am the ward sister,' the woman corrected her imperiously, then looked doubtfully at Oliver. 'Mr Laing?'

He nodded, unable to conceal the wince of agony the slight movement caused. 'Let her stay, Sister. Please.'

'Two minutes. Not one second more.' The starch in her skirt crackled as she turned away.

'You really didn't know?' Oliver asked, his voice low and hoarse. But his hand gripped hers fiercely and his eyes bored into hers.

'Not until this morning. It was in the paper.'

'My mother said . . .'

'I know what your mother said. I went to see her before I came here.' She raised his hand to her lips and kissed it. 'Did you really believe I would be so cruel, Oliver?' she asked.

He looked away. 'No one would blame you.'

'I love you, Oliver. Nothing will ever change that.' She was begging him to believe her now.

'You might feel differently when you see what they've done to me.' Still he looked away.

'You've lost a leg.' The words sounded cruel in the silent room.

'I'm a cripple.'

'Who says?' He didn't answer so she repeated it. 'Who says, Oliver? Who says you're crippled?'

'It's obvious, isn't it?' he asked, his voice strengthening with anger. 'You don't want me as a husband. Not now. I'll never walk again.'

'Look at me,' she ordered furiously. 'Look at me, Oliver.' Reluctantly, painfully, he turned his head towards her. 'If that's the way you're going to think, then you're right, you will never walk again,' she told him firmly. 'If you want to be crippled, you will be.' She knew that would sting his pride and smiled when she saw the slight frown which furrowed his brow.

'You'd better go, Meggie. It'll be easier for both of us.' He closed his eyes, blotting out her lovely face.

'I'm not going anywhere and you're not in any position to make me,' she laughed softly now. Tenderly she put a hand up to his face, then leant over and kissed him on the lips. 'You don't get rid of me that easily,' she told him.

She was rewarded by the faint flicker of a smile.

'You really must go now.' The sister, who had been standing in the doorway, listening, came to the bedside. 'The young lady's quite right, you know,' she said, unnecessarily tidying the bedspread. 'Your recovery will depend on your own determination.' She straightened and smiled. 'I know it's a terrible thing to happen to a young man like you and it will take time for you to come to terms with it. But there have been some marvellous advances for injuries such as yours. There were so many of them, you see, in the war. What you need is a goal. Tell yourself that you'll be walking again in, say, nine months, and then work towards it.' She walked back to the door and waited. 'You really must leave now, lass. Mr Laing is very tired.'

Meggie saw Oliver's drooping lids and knew the sister was right. Quickly she dropped another kiss on his mouth, pleased to feel him respond slightly. 'You will walk out of the church with me on our wedding day, Oliver,' she told him. 'And I will be the proudest woman in the world.'

'I promise,' he murmured, drifting back to sleep.

Harry Keir, back in the Netherton Bridge, scowled at his copy of the *Inverannan Press*, the town's own weekly paper. What he did next was unprecedented and so out of character that the barman wondered if he had been taken ill. Harry abandoned his half-finished pint and ran out of the pub, the paper flapping in his hand.

'Oh my . . .! What is it, Harry?' His wife was equally startled by the sight of her breathless husband. 'Are you not feeling well?'

'Look at this.' He thrust the paper at her, rattling it angrily. 'I knew that wee bastard was up to no good.'

'What on earth's the matter, Dad?' Sally, here with Ronnie to visit her parents for the evening, hurried to her mother's side.

'Read it!' Harry ordered. 'There,' he jabbed with his finger. 'The headlines!'

'VICIOUS ATTACK ON INVERANNAN BUSINESSMAN,' Mrs Keir read the headline aloud.

'Oliver Laing!' Sally exclaimed, reading her own way through the report.

'Isn't that who Meggie McPherson's engaged to?' Mrs Keir asked.

'Aye,' Sally, still reading, nodded. Her pleasure at hearing of Meggie and Oliver's reconciliation had been genuine.

'That explains it,' Harry said, thumping his fist on the table. 'Och, aye, I knew there was something going on.'

'What are you talking about, Dad?' Sally asked, puzzled.

'I was having a wee pint in the Netherton the other night, a week or so back, when Matty McPherson comes in and gets talking to the Drummond twins.'

'Bloody hell,' Ronnie muttered. 'They're an unsavoury pair.'

'Aye,' Harry agreed. 'Just new out of the jail and looking for trouble. Anyway, I just happened to overhear what they were saying. Couldn't catch it all mind, but enough.'

'What?' Sally prompted him impatiently. 'What were they saying?'

'Matty McPherson gave them some money, asked them to teach someone a lesson. To give someone a good thumping. I knew some poor sod was going to get a beating but I never thought it would be the likes of Oliver Laing. What can Matty McPherson have against him?'

Ronnie grunted. 'Matty McPherson's a poisonous little shit. He's not right in the head, that one. Jealous of any one who even looks at that sister of his.'

'Young Vera's mother said he had a go at her, that's why she left the shop,' Mrs Keir added her own titbit. 'Got her in the back room and all but raped her, he did.'

'Aye, I wouldn't put it past him,' Sally agreed. 'Right nasty piece of work he is.'

Later, as Ronnie and Sally walked home, the baby snug in her arms, Sally said, 'I wonder if Meggie knows Matty was involved.'

'Not her,' Ronnie sneered. 'As far as she's concerned the sun shines out of his backside. If only she knew!'

'And what is that supposed to mean?' Sally asked curiously.

Ronnie looked uncomfortable. 'It was him who told me about Meggie. Not that that makes what she did right, mind, but for her own brother to say things like that.'

'He used to help himself from the till, too,' Sally said thoughtfully, shifting the baby's weight to the other arm.

'And remember the cigarettes?'

'Aye. You know, Ronnie, it's not right what Matty's doing.'

'As far as I'm concerned they deserve each other,' Ronnie insisted, his bitterness against Meggie as deep as ever. 'And don't you go poking your nose in either. Leave them to sort out their own problems. They're nothing to us now, Sal.'

'Well, well, look what the dog's sicked up,' Matty grinned unpleasantly at Sally. 'You can't bring that thing in here. There's not room.'

Sally turned a look on Matty which would have frozen the blood of a more sensitive man and steered her pushchair round the counter and through to the storeroom.

'What the hell do you think you're doing?' Matty blazed, all trace of a smile gone.

Sally extricated her sleeping daughter from the nest of blankets and hoisted her on to her shoulder. 'I want to see Meggie. Where is she?' Her voice was absolutely flat.

'She's upstairs, having her lunch. What do you want to see her for?' he demanded, blocking her way.

'Mind your own bloody business,' she spat at him and barged up the stairs. The baby, woken by her mother's harsh tones whimpered, then broke into a wail.

Meggie, in the middle of her lunch, hurried to the door. 'Sally!' Her sandwich dropped messily to the floor. Flustered, she fell to her knees and picked it up.

The baby, recognising food, decided she was hungry, and stretched out a delicate hand towards the crumpled bread. Meggie saw a pair of beautiful, vivid blue eyes, the lashes dewed with recent tears, and a tiny, rosebud mouth. Instinctively she put her hand out and touched the child's soft cheek. The baby smiled but her hand stayed resolutely outstretched towards the remains of Meggie's meal. Sally and Meggie laughed and what could have been an awkward meeting was saved by the charm of Sally's baby daughter.

'Can we come in?' Sally asked.

'Aye . . . yes . . . sorry, Sal. I was just so surprised to find

555

you on my doorstep.' She looked back at the baby, who was starting to fret. 'She's beautiful, Sal. What's her name?'

'Freda,' Sally said proudly, rocking the child gently.

'Sit down, Sal.' Meggie hurriedly smeared a crust generously with butter and handed it to the baby, who applied her four teeth to it with total concentration.

'That'll keep her quiet for long enough for us to have a wee talk,' Sal said, settling her daughter on the settee.

Meggie sank down opposite her old friend. 'I heard you'd had a daughter. I was going to come and see you but I thought Ronnie wouldn't want me to. I'm really glad you've brought her to see me, Sal.'

Sally smiled, wondering how to say what had to be said. Looking at Meggie closely now, she thought she looked pale and strained. 'I didn't really come to show you Freda,' she admitted. 'I heard what happened to Oliver. I wanted to tell you I'm sorry.'

'Thanks,' Meggie whispered.

'How is he, Meggie?'

Meggie sighed. Once the initial shock of Oliver's accident had subsided, she had been left feeling depressed and lonely. Visiting hour, every night from seven until eight, was a strained affair, normal conversation quite impossible in the unnatural atmosphere of the hospital, particularly if Mrs Laing was also there. 'He's still in a lot of pain but he's a wee bit better every day. He's terribly upset about losing his leg.'

'Oh no . . .' Sally breathed. 'Oh, Meggie, I didn't realise.' The horror of it made her feel quite dizzy, especially knowing what she knew.

'Sal, are you all right?' Meggie, startled by her friend's sudden pallor jumped up and got her a glass of water. 'I shouldn't have said it straight out like that. I know it's an awful thing to think about.'

Sally gulped at the water gratefully. 'I'm all right,' she insisted.

Meggie sank back into her chair, finding tremendous relief in having another woman to talk to. 'I just wish they knew who did it, Sal. Why would anyone want to hurt Oliver? He's never done anything to deserve this.'

Sally took a deep breath. 'That's why I'm here, Meggie.'

'Thanks, Sal. You've no idea how much I've wanted someone to talk to.'

'That's not what I was meaning.' Sally fiddled with her fingernails. 'Look, Meggie, someone's got to tell you this. It might as well be me.'

Perplexed, Meggie frowned at her. 'I don't understand. Tell me what?'

'I know who attacked Oliver.'

Now it was Meggie's turn to blanch. 'You know? How could you know?'

Quietly, keeping her voice carefully neutral, Sally told Meggie what her father had overheard. 'I'm sorry, Meggie. I almost wish Dad had never been near the Netherton. But when I knew, I had to tell you. Meggie . . . if he can do that to Oliver he could do it to you.'

Meggie knew Sally well enough to know she was telling the truth. A chilling shiver started in her scalp and travelled through her body. Too late she made the connection between Matty's damaged hands and the attack on Oliver, remembered too the strange atmosphere in the shop the night Matty had apparently fallen over. And then she felt as though the air was too thick to breathe. Her stomach heaved, her mouth filled with a rush of saliva. Leaping up so suddenly that she frightened the baby, Meggie dashed to the toilet and retched until she thought her heart must surely come up.

Sally, for once ignoring her wailing daughter, put an arm round Meggie's heaving shoulders and waited until it was over. Gently she wiped her friend's face with a wet cloth, gave her a drink and helped her back to the chair. Meggie sat huddled over her knees, shivering convulsively.

'Oh, Meggie. I'm sorry. I wish I'd never said anything,' Sally cried.

Meggie made a huge effort and sat up, clasping her hands together to stop them from shaking. When she looked at Sally her face was chalk-white but controlled. 'I'm glad you told me. I needed you to make me see what's been staring me in the face all this time.'

Sally, rocking her daughter, whose eyes were closing, reached out and took Meggie's hand. 'Then I'm glad. I hate to see you hurting, Meggie, but Matty's rotten, through and through.'

'I knew he was stealing from me. I knew he told lies. I should have asked him to leave, back when you left.'

Sally gave a small laugh. 'I suppose I should be grateful to him really. If it wasn't for Matty, Ronnie and me wouldn't be married. It was Matty who told Ronnie about you.'

Meggie gave a hugh sigh. 'I suppose I should be shocked. I'm not. Nothing you can tell me would shock me now,' she said wearily. Then, 'What about you, Sal? Are you happy?'

Sally smiled softly. 'Aye. I am. Ronnie's a good man, Meggie.'

Meggie nodded. 'I'm glad. And I'm sorry we can't see more of each other. But we can't, can we?'

Sally shook her head. 'Ronnie wouldn't like it. I've gone behind his back to come here. I've never deceived him before and I won't do it again. I don't like having secrets from him'.

'I understand that.' Meggie squeezed the hand that held hers. 'But we'll always be friends, Sal? Even if we don't see much of each other?'

'Aye. In our hearts. Always friends.' She stood up, lifting the baby carefully. 'I'd best get home. She'll be needing fed and changed.'

'Aye.' Meggie was almost too tired to walk to the door with them.

Sally paused, seemed to consider something. Making her decision she said, 'You may as well know it all. Did Vera ever say anything to you about why she left?'

'No. I was through in Glasgow that weekend. When I got back, she'd gone. I've never seen her since. Why?'

'Matty attacked her. From what I heard he tried to rape her. Och, these things sometimes get exaggerated in the telling but Vera's Mam told my Mam and she's not the type to make a fuss about nothing. And I know Vera liked it here. She wouldn't have left without good reason.'

Meggie couldn't even find the words to comment. Silently she kissed her friend's cheek and opened the door.

'My Mam's always there, Meggie, if you need her. She'll always send a message for me.' And then Sally ran down the stairs, tied the baby in the pushchair and hurried away before Matty could see her again.

Upstairs, Meggie sagged for a moment against the door frame, her eyes closed. But after a minute she straightened and went to wash her face at the sink. With trembling hands she tidied her hair, put on her coat and shoes and crept out of the house.

CHAPTER TWENTY-NINE

Meggie spent the rest of the day sitting in the park, deep in thought. But when the town clock struck six she got up, straightened her clothes and started to walk towards the Netherton Mill.

The narrow streets where Sally's parents lived seemed alive and friendly now and the Keirs' small home was warm and welcoming.

'Come along in, Meggie.' Mrs Keir took the girl's arm and drew her inside. 'By and you're frozen!' She was shocked by the icy feel of Meggie's skin.

'I was wondering when Mr Keir would be in?' Meggie asked, shivering depite the warmth from the small fire.

'A wee while yet, hen. He aye goes for a wee half before coming home.'

'I need to talk to him about something,' Meggie's teeth chattered.

'Aye, and I can guess what it's about. But it can wait until you've got something hot inside you.'

Meggie looked at the clock, resolutely ticking towards seven o'clock, and knew that Oliver would be waiting for her, having been looking forward to her visit all day. But, much as she loved him, she couldn't face him. Not yet, not knowing what she did. There was something she had to do first.

'Right, Meggie. Get that down you and then come to the fire and heat yourself through.' Mrs Keir sat a bowl of soup, rich with meaty stock and vegetables, in front of Meggie.

Meggie lifted the spoon, sipped at the savoury liquid and almost gagged.

'Now then, lass, it's not that bad!'

'I'm sorry. I'm just not hungry.'

'Rubbish. Get the first three spoonfuls over and you'll manage the rest no bother. You'll feel better for it and I'm going to sit here until it's eaten. No one wastes good food in my house, Meggie McPherson.'

Mrs Keir stationed herself on the other side of the table and glowered at her guest. Conscious of Sally's mother watching her every move, Meggie scooped up a small spoonful of liquid, then another, and then a third. By the fourth spoonful there was a small knot of heat in her empty stomach and suddenly she was ravenous.

'See, what did I tell you?' Mrs Keir beamed.

'It was lovely,' Meggie admitted. 'And I do feel better.'

'Aye, now come and sit by the fire and get yourself properly heated.' She handed Meggie a cup of tea, pale and sweet with condensed milk.

'I'm sorry to turn up like this,' Meggie started. 'But . . .'

'You're always welcome. Now drink your tea and sit quiet. I know what's happened. I even know why you're here. You've no need to explain anything to me. Just close your eyes and have a wee nap till Harry comes home.'

Meggie smiled and sipped at her tea, grateful for this kind understanding, but sure she couldn't sleep . . .

'Meggie.' A gentle hand shook her shoulder. 'Meggie, hen. Wake up.'

Meggie blinked, sleepy and disorientated. Looking up at Sally's mother's concerned face brought a flood of memories. She closed her eyes again, wondering if this could all be some terrible nightmare. 'Harry's home, lass. If you want to have a wee word with him, now's the time.' Mrs Keir shook her again and Meggie forced herself to face the most difficult decision of her life.

'Come and talk to me while I eat my dinner,' Harry invited, already spooning soup.

Meggie, warmed now and feeling the worst effects of shock receding, settled herself opposite Mr Keir. 'Is it true, Mr Keir? Did my brother do this to Oliver?'

He looked at her sadly. 'I don't know how a lassie like you comes to have a brother like him.' He stuffed his mouth full of bread and then sucked soup in with it, making his cheeks bulge.

Meggie waited while he chewed and swallowed. 'Will you tell me what you know?' she asked.

'I'm warning you, you'll not like it.'

'Just tell me.'

Harry hastily shovelled the remaining soup into his mouth, chewed, gulped and sat back to repeat his story.

'You're absolutely sure it was Matty?' Meggie asked. Only the way she clenched her hands together gave any clue to her inner turmoil.

'Aye. I've come across that brother of yours often enough. There's no mistake.'

Meggie got up and walked to the fire. She stood there, staring down at the crackling flames, until the smell of her scorching skirt forced her to move away. Mrs Keir took a step towards her, meaning to steer the obviously stunned girl back to a chair. When she saw the expression in Meggie's eyes she backed away. Gone was the confusion, the hurt; in their place was implacable anger and absolute determination.

'I am going to the police,' Meggie announced. 'I'm going to tell them it was Matty who attacked Oliver. And I hope he rots in jail.' Her voice was rock steady.

Mrs Keir was unable to hide her shock. 'The polis? You'd turn your own brother into the polis, Meggie?'

'Yes!'

'Och, lass. You're family. You can't do that.' It was unthinkable. No matter what happened, families stuck by one another.

'I can, Mrs Keir, and I will.' She picked up her coat and started to put it on.

'Meggie, it's near ten o'clock. There'll be no one at the polis station to hear you the night.'

'There'll be someone there,' Meggie insisted.

'No, lass.' Harry surprised them both by solidly blocking the door. 'I can't tell you what to do, lass, but I can ask you to wait until morning. Something like this shouldn't be done without a lot of careful thought.'

Meggie met his gaze defiantly but Harry Keir refused to back down. 'All right,' she conceded at last and he moved aside.

It seemed to Mrs Keir that Meggie opened the door with slow reluctance. A moment's reflection told her why. 'Meggie!' She hurried across the room. 'Where are you going?'

Meggie looked down at her feet, embarrassed and not wanting to impose any further on this good-hearted woman.

'Are you going home, lass?'

Meggie's face, eerily lit by the street lights, seemed etched with sadness as she replied, 'I can't. I can't go back. Not while he's still there.'

'Then you'll stay with us the night. There's plenty room. Och,' she cut short Meggie's automatic objection, 'what's the point in arguing? Where else would you go?' Firmly she led the girl back inside and took her upstairs to the boxroom where a single bed waited invitingly.

'Thank you,' Meggie managed to smile.

'Sleep well, lass. And think on what Harry told you.' Mrs Keir closed the door, shutting Meggie in to grapple with her problems through a long, sleepless night.

'You do understand what you're saying?' the police sergeant asked.

Meggie, her eyes gritty from lack of sleep, her mouth dry with nerves but her resolve iron hard, nodded. 'Yes.'

Three hours later, Meggie had repeated her allegations to two different officers.

'Just sign here, Miss McPherson.' The sergeant pushed the three-page statement across the table at her.

Meggie wrote her name carefully. 'What will happen now?'

'We will bring your brother in for questioning.'

'You'll arrest him?'

'If this Harry Keir can confirm your statement then I think there's a good chance of that.'

'When will you go for Matty?'

'Two officers have already been sent out, miss. They'll be back any minute now.'

Meggie sighed, leant back in the chair and closed her eyes, feeling the tension drain out of her.

'Right then, miss. I'll show you out.'

Meggie followed him through the building and out, past the main desk. 'We'll be in touch,' he said, opening the door for her.

Meggie walked away up the street, missing Matty, who was brought from the back of the building by two uniformed officers, by seconds.

The walk up the hill to the shop seemed intolerably steep. Meggie approached nervously, frightened that Matty might still be there. Outside, a small knot of women had gathered, their heads together. When they saw Meggie they drew apart slightly and watched her in silence. Meggie tried the door and found it still open. Her heart hammering, she went it.

'Och, there you are!' Mrs Telfer hurried to greet her. 'Och, Meggie, something terrible's happened.' When Meggie made no reply she went on quickly. 'It was the polis. They came and took your brother away, lass. Kicking and shouting he was. Never seen anything like it! And the language! They didn't even give him the chance to close up the shop so I thought I'd better stay and keep a wee eye on it for you.'

'Thank you, Mrs Telfer.'

Behind them the door opened and three or four other women came in. 'Are you open, lass?' one of them asked. 'Only I'm all out of tea.'

'Aye, I'm open,' Meggie decided, walking briskly to her place behind the counter. What better way to keep her mind off the day's traumatic events? And as well to face the women now as later.

'Just two ounces of the usual,' the woman said, setting her bag on the countertop. 'What's your Matty done then, hen?' The other women gathered round avidly.

Meggie looked up and smiled brightly at them. 'He got into a fight,' she said, her brown eyes meeting their suspicious ones steadily, daring them to challenge her.

'Who with?'

'I really don't know,' she said, with grim finality.

Disappointed, the woman handed over her money and Meggie served the next customer.

Meggie knew that word of what had happened had spread quickly round the streets. All afternoon women trickled in, some buying their usual weekend messages, but others for an ounce of this, two ounces of that, anything which would give them the excuse to visit the shop. She greeted them all with a dauntless smile. Those few women who were brave enough to mention Matty's name were given the same, unchanging reply in a tone of voice which made further enquiries impossible.

Meggie was glad of the excuse to close the shop half an hour early so that she could visit Oliver, but the visit itself filled her with dread.

'Where were you yesterday?' he asked, raising himself awkwardly in bed as soon as she came into his room.

'I had something to see to,' she said, standing by his bed but too far away for him to reach her.

'I missed you,' he smiled, looking much more like his old self now. Though he was still pale, his face no longer had that grey, sunken look. His eyes were brighter now, his whole mood more hopeful as the pain receded.

'I missed you, too,' she told him. 'How are you, Oliver?'

'My arm's out of its sling.' He waved it triumphantly at her. 'And I was up out of bed today.'

'Out of bed? Already?' Excitement overcame her darker thoughts for a moment. 'That's wonderful, Oliver.'

'Only to sit in a chair, but it's a start. They're bringing me crutches tomorrow. Then I'll be hopping around fine style, you'll see.' He watched her, expecting some encouragement at this hopeful news but to his dismay the light had died from her eyes and she was staring blankly at the counterpane. Oliver's gut twisted. Was this what he had been living in fear of ever since the attack? Had she finally understood the extent of his injury? The startling progress he had made was due solely to Meggie, her fierce determination that he would recover infecting him, making him refuse the pain-killing drugs he was offered, forcing him to sit up in bed, to move cautiously and finally to demand the crutches. Without her the effort would have been for nothing. 'Meggie,' he asked apprehensively. 'What's the matter?'

She looked at him, her eyes too bright in a face which seemed pinched and tense. 'I've got something to tell you.'

He steeled himself to take it without making a fool of himself. If nothing else, she would remember him for his bravery. 'Go on.'

She lifted her chin stubbornly, trying not to think about his possible reaction, knowing only that she had to tell him. 'It was Matty.'

Oliver heard the words and closed his eyes, knowing he couldn't let her see how relieved he was. 'Matty?' he repeated.

'Matty did this to you, Oliver. Matty attacked you.' She stood back defensively, waiting for the accusations, the recriminations, the bitterness he was bound to feel.

'Meggie, I'm sorry.' His heart bled for her.

'Sorry!' She looked at him in bewilderment. 'Why should you be sorry? I'm the one who should be sorry, not you.' She slumped on to the edge of the bed, accidentally jarring what was left of his leg.

Oliver winced but ignored the upsurge of pain and reached out a hand to touch her face softly. 'It's not your fault, Meggie.'

'But I feel responsible.' Her eyes were luminous with unshed tears as she choked out the words.

'Are you sure it was him?' he asked softly.

She nodded, took a deep breath and, keeping her eyes fixed on the bedspread, her voice tremulous, told him everything. 'The police have taken him for questioning. He'll probably be charged later today,' she ended, a tear finally running slowly down her cheek.

'Oh, Meggie . . . come here.' He raised an arm and she laid her head against his shoulder. 'You mustn't ever think I blame you for any of this,' he reassured her gently, stroking her hair.

'But . . .'

'But nothing. Don't torture yourself with it, Meggie. You are not responsible for Matty. If there's any justice in the world, he will go to prison for a very long time. All you have to worry about now is getting the wedding planned. Unless you've changed your mind?'

'Never,' she assured him softly.

'Good.' Very slowly he lowered his mouth to hers and kissed her deeply.

'Mr Laing!' They broke apart guiltily at the sound of sister's shocked voice. 'Visiting time is over, Miss McPherson.'

Meggie walked out of the hospital feeling almost light-headed with relief, but the walk home drained her of her last reserves of energy. She let herself in through the back door, her shaking hands fumbling with the locks, then made her way up the stairs on legs which would barely support her. Five minutes later she was in bed, gratefully surrendering to the sleep of utter exhaustion.

She woke some time in the night, knowing that something had broken through her sleep and disturbed her. Cautiously she slipped out of bed and opened the door to the sitting room. It was deeply shadowed, perfectly still and silent. Then, as her eyes adjusted to the dark, she saw that the landing door was open. The catch was stiff and sometimes, if it wasn't closed firmly, the door would blow open with a loud click. That must have been what had woken her. Yawning, she walked across the room and slammed the door. But as she turned round again, she saw something that made her heart stop. There, sprawled on the sofa, easily identifiable even in the darkened room, was her brother.

'Matty?' she whispered fearfully, backing towards the window and hauling back the curtains, letting in enough grey light for her to see him clearly.

'Meggie.' It was soft, almost friendly.

'What are you doing here?' she asked, her stomach churning with fear.

'This is my home. I live here.' He stood up, laughing, a wild, bitter sound.

'No, Matty. Not any more.' She spoke out bravely, but backed away until she was up against the wall, her whole body tensed, ready to run.

'You set the polis on to me,' he snarled, all pretence of pleasantness abandoned. 'You set the bloody polis on to your own brother.' He stepped closer to her with each word, finally shooting out a hand and grabbing her hair. 'You bitch. You bloody, fucking bitch!' He jerked on her hair, forcing her face upright, then struck her hard, across the cheek.

Meggie gasped, tasted blood in her mouth and writhed desperately. There was the glitter of madness in his eyes and his teeth were bared, his lips drawn back like an animal's. 'No,' she screeched, then screamed as he hit her again. 'Stop it,' she begged. 'Matty, stop it.' She managed to raise an arm to protect her face and then twisted away from him, getting the sofa between them.

Incredibly, he laughed. 'You'll not get away from me,

Meggie,' he told her. 'I'll make you both pay, you and that stinking boyfriend of yours.'

'Pay for what?' she demanded. 'I've looked after you. Done things I will always be ashamed of, just to give you a home. I took you in here, gave you a job, and place to live. And you repaid me by trying to kill the man I love.'

He dodged to the side but she matched his movements, still standing opposite him. 'I'm the man you love!' he yelled at her, the words sending ice to her stomach. 'Not Oliver Laing or Ronnie Sandys. Me. It's always been you and me, Meggie. You didn't need all those other men. You shouldn't have done what you did with them, Meggie. Dirty things. You hurt me, Meggie, going with other men. You know you belong to me. That's why I had to stop him. I always loved you, Meggie.'

Appalled, sickened, she realised he was crying. 'No, Matty,' she said, striving to keep her voice controlled. 'It can't be like that. Not with us. It's wrong.'

'It's you, you're wrong!' He flung it at her viciously. 'You lied to me. You promised you'd always love me. You lied, Meggie. You lied.' Again he lunged at her, again she darted away, still facing him, aware now of how truly dangerous he was. 'I won't let him have you, Meggie,' he said, the words hissing between his teeth.

Meggie dodged from right to left, keeping him moving while giving herself time to think. 'Matty, if you really love me, don't hurt me. What will you do without me, Matty? You know I'm the only one who cares about you.'

'You don't care. You told the police.' Then he laughed. 'But it didn't work, Meggie. They couldn't prove anything. I've got witnesses, people who saw me in the pub that night. So I couldn't possibly have been anywhere near Oliver Laing, can I? And there's no one, not one single person, to say different. Not even Harry Keir. He doesn't know anything about anything. Not seen me for months, that's what he told the polis.' So pleased was he to be able to tell her this that he dropped his guard. Meggie grabbed her chance and shoved the sofa over, knocking him off balance, then rushed for the door, grabbing her keys from the small table as she went. Matty was still on his knees when she slammed the door shut. Fumbling desperately she found the right key and got it in the lock. Even as she turned it he crashed against the door.

'Matty,' she called, desperately, knowing it was only a matter of time before he broke down the door. 'Matty, listen to me.'

'Bitch,' he yelled back, thumping into the door again.

Desperately frightened, Meggie hauled the heavy oak cabinet which stood at the top of the stairs along the landing and rammed it hard against the door.

'I know about you stealing from me, Matty. I know what you did to Vera. You turned Ma and Pa against me with your lies. You drove Sally away from me. You came between me and Ronnie. And now you have tried to kill Oliver.'

The door juddered again, more weakly this time, but he made no other response.

'I know it was you, Matty,' she yelled. 'I saw the mud on your trousers and your cut hand. But I didn't tell the police about that.' It was, she realised, a crucial piece of evidence and one which, in her distress, she had forgotten about. 'If I go and tell them now, they'll arrest you and this time they really will charge you.'

'Open the bloody door.'

'No, not until you make me a promise.'

'What?'

'I want you to go away, Matty. Get out of Strathannan.'

'No!' It was an anguished wail, the protest of a thwarted child. 'Don't send me away, Meggie.'

But Meggie had seen the other side of her unstable brother, facets of his character which appalled and sickened her. 'If you don't go away, Matty, I'll go back to the police. I'll tell them everything I know. And Oliver will tell them he knows it was you who attacked him.'

'He never saw me!'

'Yes he did.' She had no hesitation about lying. 'Even if you manage to get out of this room before the police get here, they'll still find you, Matty. You'll never be safe.'

'I live here.'

'No, you don't. Not any more. I don't love you, Matty. Not after what you did to Oliver. I don't want to see you again. Not for as long as I live.'

'Meggie. . .' It was a choked sob.

'You hurt me, Matty. I'll never forgive you.' She was relentless, cruel, knowing that she had to drive him away, force him to hate her, to forget his unnatural feelings for her and start a life of his own, somewhere else. Somewhere where he could never hurt her or Oliver again. She listened at the door, heard nothing and went on. 'I'm going now, Matty. I won't be back until Sunday night. You're to be gone by then. There's money, the takings for yesterday and today, under my bed and there's ten pounds in the till. Take it.' Still silence. 'Goodbye, Matty.'

Resolutely she turned away and walked steadily from the shop, leaving the keys still turned in the lock.

'Are you sure you should go back?' Bertha Cruickshank asked.

Meggie nodded. 'I have to. I won't let him drive me away.'

'There's always room for you here, lass. You know that?'

'I know, but I belong in Inverannan. With Oliver.'

'Och, Meggie,' Netta sighed, giving her daughter a perfunctory kiss on her cheek. 'Always trouble. Never anything else with you.'

'I won't let you blame me for this as well, Ma. I've always tried my best. If you won't accept that, well, I'm sorry, but I don't really care any more. All I care about is Oliver.' They were harsh words, but the last weeks had changed Meggie. She was no longer prepared to let her mother feed the guilt which had dogged her for so long.

Netta opened her mouth, a sharp retort ready, but, recognising the new steel in her daughter changed her mind. 'Don't forget to send me a wedding invitation,' she called, as Meggie walked down the front path.

Meggie heard but didn't look round. Bullies, manipulative people, people like her mother, like Oliver's mother, like Matty, they were all weak and frightened underneath and she would never forget the lessons they had taught her.

Getting off the train at Inverannan station, Meggie felt a shiver of fear run through her. If Matty hadn't gone, then he might be waiting for her and he was unbalanced enough to do her some real harm. She actually turned towards Netherton, fully intending to ask Harry Keir to come home with her. But then she stopped. Harry had already proved himself to be a coward by refusing to give the police the evidence they needed to charge Matty. How much use would he be in a real emergency?

Grimly, she turned left and started towards the town. At the bottom of the hill she looked up towards the shop.

Despite the evening darkness no light showed. Her heart hammering she turned off the road and followed the lane which went between the backs of the houses, only emerging when she was well above the shop. If Matty was still there, watching for her, he wouldn't expect her to come from this direction. Keeping to the shadows she edged towards the back gate and, very cautiously, lifted the latch. Easing the gate open a fraction, praying the old hinges wouldn't squeak, she crept quickly to the back door. It was still unlocked. The stairs seemed interminably long, every tread complaining with her weight. And, on the landing, the old oak bureau was still firmly placed across the unbroken door, the key still in the lock.

Meggie felt sudden panic and ran back to the top of the stairs where she stayed for five minutes, sweat pouring between her breasts. Then, summoning all her courage she shoved at the bureau. It moved reluctantly, scraping across the floor and banging against the door frame loudly enough to alert anyone inside the little flat. With the door still locked she leaned against it, listening. There was no sound, nothing at all, but she hadn't expected there to be.

'Matty,' she called. 'Are you in there?' Again, nothing. 'Matty! If you're in there, answer me.'

Slowly she sank to the floor and sat there, her face close to the wood, listening for the slightest sound. An hour passed, and then another. Her legs ached, her neck had stiffened and still there was no sound. Surely no one could stay so absolutely silent for so long? But what if Matty was on the other side of the door, waiting for her?

Meggie eased herself up, wincing as restored circulation caused pins and needles in her feet. She waited, gritting her teeth until the agony passed, then, with one sharp movement she unlocked the door and threw it open. She thrust a hand into the room and switched on the light, blinking in the sudden brightness. She darted back, almost expecting Matty to pounce on her and, when there was no sign of life, finally looked inside.

The sight that met her eyes was one of total chaos. Every item of furniture had been overturned. Drawers had been ripped out of cupboards and emptied on the floor, her crockery was smashed, the curtains torn down. Strangely, Meggie felt no sense of surprise, just overwhelming sadness. She crossed the room, carefully avoiding shards of broken glass and looked into Matty's bedroom. Here everything seemed perfectly normal, the pillow still bearing the indentation made by her brother's head but, when she opened the wardrobe, it was empty.

Her own room had been systematically wrecked. Even the mattress had been ripped apart, its stuffing spilling over the floor. The doors of her wardrobe were hanging open, sagging on broken hinges, the contents scattered round the room, her dresses ripped, her underwear desecrated by the most foul acts. And there, on the floor, in the corner, was the suede case, its lid ripped off. Of the jet-and-diamond-studded bracelet there was no sign. Meggie shivered as a breath of cold air touched her skin and she realised that the sash window was open. It looked out over the storeroom roof just two or three feet below and explained how Matty had got out. Clambering over her ruined possessions she slammed it down and rammed the clip across.

Looking round her room, dry-eyed and calm, she thought that none of this devastation mattered. Apart from Wallace's bracelet, there was nothing that couldn't be repaired or replaced. All that mattered was that Matty had truly gone and would never come back.

CHAPTER THIRTY

Oliver eased himself out of the car and grappled awkwardly with his crutches. Meggie stood back, knowing better than to offer any help. When she was sure he was steady, she walked ahead of him and opened the front door.

'Well?' she demanded, as soon as he got through the door, unable to contain her excitement any longer. 'What do you think?'

He grunted a laugh. 'Can't tell much from a hallway.'

She laughed back and held the sitting-door open for him. 'Come on, I'll show you round.'

He hopped after her, going from one room to the next, saying little but noting every detail.

'I wish you'd say something,' she said anxiously, when they had completed a circuit of the ground floor.

'I haven't seen it all yet.' He looked pointedly up the staircase. Then, to Meggie's consternation, placed both crutches on the first stair and swung his leg up after them. She held her breath as he repeated the manoeuvre twelve times. At the top, he turned round triumphantly. 'You didn't think I could do that, did you?'

She laughed, ran up the stairs and kissed him so enthusiastically that he wobbled dangerously and dropped one crutch, grabbing hold of her to steady himself.

Together they examined the four bedrooms and bathroom that comprised the top floor of the double-fronted, sandstone villa which the builders had only just completed. 'Well?' she asked again, seething with impatience.

He hopped across to look out of the large bay window of one of the back rooms. 'What a view!' Propping up his crutches, he put an arm round Meggie's slim waist and drew her to him. 'You can see the Forth from up here. And away across the hills on the other side.' In the still, summer air the distant hills were misty, the wide river estuary a deep, sparkling blue and the sky above perfectly clear. In front of them stretched undulating fields, a patchwork of gold and green, broken here and there by a farmhouse, a copse of trees or a road as the land fell steadily towards the river. 'You'd think we were in the middle of the country.'

'I suppose we are,' she said. 'There was nothing here until they started building these houses. Do you think it's too far out of town?'

He turned and looked into her eyes. 'I think it's absolutely perfect.'

'Honestly?' With Oliver in hospital until two days ago but stubbornly insisting on a September wedding, Meggie had taken on the responsibility of finding them a house. This modest, four-bedroom villa was part of a ribbon of new houses being built along one of the main roads out of the town. Meggie had loved it from the moment she saw it, but had worried that Oliver might prefer something older, or more grand, or even want to be closer to the office, or to his mother.

'Honestly. Now that you can drive it doesn't matter that it's outside the town. Until I get my new leg you can drive me to work, so that's no problem. And it's too far for Mother to walk so we'll be spared from having her popping in to find fault every time she's got nothing better to do.'

'Don't be too hard on her, Oliver. She's doing her best. It can't be easy for her, seeing her only son getting married and moving out. She'll be lonely in that big house all on her own.'

With the support of Oliver's cousin, Robbie, Meggie had ruthlessly imposed herself on her future mother-in-law, forcing the older woman to accept the marriage and convincing her that Oliver would be in good hands. It was an approach that was finally paying dividends. If not precisely enthusiastic, Elsie Laing appeared to have conceded defeat and no longer wasted her energy in trying to snub a girl who so resolutely refused to take offence.

'You'll buy it?' Meggie asked excitedly.

'No,' he corrected her. 'We'll buy it. We're partners, Meggie. In everything.'

'We'll need to see about furniture. And carpets. And curtains. I'm so glad you're home, Oliver. You can help me choose.'

He wrinkled his nose. 'I won't have much time. I've got to get back to work. Robbie's been marvellous, putting off his own wedding and taking over like he did, but it's not fair to keep him up here for any longer than I absolutely must.'

'I like him,' Meggie said dreamily. 'He's very like you. Says what he thinks. You'll miss him when he goes back to Wales.'

'Oh! Like him, do you?' he teased. 'Well, he's spoken for so you'll just have to make do with poor old me. Second best.'

Meggie flushed faintly. She had indeed been very taken with Oliver's charismatic cousin. Robbie, the son of Wallace's brother, had his full share of the undeniable charm that seemed to be the hallmark of the Laing men. There was something in him that reminded her both of Wallace and Oliver. Loving Oliver as she did, with her affectionate memories of Wallace, it would have been quite impossible not to like Robbie, who, in addition to his easy, unaffected friendliness, was also exceedingly good-looking.

He had arrived the same weekend that Matty had departed. Visiting the shop to introduce himself, he had been appalled to discover the devastation Matty had left in his wake but, cheerfully rolling up his sleeves, he had set about clearing up the mess. Then, explaining Meggie's predicament to his aunt, he had employed a combination of charm and bullying which had eventually resulted in the bewildered Mrs Laing taking the unprecedented step of walking down the hill personally to offer Meggie a room in her own house, until such time as her own home was habitable again. In fact, Meggie had never moved back and the small flat with all its memories was now occupied by a jubilant Vera, who was back helping in the shop. All in all Meggie had good reason to be grateful to Robbie and thought of him as a true friend. And that was as far as it went.

'Jealous?' she asked, teasing him.

'Yes,' he admitted, only half-joking. Then, almost roughly, he kissed her, twining his tongue round hers and caressing her breasts with one hand, gratified to feel her eager response as she pressed her body against his.

'Hello! Anyone there!' The builder's agent called up the stairs.

'Bloody hell! We never get a minute to ourselves,' Oliver complained, feeling the frustration of months of enforced separation.

'Up here, Mr Douglas,' Meggie called, giving Oliver a resigned smile and quickly smoothing her dress.

'Och, here youse are. Well, do you like it?' Mr Douglas asked, rubbing his hands together.

'Yes, Mr Douglas,' Oliver answered at once. 'We certainly do. I'll instruct my solicitor tomorrow.'

Meggie listened to the house settling down to sleep. Only when a full half-hour had elapsed since Elsie Laing's footsteps had passed along the landing did she slip cautiously out of bed and open her door. Elsie's door was on the opposite side of the landing. No light showed from beneath it and, just audible, was the sound of gentle snoring.

Meggie wrapped herself in her housecoat and crept down the stairs. As she reached the hall, the light under the morning room, temporarily being used as a bedroom for Oliver, snapped off. Smiling, she turned the handle and edged inside.

'Meggie!' Oliver knew no one else would sneak into his room at this time of the night.

'Of course it's me,' she giggled, then shivered. 'I'm cold.'

'Then come over here,' he ordered in a loud whisper.

Meggie ran across the room and slipped between sheets which were already warm. In the darkness, Oliver propped himself up and looked down at her. 'I've missed you,' he told her, his voice already unsteady with passion. And then his mouth was on hers, devouring her. In his urgency, his hands tore at their clothes until their bodies touched. Oliver pulled her closer and she felt him hot against her hip. His hands worked, rousing her until all she was aware of was her intense need for him, the longing to feel him inside her again at last. He pushed her back, heaved himself up, then, to her dismay, gave a cry of pain, fell back and lay absolutely still.

'Oliver?'

He grunted, turned his face away in despair. 'I'm sorry,' he mumbled.

With great tenderness, Meggie rolled the sheet back, pulling it firmly from his fingers when he would have kept it over him. Then moving carefully so as not to hurt him, she straddled him. Bending her head she kissed his throat, moved down to the hollow of his shoulders and then ran her mouth down to his navel, kissing him lightly, teasing him with her tongue. Oliver groaned, but kept an arm flung defensively over his head. Exercising enormous self-control Meggie limited herself to a few fleeting kisses between his thighs, then moved down to run her mouth along the length of his uninjured leg. As she moved to kiss the other one she felt him tense beneath her. One hand gripped her shoulder so tightly that she would see the bruises there in the morning.

Gently, she sank her face to the warm skin of his damaged limb. With infinite care she ran her tongue over the soft flesh near his groin, then down, feeling the skin become tighter, drier and more fragile. She let her mouth linger, dropping the lightest of kisses as she neared the thin protective dressing he wore at night to protect the stump. Even then she did not stop but fluttered her tongue there before working her way up again. Gradually the pressure from his hand lessened. When she felt it fall away she kissed his leg again, then moved her hand up, finding him hard and ready for her again. Shivering with anticipation now she lowered herself on to him. Oliver groaned, gripped her again and thrust up at her.

Later, much later, they stirred, dragging the dishevelled covers over their cooling bodies. Oliver dropped a kiss in Meggie's tangled hair, his hands drawing her even closer to him. She nestled against his side, her head on his chest, one leg thrown across him, careful, even in sleep, not to hurt him. The gentle light filtering through the curtains showed a smile of absolute contentment on each relaxed face.

Two months later, Meggie, breathtakingly beautiful in a dress of cream lace, walked down the aisle on the arm of Robbie Laing. There were suppressed gasps of admiration from the large congregation and no one was more proud of the bride than Netta McPherson and Bertha Cruickshank, sharing the front pew. On the other side of the aisle, Elsie Laing hid her regrets under a stiffly veiled hat, while further back, Ronnie Sandys held his little daughter on his knee and smiled affectionately at his wife who was proud to be best maid at her friend's wedding.

As Meggie neared the front of the kirk where Oliver was waiting with his best man, Iain Sutherland, she felt a moment of longing for her father, who would surely have been proud of her today; for Wallace who had changed her life and made this moment possible. And for the baby daughter she would never know. For a moment her eyes misted. But then audible gasps from the onlookers as Oliver rose from his seat and stepped firmly into the aisle, reclaimed her attention. In that second the past was put aside and Meggie's thoughts were concentrated on the man she was about to marry. Her regular step faltered and her hand tightened with shock on Robbie's arm.

Smiling, whispering a word of encouragement, he drew her on and, at the minister's invitation, handed Meggie to her future husband. Oliver extended his arm and Meggie laid her hand on it, feeling him reassuringly steady beneath her. Without the aid of crutches, his artificial leg hidden under the knife-edged creases of his new suit, Oliver turned round smoothly to the minister.

Twenty minutes later, Oliver walked up the aisle with his new wife, his step surprisingly confident. Behind them came Robbie, who had worked in secret every afternoon to help Oliver with this ultimate wedding present for his new wife, and had seen the pain, frustration and sheer effort involved, his generous heart bursting with admiration.

Outside, while the photographer fussed with his camera, Meggie looked at Oliver, barely able to speak for the emotion which was choking her. 'I didn't know,' she whispered at last.

'Didn't I promise you that I'd walk down the aisle without crutches?' he said softly. 'I love you, Meggie Laing. I'll never let you down.' And he kissed her on the lips, just as the camera captured the first picture.